FORBIDDEN LORE I REVIVAL

Book 1 of the Forbidden Lore Series

Author: Shobhit Dabral
Published by: Shobhit Dabral
Printing by: Panthera Uncia LLP, Dehradun

www.shobhitdabral.com

ISBN: 9798582215905

Regn. No. TXu 2-068-420 US Copyrights Office for First Draft

FORBIDDEN LORE

- REVIVAL -

SHOBHIT DABRAL

—-
For DADU
—-

The one person who never had any doubt in me.

The one person who impressed me much more than anyone else in life.

Acknowledgements

I am grateful to be born into the Dabral Clan and couldn't have asked for a better family. I thank my parents for being patient with me always - heavens know they've needed to be. My sister, for being the best sibling anyone can ask for. My wife, for being the rock of my life - calm and steady.

A special mention for Amit, my brother more than my friend - for pestering me to realise this dream of mine.

To all my family around the world and my friends - you are what makes the world a beautiful place.

Thanks also to:

Tanya Kotnala (BHULI DESIGN STUDIO) for the cover design.

Jessy Mills for editing (and causing me pain) in order to help out.

Revival

00

«« « PROLOGUE »» »

It was a very dark night. The darkest Dr Chhibbar had ever seen in his life. He could barely see anything past a yard from the window. Or maybe it was the heavy rain that caused poor visibility? It hadn't rained like this in Kasauli for as long as he could remember. The baby was in sound health – except for the obviously unexplainable. There was no physical concern at all; in fact, he was right as rain. It was the mother he was worried about. He had no explanation for her deteriorating condition.

He turned around to have a look at the monitor again, then arched his head leftward to peek out to the portico. There he was standing – looking away into the distance. Lost. His overcoat's left shoulder wet with spray from the hammering rain. He was an enormous, dark figure in a hat and a coat. The man was not someone you would want to be in trouble with. Standing over six feet tall, he looked massive with broad, heavy shoulders, a full chest, and a slim waist. His hands were all muscle; big hefty arms that were rumoured to have strangled a python once. At less than 30, this man had made himself a name to be regarded in the construction industry as one to be respected and to watch out for. As an orphan from a village near Kasauli, he had established himself well in Delhi and Uttar Pradesh. The turn of the century was just around the corner, and he was being hailed as a pioneer of intelligent building in the twenty first.

Yes, it was the mother's falling statistics that worried the doctor. The very man's wife. 'Call me when I can talk to her. No sooner', he had said. 'And mind you, doctor, you'd better make sure she's well'. The man had fire in his eyes. It was common knowledge how much he loved his wife. How would he ever tell him she couldn't be saved? And who was this person he was so frantically trying to reach on the phone? So busy was he in connecting to this person, he didn't even hear the baby!

Dr Chhibbar said his prayers and stepped outside. 'Sir,' he said, clearing his throat. 'Excuse me, sir.'

The man turned around, looked at the doctor through blood shot eyes and growled, 'What?'

Gulping down half his words, he mustered, 'She...I'm sorry...doesn't look like...I'm sorry we can't save her.'

In one big stride, he was across the doctor and into the room. 'Sumi!' he called out, in an urge to get her to talk to him. 'Sumi get up. You cannot abandon me, you hear me? Get up now, our baby...where's the baby?' He turned around.

It was difficult to say whether it was from rage or fear. Maybe both, thought the doctor.

The man uttered a more urgent, 'Where?'

'He's in the next room,' he replied as he was halfway there...'Yes, a boy. We're trying to figure out...'

He just stood at the door watching the boy for a moment. 'Is he...is he well?'

'In perfect health, sir.' The doctor had a nervous smile on his face. The man went to the baby to examine him. As he touched the baby's head, he looked back at the doctor, bewildered.

The doctor was his shaken self again. 'We've no idea, sir. That's what we're trying to find out.'

'She's awake!' shouted the nurse from the other room. They both rushed back, the man to his wife and the doctor to his monitors.

'We're losing her,' panicked Dr Chhibbar. 'Nurse...'

He was cut short by Sumitra Devi's hand in the air, clearly signalling for all to stop. For a few seconds, there was no sound but the rain thrashing down on everything outside, and the continuous 'bip...bip...bip' of medical instruments indoors.

'Tell them...leave,' she murmured. With a quick gesture of his hand, the man signalled them out. The doctor had a mind to resist but then decided otherwise.

Once alone with his wife, he let a tear roll down his cheek. 'You can't abandon me Sumi. What will I do without you?' he said, holding her hand dearly in his.

'I have to go' she replied, 'promise me you will love him for the both of us.' He couldn't stop crying. 'Brij...promise me.'

'No Sumi...we will both love him. I won't let you go.'

'There's nothing you can do Brij. I can't stay any longer.' With her last breaths, she said 'prepare him...'

'What?'

"Prepare him for when they come...' She barely managed the last words and closed her eyes forever.

The doctor could've sworn the entire lot of humanity heard the cry of 'Nnnooooooooo...'

Fifteen minutes later he entered and saw the man sitting next to his dead wife with his boy in his hands, staring at his head. When he looked up, he had the look of a man so resolute, it was inconceivable to imagine the man had gone through what he just had.

'No one, doctor; no one hears a thing about this. My wife died in childbirth, and I left with the baby. That is all you ever say of it...you understand?'

01

««« ONE »»»

'Wager for T20,' shouted a scantily clad young female. 'T20?'

'How come you don't know me?' he asked, with a smirk on his face.

'Should I?' replied the girl, teasing him, fanning the voucher.

'Who's the poor bastard?' He nudged her on, scanning the crowd behind her. She just looked at him blankly. 'Doesn't have a name, darling' he said, never looking at her, waving it in her face.

'And?' She drew another blank.

'You're new, aren't you love?'

'Talk to Kaka,' she said, smiling as she walked away.

He hadn't had a blank voucher in a long time. There weren't too many who'd wage him unannounced. Most racers would take pride in challenging him and show up even before the voucher was drawn. Who would want to race him without making a show out of it? He wondered as he walked over to Kaka.

Kaka had been in the business for a long time now. There wasn't a race in Delhi he didn't have a hand in. Built like a wrestler and dressed like a pimp, Kaka was never too difficult to locate. One simply had to follow the sound of blaring music and spot the largest concentration of females. That is where he'd be – the dreadlocks were hard to miss under a bright tennis cap and a dark track suit.

'My man!' he exclaimed as he greeted Trish with open arms.

'Stop acting like you're a gangsta rapper man, Jesus!' Trish liked the man and had immense respect for him. Despite running all his business on the sly, Kaka had always been known as a man of his word and was honourable in the racing circuit. His word was the last, and his decision final. No racer ever questioned it for the sheer need to be able to race again on the roads of Delhi.

'I hear you got a blank.'

'Stop it with your games, Ka. Just tell me who it is.'

'I haven't a fucking clue, man. New rider. Won't talk. Paid a granny for this one, man. Looks like he's desperate to lose to ya.'

'What does he look like?'

'Black Shoei helmet with a reflective visor. Wears red and black leathers and rides a sweet ass red Panigale R. Never took off the helmet. Never saw no face! Money comes out the tank pocket, and that's all I could be bothered about. I'll have his pedigree for you by tomorrow though.'

'No need. I'll let you know if I need it, thanks. What's with the new bird?'

'Natasha? She's a friend of my cousin's, came over last week, wants to be seen and noticed. She heard about that bird from last year...what's her name again – Kiara, was it? Yeah, so she thinks she might end up in a film career too.' He smiled and winked at Trish.

'Well, in the meantime I'll introduce her to myself and take her for a treat. I deserve one as well I guess. I will be racing as T21 starting tomorrow after all.'

'No way man! Already? That's just fucking awesome bro! I'm

so sorry I didn't remember. My sincerest apologies and a hundred percent off on all bets from your end. Tonight Kaka bets for you!' Kaka hugged Trish and signalled for a megaphone. 'Ladies and gents, boys and girls, one round of drinks on the house for my beloved, the one and only, Trish...Who, by the way, turns 21 tonight!'

Fireworks lit up the sky as the free drinks did their round. Trish started walking to his bike when Natasha came up to him with a drink in her hand. 'Why didn't you tell me you were Trish?'

'I never got the opportunity to introduce myself. You were too quick to leave.'

'You can try now.'

'Trishul Negi. Friends call me Trish. I race under the call sign T20, which will be T21 starting tomorrow. And whatever people say, I had no hand in Kiara's success.'

'Is that why you think I came over?' She looked annoyed, maybe even disappointed. 'I've heard about your magic trick. Lights out, eh? That's what intrigued me. They said you were a dickhead. Wonder why I never listen.'

'Maybe because you have a brain of your own,' he said, catching her hand as she turned to leave. 'I'm just saying. That's why *I* don't listen.'

She smiled. 'If you smoke that racer, I might not listen to some of the other stuff they say and risk leaving with you tonight. See ya after.' She freed her hand and started walking away but turned after a few steps and walked back to him. 'By the way, I have your helmet. Wanted to check if you have some night vision thing in there or something, you know, for your special trick.'

'Okay, so can I have it back then? The race is almost on

now. They won't let me race with gadgets I don't declare, you know. Everything goes through a thorough check anyway, so what was it you were looking for?.' He threw up his hands in disapproval.

'But you're Trish! I'm sure you can manage without a helmet too.' She winked at him and smiled foolishly.

'It's a matter of resolve; I don't expect you to understand, but just so you know – outside my own territory, I never ride without a helmet. There is nothing manly in it. Now get my helmet and meet me at the start line in five.'

+++

There were still three minutes to flag off. Trish was at the start line toying with his helmet and looking around for his opponent. It was unusual for people racing him not to show off. Natasha whispered something in his ear. He smiled, but his mind was on the space next to his bike. Two minutes remaining now...could the guy forfeit? Maybe he wanted to make a grand entry at the last minute with a massive stoppie or a couple of doughnuts or something. *Punks!*

He put his helmet on and gunned the engine on his Erik Buell 1190RS a few times even as Natasha whispered something again and slipped a chit into his breast pocket.

Thirty seconds to go...

The sweet hum of the Panigale closed in from behind. A slow, majestic ride-in. This was no punk; he was just fashionably late. Trish caught a quick glance at the rider – a little shorter than he expected and very lithe. He never looked back at Trish.

'Three...Two...One...'

Both riders roared off at the drop of the scarf together as

watchers shot videos of them taking off. Some were streaming live on the racing blog under the "sub-1200" race. Big flat screen TVs showed a live feed at the base camp, which was covered by drone cameras. The route would keep changing while traffic was handled by crews across the city. Detours would be indicated by square, three feet high reflective arrow boards – red mandating a turn, blue giving options, and green advising shortcuts. Shortcuts were never well-paved roads, so it was up to the riders to decide whether they wanted to take them, or to keep going on asphalt slabs.

After the third turn, Trish began to slow down a little. 'Lights out! Lights out!' shouted everyone witnessing the race from wherever they were in unison. Trish switched off the lights on his bike, carried on at a slowed pace for a couple of seconds, then sped on again into the dark. There was a roar of admiration at base camp.

This was his secret weapon. The other rider could barely make him out at the speeds they were doing, while Trish rode on like it was no different. Every racer in the circuit knew of this and was wary of him. He still remained the undisputed champion of the "sub-1200" contest. Others just fought for a record of how close they got to him even as they lost money on the race, making side-bets to rake in bigger sums.

Even though he could see as clear as day, Trish couldn't stop admiring how talented the other rider was. He was never far behind, and whenever he opted for a different path in the route, he always joined back at Trish's heels. He manoeuvred extremely well...better than Trish himself would have, at times. He had to concede that this mystery rider was better than him. The only reason he was ahead was that he wasn't offering himself to this guy visually. But this wouldn't fly at all times – most places en route were so well lit that it was hardly an advantage. The secret to Trish winning all these races was when he managed a massive gap in the darker regions, however, that wasn't happening today. The last leg of the race would be lit like a Christmas tree, and if he hadn't enough lead on the other guy, the race could go anywhere with him displaying great riding skill throughout the race.

As they approached the last leg of the race, it was evident to Trish that it would be a close call. The other racer was almost at his rear tyre, and even as he tried to outmanoeuvre him, the guy kept right at it.

There was utter silence at the base camp. *Could this be it? The race Trish would lose? Who was this guy?* Awe-struck faces had their eyes glued to the screens on display. They were almost at the finish line. The Panigale was gaining on Trish. He knew he had lost the race when he realised the other guy had stopped accelerating any more.

As Trish zipped past the finish line with him in tow, he knew he'd been given the match. Both bikes decelerated rapidly as Trish finally turned around on a stoppie. The Panigale circled him twice, the guy took a bow for his effort, then rode off.

Trish kept looking at him riding away while he heard the cheers around him...the crowd flocked in, and foam streamers went around in the air. Bottles popped, music blared, and almost everyone wanted to shake his hand. Kaka came over with the spoils, neatly rolled up and held with a rubber band.

'He gave it to me,' he whispered in Kaka's ears.

'What? You won it...fair and square...we all saw it!' exclaimed Kaka to Trish as he rapidly shook his head. 'Listen up, yo. I don't give a fuck about anything other than who crossed the line first. Stop imagining things, man! Enjoy the spoils.'

'I don't deserve it, Ka,' said Trish, grabbing the megaphone from the girl behind him. 'This is community fund right here...everything, till the party ends, is on the house!'

A huge roar went up, and people jumped and clapped in acknowledgement. Trish rode off silently, trying to understand what had just happened. Why would anyone make a hefty wager only to give the race away? He rode the bike up the ramp on to Kaka's truck, locked it, climbed down, and went to the edge of the bridge to his car. As he took off his jacket, he pulled out the chit in its breast pocket. It had a number which he dialled, smiling.

'Behind you,' Natasha answered. 'My place?'

Trish walked her over to his car while they made small talk. He never mentioned to her that he thought he had been given the race by the other rider. He didn't know her well enough. She held his hand and kissed him before he opened the door to his car for her. 'Okay,' he said, grinning, 'let's get home then.'

He stopped the car on the way to her house, rushed over to the chemist across the road, and came back with a small packet he put in the glove box. 'You don't need those,' she said, 'or don't you think I'm clean?'

He smiled. 'You forget too soon, babe. Outside my own territory, I never ride without a helmet.'

02

«‹« TWO »›»

Natasha woke up, rubbing her eyes, to the sounds of him murmuring. She noticed him through the glass door to the balcony, talking on his phone. Trish waved at her and smiled as he saw her sit up, and signalled 'two' with his fingers. While he turned and turned again, pacing around in a pair of boxers on the small balcony, she admired his tattoo in daylight.

A shaft ran up from halfway between his elbow and his shoulder on his left arm and across his left shoulder where a '*damroo*' (the small two-headed drum) was inked with its heads spilling to one on each of his left upper chest and upper shoulder blades. The shaft itself culminating into a trident across his left shoulder blade to the middle of his upper back.

It was a magnificent piece of art. Very intricately done, its darkness seemed to compliment Trish's fair skin and lean, muscular body. He ended his conversation, slid the door open, and stepped inside. 'Dad. He just landed in Delhi and will be home soon. He was out for some urgent business but came back for my birthday.'

'Oh yes! Happy 21st Trish.' She rose up and gave him a peck on his cheek. 'Good to know that the famous Mr Brijbhooshan Negi puts his son's birthday ahead of business. You don't see that very often these days.'

'You know my father?' He looked surprised. 'You know me quite well then!'

'Listen, Trish,' she said calmly. 'I just happen to know of him. There's nothing fishy here, okay? Last night was fun; I really wanted it. You...you're a nice guy too, and I'd love to hang out with you if we bump into each other again, but there's no more to it. I hope you understand, right? I'm not looking for anything.'

He was a little taken aback. 'No, no...I know. No, I didn't mean...' He gathered himself and said, 'I know what you mean. I didn't mean it to sound like that; I just meant that you actually knew who I was, not just that I race or where I study, you know? You knew who my father was. That's not routine, that's all.'

'Ohhh, and that's what all *this* is, huh?' She beamed, pinching him wherever she could while he evaded.

'Will you have breakfast before you leave?'

'Depends on whether you can *make* me some...bacon, eggs, nothing too fancy.' He smiled as she started to get up.

'Sure. What's up with the tattoo?'

'What? It's a trishul.'

'Just that, eh? Coffee?'

+++

As the gatekeeper opened the gates and he drove in, Trish noticed there were four extra cars parked beside the usual two that lingered around his father's place. This was out of place unless they were hosting guests, but his father never brought home guests unannounced. He was a man of meticulous planning, and this was out of character for him.

Trish took off down the paved driveway and parked on the gravel, allowing for more movement of cars. Getting out of his car, he saw a couple of people in the garden. A man dressed in an expensive dark suit who had his back turned towards him was on a phone. And a woman, who was facing the man, looked at Trish with a blank face as he walked on to the patio. She was dressed in an expensive black dress too, with a neatly tied bun on her head.

He wondered why these people were in the house looking like they were going to a ball in the middle of the day. His father never conducted business at home. It was making him uncomfortable.

Brijbhooshan Negi walked towards the door to the hall and threw his arms open for his son as he entered the house. 'Happy birthday, son,' he said, hugging him tightly.

Trish thanked him and noticed over his father's shoulder that there were nine people in the hall. Seven men and two women, all dressed in expensive looking, dark, formal clothes. None of them looked extremely happy, he thought.

'So, what's up, Dad?' Trish asked as his father loosened his grip around him. He always thought no one could ever 'un-hug' his father if he didn't want it. His hug was so firm that you could feel the power in his arms and shoulders. A gentle squeeze more, and they'd crush you.

Mr Negi didn't seem ecstatic either. 'Please take a seat, son,' he said. 'I...We have something to discuss with you.'

Trish felt really uncomfortable with the movement around him. Taking a seat on the sofa, he noticed how the others in the room were suddenly at work like stagehands arranging other furniture, taking positions, some already in their spot, folding hands, or leaning on to something and looking at him as if waiting for their cue to start. The two from outside also walked in and took positions. His father took a seat directly opposite him, waiting for the others to settle down. Everyone was then looking at him.

'Dad, what is this?' he asked, unsure of whether he was amused or anxious. 'Really, what?'

Brijbhooshan took a deep breath. He looked at the oldest of the ensemble, who nodded to him as if granting his approval. 'Son, this here is Mr Adipati Srivastav and the others are his most trusted team.'

'Dad?' His father wasn't someone who would seek approval from anyone anywhere before saying his piece, leave alone his own house! Trish was beginning to get edgy.

'Let me finish, son. These are the people I was meeting with last week. What they're going to talk to you about may not make any sense to you immediately, but you must know they have my complete trust as they did your mother's.'

Now Trish was *very* uncomfortable. He realised he was thirsty. He gulped for a little air, tried to sit back to hear what had to be said, then readjusted back to sitting straighter. His father had *never* mentioned his mother himself. He never talked about her much, except for when Trish asked him specifically. He loved her a lot, that was apparent; but somehow he'd never been forthcoming with the many details of their life. As he grew up, Trish assumed it must've caused him pain to talk about her as he missed her a lot, and let it be. But he'd never met family from his mother's side. His father said he didn't know anyone from her life before him and didn't care. Who then, were these people?

'They've been deciding on how to go about this,' Brij continued, 'we have all agreed unanimously that you can no longer be left in the dark. You have to know so you can cooperate and help us, and without that, we'll never succeed.'

'Cooperate in doing what? What on earth are these people here for, Dad?'

The old man stepped forward. He looked like he was in his sixties, but he stood like a young man who had a calm about him that was unsettling. 'We're here to save you, son.'

+++

Brij was facing Trish as he paced up and down the study. He had jumped at the suggestion of his life being in danger and wouldn't listen to the other man at all. Brij had decided it would be best if he tried speaking to Trish alone for a bit.

'Is this some prank you're pulling on me for my birthday? Is that it, Dad?' Trish asked his father while everyone else waited outside the study. He wished against all odds that were the case. 'I'm an engineering student, and the worst thing I've ever done in life is race on bikes!'

'You've been racing again?' Brijbhooshan lowered his voice and sounded more disappointed than angry. 'How many times have I told you to stay away from such stuff? Who the hell's been giving you their bike?'

'Not now, Dad! Tell me what the hell's going on? Who *is* that guy? What's he doing with a team claiming he needs to save my life?' In a hushed tone and leaning closer to him, Trish asked with concern in his voice, 'And what has any of this got to do with Mum?'

Brijbhooshan looked grim. 'I'm sorry son, I never wanted you to learn about any of this in this manner. Even I don't know much; Adipati and his men know a lot more and will explain everything to you. But before we learn the whole truth, I want to come clean with you first. No matter what happens next and no matter what we have to face, you have to know that I love you and I'd bring down the gods themselves before I let anything happen to you.'

'Dad, you're scaring me now. What do I not know?'

Brijbhooshan placed his hands on Trish's shoulder. 'All I know son, is that your mother was "special". She was not like everyone else. There were things about her I could never explain. I don't even know what they were, but there were things about her...I could always feel it,' he muttered. Trish saw him looking into oblivion as if peeking inside his past.

'When your mother first met me, and we fell in love, I promised her I wanted to know nothing of her past, as it was something that always deeply disturbed her. She said it would eventually catch up anyway – that I would have to face it someday and so would our child.'

'During our life together, she used to tell me to take good care of, and train, the child we would one day have; well enough to defend himself against enemies that life might have in store for it – for you! I thought there must've been some dangerous people in her past life that she couldn't defend herself against or someone she loved. That explained all the martial training I've always insisted you have and also why I don't want you racing or getting anywhere near trouble.'

'However, her behaviour after she conceived you changed, and deep down I somehow always feared that what she'd be warning me against was far more than some vicious people. She somehow knew right from the day she had you that she wouldn't survive your birth…'

'When she died, the last thing she said was to prepare you for when *they* came. How does one prepare for something one knows nothing of? I did whatever best I could, son, but I'm afraid it might not be enough...'

'What are you saying? This can't be happening...I was only an ordinary boy an hour back! Who'd want to harm me? And

Mum...Who was she? Where does this gang sitting outside fit in? Dad...' Trish suddenly frowned. 'How do we know these aren't the men trying to harm us? Maybe they're the ones she warned you about and are now just using this as a pretext to get us somewhere?'

'I have seen Adipati once before...only very briefly with your mother. She told me after he left, that if there was anyone I could trust for anything at all in her absence ever, it was him. But I was never to contact him. I never heard from him after that until last week when he met me and said it was imperative I come with him to discuss your safety'.

Trish didn't even know what to think. It was all too much to take in at once. 'But what do you mean you couldn't explain things about Mum, and why do you think it is anything more than just some thugs?'

'There were several instances throughout our life together when I knew she was capable of much more than regular people...I knew for sure she was special, but I was just so in love with her, I wanted to have nothing to do with it. And then...' Brijbhooshan's eyes moistened as he reminisced. 'Then there was this thing when you were born...when I looked at you for the very first time…'

'What then?' Trish demanded.

Brijbhooshan bit his lip. 'Nothing, my son. You were such a sight to behold, I forgot everything all over again.'

'But Trish, I have no doubt that there is danger to you. Of what magnitude, I do not yet know, but these people outside showed me surveillance of people surveilling you! I saw it live with them as well. That is what they showed me in the past week. Teams of men taking pictures of you, making notes, talking on radio to each other – some of them armed!'

'But why is it you think you can trust them?'

'They also had a video of your mother recorded for me. She was sitting with Adipati on a sofa and she addressed *me* in the video. She said that Adipati would come to us one day and would ask us to put our trust in him. She said he would have answers for us in time, but asked me not to press for them immediately as what we were to learn would be far greater than what we would be prepared for.'

Brij's lips trembled as he held back his tears.

'I can not shake off her trust in this man, son. I am going to trust him, at least for now. I don't expect you to trust him at all, but just have faith in *me*. She said to trust him and I'm going to, but I have back up as well. She didn't say don't have back up.'

+++

When they walked out again and were ready to talk to Adipati and his team, they were met with a plea more than a suggestion.

When they sat down, Adipati folded his hands as he addressed them. 'You don't have much to go on in order to trust me,' he said. 'I know I probably wouldn't trust me either, in your position. There is also a lot that you don't know and I understand you would think it would be easier to trust us if we were to tell you everything there is to know. You couldn't be more incorrect. If I were to tell you now, the things you must know, and will, you wouldn't believe me. Not any of it. If you wouldn't believe me, there would be no chance of trusting me. So for now, I must lean in on your mother's faith in us for you to trust that we are here to help.'

Brijbhooshan and Trish looked at each other. Brij put his hand on Trish's knee and nodded.

Adipati's eyes widened with promise. 'I give you my word – I will have answers for you, and I will explain everything in time. But it may not be before. Things you will learn in the next few days are best understood once you've seen or experienced some of them. For now, please believe me when when I say there are people out there who want to get you and most likely harm you. But if we manage to keep you out of their hands for a while, it shall pass.'

He got up from his chair and looked at the father and son with folded hands again.

'It is therefore imperative that we leave at the earliest and be on the move.' He then turned to address Trish alone. 'What I ask of you is your patience for the next five days. If at the end of five days you are not certain of our objectives and are not working with us willingly, I will myself bring you back here.'

It was night by the time Trish was convinced he should trust what was being done. If nothing else, he trusted his father. His father trusted his mother who trusted this man.

'We must leave immediately, Brij,' Adipati said, then looked at Trish. 'I know you're trying to make sense of everything, son. You'll learn it all in time, but we just have to get a head start.'

'What can I keep with me?' asked Trish.

Adipati was impressed. *He was thinking ahead already.*

'Anything that can't help someone trace you...no cards, phones or laptop, no—'

'Yeah...got it.' Trish cut him short.

'Another thing...' Everyone looked at Adipati even as he addressed Trish. 'We'll only take three cars. Mugdha will drive one, Vishwas will drive another, and you Trish, will drive the third.' Mugdha and Vishwas looked just as puzzled as the rest of the room, including Trish.

'Oh, I'm also your driver now?'

'We need you to drive. We don't have a third person who can drive without the headlights on.'

+++

Three cars left the premises as he looked from the top of the building. No lights on any of them. 'Blip, blip' went the radio just as he spoke into it. 'Package on the move. Three units, thirteen counts in all, four counts in unit with package.'

He drew one of his big cigars as he waited for a response, caressing his bald head with the other hand. The men behind him strained their eyes to see exactly what he'd reported to no avail.

'Aite,' came the reply on the radio. He signalled the men to pack things up. The thirteen-hour stakeout had come to an end. The men could see him following the cars without any aid, and they thought to themselves, *How the fuck does he see so far and in such darkness, so clearly?*

03

««« THREE »»»

'The boy's fast,' said Vishwas into his phone, 'and good!'

Mugdha's voice boomed from the car's speakers. 'He can see, don't forget. He's one of *them*. We've all heard this a zillion times, but it's still a lot for me to sink in. It's finally time for the eventuality we have all been hearing of and training for!' They were having so much trouble trying to keep up with Trish; he often had to slow down.

In the backseat of the lead car, Brijbhooshan was having a difficult time getting to terms with his son's feat. Even in areas of absolute darkness, Trish was driving as though he could see as clearly as if it were broad daylight. Sure, he'd suspected Sumitra to have had better vision than normal at times, but this was insane! Even Adipati was somehow able to understand where they were exactly and when they would be approaching a turn, what Trish was doing had surprised even him.

Brij noted astonishment followed by a wry smile on his face soon after they'd left home. The two people with him in the backseat hadn't spoken much, but Brij could gauge from his accent that the man to his left was a Russian. Adipati had from time to time looked back at the woman to Brij's right. He held her gaze and smiled before looking ahead again. One time Brij could have sworn he heard her voice in his head saying '*clear.*'

Maybe he was imagining things? Yet, not much of last week made sense to him. All he had to go by was his wife's advice of trusting Adipati. Trust him to what end? What was happening? The only thing he knew was Trish needed saving from someone. Or something?

After they had exited Delhi, they were immediately on the highway to Agra. It was one of the stretches of road that Trish loved. 'Where are we headed?' he asked, to a smile from Adipati. 'What? You're supposed to be saving me, but I can't know where we're going? This is turning out to be quite the opposite of a good decision'.

Adipati was about to say something when the woman at the back leant forward and shook her head at him. Adipati signalled to Trish with his finger over his lips, then they turned back towards Brijbhooshan to indicate him to remain quiet too.

'What's that again?' Trish said. 'Are you threatening us to shut up?'

But then the voice of the woman said in all their heads, *'Guys, please. We need to maintain silence for a bit. I think someone might be honing in on us. I'll explain everything as soon as I can, but for now, I'm begging you to give me some time of complete silence.'*

As Trish noticed Adipati pleading silently with folded hands as a gesture, the instructions he'd just heard seemed unusual somehow, as if he heard it in his head and not through his ears. Brijbhooshan, on the other hand, was utterly bewildered. He heard the complete instructions too, in his head. He was, in fact, looking right back at her as she looked to him while giving the instructions, without uttering a word from her mouth, or even moving her lips.

+++

'Silence' he said. 'The fuckers know!' He threw his glass away. There was total darkness in the room. The guards only heard his harsh voice and the sound of the glass hitting a wall and break into pieces. They had no clue what was going on; they'd just been standing in total darkness without a sound for the last couple of hours, guns at the ready.

'They're going to keep silent long enough to throw us off, so when they start talking again, we won't know which ones they are. Must be that bitch! She's come out remarkably well for them.'

He realised he never got a reply from the boy. *What the hell was he doing?* He switched the lights on and went to check on him at the other end of the room and found him still at it, with his head lowered into his palms, and his elbows resting on the table; he was concentrating hard.

He noticed a bead of sweat rolling down his forehead. *What the hell was he tuned in to?* They'd been silent for five minutes already. Then it dawned on him. *The brilliant son of a bitch...*he knew the people were taken care of, so he tuned to the engine. A smile broke on his face. The boy was everything he said he'd be. Now as long as they didn't stop the car, they still had them.

+++

It was breaking dawn. There had been complete silence in the cars for over two hours now. Adipati had been signalling Trish for any instructions he wanted to give. Every person in the car had their minds working overtime. They had bypassed Agra and were headed towards Lucknow. As they approached Etawah, Adipati signalled for tea. Trish nodded, and everyone on the back seat nodded too as he looked at them. They pulled over at the next *Dhaba* that had any indication of activity and got out. The other two cars pulled over one, after the other, and as they got off a kid from the shack approached them. 'Chai, sir?'

+++

The kid had tuned out after losing the engines and was standing in front of a map of the Archaeological Survey of India posted on the wall. He manoeuvred the map with a set of dividers, marking, then marking some more, then finally drew a circle around Etawah. 'Five kilometres around Etawah', he said.

He had the same look on his face as when he first came to RD, determined to prove himself. He had done exceptionally well tonight. Even if they didn't turn the engines off, they'd have been too far to be tracked soon anyway.

'Lucknow', RD said. 'They're headed for Lucknow. Tell them to keep an eye on Dr Surbhi. They're seeking help, and with Vashisht out of the picture, she's their closest bet. They'll try and find the ideal time for it first thing, then see if she can help them with procedure for the boy.'

'But what about Benares? They could–'

RD cut him short. 'With Vashisht out of the picture, they'll avoid Benares like the plague. They'll try and not go anywhere near any place that has a gateway. Vashisht was the only reason they'd even consider it. Make the call. Tell them to have the twins at the Kanpur – Lucknow road.'

+++

'Do you think they made us?' the Russian from the back of the car asked Adipati as Brij was taking his glass of piping hot chai.

'I don't know, Lyosha' Adipati said, 'we kept silent long enough, but they knew the direction of our travel. It's highly improbable he picked up anything after we went silent, but he is *the* Rai Dutta.'

'Wait a second; there's only one Rai Dutta that could mean,' Brijbhooshan interjected. 'Shujoy Rai Dutta of Rai Dutta Industries! RD? Was he tracking us? He's not into any technological businesses at all. He's a good businessman, but that's it. I don't think he has the means to track anyone, leave alone technology that'll track us through the sound of us talking!'

Lyosha looked at Adipati for approval, which he got with a tilt of the head. 'You don't know the half of who that man is. He doesn't need means; he was born with them. He's also the best of his kind around, probably the only of his kind around now. Can't believe he was one of us and—'

'We can discuss him later,' Adipati said, cutting him short and acknowledging Brijbhooshan's look. 'And we can discuss us later too. I know you have questions about what this one here means by "his kind and "our kind" along with others. Bear with me a tad longer. We're doing famously so far, Brij. You don't mind me calling you Brij, do you?'

There was a nod from Brij and he carried on. 'Right now we need to focus on our next stop, replenish some energy and continue with our onward trip. Before you ask me, plans will start unveiling themselves today, and we will all be on the same page pretty soon'. He looked at the sky near the horizon. 'The time isn't far.'

Not long after everyone had had tea, and some had omelettes and pan-toasted bread, the cars continued to speed down the road again. A lot of questions remained answered, some new questions added to them. *What was this kind they were talking about?* Some acknowledgements were made - Adipati addressed their discomfort over not knowing, but reiterated his need for time and things to unfold themselves. Very few more words were shared and the motley crew was back to being awkward.

'We'll stop and rest at a place in a couple of hours,' Adipati said, breaking the silence. 'Can't pause for too long, but we all need a few hours sleep.'

The rest of what was close to two hours went by in total silence, till Adipati spoke again. 'Take the next slip road off the highway.' In two minutes, they got off the highway into a slip road. 'Take the second left, then take the first left.'

Trish turned as instructed on to a dusty road that was breaking up in places. He wanted to ask Adipati why he still needed to drive when it was broad daylight, but he kept it to himself.

'Now, keep on this road till you see a mosque to your left. We park there.'

At the mosque, Adipati went to ask for someone. He returned with a boy and said that they needed to walk to another mosque nearby.

'*Abbu* is at the *Bagh Wali Masjid*,' said the boy. 'It's close, we can walk.'

Adipati decided not to let everyone step out. 'We will have to come back here after meeting him. I can go see him and be back while the rest of you can wait in the cars. Jameel Bhai will get you water and some fruit.'

He nodded at a young man coming out of the mosque.

'I'll come' Trish said. Adipati smiled.

They crossed the road and started walking back to where they came from. Not even 100 metres down the road, they turned left onto a dirt road winding around a small cluster of houses.

Adipati put his hand on Trish's shoulder. 'We're going to see an old friend of mine. Do not be fooled by his appearance or demeanour. I'd like to tell you right now; he's a man educated in Applied Linguistics from the University of Cambridge, lest you make a fool of yourself.'

In another 100 metres, they approached a grove of trees. A man on a plastic chair had his back towards them and sat under the shade. A few people, who looked like they were related, sat around him.

'Fakru!' Adipati exclaimed.

The man sprang like he'd been waiting for that cue forever. He turned around with his arms thrown open. 'Adi, my dear friend!'

He had the skin of a very young man, yet he had some silver hair and eyes that had seen many years, Trish could tell. They hugged for a good thirty seconds if not more, patting each other's back. 'Is he the boy?' Fakru asked. 'You sure he's up for it?'

'What's he talking about?' Trish demanded.

'I was going to ask you, Trish, but now that the subject is in discussion, I'd better ask you now; would you be willing to show us what you've got inside you in case you need to defend yourself?' Adipati asked.

'I can fight,' Trish retorted. 'I've had training.'

'The very best, I hear,' Adipati added. 'And we hope to see some skills ourselves, that's all I ask. It is a treacherous journey ahead, I assure you, and a good display of skills will boost up my morale a bit; if you don't mind. It will ease my unrest if I see how well you can take care of yourself. I've heard no student of Sikhni Amrat Kaur Ji ever backs down from a worthy challenge.'

The mention of Sikhni Amrat Kaur Ji brought a look of admiration on Fakru's face, and a smile.

'Then you better make it a worthy challenge,' Trish announced, stepping forward. 'I'm not backing down till I put whatever you throw at me to the ground.'

'Early evening then, after everyone's had some rest,' Fakru exclaimed.

He then turned around and whispered to Adipati. 'How many?'

'Up to ten of the best you have. Are they ready?'

'Standing by. How bad do you want it to be?'

'If he lets them, they should kill the boy.'

Fakru was taken aback for a moment. Then, smiling, he said, 'He must really be special, this one.'

04

«««« FOUR »»»»

Fakru Rehman Ali, as Adipati had introduced him, guided everyone to an abandoned looking warehouse in the fields nearby where he had *charpoys* with pillows and sheets for everyone to rest on, after a meal of *paranthas*. He and Lyosha had got along really well since Russian was his favourite language. Adipati had been right – no one could have ever guessed this guy was such an educated man. He wore a *khadi kurta* and pyjamas, rubber slippers, and a skull cap. Nothing about him gave him as a man more than a local of the nearby Akbarpur where he lived. Trish wondered why he'd chosen to live here of all places, but since the day before, this was the least surprising fact to come to light.

Six hours of sleep later, Trish woke up noticing he was the last one asleep. Everyone had changed into more comfortable clothing, which was a refreshing change from their dark formal attire. His father was talking to Adipati and didn't look pleased while Fakru was helping his son set up tea and refreshments. Apparently, Brijbhooshan wasn't entirely convinced of the whole "display of skills" event.

Trish wondered if his father actually believed in his training. He had been offered to train with some of the world's best martial artists, but Trish had decided he wanted to learn only from Sikhni Amrat Kaur Ji. He'd been immensely impressed with the display of skills some students of hers had put up in a martial arts show at the Talkatora Stadium, which he attended as a school excursion. He'd walked up to her to ask if and how he could learn from her.

'Think about why you want to learn to fight. Tell me when you have an answer, and we'll see if we can get you sorted,' she had said.

But Brijbhooshan hadn't been sure about Trish's choice from the very beginning. 'Are you sure about this Trishul? If you ever change your mind and want to learn elsewhere, just say the word.'

He'd asked this a zillion times, till he had to give in to the boy's persistence, and not once did he visit her school while Trish was training.

Trish walked up to Brij. 'Dad I've got this. Please believe me. I want you to have faith in me, and I promise I'll show you.' He hugged his father.

'He says there'll be ten of them, Trish,' he said. Then he looked at Adipati and frowned. 'They'll be fighting him one at a time like gentlemen, I hope. Not two or three, or all...I won't allow that!'

'Well, at some point in time, if Trish is good enough...'

Trish turned to Adipati. 'As many as you want, and if they have any skill I won't be able to break their bones before they concede.'

Adipati smiled. 'At any point, if you want to stop it, just signal me. To the yard then, shall we?'

In the yard outside the warehouse, seven men and three women stood tall. Fakru walked up to them and introduced each one while they folded their hands as their names were being said.

'Bhairavi, Sunitha, and Ritu practice Brazilian Jiu Jitsu, Kalaripayattu and Kickboxing respectively. Namdourei practices Thang-Ta. Vaibhav and Brian practice Wing Chun and Yiquan styles. Nathaniel practices Krav Maga. Kuldeep: Tae Kwon Do. And Bosco and Nagesh are mixed martial artists.'

'I've had the good fortune of knowing their families and themselves. I thank you all for this at such short notice'. He bowed to them with folded hands as they reciprocated the gesture.

'You shall be fighting Trishul here; he is trained in Shastar Vidya. There are some primary weapons on the table there, though we'd like it if you used them only if you trust you will not be able to win without them. In other words, whoever picks up a weapon admits not to be able to cope without a weapon any more. Please, take a moment before we begin.'

Trish closed his eyes. He remembered the time he was at Amratji's school. 'You want to learn to fight so you can forgive others? Could you explain what that means, boy?' Amratji, as everyone in school called her, had looked at him quizzically. 'Is beating others your way of forgiveness?'

Trish was nervous. He was only eight at the time. 'I don't want to hurt anyone. But if I don't have the strength or skills to beat someone, what good is it forgiving them? Only a person in a position of strength can forgive another. If I knew I'd get beaten up, I'd run, not forgive,' he mustered.

The way Amratji laughed had made him smile too. Then she said, 'Forgiveness doesn't come from physical strength, Trishul Ji. It comes from emotional strength. I will teach you. In time, you shall have both.' She hugged him. No one had called him Trishul Ji before.

'Move only enough to misalign your opponent; there's no point running around. Save your energy, let them fight. The slightest touch can produce maximum impact on the other person if you know when and where to make it. It's like a dance. Do you know how to dance Trishul Ji?'

She always kept pushing, trying to make them perfect their every move.

'No! What kind of idiot meets the edge of an opponent's sword with their own? You're ruining both blades! Use the flat of the blade to deflect his blow and turn that move around to bring your own edge on to him. Here, watch me.'

Trish always looked at her and wished he'd have half of her grace someday. Her turban was always blue, her clothes white. She was widowed six months after her marriage at the tender age of fourteen. Her parents-in-law noticed her keenness in the martial art their son was learning to practice and encouraged her to learn it herself.

'She's our son,' they would say when they attended her school every month.

After nine years of learning at her school, Trish finally got the highest honour bestowed to anyone in training – a duel with Amratji herself. Not everyone who graduated from her school got this honour. The last time it was presented to a trainee was before Trish had even joined. He was ecstatic. There was every chance he'd lose, *but just to be able to fight her!*

When the day came, the battleground was packed. People from all over had come to witness this rare event. Distinguished guests lined the seats set up around the grounds. It was a big affair, and the school left no leaf unturned in trying to make it as grand as possible.

After the duel had begun, the only sounds were the periodic 'ooohs' and aaaahs' of admiration as they both danced in perfect sync. It went on and on, and in what was generally pin drop silence; they danced for an hour and a half like boats in a storm...until she drew blood.

Trish slashed his sword upward across her chest, but the blow was deftly parried by Amratji as she moved across his line of attack. He'd lunged forward a bit too far, and she took good advantage of this, kicking the small of his back as she manoeuvred past him. While that had the desired effect, it wasn't to the extent she'd wanted.

It did throw him off balance just a little but he recovered, and she noticed him over her shoulder beginning to crouch as he started pivoting around his right leg. She had taught him well. She expected the leap any instant and spilt her centre of gravity ever so gently, angling downward as she began twisting around herself.

He was watching her too, and she noticed he never lifted his sword. Clever boy.

Even as Trish leapt into the air, she noticed he'd changed the grip on his sword and was holding his thumb away from the blade, never having lifted it. It was just what she'd anticipated.

Amratji slid under him holding her sword flat above her body to check the intended cut and deflected it sideways. What she noticed too late, was that he was gripping it rather hard. Whilst she slid past him under his sword, she had deflected it enough to make it nick the inside of his left thigh.

When she turned around, she saw his back with his right knee dug into the ground. His body weight was on his sword buried three inches deep at the tip just ahead of him, while his left leg stretched behind him, blood dripping from his thigh.

'Medic!' Amratji shouted. 'Ring the bell! Fight's over!'

'NOOOOO!' Trish roared as he turned around. 'FIGHT ME!'

He had rage in his eyes; a madness no one had ever seen in him. He'd started breathing heavily and looked at her as if he was waiting to rip her apart. He lifted his sword high above him.

Amratji threw her sword away. 'Drop it. I will not fight you.'

'THEN DIE!' he roared again as he lunged towards her.

'TRISHUL!!!' she half shouted in fear and disbelief as she stepped back, never looking away from his eyes.

'Trishul? Trishul?' He snapped himself away from his memory and saw Fakru looking at him quizzically. 'What happened? Are you ready to fight?'

'I am,' he said calmly.

Everyone saluted each other and Trishul in their own way. Trish brought up his arms in a circular motion and held them together in front of his chest, with his left palm facing up and right fist resting on it in a ball with his thumb sticking out. He then bowed his head and stood upright.

Ritu stepped forward first. Trish held his arms behind his back and never struck once, while she kicked, boxed, then kicked again. But not once could she touch him. All Trish did was twist and turn, then he bent and stepped aside. After this had been going on for a few minutes, Kuldeep stepped in as she stepped back. Brian came next, then Nagesh and then everyone else one after the other. The only person to make contact with Trish was Nathaniel, and he never made an impact either. He just managed to scrape past Trish's arms every once in a while. Through the entire time, Trish still had his hands behind his back.

Fakru clearly appeared pleased. 'He's really good. What do you think?'

Adipati smiled. 'I'd pay to see him dance. It's beautiful.'

'So what is this really about?' Fakru asked him. 'Clearly you know the boy can fight, or else you wouldn't ask me to let ten of these fighters attempt to kill him, even figuratively. You said you had to keep him safe and avoid capture. So why this charade then? Why not head straight for safety?'

Adipati took turns looking at Fakru and the fight when he replied. 'I'm hoping something dramatic will happen here when he's fighting. Something that triggers him to turn into who he really is. I want to see how much of this transformation occurs, and whether he can control himself when he turns. What we might find should decide whether we need to make a detour before our final stop. Time to up the game a bit, don't you think?'

Fakru let the man's words sink in, then nodded and blew twice on his whistle.

They came at him two at a time now, as they took up a stance in front of him. Trish brought his hands forward and folded them against his chest. The result remained the same. He opened his arms up to balance off his sharper twists and turns now, but no one made contact with him for the better part of ten minutes. Then, as Bhairavi and Namdourei teamed up, he started parrying their blows by using his feet, arms, and whatever other part of the body he wanted. He was clearly playing them.

Fakru blew twice on his whistle again, and they now came at him a few at a time, one backing as the other stepped up. Trish continued manoeuvring around them till Bosco managed to land his fist on his ribs. That threw him off balance, and Sunitha crept under him and managed to roll him over her back. Trish found ground for his feet and steadied up. He appreciated the moves with a nod and opened up his feet a little, exposing his full body to his attackers.

'That's a daft move,' muttered Fakru. Adipati continued to smile.

Trish lowered his head a little towards the nearest opponent while looking at the farthest. He slapped his thighs and then his chest, moving towards the most distant person.

Kuldeep, being the nearest opponent, came in and saw the opportunity with a kick to the back of Trish's head. Trish slapped his shin with his left palm, then moved towards him as his leg slipped past his skull. When he was near enough, Trish hit his cheekbone with his elbow and in one quick motion, turned to hold him by the collar with his right hand, still turning as he put him in the way of an incoming blow from Vaibhav. Vaibhav hit Kuldeep hard as he met him halfway to where he was expecting the impact. This threw him off guard too.

Trish rolled over on to Kuldeep's back and landed a kick on Vaibhav. He managed to block it, but was sent down to the ground as he fell off balance. Trish then started ripping through the others. He broke their chain and put himself between them from one side and then the other. For the first time since the fight began, people started getting beaten up and fell to the ground.

'Hail *Varah*, the boar!' Adipati said to Fakru. This time Fakru smiled.

They came at him from all directions now, as many at a time as they could. Trish's lowered head turned upward as his stance changed. He suddenly looked broader, and opened himself up like the sails on a boat. With shoulders lifted, his arms opened up a bit more; he was moving more fluidly than before but now took them head on like a wall rather than penetrating their formations. Twisting around the spine, he compressed his body more, then shifted to the offensive. Everyone around him kept getting hit and falling. He was plundering through them all.

'*Nandi!*' Adipati exclaimed. Fakru noticed an excitable Adipati for the first time in very long. Adipati turned to Brij, who was biting his nails. 'The boy is much better than I expected. My congratulations to you, sir.'

Fakru's fighters had had enough. They were all on to Trish now. He'd still not been hit once, while the others already had bruises. They all individually looked great, but as a team against Trish, they were falling to bits.

Nagesh was the first to realise this as he seemed to start taking control of the attack. Others followed his lead and not long after, they looked much better as an offensive unit. Trish smiled; he knew the game was getting to the next level. Fakru noticed the next change in his stance and looked at Adipati to share his brilliant observation, but saw him smiling as he nodded back in acknowledgement.

The blows were far more coordinated and much stronger than before, but Trish was as fluid as water. Spilling all over, he remained at the periphery of every blow and moved like he wasn't made of solid matter at all. If there were no people around him getting hurt, and if Trish were alone on that ground at that very moment, no one could have said he wasn't dancing. There was movement within his movement, and people still kept hitting the ground while he moved through them like a breeze through the woods.

Adipati folded his hands in a *namaste* and bowed. Then he turned to Fakru to explain.

'I know the SHIV when I see the SHIV,' Fakru quipped.

Adipati bowed his head again; silent and full of admiration for the boy.

'What about extraction?' Fakru asked him. 'Why are you still travelling by road?'

'They have hit a technical snag with the new variant,' he replied, never taking his eyes off Trish. 'The timing couldn't be worse if you ask me— Oh! How wonderfully he moves.'

Sunitha was the first to pick up a weapon. They'd been fighting for long enough, and Trish hadn't lost his balance completely, not even once. All the others had tasted dirt several times. *How do you throw someone off balance when their centre of gravity isn't in one place?* Trish was like a mass of fluid around his apparent body, with his body weight all over the place.

She had to admit it was beautiful, but someone had to do something to end the prolonged agony of trying to get one decent chance at triumph. If she could injure him ever so slightly, it could give them an edge.

Trish plucked the incoming blade with his index finger and thumb, pulled it along its line of movement while pulling out his shoulder, then landed his elbow on Sunitha's forehead. More weapons poured in, and soon everyone but Trish held one.

'He should have a weapon too!' exclaimed Brijbhooshan.

'He can pick one if he chooses at any time,' Adipati reminded him.

However, Trish never looked interested in picking one up for himself. There were so many of them around him that he was using them against each other anyway. His fluid body was now in and out of their lines of attack from the various weapons swinging left and right. He was the wind, and if he didn't know any better, Brij would have thought a few weapons went right through him without touching his body. They could barely see him anymore with the speed he was moving at.

'You have to stop this now.' Brij said.

Adipati retorted. 'He can stop it anytime he wants. Your son is incredible, but can *you* enjoy his brilliance for just a moment? I know you're his father, but for that very reason there must be a part of you feeling incredibly proud too, right?'

Fakru went down on his knees. 'Allah, bless this boy. I thank you for this chance to watch him.'

There was an axe in play, with a few swords of different styles, some spears, and a hammer. But it was the knife that did it. Trish had just pushed a sword away from his shoulder with a smack from the back of his hand, when a knife clipped his triceps. He didn't even realise it at first, but the look on some of the faces in his opponents and a slight discomfort while wielding his arm made him look at his wound. He saw blood – his own blood.

No one missed his roar. It struck fear even in those who weren't fighting him. 'His eyes!' exclaimed Ritu. The others stepped back.

Everyone watching saw the change in a split second. Trish wasn't playing with his opponents any more. He was striking them; with might. They heard a couple of bones crack. There was blood next to those who were on the ground.

'DIE!' Trish shouted.

'Call it off,' shouted a terrified Adipati to Fakru. 'He's found himself!'

Fakru blew into his whistle rapidly, and everyone scurried from the field. Adipati yelled, 'Run, abort, save yourselves!'

Trish turned towards Adipati. 'YOU!' he bellowed. He picked up an axe, pivoted on his toes, and hurled it towards him. 'DIE!'

The axe came straight for Adipati's throat, turning the blade around several times till its sharp edge was inches away from him. Then it stopped in mid air. Trish looked at him and roared again, breathing heavily. As Adipati walked around the suspended axe towards Trish, Lyosha raised his arm, and the axe flew into his open palm. Brij was too stunned to react to any of this.

Adipati walked up to an enraged Trish and shouted, 'Trishul! You listen to me boy! Trishul!'

+++

When Trish came to, he was being nursed by her. The moment he opened his eyes, she got up, startled.

'I'm sorry Amratji. I don't remember it clearly, but I was way out of line,' Trish said.

She eased up a bit.

'Please forgive me. I don't know what got into me,' he continued.

'What happened to your eyes?'

'My eyes? I don't know. What happened? I swear I don't remember it clearly. I gave in to anger. This is not what you taught me, and I'm ashamed of myself. I promise I'll never repeat this. Please forgive me,' Trish said.

'You leave on Saturday. I have nothing more to teach you. Practice what you have learnt, Trishul Ji. All the best for your life.' She walked away, leaving Trish in tears.

Outside, she wiped her own.

05

«« « FIVE »» »

Brijbhooshan hadn't said a word in more than three hours. He sat wondering what was going on and what kind of people they were really involved with. *Had Sumitra been right in trusting this man? How did she even know to trust him? Where did she come from?* This was the first time in his life Brij was regretting not knowing enough about his wife's past.

'*Prepare him...*' her whisper said in his ears, as he remembered her last day like it were yesterday. He had no idea of the magnitude of their predicament, and he doubted he realised it fully even now. But with what he had just seen, he was sure it was not just men who wanted to kidnap or harm his son. Trishul had just exhibited a side of himself Brij had never known. *That rage! And his eyes - what had happened back there?* Then the flying axe came to a halt in mid air! He wasn't sure what to make of any of it, but things beyond comprehension were at play here.

Adipati's words played back in his mind. *"If I were to tell you now, the things you must know, and will, you wouldn't believe me. Not any of it. If you wouldn't believe me, there would be no chance of trusting me. So for now, I must lean in on your mother's faith in us for you to trust that we are here to help."*

He watched his son lying on a mattress on the floor a few feet away, sweating and asleep. *What have we have we got ourselves into? What is it about you, son? What was it about your mother...and what do these people really want,* he thought, looking at Adipati, Lyosha and Sveta — as he had heard them call her — sitting huddled up on a *charpoy* in the far corner. Mugdha, Vishwas and the others stood close by.

He didn't even want to hazard a guess at what they were discussing.

'It wasn't just an interference,' growled Adipati. 'I know that could have been from the boy. It was much stronger. Someone was there; the shift in energy was massive...the presence was most certainly nodal. When I shook him up, just before Trishul fainted, I felt the energy surge.'

'But that's impossible,' Lyosha said. 'They have what... eight nodes left, maybe ten? All of them are really important to them. There's no way any of them are here permanently and none can cross over just yet...and to do what? Observe? That's not like them at all! Could it have been...'

'You're not saying I don't know what I'm talking about, are you?' Adipati said through an almost tightly clenched jaw. Everyone moved their heads back a few inches as if he was going to explode. 'Sorry, I don't mean to be cross with you. I am disturbed too. You are right; it is highly unlikely, but I know what I felt, even if for the life of me I can't make sense of any of it. Whoever it was that commanded the energy, they were really close too. But they muted immediately after the boy fell. Maybe even left, it's difficult to say.'

Their discussion was ended by Trish's moaning as he came to. At first, he looked around bewildered, trying to get his bearings, then he smiled at his father who had a rather concerned look on his face. Adipati walked up to him.

Trish started to speak. 'I'm sorry I...don't remember...got cut...blood...axe...the axe...' His eyes widened. 'How did you...' He looked at Adipati with astonishment.

'You have a lot to take in,' Adipati said while he helped Trish upright and made him sit in a chair. 'Just take a seat and let me explain as best as I can.' He then turned to Brijbhooshan and offered him a seat next to Trish with a desperate smile on his face.

It was like the time when Adipati introduced himself to Trish back home. They were all standing this time though, and Brijbhooshan sat by his side, just as lost as him.

'So,' Adipati started. 'Since you have now experienced some things first hand that will have increased your appetite for the unbelievable, I think we might be ready to share some things with you. Have you ever heard of THE CIRCUIT?'

Trish shook his head.

'It's a myth' Brij said, throwing up his arms. 'An urban legend, if you will. They are a group of investors and powerful men empowering shelved projects and investigations. Every now and then, when there's something no one can explain, their name comes up. But they haven't influenced any decisions taken by governments or any major organisations. So basically, they're a name people whisper when they have no idea of what's going on. Like "Mr. Nobody". It's a farce, they're not real.'

'Oh, but they are,' Adipati interjected. 'It is anything but a farce. They have existed as individuals for as long as one can think of, and as organisations, at various points in time. These people have mostly stayed hidden, burdened by their knowledge and their quest for answers that religion or science couldn't provide them with.

'They have also been known to come together time and again in human history in a bid to better understand us, as humans, and the purpose for our existence. It is believed that the first time of any such organisation came into being was thousands of years in the BCE era when a peril came to present itself to humanity. A few showed themselves, and word spread about there being others like them...'

'So, you're saying The Circuit has existed as far back as the BCE?' Trish said, half mocking Adipati's tale with a raised brow.

'No,' Adipati replied. 'They had since disbanded for reasons unknown, and were most definitely not known as The Circuit. But since then, they've been aware of each other and in touch with others like them. They have lived normal lives amidst people while striving towards their goals.

'The need for an organisation in themselves has arisen from time to time, and they have collaborated on several instances, but there had never been a structure to their organisation till the middle of the eleventh century. Have you heard of Al Biruni?'

Both Trish and Brij looked at him blankly and then at each other. 'Who?' asked Brij.

'During the conquests of Mahmud of Ghazni, one of the most brilliant minds in the human world at the time was brought to India. Al Biruni was a scholar whose quest for science and truth got fuel in the years he spent in India learning from Sanskrit scriptures and gurus, while acquainting himself of the Indian system of astrology, sciences, and mathematics. At this time, he met with the brightest people working on these sciences in the region. Through him, a lot of these people came to interact with one another.'

'Now, within them were some who knew a lot more than anyone at the time could have handled; probably not even today. These people got together more often and soon, after the demise of Biruni himself, they realised the need for working together under a structured organisation. Thus was born SUKRIT, or *pious creation,* the first known structured organisation of these people. They have since devoted their lives to pure science, and the truth of our existence and evolution.'

Adipati reached for a glass of water just as Brijbhooshan was looking to interrupt, as if he would pounce on him.

'So what are you getting at? Are these the people my son is in danger from? Because of what he can do...see clearly at night, I mean?' asked an incredulous Brijbhooshan.

'Oh your son can do much more than just see clearly at night, I am sure. Part of which you have seen today. But no…' Adipati looked at his people over both his shoulders before continuing. 'I am comfortable to let you know now that these are the people who want your son alive and happy. *We are* The Circuit.'

'So Sukrit became The Circuit, eh?' Trish asked. 'Modernisation?'

'Sort of...' Adipati replied. 'During the last crisis we had a difference of opinions within Sukrit, and soon after the crisis was over, some members dissociated themselves from us. It was a huge blow to the organisation, since some of the ones to leave us were pioneers and influential people. But the dissolution of Sukrit gave birth later to The Circuit as a conglomerate in the early nineteenth century.'

'Our structure became modern, and we started doing really good work on sciences very soon. There was also a significant reorientation in our financial goals, which led to us being monetarily stable and self-sufficient. We've grown stronger ever since.'

Trish's interest peaked. 'When you say over and over again that *these people, people like them* and so on, what do you mean? What was so special about these people? What's so special about *you*? You say The Circuit's goals are aligned with scientific progress and *pure science*. What does that mean? Isn't that everybody's goal? We all are advancing technologically. Do you have stakes in big tech firms or something? Is that your business?'

Adipati took a moment to frame his next words and looked away. He knew the boy had many questions and would have many more. There was no correct way of breaking down the information, yet he had to be informed. His world was going to turn over in the days to come.

'The ones before us, as well as our group, have been able to harness, let's say, more of the capabilities of our minds than what is the norm. We are, Trishul, in the right sense of the word - yogis.'

'Yogis?' Trishul asked.

He received a nod from Adipati.

'Yogis?' he asked again. 'Seriously? You guys are yogis? In your dapper suits and dresses, your perfectly gelled hair and perfumes, your expensive cars and big conglomerates? What kind of yogis does that make you? Aren't yogis supposed to shun worldly pleasures and give themselves up to God and live in the mountains wearing only cloth?'

His rant got a muffled titter from the people in front of him, but Adipati cleared his throat, and there was silence. With a wry smile on his face, he pulled up a chair for himself and leant towards Trish as he sat. 'What do you think yog is, son?'

Trish was uncomfortable and he shifted in place just a bit. 'Yoga? I don't know...health through exercise...devotion to God...giving up worldly desires...everything else you guys do not seem to embrace?'

Adipati patiently smiled, which was a quality all his peers admired. Trish, however, was beginning to like his ever patient smile less and less every day.

'All these perceptions, my child, came along with the metamorphosis of yog into yoga as you like to call it. Or of aasan into asana, or Ram into Rama and so on. Yog, in its essence, means to liberate yourself from the limitations of your body and unite with the one true energy that drives everything we know of; the ascent and augmentation of consciousness and the course to the omniscient.'

'When consciousness leaves the entrapment of the body, it is able to do what the body could never imagine. To this end, to be at one with the universe is the path of yog. To achieve that level of consciousness, aasans are employed as a vehicle to channel energy through the body, which in turn heals the body itself as a by-product of the entire exercise. The goal, however, is not merely better health of the body, though it becomes an important checkpoint on your way to the goal itself. Most people, more so in western cultures, are beguiled by the misunderstanding of yog as an exercise regime for fitness. If aasans are the vehicles to this end, meditation and concentration are the drivers.'

Brij was listening to him as intently as Trish. The others seemed to listen in as well, with the odd whisper to one another at a distance from them.

'Meditation and concentration are described as *dhyaan* and *samadhi,* which are easily misconstrued to religious effect,' Adipati continued. 'The discovery of, aspiration to understand, and advancement in yog may have been born in the Hindu faith, but it is understood and practised to good effect by people of all races, creeds, and religions as already demonstrated to you by Lyosha.' He looked at the big Russian disapprovingly.

'What?' Lyosha retorted. 'Three inches...that's when I held it...three inches from your face!'

'And I told you there was no need for it.'

'Yeah, next time that happens, I won't even hold your head off the ground after it's been sliced already.'

'Hold on a minute,' Trish said, breaking their conversation and addressing Adipati directly. 'What was that trickery anyway? I knew I threw an axe, though I have no recollection of what led to that, and I know it stopped in mid air before it reached you.'

He then turned to Lyosha. 'And you're telling me you stopped it there? And you say this is Yoga?'

'Yog,' said Adipati, correcting him. He then put his hand on Trish's knee and continued, 'not really. This is what Lyosha can do as a result of yog and his ability to exercise it. This is a manifestation of yog, not yog itself.'

He turned to Lyosha. 'This is why you shouldn't have done it. There's a time to tell the boy a thing. First off, there's no perfect way of doing this, and I'm trying my best to plan and break things to him, so he best understands them one at a time. Then you just go ahead and screw up the time line in my plan.'

'Here kid,' said an evidently agitated Lyosha, looking grimly into Adipati's eyes with his hands folded across his chest. 'Do it again!'

An axe flew from across the room and stopped in front of Trish's face.

'What the fuck?' Trish moved back and almost fell off his chair. Adipati hit his palm on his forehead, shaking his head deploringly. 'How are you doing that?' Trish demanded.

Lyosha looked at him for an instant, then said, 'I can move things with my mind; I thought you'd figured that out by now, Einstein.' Then he focused back on Adipati. 'Looks like it'll never be time enough for this one...the one thing we don't have plenty of, in case you forgot.'

Trish was still petrified. 'But you're not even looking at it. Even your hands are folded.'

'This is not a movie, boy. It's not really controlling by mind if I have to make gestures, is it?' The axe started to back up, then glided back to where it came from. Lyosha shook his head. 'I need air. You have to realise he has to know. The sooner, the better, Mr Adipati. Time is of the essence.' With a finger held out above his head, he started to walk out. 'Tick tock, tick tock...' he mocked as his finger moved from side to side.

'Sorry about that. He's improved a lot, but he's always had a temper,' Adipati said, looking sheepish. 'Comes out when he's stressed sometimes.'

Trish sat there awkwardly holding his folded knees with his eyed widened. 'You're yogis, eh? What can you do?' He asked Adipati.

'Not everyone here has tangible skills like Lyosha, Trish. But we can all use the mind to a far greater degree than is, shall we say...normal,' Adipati replied. 'Some things I can do too. You'll see in time.'

'And you?' Trish asked Sveta.

"*I can talk to you.*"

Trish was awestruck. 'No way!' he exclaimed. Sveta never uttered a word from her mouth, but he could hear her loud and clear in his head. *"Can you hear me too?"* he thought in his mind.

"Yes."

"Raise your right hand."

She lifted her right hand up and waved at him, throwing her head to the side. Trish was clearly impressed. He was beaming. Something inside him wanted to trust these people, like a kid in a magic shop. He looked in awe.

However, Brijbhooshan did not.

06

««« SIX »»»

'Hurry up, we must leave now,' came Adipati's instructions as everyone scrambled to leave. 'Where's Sveta?'

Brijbhooshan went back inside to find his son fully healed of his wounds. There was not even a sign of a scar left on his body. Just under a half hour, Mr Fakru had healed him completely. Trish looked more and more pleased with these people by the minute, but there were so many things on Brij's mind.

'Look Dad,' he said, opening up his arms and turning around. 'Not a scratch! No pain, no nothing. I still don't think I understand much, but this is way beyond cool.' He beamed. Fakru was on the far side of the room, praying.

Brij was serious and spoke in a hushed voice. 'I don't trust these circus freaks much, Trish. If they are indeed capable of these things and say that they are still struggling to save you, can you imagine what kind of danger you may be in?'

'But Dad...'

'You said it yourself Trish, what is to say we can completely trust them? What if this is an eyewash? Who knows what these people really want?' His eyes narrowed and he lowered his voice to a whisper. 'However much I might trust your mother's word, I've hired help Trish; the best that's available. Trust me, son, I won't let anything happen to you. For now, we do as they say.'

'I trust you Dad, completely. I'm in this with you,' Trish said.

Fakru finished his prayers and walked them out as Sveta appeared. She went straight to Adipati. 'Twins off Unnao, close to Ajgain. They didn't feel me.'

Adipati looked at Mugdha and Vishwas. 'We get off the highway at Dharau and take the inside roads via Pukhrayan and Ghatampur to join back before Fatehpur. We want to give Kanpur a wide berth.'

While everyone else was taking seats, Adipati went to Fakru and hugged him. "Thanks again, my friend. I wish you could come with us, you have seen the light. I never understood what you're still doing in a mosque and living here of all places, helping people who don't want to be helped.'

'I had Allah before I... how do you say it, *saw the light*. He is all these people have. They may not want my help, but He will not let me ignore the fact that they need it. He is hope; I can abandon neither him nor his people,' Fakru said. 'But I am just a wish away my friend, we are all in this together, and I identify with your quest. If and when I'm needed, you'll find me standing right beside you as always. For now, head for the well; I understand what you must do to help him control himself.'

Sveta opened the rear door and offered Trish to sit beside her. 'Lyosha will drive,' she said, 'and we'll be at our stop before nightfall. After that, you can take over.'

'Our stop?' Brij inquired.

'We're picking someone up on our way,' Adipati replied as he signalled to Gurung, one of the quietest guys of the lot. He handed him a piece of paper and said, 'Gurung, this text, that number and this origin.'

Gurung nodded.

'On our way to where?' Brij demanded.

'Benares.'

+++

'She got a text,' Bijoy announced.

'Display it please,' Shujoy Rai Datta said.

The screen on the wall lit up.

> Sender: LM-569874
> "Worship the vehicle of Lord Yama
> and win over life.
> For astrological help reply 'YES' and receive
> weekly advice for Rs 5/- only."

'You're showing me spam now? You think this is funny?' RD complained.

The young man looked rattled. 'I'm sorry, you said everything...She's deleted it. My bad.'

'Of course, she's deleted it. Nobody keeps spam on their phone,' Rai Datta shouted. 'Don't bother me with this shit again and tell the twins to be on the lookout. They must be on their way to Lucknow soon. Tell them to have eyes on her too when they can. They *will* try to contact her somehow. And what's the news from Etawah? Has someone reached there or not?'

+++

Dr Surbhi Tripathi was an alumna at the university she taught in. With degrees in *Ancient Indian History and Archaeology* and *Jyotir Vigyan* (Science of Astrology) from Lucknow University, she was also a celebrated author of a series of books exploring commonalities in the two fields of study. Married at the age of twenty-one, she raised three children and led what she thought was a rather mundane life. The only thing she would never compromise was her studies of the subjects she loved so much.

Despite her otherwise engaging life as a wife, mother and a loveable daughter-in-law, she always found time to go through a Master's degree in both disciplines and a doctorate in one. At the age of fifty-two, she lived by herself with her children studying and working abroad. Her husband passed away after her youngest daughter left home for studies in Europe. Now she had all the time she wished she'd had earlier in life. She followed a routine and her days went by like clockwork. She was busy teaching what she'd written to her students and had little to no expectation that anyone would work on these fields.

However, seven months ago, a man came to see her at the university. He introduced himself as the CEO of a private company that was interested in her work and wanted to share what his company had done in the field as a project of interest. He seemed to know everything she'd written and worked on, and he showed her some of their own work that left her awestruck.

What he suggested seemed outlandish in the beginning, but when she looked at what they had to offer, she could argue no more. They were ready to share their work with her if she promised confidentiality. Soon after, she urged that the discoveries they had made and the history they had uncovered belonged to the world, and it was something that had to be shared. It was then she was introduced to Adipati Srivastav.

The man talked with her for over a week and made an offer that changed her life. She could work with them on a strictly confidential basis, and could work on her own times as long as she cooperated with them on their upcoming project. Over the next few months, she learnt of things she had never thought were possible. The existence of people such as the ones she was working with was nothing short of surreal in itself. But it was the study and research that she was in for. No amount of access would have got her the information these people had. She couldn't do the things that they could, nor did she understand everything they meant, but her work with them was valuable and intriguing. It brought out the girl in her that never got any real excitement, and today was the most exciting day so far.

She was waiting for it since she awoke; she knew it would come. Her phone beeped late in the morning. It was a text, just as she had expected. She read it and noted everything on a piece of paper with a racing heart. Then she deleted it and headed for her car. The driver was waiting as instructed.

'Start driving,' she said as she took a seat and opened a map in the rear of the car.

On the map, she placed a small notebook. She opened it to a page that had "texts" written at the top followed by abbreviations, then scrolled till she came to *LM*. She opened up to a blank page and took out the piece of paper she had written her text on.

Sender: LM-569874
"Worship the vehicle of Lord Yama
and win over life.
For astrological help reply 'YES' and receive
weekly advice for Rs 5/- only."

She started writing on the blank page: *Leave Moving 5 6 9 8 7 4*

She took the map to Lucknow, then began panning in all directions looking for '5'. Due south east, she found the road – number 56 and circled '5' and '6' on what she had written. She traced it going south east on the map through Jaunpur, then further south east, looking for a '9', or a '9' followed by an '8' on either side of road 56.

At Babatpur, she saw a road numbered 98 going west, then heading southward. She circled '9' and '8' together as well and started tracing that road till after it had crossed the AH1 highway, where it changed to road 74. Her heart beat so fast she thought she'd have a stroke as she circled '7' and '4' together as well. As she started following this new road on the map, she came across a place named Bhainsa.

'Toward Sultanpur for now...keep going straight. I'll tell you where to head when we're there,' she instructed the driver. She switched her phone off, smiling to herself even as her heart exploded with excitement.

Bhainsa...Buffalo! The vehicle of Lord Yam!

+++

'Are you religious?' Adipati asked Trishul as Brij listened intently, even though he appeared to be lost in thought.

'Not particularly,' replied Trish.

'Well, do you believe in God?' Adipati said, egging the boy on.

'I guess...' he replied. 'I don't pray or anything though, you know? Like, I don't tie myself to religious practice or whatever, but there's so much we can't explain and don't know about. I can't reject the notion that someone is running the show. How else is the world working? Who put us here?'

'Now that really is the question, isn't it? Who put us here?' Adipati looked pleased with his response. 'But just because we don't know or can't explain some things, does it mean gods are running the world for us? I mean when we didn't know that the earth spins on its axis, didn't we think that the Sun was a god that showed himself every day and rode a chariot of horses across the skies? Now that we know what's actually happening, now where's that God? What is to say we won't find more and more answers to everything we cannot explain now, and that gods then will lose their relevance one after the other? Should we then consider God as unexplained science?'

'So you're saying there is no God, just science then, aren't you?'

'That depends on what *you* mean by God, Trish.'

'What are you saying exactly?'

'Just think about this, what is the one thing that humans want to do that we tend to think would be the pinnacle of our scientific evolution?' Adipati half turned toward Trish. 'There have been countless books written on the matter; men have spent their entire lives trying to achieve the one goal that has eluded us forever. Who do we aspire to become by achieving this one feat?'

'What are you talking about?'

'Frankenstein.'

'Creating life?'

'One in our own image, that too. Why are we so obsessed with it?' Adipati asked. 'Who, I ask again, do we want to become?'

'Gods?' Trish smirked.

'Which is why your question is so interesting, don't you think? Who put us here?'

Brij no longer pretended to appear not to listen. He turned toward them and looked at them as they talked.

Trish shook his head. 'But we were not just *put* on earth though, were we? I mean unless you want to go with religion. I know why you mentioned *own image,* but that's from religion. Science says we evolved from a single cell to fish to reptile to ape and man. So it's a bit of a paradox if you're trying to sell science as opposed to religion, while basing your arguments on religious text, so I'm not really buying that.'

'As you shouldn't. I don't advocate ever buying into something you're not convinced of, be it a decision between science and religion, or an Apple and an Android,' Adipati said with a smile that was reciprocated in a chuckle.

'We evolved from a single cell to the supreme species of the planet so determined to be gods of our own, that we won't stop at destroying every other species. I am not contesting that. Neither am I contesting that it all actually happened here on earth. But would you consider at all that we might have had help in this *evolution*?'

'How do you mean?' Trish asked, and took the bait to engage.

'What is the one thing common to all life forms?' Adipati asked. 'What is it in us that is in plants and animals and insects, but not rocks, or rivers, or air? With life as we know it, what's at its core? Yes, we evolved. All living things evolved and are evolving right now. But what is it that allows evolution? How did the one cell become the tree, the butterfly, the tiger, and also man? And when it evolved, what determined what it evolved into? While we all have it since we came from the same cell, why are we all so different as species that live?'

'Umm...Are you hinting at DNA?' Trish seemed to enjoy the discussion and was grinning, but wasn't quite sure if he was really contributing to it. He couldn't tell one smile on Adipati's face from another. *For fuck's sake, stop smiling.*

'Do you know that by the latest acceptable standards, your body has many trillions of cells?' Adipati wasn't asking; it was a statement more than a question. 'Each cell has a nucleus. The nucleus consists of a number of things out of which, chromosomes are one. The chromosomes have in them our genes, which in turn, have our DNA.'

'Agreed,' Trish said. Even Brij nodded.

'DNA is a chain of repetitive nucleotides. In living organisms, the DNA – or the biopolymer chain – occurs in a pair, entwined in a double helix. Let's not even get into mRNA, tRNA, and rRNA for now, but let's just say RNA is created through a process called transcription, which is possible only by exact enzymes using DNA as a template. Our DNA is written as a code comprising four chemical nucleobases that you know as C, G, A, and T, plus sugar and a phosphate group.'

'The bases pair with each other through bonding; C with G and A with T, joining the two biopolymer strings. These DNA biopolymers *need* to exist in a double helix so they can squeeze in volumes of code into a chromosome! The only way it can exist as a double helix is by both strands running in opposite directions or being anti-parallel. Related DNA base pairs on earth are approximated to the amount of 5×10^{37}.'

Brij's eyes squinted in a quizzical look at first, then he pursed his lips and nodded in appreciation.

Adipati addressed him directly this time, before he looked to Trish as well. 'Imagine the possibilities! How these bases are sequenced determines the code for what they make; a tree, an animal, a human, or an insect. It also determines what kind of human you are, or which butterfly with what colours, or whether it's a herb or a tree! Meaning for instance, if you have black hair, it's written in that code.'

'Everything is in these codes. So when you say evolution from a single cell organism occurred, I say it did but not by chance. The odds of that happening would be akin to dropping symbols of musical notes in a drum and hurling it out to sea, to be found several thousands of years later, with the symbols coming out in order of Beethoven's Fifth!'

'So you're saying God or gods wrote the code?' Trish asked, wide eyed. 'So religion's been preaching the truth, and science is fiction?'

'All of what I just said is science!' Adipati exclaimed. 'Why do we think one is right and the other is wrong? They are both right, Trishul, and they are both wrong. All the science happened, and it was helped along by gods; but only because convention calls them that.'

'What should we call them then? Because it's difficult to believe in gods as the engineers you say they are, with your theory suddenly in my face,' Trish complained.

Lyosha had had enough. He mumbled over his shoulder, 'Why don't you just wait and watch? You are bound to get your answers soon enough!'

07

«‹«‹ SEVEN »›»›

'I have her. I can guide her here, but it'll take her another couple of hours to reach.'

They all heard Sveta even though she appeared to be in deep meditation on top of the SUV. After they had got off the AH1 heading south, Adipati had nodded to everyone in the car, and since then they had all been quiet. They kept heading south till they crossed a railway track, after which the road swerved left where they got off to the east-side and headed straight into a thicket where they stayed hidden.

Twenty minutes later two men brought refreshments on bicycles and disappeared. They left a plastic drum out for litter. Not long after that Sveta had perched atop the car and was in a state of meditation. Others followed suit and took up positions to meditate around the cars except for Adipati. He just wanted to keep talking to Trish.

Brij took out a book from his bag and began reading as Adipati leaned his back against a tree trunk to take a seat next to Trish.

'So, we have another couple of hours here,' Trish said.

'Yes we do,' Adipati replied.

'Mind telling me what Lyosha was on about?'

'You know how he is. He exaggerates everything and is temperamental. I wouldn't go by everything he says.'

'So you're saying what he said meant nothing then, are you?'

'Well, now that you put it that way.' Adipati took a deep breath. 'You know how I said what is documented as religion is not much different from science? We're all sons of gods in a sense, only some more so than others.'

'What do you mean?'

'Trish, this is going to be a lot for you to process within a short time. It has taken us our lives to come to terms with what we have discovered, and we still end up astonished more often than not. You have not been exposed to any of this, and have very little time to understand it all. On the other hand, understand all this, for *you must.* As you will see, first hand, things you cannot begin to explain. You must, therefore, realise that I'm in a very awkward position here. I have to do the best at making you grasp everything in a few days, the things that took me more than a century to learn.'

Trish smiled mischievously. 'I know you did that on purpose. What do you mean *a century to learn?*'

'Yog prolongs your years, son,' Adipati said. 'The more you are at one with the universe, the less you age physically. The aim of the yogi is to be completely unified with the cosmos to become free of space, time and physicality of material or mass. To harness the energy in the universe and channel it through oneself. However, it is easier said than done.'

'So how old are you saying you are then?' Trish asked.

'Let's keep that for another time shall we?'

'Humour me.'

'Knowledge of me will get you nothing, Trish. We have little time. I have to make you appreciate a lot; we can't afford small talk much longer.'

Adipati looked serious for a change. Trish nodded.

'So, as I was saying, everything written in the texts from our ancestors cannot be gibberish. They may not have been entirely aware of what was going on at the time, but they were by no means foolish. Holy scriptures from around the world describe as best they could, of how science was used by gods.'

'An aircraft does look like a giant bird that carries *gods* around if you have not even yet domesticated animals in a world over which it flies. How do you explain a gene bank to someone who still uses a stone axe as the most advanced technology for his time? You can at best tell him there's one of every species in there if he asks!'

'You don't really think arrows caused the kind of destruction they are documented in our texts to have caused at the time? But if one was told that it resulted from a weapon, what should one have equated that to? A weapon meant an arrow in that age. Are you getting my...drift? Is that what you say?'

'Kind of...' Trish said, thinking.

'We've already established that our *evolution* was controlled, right?' Adipati continued, but Trish interjected.

'No, you've established it, or so you claim. I'm still processing that theory. You have to admit, it does sound outlandish. Evolution is the most widely accepted theory in the world of science. Nobody would take what you're saying seriously. You just sound like one of those bogus alien theorists.'

He smiled again, but it was slowly growing on Trish. 'Let us not forget that a theory, whether accepted by almost all of mankind, or by a couple of men, remains just that. A theory.'

'But let me tell you Trish, acceptance of scientific theories is more of a result of convenience than anything else. If you were to consider every new theory seriously, can you imagine the amount of work that the scientific community would have to redo over and over again? That is why, even if a theory is promising and has enough to back itself up, it is generally dismissed outright at first. Then, if some nutjob perseveres with it and takes it to a point where it cannot be refuted anymore, only then does it start gaining acceptance. And then you have to re-discover everything in a new light, or in other words, admit that we know nothing, and all we are doing is pursuing another theory which might be overturned again in the future.'

'Our species cannot live with that. We have to know as a collective that we know whatever there is to know. The unknown scares us to no end. For the other part of your remark, take any *genius* from our history. Anyone whose work is unanimously accepted and regarded by the scientific world. I will tell you how he was ridiculed when he first came out with the same idea.'

'You're saying you're a nutjob?' Trish chuckled.

'No,' Adipati retorted. 'There are thousands of others who believe in theories on these lines. I just happen to know things they don't, which makes me say they aren't just theories. Let's talk about something that might get you comfortable with my ideas. Take any religious text from around the world and think before you tell me. Where do god's live?'

Trish played along. 'The heavens? *Devlok* as we call it, I guess.'

'And just where is this *devlok?*' Adipati asked, urging him on. 'Again, every civilisation/religious belief will tell you the same thing. Across continents and from the remotest tribes.'

'In the skies up above? You're trying to sell me aliens again, aren't you?'

'I don't know what you understand by that term, or why you would say I want you to think of any such thing,' Adipati replied. 'I'm just saying all peoples tell us the same thing, throughout our existence gods came from the skies. They didn't know space as a word, they just knew the sky. That is all I'm saying.'

'Who might arrive from the sky in giant birds that breathed fire and big chariots that made sound and smoke and could fly, I leave entirely for you to ponder over. I don't even want to know who you think they were as long as we can agree that our ancestors across the globe were not idiots and someone did come.'

'These *gods* who came and created us had powers we didn't understand, and weapons of mass destruction. If they so wished, they *gave* us powers, had offsprings with humans by way of procedures that did not involve sex at times, and helped us progress and protect us. They also punished us if we didn't follow their guidance and even wiped out humanity to start over in some instances!'

'Okay,' Trish said, 'I'll bite. Where are you going with this?'

'Just as they did not know space as a word Trish, just the *sky* where they believed the gods had their residence, they did not know a lot else in terms of how we define things today. What I'm saying is, if the earth was our place, and the gods were above us, any other place by this understanding would be *below* us, right? Thus the concept of the Underworld, or *Patal Lok*, or the Netherworld. People have been there. It has been written in every text, yet still today we choose to believe in it while ignoring how ironic it is.'

'Below us is solid rock until there is molten lava. There's no world or life *underneath* us, yet the place exists in every civilisation's understanding of the world. Every text has a mention of this place and has tried as best as it could to explain it. Only, there are follies like "it's beneath us", a derivative from the gods being above us. But how do you explain where it is with the limited understanding at the time of terminology that we, the ones form the future, would employ? We as a people still don't have enough understanding to fully appreciate what they were trying to say.'

'So, where is it?' Trish apparently took Adipati by surprise. He fell silent and started pondering. '*Maybe he's lost the plot,*' Trish thought. '*It doesn't look difficult to get lost in after all.*'

'She's here,' Sveta broke the silence. 'I've told her to stop the car no more than five seconds on the road and walk down here.'

'Good,' Adipati said to her with a nod and turned to Trish. 'Dr Tripathi will help us understand when it is we must go to Benares. Remember how you lost yourself at the end of the fight at Fakru's place? We will try to remedy that in Benares. You should never lose control of yourself again.'

+++

'Why aren't they there yet?' RD asked, appearing agitated, sitting on the plush leather seat at the back of his van that was his mobile office.

Bijoy had been lost in finding something. He'd spoken almost nothing, but was writing and scratching on a notepad. The boy was up to something, but RD knew he wouldn't say what it was till he was sure. He turned to the man sitting opposite him and said, 'Odogwu, are you sure you've got the right men for this?'

Odogwu was a veteran at his job. He had seen everything a profession like his could throw at a person. Men hired him for his expertise since they knew there were not many who were better at the job. Yet they would question his methods and ability, even after hiring him. After being in the business for thirty-seven years, it didn't bother him any more.

'Would you have paid what you did for my services if you thought I wouldn't have the *right men* for whatever it was I was doing?' he said calmly.

'Yeah, yeah, all right. Just know they had tea at that stall, then they went missing. They were headed to meet Dr Tripathi for sure, but they haven't shown on the route yet, and Tripathi's missing too,' RD said. 'What's going on here?'

'Ummmm...' Bijoy raised a pencil in the air. 'The text. She left within five minutes of receiving the text, then her phone switched off.'

'So?'

'So I thought there might have been something we missed,' Shujoy replied.

'Shujoy, young man, there's a team on standby at PatalPani to get the boy there so transport can be arranged. They would not dare go anywhere near Benares, and they want to meet up with Tripathi.' RD was clearly agitated and grinded his teeth. 'Are you telling me you find that spam more exciting than finding them around wherever they are near Lucknow?'

'Technically the team is in Mhow, just so that everyone is on the same page,' Odogwu clarified. RD looked at him with a tilted head and spread out his right palm as if to say '*seriously now?*'

Bijoy pulled out a map while he spoke. 'But let me explain. They are headed toward Benares.' He pointed to a place that was circled in pencil on the map.

Bhainsa.

+++

'Your phone needs to remain switched off, okay Mandhar?' Dr Surbhi asked her driver.

'I left it at home, madam. Never brought it with me.'

'Good. Slow down after the railway crossing. Do not stop. I will tell you to keep slowing down, and as soon as I get out, you are to continue driving straight ahead, till you find a shop or somewhere you can ask for directions. Ask them how to get to Parsottampur. They will tell you to turn around, which you will do and go back the way we came. Do not stop anywhere and don't go back to Lucknow. Go visit your family in Faizabad and take the week off. Do you understand?' she said, sounding concerned.

'But madam, where will you get off? There's no safe place anywhere after the crossing.'

'Do what I'm asking of you Mandhar. Please trust me. Do not speak to anyone about this. I will get in touch with you when I'm back. Here take this...' She handed him some money, which he initially refused. When he finally accepted it, they were crossing the railway tracks. 'Start slowing down now please.'

+++

'Is he the boy?' she asked as she looked at Trish, bewitched.

'Okay, everyone's got to stop saying that,' Trish complained as Adipati nodded to her question. Dr Surbhi spent another moment or two looking at him. Trish wasn't sure what to make of it.

Adipati cleared his throat and intervened. 'Do you have a *tithi*, Dr Tripathi?'

Dr Surbhi looked flustered for a bit, but took out a small notebook from her bag. 'I'm sorry' she said. 'There is an excellent opportunity we have next week—'

Adipati cut her short. 'We do not have that kind of time, madam. I thought I was clear about that.'

She looked flustered again. 'It is my duty to tell you there exists a better opportunity so close to us. I have for you, however, a time for the morning on the day after tomorrow. You may see them both and find out for yourself that it is not nearly as auspicious as next week. There...'

She opened the notebook to the facing pages that had identical drawings on them. The figure was that of a square, the centres of the sides which joined to form another square, only this time oriented like a diamond. Across the first square were drawn diagonals dividing the entire figure into four small squares in the centre, and eight triangles around them all within an outer square. Inside each of these sections was the Hindu name of one of the planets. They all knew what it was, but Trish just shook his head in disbelief and looked away.

'The morning after tomorrow will have to do,' said Adipati. 'They might get on to us soon, and we cannot be found in Benares under any circumstances. We must proceed now.'

'What has to be the day after?' Brijbhooshan asked.

'The procedure for your son,' Adipati replied. 'We must try to get him to be in control of himself at all times. Whenever there's an attack on us, it will be key for our survival for Trish to be focused. There is a place I know of where we might try to achieve this.'

08

«‹« EIGHT »›»

'You say his safety is your utmost priority and yet it's him driving at night every time in the lead car,' Brijbhooshan complained.

It was into the wee hours of the morning, and they could have already been where they were headed and sleeping, but Adipati insisted that the travel be swift and at a time of minimum traffic since they'd be driving without lights again. Brij was getting more concerned about this entire adventure with every passing minute. What started as blind faith in his wife's advice, and a real concern for the safety of his child from unknown dangers, was turning out to be something that constantly made less and less sense every step of the way. He couldn't help but think that so far, the only real danger his son had been in was a result of their own arrangement.

'Believe me, I only have the best interests of your son in mind. There's a reason we have to lay low and under the grid,' Adipati said. 'Not only are we not to be found; we cannot be found dead with where we are going!'

Trish was in the lead car, and it was the first time Adipati wasn't right next to him, but he chose to be in the following car with Brij. He'd thought it was best to stick with Brij for a little while and see if he could be pacified. He hadn't been as comfortable as the boy surprisingly was. *Maybe if he talked to him more...*

Brij wasn't the least bit calmer. 'What is in Benares? What are we going there for? Why is it so important that we go there?'

Adipati drew a deep breath. 'You saw what happened to Trish at the grounds, right? After the fight, I mean. He didn't know who he was or what he was doing...all he seemed to care about was ripping people apart. He had no control over himself. And his eyes. Did you notice his eyes?'

'Yes, what really happened there? I've never seen him like that. It was scary.'

'He was realising his true self; his inner instincts and reflexes were taking over. Now that is a good thing, mind you. We want that, but he has to be in control. What he was turning into can help him, as long as he doesn't lose himself to it. It's all about harnessing what his strengths are and having full control over them. That's what he needs to do,' Adipati said.

'It's from his mother, isn't it? I knew she was different. What's really going on with him?'

Brij was obviously concerned as was expected of a loving father, Adipati thought.

'You will know it all. But right now, we need to focus on the things we need to do to make him right. To put him in control of himself. Imagine how formidable your son would be with the energy he showed in the end, combined with the skills he showed us earlier. He needs to be strong for the events to come. The people surveilling your son will try to attack us and get to him, and he will need to hold himself together when he turns. The only place I know of where he can harness control is in Benares. It is the only way I know. To put him in the very place I am aware will help put him in the driver's seat of his own being.'

Brij nodded. 'Why is it then, that you keep saying we cannot be found in Benares?'

'Because if they were to get a hold of Trish, out of all the places they would take him, at the very top of the list would be the place we need to go to in Benares.'

+++

'You must be Adipati Ji,' the man waiting for them at the gate said as they pulled up. 'Sharma Ji told me about you. Please don't mind, sir, but could you show me some ID? You know how he is about these things.'

Adipati pulled out his driver's license.

'You are Kundan saheb's friend, right? You know Vashisht Ji? Please step inside and sit in the hall. We will get your luggage from the cars. Fresh tea is brewing as we speak and we are making some *pakauri*. There are two of us, sir. We will be at your service here at all times. My name is Jagan, and Murli is seeing to your tea inside.'

'The cars will go away, Jagan,' Adipati replied. 'I spoke to Sharma Ji, and it isn't our intention to cause inconvenience to the neighbourhood. These guys will come back later in a smaller car in the afternoon. The rest of us could really use the refreshment. Thank you for your kindness.'

Jagan beamed. 'No sir, please don't say that. It is our pleasure. Sharma Ji's guests are welcome here anytime. Come whenever you want, you can call the house directly or call my number. We will be glad to accommodate you and what guests you have. He is out most times anyway.'

He reached out and took his bag.

'Oh, and I almost forgot, your nephew arrived late last night and is resting in the bedroom upstairs. He asked me to wake him when you arrived, I'll go and tell him too.'

'Don't bother with Rakshit just yet, Jagan. Let him rest for now,' Adipati said as they stepped inside. 'We'll wake him up later. Thank you again.'

Jagan folded his hands and smiled before leaving to get the luggage.

'Rakshit?' Trish inquired.

'He was supposed to accompany us from the start, but he couldn't make it in time to your place. And no, he isn't really my nephew.'

'What's with the cars being dumped for a smaller car?' Trish continued.

'A smaller car befitting the locality is what we need. We don't want to stand out. We will head for the procedure very early tomorrow morning. Some guys will use the car along with Surbhi Ji. The rest of us will be on scooters in plain, non-flashy clothes.' Adipati said, informing everyone in a *matter of factly* tone. 'You are not to leave the house or even step outside before that Trish, do you understand?'

Trish nodded just as Murli stepped out of the kitchen with a tray in his hand, bowing to each one with a smile. Tea was served with onion and potato *pakauri* and *chutni.* Everyone eased back as the house help went back into the kitchen. Adipati was impressed with their warmth and respect for their guests' privacy. He addressed everyone once both Jagan and Murli were in the kitchen having tea themselves.

'I do not wish to alarm anyone, but if for any reason we are found to be where we are going tomorrow, we might end up in a rather worrisome situation. Now, however unlikely this may be, I want those of us not carrying any weapons to let me know their choice of arms so it can be arranged by this evening. The professor is coming in tonight, and I'll ask him to get what you need from the armoury.'

'Which professor is this one now?' asked Brij. He turned to Prof Tripathi. 'No offence.'

'He's one of us. We just call him professor because...well, because that is what he's called, really. You'll see,' Adipati said. 'So...weapons anyone?'

Most just said no since they were carrying what they preferred. Trishul had a question though. 'What's the combat area like?'

Adipati appreciated his question a tilt of his head and a raised eyebrow. The boy was asking the right questions at least. 'We will be in and out of a small, closed compound in the middle of one of the busiest markets in town. The compound itself has a pure line of sight throughout with no pillars. But they will not fire in there. I can assure you of that. Once outside, we will be on a very busy, crammed up street. Hence the scooters to blend in while retaining manoeuvrability for better chances of escape.'

'I need a set of two short swords, or rather long knives, preferably with blades broadening toward the tip, and sharp enough to finely chop a ripe tomato. No longer than three feet at maximum, pommel to tip. Please.' Trish asked smugly, acknowledged Adipati's expression, then added, 'What? You asked...'

Everyone chuckled, and Adipati said in a teasing manner, 'I'll see what best I can do, sir.' He turned to Brijbhooshan. 'And what about you?'

Brij thought for a moment. 'I wouldn't mind a couple of Desert Eagle 50 Cals,' he said with a sheepish grin.

'We are hoping not to make a bang, Brij,' Adipati said.

'Then get me ones with fucking silencers, right?' Brij was edgy and had his fists balled up and resting on his thighs. 'Listen, she said to prepare him, not be prepared myself! I didn't even know what she meant. It's good the lad knows what he's learnt, but where would I find time to learn to fight like that? I can shoot a gun, that's it! And don't you dare think you're going to keep me away from my son for a second, weapon or not.'

'Handgun with a silencer it is. Sorry, two.' Adipati said reassuringly. 'Now, will all of you please rest while I make a call to the professor?'

Trish stayed where he was while everyone made their way to the rooms, guided by Murli and Jagan. Brij tried to convince Trish and insisted he needed rest, but he wanted to stay a bit, so Brij nodded at Adipati and moved on upstairs.

'Finely chop a ripe tomato, eh?' Adipati prodded. 'I was of the opinion nobody uses blades that sharp in combat. It wears out faster, you can barely hack or cut a few times till it starts dulling. Not to mention if the edge makes contact with another blade or metal it damages itself.'

'Well then, we'll have to make sure the edge doesn't make such contact, won't we?' mocked Trish. 'And I don't hack. It's a waste of energy.'

'Well, I've seen you fight. I'm sure you know the science of it.'

'Speaking of which,' Trish said, frowning. 'How come you keep preaching about the science behind everything and yet believe in *Kundlis* and *Tithis,* and have an auspicious moment selected for whatever it is you want me to do?'

Adipati sat down next to Trish. 'But who says there's no science in that? The orientation of celestial bodies affects cosmic energies in every one of us. Religion from the world over wasn't wrong in studying these celestial bodies and acknowledging their significance. There's science behind it.'

'Where Mars is in the celestial sphere at a point in time, will affect you and me differently combined with the orientation of other bodies. It may augment energy that flows through your body or weaken it; this is all science.'

'You can, therefore, decide whether to do something on a said day at a said time, or avoid it for the best results, if you will. However, giving away a certain colour of food as alms on a certain day is not going to make Mars change its position in the celestial sphere. This is where religion departs from science, and this is the doing of preachers of religion, for their own agenda.'

'Yeah. I'm not buying it.'

'Okay, let me put it another way. Do you remember your paper for your first-year vacation project? What was that about?'

'Magnetism. You know my paper? How much *do* you know about me?' Trish threw up his hands and shook his head in surprise.

'Magnetism,' Adipati said, dismissing his query. 'In your research, you mentioned in the chapter about shipbuilding how the compass on a ship needs calibration based on magnetic properties of the ship itself. When the ship is being built, a tremendous amount of energy is transferred on a daily basis. I say transferred, as energy can neither be created nor destroyed. Conventional science. Do you agree to that at least?'

'Yeah, go on...'

'Owing to this immense transfer of energy through the ship's steel and due to the earth's magnetic field, depending on which hemisphere the ship is built in and what direction it is facing, it acquires magnetic properties. So north can be the bow and south the stern or vice versa. That's fore and aft, while the same applies to the transverse and also to the vertical. You have to agree to this, right? It's from your own paper.'

'Yeah yeah...the P, Q, and R forces. I know, go on...'

'Okay. So to compensate these magnetic forces the ship's compass needs calibration with the help of small magnets placed around it so as to help it keep pointing north, despite its own acquired magnetism, which would otherwise interfere with the compass. The orientation of these small magnets that are placed around it depends on where the ship was on earth, and where it was pointing when the energy was going through its body. Correct?'

'Absolutely. Your point being?'

Adipati stepped closer toward Trish. 'Do you have any idea of the amount of energy at play when a child is born? Compared to where he's born and how the celestial bodies are aligned at the time over that place, combined with the earth's effect on it, can you begin to understand why a person would acquire certain, shall we say, properties?'

'If this person has to keep pointing north, would it make sense that any major alteration in his life be done at an opportune moment where celestial bodies are in certain positions? We can't put objects in our bodies to calibrate ourselves, but other bodies – celestial or people's orientation – might affect him or her in a certain way.'

'That is why when two people were brought together back in the day it was diligent to check how they'd influence each other. And when they were, they were brought together at an opportune time to have them *calibrated* enough to accept each other's permanent proximity. This is why *kundlis* were so important for marriages in the old days. Of course, this was helpful when people were married without knowing each other. If you know each other for a while and then decide to come together, then you already know you'll work together as a couple, or else you would've fallen apart by that time. But there was an exact science behind this.'

'The gods practised it, and so did the ancients. However, the science was very precise. It is lost on people who think the world can be divided into twelve types of beings, and what works for one, works for the rest.'

'You've got an answer for everything, haven't you?' Trish asked, smirking.

'No son, I have answers to what I know. What I don't know for myself, I refuse to believe for someone else's word.' Adipati said calmly. 'Dr Surbhi has immense knowledge in this regard. She may not be as well versed in these sciences as our ancients were, but she is the best we have got. So, are you satisfied now that I'm not some blind follower of religion and still stand by knowledge we can use?'

Trish shrugged, but nodded.

'I suggest you rest, if you please. You need your energy for tomorrow. I mean it. Besides, you can wake up in time to meet the professor and Rakshit. Though I have a feeling he'll insist you call him Raka.' Adipati chuckled. 'You'll like him.'

09

«««« NINE »»»»

'The damned birds. They always make a ruckus in the evening,' Murli said apologetically when the guests gathered themselves in the hall. Everyone but Trish was waiting for tea and refreshments. 'These trees we have outside always attract birds no matter what time of year it is. Beyond the line of trees is the university, sir...Benares Hindu University? You know, right? It's a very big university. The most famous one in the world.'

'We know,' Adipati said engaging his exaggeration. 'Who doesn't know BHU?'

'Right sir.'

'It's all right Murli, we don't mind the birds,' Lyosha said and picked up a small plate of *samosas* for himself. 'We love nature.'

'Very good, sir,' Murli said, quite pleased. 'Cities are ruining everything. People just want buildings, malls, and new technology. We are moving away from mother nature every day. There used to be so many trees here when I was a kid. Now, if it weren't for the university, even these trees would have long since vanished to make space for more buildings.' He looked at the stairway. 'Look, the damned birds woke up *saheb* too.'

Trish came downstairs rubbing his eyes. 'How long was I asleep?'

'*Thirteen hours,*' Sveta said, her voice echoing through their heads. Murli looked at her suspiciously. She smiled back at him, then he retired to the kitchen, leaving tea and the refreshments on the table.

'Why can't you just speak? You show off,' quipped a young man not much older than Trish himself. He looked at Trish and nodded. 'Hi I'm Raka.'

Everyone laughed.

'What?' he said, shrugging.

Trish smiled and waved at him. 'Hey, Rakshit.' He looked at Brij and continued. 'I don't think I can sleep for another day at least.'

'Well, you needed the rest, son. Besides, you never know when they need a midnight chauffeur next,' Brij said, looking at Adipati.

Mugdha picked up a plate and walked toward Trish. 'Here, you need something to eat.'

Vishwas brought him a cup of tea. They talked for a while as Raka played with a tennis ball. Trish had half a mind of asking him what he could do as part of their team, but decided against it. It was nice to feel normal for a bit.

Almost an hour later everyone was laughing at the jokes Raka made. He was a funny person, even causing Adipati to crack up every time. Trish was glad someone his age was around. He'd finished his tea a while ago, and he held the empty cup listening to the guy's jokes. Finally he got up, and together with Mugdha, they took the serving trays to the kitchen.

'Oh sir, you should have called out,' Jagan said. 'We thought it best not to intrude, so we just sat here drinking our tea instead.'

'Don't worry about it, Jagan,' Trish said over his shoulder, walking back out to the hall. Right when he was passing the front door, the doorbell rang. 'I'll get it.' He walked to the door and opened it.

A dark man dressed in a crisp grey pinstripe suit stood at the door. He looked like he was in his late fifties, and had an air about him. He wore a pink neck-tie and pocket square. The only thing that didn't go well with his appearance was a duffel bag slung over his shoulder. The moment he saw Trish, he grinned like a Cheshire cat, closed his eyes, and drew in a deep breath. Trish looked back at the others, then at him again, but the guy continued to grin with his eyes closed and hands folded in front of his waist.

'May I help you?' Trish finally asked.

The man opened his eyes while still grinning, and said in a thick British accent, 'You have to be Trish. You can be no other. I can feel it.' Trish gave him a half smile, bemused. Then after a slight pause, the man continued. 'How rather rude of me.' He extended his hand and Trish shook it. 'I am Maurice Mburu. I cannot begin to explain what a pleasure it is to meet you.'

'Hello professor,' Trish replied.

The grin disappeared, and the man stepped forward. 'This must be Adi's doing. How many times must I make it clear I am not a professor, and must therefore not be addressed as such? It is an insult to people who've deserved the privilege to be called one! Now there's a real professor...' he said turning to Dr Tripathi. 'How do you do, my fair lady?'

Dr Tripathi smiled sheepishly. Trish wondered how she must feel in the midst of all this, surrounded by these people with incredible abilities. She appeared to be quite at ease with them though. It was strange but delightful to see her appear to be comfortable.

'Mr Brijbhooshan Negi,' continued Maurice to a bewildered Brij, 'what a delight to finally meet you, sir! I must admit that the new building of yours in Pune is a marvel, to say the least. You, sir, have single-handedly redefined reduction of energy waste by designing the best buildings I have come across from all over.'

'Thanks,' Brij replied, stealing looks from the others. 'I'm trying to make the best of natural light, and with our architects, we're trying designs that reduce the need for heating during winter, and cooling during summers. We're calling it EASE, or Energy Adequate Sustenance Engineering. I'm glad you know of it.'

He was, in fact, glad he could speak about his work for a change, and about anything but yogis, danger, and stuff he'd never known existed.

'Oh! I more than just know of it though. We took a floor for our office in that building just yesterday,' he said as he seated himself.

'We what now?' Adipati asked, lowering his head to one side and not hiding his surprise. 'I thought you'd at least discuss something before making such a decision.'

'But mate, have you taken a step into that building? You enter, and you can just feed off the energy flowing inside. It's a phenomenal achievement. I wonder why none of our enterprises worked in this direction before. The flow of energy is so strong in there, I could swear I'd grow younger just standing there.' He turned to Brij again, who looked as pleased as a kid taking a joyride. 'It is spectacular.'

'Did you get their toys?' asked Rakshit.

'Hello to you too, little one,' he said, reaching into his duffel bag. Then turning to Brij again he drew out his weapons of choice. 'Handguns, silencers and extra magazines for you, sir. Oh, I wouldn't mess with you, no no.'

Brij shrugged.

He then turned to Trish and drew out two blades in wooden scabbards. 'This is the best I could do in this rather short time I was afforded. Two Moro blades befitting the description I received; only the build quality isn't the best, but I'll change them in the first instance we get.'

Trish held one and drew it from the scabbard. 'They'll do just fine,' he said, with a nod. Then he drew the other out and began playing with them. The more he moved the blades, the deeper Maurice drew his breath. His eyes closed and pleasure was written all over his face.

When Trish was done, he placed them back in the scabbards, put them aside, then slumped on the couch. Maurice sat next to him, beaming.

'What's your deal?' Trish asked. 'You high?'

'Something like that. You see dear, I don't very often come across individuals such as yourself. Undoubtedly there are others with strong energies around, but yours are off the proverbial bloody charts, aren't they? I mean, there you are sitting a foot and a half from me, and the bloody rush is driving me insane. You've felt it, haven't you mate?' he asked Adipati. 'Of course, you have. Maybe not nearly as much as me, but you couldn't have missed it if you tried, right?'

'Some tact, professor,' Adipati interjected.

'What do you mean?' Trish asked Maurice.

"You don't know energy like I do lad,' Maurice said, his eyes glinting with excitement. 'It is the one single truth. You and I, this table, that wall, the water in your glass...this is all illusion. The only certainty is energy. It's running through everything, you see? The one thing that can neither be created nor destroyed; the one true God.'

'Professor,' Adipati snapped curtly. 'There is a time and a place for everything. I've been trying to get him to grips with what's going on at a certain pace. What's gotten into you? Do you want to ruin everything?'

'I thought you were trying to make me understand,' Trish said. 'That's what you've been doing all along. You think I asked for all this? You've been feeding me self-endorsed knowledge about how *you think* the world really works and I've tried to take it all in. I'm not in this by choice. For all I know I'm in it by your design. But in this entire situation, I know of nothing, and I want to be in the know.'

'Trish, son—' Adipati said, trying to calm him down.

''The young lad's got a point, though.' Maurice cut in.

'Professor...' Adipati was not amused.

'I want to hear what he wants to say,' Trish insisted. 'Go on professor.'

'Yeah! Maurice is just fine lad, and let's not let Dr Spoilsport gybe us here,' Maurice said as he turned back toward Trish. 'The one truth...energy. That's what makes you, well you; and me...me. That's what makes this table what it is, that wall, the water in your glass. *Shakti* as they say in Sanskrit. You must've heard the aphorism *Without Shakti, Shiv is Shav*, Shav meaning a dead body...You do know what that means, right?'

'And you must've heard professor, that he who begins many things finishes but a few,' Adipati interrupted his flow as he got up with a start, clearly not pleased with him.

'There we go again,' Maurice retorted with a gesture of his palm. 'You go on lad.'

'That without energy, even the gods are lifeless?' Trish tried.

'Now, where did the gods come in here?' Maurice complained.

'I don't know...you said Shiv.'

Maurice looked appalled. 'But the Shiv is not...what in the world have you been doing with this child, Adi? Have you no sense of responsibility? Don't you know what he faces? Wait, does *he* know what he faces? Does he know *who he is*?'

'Well, if you just let things play out the way we have been setting them up, and if we are successful tomorrow, then he will, won't he?' Adipati said, raising his voice. 'There has to be a method to this madness. You can't just waltz in here and derail his learning process. He is under my tutelage.'

'Who am I?' Trish spoke as he got up.

'What?' Adipati demanded.

Trish looked at Maurice. 'Professor, you asked if I knew who I was. Who am I?'

There was a moment of uncomfortable silence that felt like eternity. Brij finally broke it. 'You are my son. You were born to your mother and I; we didn't adopt you, so there is nothing else you can be. Our blood runs in your veins. I don't care what new chapter unfolds next, and I don't care what we learn about the truth of this world we live in. The one thing nothing can change is the fact that you are my flesh and blood.'

Lyosha got up from the far end where he had been sitting with the others. He gave Maurice a look and then turned to address Trish and his father. 'I know I haven't been the best example of mentorship, but let me just step in to say Adipati wants knowledge to imparted at a certain pace so nothing overwhelms the boy. He is correct in doing so I think and I believe Maurice may be under the influence of Trish's energies a bit. But he means well and what he has to say must also be understood, I think. We all want the best for you Trish, we are none of us certain exactly how, though. Please bear with us.'

Sveta clapped. '*Bravo,*' they heard her voice in their heads.

Brij turned to Maurice and Adipati. 'If you must teach him what he must know to be safe, then do it. But you dare not fuck around with his sensibilities. The moment I see my son uncomfortable, we walk.' Then furrowing his eyebrows, he growled. 'He's a kid. He's *my* kid. You understand?'

He retired back to his seat, where Lyosha offered him a drink.

Adipati pulled Maurice close to him by his elbow. 'Stick to energy and matter if you must, Professor. Leave his truth for tomorrow. Give the boy a chance.'

Maurice jerked his hand from his grasp and took a seat next to Trish. He had only just sat down, and started smiling, moving his head upward in delight till his eyes met Adipati's. He turned back to Trish. 'Sorry about that lad, but your proximity is driving me nuts. It's best I say my piece from a distance.'

He got up and walked to the other couch. Once seated, he continued. 'I am...an energy enthusiast, if you like. Energy is often misinterpreted as one of its manifestations. In truth, we don't know what energy is. We only know of its presence by whatever means it manifests itself on matter. When I say this wall and the table and the water in your glass are all illusions just like you and me, I mean it. What is this?' He touched the table.

'A table?' asked Trish. 'Wood? Solid matter? I don't know what you want.'

'That's just it lad,' Maurice continued, 'nothing is truly solid.' He shifted his weight to his other leg and picked up a drink for himself. 'See deep down inside, what is this table made of? Or that wall? Or anything you call solid matter?' He paused for effect, sipping his drink. 'All matter is made up of molecules, then atoms and quarks, and so on. So solid, liquid, gas...they're all the same really. The wood is the same particles as the wall is, and then this glass, including the drink it holds. So are you and me. Movement inside a so-called solid is not different from a fluid, we just don't see it the same way. When steel gets magnetised, the particles inside move as any fluid; only we perceive it differently. Why? The particles in all matter are the same, but their arrangement and how force binds them together is what gives properties to matter. The force...the one truth...energy.'

'Is that why you said these are all illusions?' asked Trish.

Maurice took a sip and nodded. 'What is an atom? It is an infinitely scaled down solar system of a kind. Particles that have non-existent mass revolving at immense speeds, bound together by prodigious forces. They are almost entirely empty space. Which means this table is almost entirely empty space. The wall is empty space, and so too, are you. Rakshit,' he called out.

Rakshit looked the other way. Sveta sniggered. Maurice shook his head.

'Sweet mother of...' then he paused again. 'Raka.'

'Yes.'

'Could you bounce that ball off the table to me please?'

He did. Maurice caught it.

'Why did the ball not go through the table, Trish?' he asked as he threw the ball back to Rakshit.

'I'm thinking now, it is not because both of them are solid...' Trish offered, slouching on the couch.

Maurice shook his head. 'Nothing is solid my dear. What did we just agree upon? This is an illusion. The ball did not bounce off the table, because the ball does not exist, and neither does the table. The only truth is energy. Now try again.'

'Because of the forces that bind together the ball? These forces bounced off the forces that bind together the table?' Trish looked confused as he threw his palm out and raised a brow.

Maurice nodded. 'These forces – of the ball and the table – are mutually interactive. Hence we can see the ball bounce off the table. But what if these forces were not mutually interactive? Better still, what if they were made to not interact mutually? Rakshit...Damn! Raka, will you do the honour?'

Rakshit repeated his previous feat - only this time, the ball went through the table and bounced off the floor. Maurice caught it again. Trish sat up straight and looked at Rakshit in disbelief. He smiled back and winked.

'Yeah, I can do that,' he said as he caught the ball thrown back by Maurice.

'What trickery is this?' Trish snapped. 'The ball did bounce off the floor.' Brij looked at the drink in his glass.

Rakshit, as if on cue, slammed the ball hard on the floor and it disappeared into it. 'It's now probably about five metres in the ground. Can't push it much farther. We all have limits you know.' Adipati walked over to a small bag near the stairway.

Trish threw up his arms and shook his head in cynicism. 'There we go again. Haven't we already established you are all super human beings who can do anything they want?'

Maurice shifted his weight on the other leg again and put his glass down. 'You see lad, we are all yogis. We have a single goal, and it is to be at one with the universe...to unlock our immense potential. When you are one with the universe, you understand it, communicate with it, and may even commandeer the manifestations of energy on matter.'

'But I must admit, we are all failures here. We've only managed to tap into one or the other possibility, and none of us is completely sure how we're doing it. As in if I were to teach someone how to do what I do, I couldn't. I don't know. I found I could do it merely by chance trying to unlock whatever I could within me.'

'The ultimate yogi who was truly at one with the universe, and could exploit all these faculties, could bend whatever manifestation of energy he wanted. The ultimate yogi, my son, was The Shiv. The Shiv is no god. The Shiv is a state of oneness. The one true yogi.'

'And yet he sits in temples and is prayed to,' Trish quipped. 'What exactly do you mean by "he is no god"? Are you saying he was human?'

'The Shiv my dear, is neither human nor god. He is an idea, a way of being. He who lived to be the idea, however, was most certainly human. The idea our makers could never come to terms with. That one of us – their creation – could do what he could.'

'They couldn't explain it to themselves, left alone any of us. Thus the Shiv had to be crowned a god. He didn't come from the skies like any other god. Pick up any text you like. Surely Adi would have touched on this...where did the so called gods come from? Any one of them?'

'Skies, heavens, Devlok, space...' Trish said, mocking them, bobbling his head from side to side.

'And where was it that the Shiv came from? Where was his abode?' Maurice asked, nudging him on.

'Mount Kailash? You mean he came from the Himalayas and hence was of the earth.' Trish smirked.

Maurice continued with his repartee. 'I'm saying nothing. Just pointing out facts hidden in what was not clearly written, but was written all the same. Let's say it is believed that he was from the mountains. How would those who created us explain someone designed and fabricated like everyone else by the gods, but could bend the universe to his will? How could that be known to us? What would the gods do if we all learnt that we could be the Shiv? You, me, all of us?'

'The Shiv is the ultimate yogi, better than the gods, in that he could do what even they couldn't. Completely at one with the universe. That is what we're striving for, but there has been no other yet. None of us could ever do more than a little. And all this, like the Shiv-Shav aphorism, is only possible due to the one single truth...energy.'

He raised his hand to shoulder height, then brought his thumb and index finger close together, an inch apart. Trish could see what he thought was a spark of electricity between them.

'I get your point, more or less,' Trish said. 'No need to go all Matrix on me.' Their antics were ceasing to impress him more and more by the day.

'You like the Matrix?' asked Adipati. 'Here's a translation of the original Matrix from a few thousand years ago.' He handed Trish a book from the bag.

Trish stared at the title and read it out aloud. "Shiva Samhita - By Srisa Chandra Vasu."

'Everything we are discovering now, all our science and even some of our fictional works touches on what we were supposed to know anyway. But we lost it somewhere and started from scratch again.'

They heard a yawn in their heads and looked at Sveta. 'What?' She demanded.

'We must rest a while. It is an early day tomorrow,' Maurice said.

'Oi! Matrix boy!' Rakshit shouted from across the room with a spoon in his hand. He bent his head sideways, and the spoon bent with it. 'There is no spoon.'

A cushion threw itself onto his face as Lyosha burst into laughter with the others. 'Show off!'

10

«««« TEN »»»»

Even though they woke up really early, tea was waiting for them in the hall. Sveta had echoed all of them awake and asked them to be ready in a half hour in the hall so they could gather themselves before they left.

They had barely slept a few hours and were on the move again after tea while it was still dark.

'We cannot all travel together,' Adipati said. 'We must take different routes and have no more than two scooters in sight of one another at any time. It should take us about half an hour to reach, give or take, depending on the route we choose.'

'When we reach, we will park on the street, but not too close to each other, yet being in sight of the entrance. Only when we're all there will we come over to the gym. Everyone clear?'

Everybody nodded in agreement.

'Once at the entrance, Rakshit will get us in. What are you wearing?' He looked at Trish in disappointment. 'Didn't I say we need to not stick out?'

Everyone looked at him. They were all wearing inexpensive trousers, shirts, and open sandals, but there was Trish with a broad V-necked t-shirt that was longer on one side than the other, joggers, and what looked like Roman sandals.

'Listen,' he said, looking at everyone there. 'If I might be getting into a fight, I want to be comfortable.'

'All right, we don't have time now. Let's just load up and leave,' Adipati said.

'That's not fair,' Rakshit complained. 'How come he got to wear that, and I have to look like a dork?'

'You will take Mugdha. Start your scooter around the next block. We can't afford to waste much time now, so let's leave,' Adipati commanded.

Everyone left for their transport. The car started in the distance and left. Brij checked his guns and sat behind Lyosha. Trish adjusted his blades under his loose t-shirt and sat behind Adipati. Two minutes later, they were all gone.

+++

'Do you want me to find the person who brought them supplies?' asked Odogwu.

RD was pacing around in the grove. 'Why the hell would they go to Benares?' he asked Odogwu rhetorically, then looked at Bijoy. 'Why?'

Odogwu repeated the question.

'You're sure Prof Vashisht is not there, right?' he asked Odogwu, ignoring his question again.

'There are men watching him in London as we speak,' he replied.

'No.' RD shook his head vehemently. 'There's no need to look for anyone. The poor bastards won't know a thing, and I'm really not interested in what they ate anyway'. He looked up at Odogwu. 'Get in touch with Rooftop. Ask him to reach Benares ASAP and watch over Vashisht's house. Scramble everyone you can, and we'll all convene at Phulwaria. Tell the twins to be there too. Let's go to Benares right fucking now.'

'I do not trust him. My men can handle it,' Odogwu said.

'Listen to me...' RD said, stepping forward with gritted teeth. 'I didn't hire you for advice. Get in touch with him, and get your men to Phulwaria.'

Odogwu resisted the urge to crack his elbow into RD's jaw. He ran things a certain way, which meant it was important for him to be in control. This wasn't possible if the client hired independent third party units. He had two of his men with the guy the last time, and they had nothing good to say about him. In fact, they had nothing to say about him at all. It was unsettling that they stayed with him for over half a day and could say nothing helpful about him whatsoever. But the client was the boss.

'My men will get in touch with this Rooftop guy, and will have him at Vashist's place first thing. I'll make some calls and arrange a team for us at Phulwaria. We'll be there in an hour' Odogwu said, then took his leave, dialling on his phone.

+++

'Is this really a good idea?' Maurice whispered into Adipati's ear as Rakshit stood halfway through the grille door, holding Mugdha's hand while walking her across. Vishwas, Sveta, and Lyosha were already inside. 'If they get him here, they will take him, and we'll be left to fend for ourselves to no good end.'

Adipati held Maurice by his shoulders. 'This is the only way I know. I realise full well that the entire quest will end here and now should things go sideways; but if the boy loses himself every time he turns, we're a lost cause anyway. We need to use the energies of this place at the time Dr Tripathi has provided us with. The only chance we have is if he realises himself in there. 'If you have a better idea, right now is the point of no return. Tell me, and we will bail out immediately, and move as far away from here as we can. If not, let's do this and be done with it.'

Lyosha was wrapping two large belts of *Khukuris* around himself going across his chest in an '*X*' secured by another belt at the waist housing more *Khukuris*. 'Anyone else coming?' he asked.

Trish and Brij entered first, followed by Maurice. Adipati said to Gurung, 'Nothing electronic picks us up, okay?' then he walked in himself.

Soon the nine of them came across another grille door on the floor of the gym.

Through the door, Trish saw stairs leading to an opening. 'Vishwas, could you...' Lyosha said as he gestured toward the lock.

'Can't you will it open or something?' Trish asked him

'It doesn't work like that' he replied. 'I can move things, which means I can move the levers in there too. But I don't know which levers to move and by how much and in what combination.' Vishwas went at it with a gem clip.

'And Vishwas is a lock-pick?' Trish asked.

'Mugdha and Vishwas can perceive. They feel their environment much differently than you and I. They could tell you what's behind a wall, or in a box without opening it. That's how they're able to drive at night without lights. They can see without their eyes. He can be in the lock and know what to move to open it.'

'There,' Vishwas announced as he opened the grille, folding it all the way to the top end.

Adipati walked down a couple of steps and turned to address them. 'What we are going to attempt may not work. There's no way to tell but we have to try. With Trish's energy flow I believe it should work and if it does, Trish will be much safer than he is at present.'

'Down there is sacred ground. It is a sweet spot of energies, and we want Trish to unite his flow with them. The process is physically quite simple and has been done before, but very rarely has it achieved the desired result.'

'Down there is also where our foes want Trish to be, and it is imperative they don't know where we are. In the odd chance this doesn't work, the process itself has not been known to affect anyone adversely. However, we must be careful not to disturb the sanctity of the place and most importantly, make sure that no one – especially you, Trish – sees their reflection in the water.'

'What the hell kind of place is this?' Brij growled. 'And what's in that water? It all sounds radically dangerous to me!'

'This place is a focal point of yog as we know it today, Brij,' Adipati said, trying to reassure him. 'And we are all yogis. I assure you the place or the process is not a threat. Our being here is a risk though, but we'll get out as soon as we can.'

Sveta stepped closer to interrupt. 'Dr Surbhi says we're nearing the window.'

'Come on then,' Adipati said while he walked down. The others followed. Brij cast a last glance out of the gym and then followed in last.

They entered a large enclosure of sorts, hidden from the outside world. At the end of the set of stairs from the gym was a square space with steps on all four sides that descended into a square well. Trish suddenly felt overwhelmed, though he didn't know what with. He looked around at the place, then at the others.

They looked overwhelmed too, he thought.

'Have you got the floats?' Adipati checked with Mugdha. She nodded. 'Good. Get them ready.'

'What floats?' Brij asked.

'Trish needs to meditate here,' Adipati replied.

'I asked you about the floats' Brij snapped.

'He needs to be floating in the water, partly submerged as he meditates.'

'In the same water he's not supposed to see himself in?' Brij's growl grew deeper than they'd ever heard before.

Trish cut him in. 'Like a sensory deprivation tank?' he asked, not taking his eyes off the water.

'Like a sensory deprivation tank,' repeated Adipati with a nervous smile. Then he nodded. 'A couple of floats tethered to your shoulders and thighs will keep you on the surface.'

'Or I could just float,' Trish replied, looking intently at the water.

Brij held Trish's shoulder and snarled. 'We should walk out right now. I don't know what this will do for us, but it sounds dangerous and quite simply, ridiculous.'

Trish clasped his father's hands. 'Everything we've seen in the last few days, I wouldn't have believed before. What I do believe is either something too big to understand at the moment is going on here, or that the alarm will ring soon and I'll wake up from a dream.'

'I don't need the floats,' Trish said to Adipati. 'I can float on my back. I do it at the pool to relax all the time. It'll take me a few minutes to get my breathing into a rhythm, but after that, I could float for hours. I've never meditated though. I don't know how.'

'You don't need to know Trish. You'll be half meditating already by the time you are breathing right to stay afloat. Meditation is not much different. Just close your eyes and try to perceive the flow of energy through your body. Being in there will help as well.' Adipati signalled Mugdha to stop.

'Three minutes,' Sveta announced. Brij resigned to one of the steps. It was going to be daylight soon.

Trish kept his hand on his father's shoulder. 'We'll get through this,' he said and started stripping. Once he was in his trunks, he walked down to the water.

'Face up, son. Don't look at the water. Not now, not later. Never,' Adipati said behind him.

At the last step, while looking straight ahead, Trish turned around and gradually stepped backward into the water. 'Do not go underwater, and certainly not to the bottom. Stay away from it. In the odd chance you turn and see it, there is something like a manhole at the bottom. Do not go near it if that's the only thing in life you want to do, you understand?'

Trish nodded.

'Keep your face out of the water while floating. Realisation can be triggered by acute emotion, though which emotion I cannot say. Everyone finds their own, the energy should guide you. Just float at the surface and once you're ready, close your eyes and surrender.'

Trish was now waist deep in water, trying to process what information Adipati was giving him. He looked at his father and could see he was worried. Trish smiled at him then winked.

Brij smiled back. *What kind of shamanic rituals are we getting into in the name of science or yog or whatever this is...Don't look at your reflection in the water...stay away from the manhole...what could be scientific about this. Maybe Trish is right, maybe the alarm will ring and wake me up and I'll realise this was all a weird dream'.* He thought. *What the hell was this place anyway?*

Adipati looked at Sveta incessantly, and she was deep in thought. Then, she finally nodded.

'Now, please,' Adipati said to Trish.

Trish pushed himself backward on to the surface of the water with a deep breath. He floated then held his breath for a while. Then he exhaled in a short burst and just as he was going under, he inhaled again and held his breath. His body was loose and his limbs were spread. He could hear nothing as his ears filled with the murky water of the well he was in.

What the hell was he doing here? How did his rather average life turn around so fast? What was in store for the future?

He breathed out for a few minutes till he was breathing effortlessly in a rhythm while he kept afloat. Then he closed his eyes.

+++

'We have a team of fifteen, more will join soon,' Odogwu said to RD.

They were in the office that RD had set up in the house they were in. The man the house belonged to, left it to them without question. Odogwu wondered what he owed RD.

'Is Rooftop at the location?' RD demanded.

'Not yet. The man is slow...'

'I should have given him more time. More time, you hear? The time we wasted because you wouldn't have him with us!' RD snapped.

'I offered...but he didn't want to...'

'He doesn't work like that, and you know it. All he asked was he travel alone in his vehicle. But no, you had to upset him. Have I not made it clear a thousand times that you don't inform me of a decision you've made. You ask me and I decide!'

'It was a judgement call. He wanted to know there and then.'

'And that's because you make him uncomfortable.'

RD was probably tense because they still hadn't got eyes on the party.

'You are running the show on the ground. I only want to give him specific tasks that he's best suited for. There's no interference in your work. I don't understand what your problem is.'

What kind of a man has no hair on his body? Not one! Odogwu didn't like the man at all. Neither his appearance nor his alias. *Rooftop. Stupid punk.*

'Hotline's up,' Bijoy interrupted.

'Make yourself useful for once. Tell the guys to be at the ready to move at the drop of a hat,' RD spat at Odogwu.

Odogwu was finding it more and more difficult to check his elbow lately. He turned and walked away.

'And tell me the moment Rooftop is on location.'

Motherfucker!

+++

Trish looked down at his father pacing along the length of one of the long steps to one side of the well. Others around it, standing, sitting or leaning against the walls. Adipati sat with Maurice, looking intently at the well. Trish followed their gaze and found himself floating in the water, his eyes closed.

What? How was he there? He was here...

He tried to look at his hands but couldn't see them. He looked down – Mugdha was standing right under him.

Where was his own body?

He looked around. He could see the entire place, everyone and everything. He looked up, down, then turned around in a full circle. Everything was right there but him. Well, he was there too...in the water.

But then how was he seeing it from here? What was he seeing through?

He needed to look at a mirror. There was no mirror.

The water! He could look at the water!

He tried to move toward the well, but he was stuck right where he was. He couldn't move. He saw himself lying in the water again.

How long had it been?

Everyone was silent. No one was saying a word.

Yes! This was it. Call out to them.

He couldn't. He tried so hard to cry out loud. But not a sound left him.

He saw Maurice touch Adipati's shoulder. Adipati looked at him. Maurice nodded, looking very nervous. They both looked at the sky.

Trish felt himself drawn toward the well. He was at the same height but moved horizontally toward it. He still couldn't see himself. Not from other than being in the water at least.

What was this tug he felt?

He got closer to the well. He could see the morning sky reflecting off the water. He'd be over the well in a couple of seconds.

Finally, he'd be able to see himself!

He was at the edge of the water.

Don't look at the water. Not now, not later. Never.

He closed his eyes shut.

I shouldn't look.

He could still feel himself moving. He could be over himself any time now.

Oh, how he wanted to open his eyes.

For a moment he thought his drift had ended.

Was he over his own body now?

Then, without warning, he felt as if he was sucked up by a force he thought would break his back. Of course, he didn't have a back since he had no body.

He opened his eyes. There were houses below him, shops, people. He was rocketing skyward. He could see the entire city, then more cities. In just a few seconds he saw India. He was travelling at speeds he couldn't comprehend. He found himself going down again.

Damn! Was this the end?

His heart beat so fast he thought he'd die before he hit the ground. Or the mountain, as it appeared. He closed his eyes before impact.

There was no impact.

He opened them again.

What was this? A cave? A cave, yes a small cave. What a beautiful sight! What was this peak he saw in front of him?

There was snow everywhere.

Why wasn't he cold?

He got up.

He could get up!

Still, he couldn't see his own body. He stepped out.

'I see you,' he said to himself.

What? What the hell does that mean?

He rocketed toward the sky again. Only a few seconds later he was falling back far away from where he'd been, but he was further up this time. He saw South East Asia for a split second before he started falling again.

What the hell was happening? Was that Philippines he saw last?

He didn't close his eyes before the impact this time, however, there was no impact again, and into the sea he went. He was breathing and didn't even get wet. He could still hear his own heartbeat. He saw creatures he didn't understand.

At this speed...How deep was he?

There were mountains again. Under the sea. Soon enough he was sitting under a ledge.

'I see you,' he said to himself again.

No...no...no...

He was going up one more time. This time was so fast that he only saw flashes. Mountains in the sea...the sea...the Earth. He could see trails of his path.

Stars...Galaxy? What the fuck? Galaxies!

Trish never felt so overwhelmed before. He'd been awed, but never like this. It was the most beautiful sight he'd ever known. His eyes welled up with overwhelming awe. He felt like he knew. He couldn't say what he knew, but he knew it. None of this felt new to him. He felt connected.

As a tear rolled down his cheek, he closed his eyes and wept. When he opened them, he was on something that resembled a beach. No sound other than the waves and a light breeze.

'I see you' he heard himself say.

He had to get up. The sea was calm and blue...he would see himself in it.

He got up and walked toward the water. Past the surf he went in thigh deep. When he looked down, he fell to his knees and wept again.

+++

'They're here,' Adipati gasped.

'What?' Maurice asked, confused.

'They're here. We have to get him out of there. I feel a node,' Adipati hissed at him.

'A node? This early? Are you sure? I'm absolutely numb from all this energy here.'

'We are at the seat of their plans Professor, do not forget that. They get us here, and it's a walk to the end of this for them. The very energies we are banking on for Trish to realise himself here are the ones the need to take him away for good.' Adipati looked battle ready already, fists in balls and a stance that suggested he was ready to pounce on something. 'Get him,' he said to Maurice, 'If I touch him I'll probably get fried'. Then he turned around. 'Everybody at the ready. Let's get out of here.'

Maurice almost glowed as he reached out for Trish. Brij drew his guns. *For fuck's sake.* Maurice woke Trish up from his trance, and he came to with a deep breath. The water in the well rose then fell as Maurice pulled Trish out.

'Let's dry you up lad,' he said.

Trish was in a daze. 'I was...I was...' He tried to talk, but Maurice calmed him down.

'Later, my dear. We need to get out of here.' He patted his back with a towel. Trish slumped on to the stairs as Maurice tried to dry him up. 'Put your clothes on, get your weapons.' Trish nodded.

He looked up at the sky, took a deep breath again, then started putting his clothes on. As he put on his sandals, one of them slipped and fell in the water. Trish bent over and grabbed it. Picking it up, he glimpsed his reflection in the water. Startled, he yowled as he fell back, trying to find a grip on the stairs with his hands.

'Pull him out of there!' Adipati yelled. 'Carry him if you have to...we need to leave now!'

+++

'Gather the boys! make a run for it!' RD howled, grabbing his jacket as he put the hotline down. Bijoy ran in to check on him. 'If we find them there, we can finish it there and then. This is our chance to shine, we must make haste.'

'What was that about?' Bijoy asked, looking at the phone.

'It was the twins. The fucking audacious bastards are at Sheshna. The boy just looked in the water.'

11

«««« ELEVEN »»»»

'Are you sure it was a node?' Maurice asked, straining his voice to make sure Adipati could hear. 'It's too early for any of them to show up just yet, let alone a node. There aren't many of them around other than the twins, who are permanently in our midst, and they haven't showed up either.'

'Do you think I don't know that?' Adipati snapped. 'Don't you think I know what I felt? Have I ever been wrong before? It's the second time I felt it recently, Professor. I couldn't mistake that energy shift if I tired. It was nodal.'

'And since the first time it happened was when the boy was turning in half realisation, this time when he was actually realising himself, have you considered that it might be the boy and not one of them?'

'It cannot be the boy...'

'But his mother was—'

'Has a node had an offspring with a human before, Professor?' asked Adipati.

'Many times, you know,' Maurice replied.

'And how many times out of these has the offspring turned out to be a node? How many of them have even affected half of the energy shift nodes do?' Adipati continued.

'Not once,' Maurice said. 'I know what you're saying. Just that I'm getting knots in my stomach with the timing of the boy turning and the shifts in energy. Nothing is impossible, right?'

Adipati was in no mood to listen. 'Let's just get the fuck out of here. These damned scooters might blend in well, but they could fucking well be faster!'

+++

'They've left and are headed south, south west,' Odogwu announced as he finished his call. 'One of my men is tailing them. He's a couple of hundred metres behind them, and his phone's GPS is pinging right here.'

He turned his laptop toward RD and Bijoy, then pointed on the screen.

'He will be replaced by this one here, and we'll know as they meet and when the first one stops. Then the third will take over. As our team finally approaches, we'll divide and cut them off at a tight spot from both forward and behind on Durgakund Road. They're slow, and my men are ahead of us.'

'How are your men already there? I thought we had all locally available manpower right here with us?' RD scorned.

'Save a few,' he replied. 'These few remained scattered in the city for the purpose that's serving us now. It worked, that should be important.'

'What is important is that you *listen* to me. We need the boy alive, Odogwu. I don't care if you kill the rest,' RD said.

'No one hurts the boy.' He nodded.

RD narrowed his eyes, brought his face right in front of him and hissed, 'You do not listen, Odogwu. That's the fucking problem.'

He looked back, confused.

RD continued as Bijoy watched on in horror. 'I said I need the boy alive. I never said don't hurt him. I couldn't give a flying fuck if you chop off his limbs so long as he can survive long enough to see the next few days.'

+++

'I heard you fight really well?' Rakshit asked Trishul, who was riding with him.

'I can defend myself,' he replied.

'Shastar Vidya, huh? You sure you learnt everything right? I've never heard of fighting with two short-swords in that regime.'

'My teacher taught us what the style had to teach, but always maintained that we should use our knowledge of something and grow, and not instead be limited by that knowledge,' Trish explained. 'I may not fight exactly how I'm supposed to under the fighting style she taught us, but that style is the backbone of my knowledge. What I do branches from it, and how I grew with the knowledge was always left to me. You will see no two fighters from her school fight alike.'

'Contemporary Shastar Vidya then, eh?' Rakshit smirked.

'Something like that.'

'So, what happened back at the well?'

'I don't really know...nor do I know how or what I'm feeling, if you want to know that next. Something is different, I know that. But I don't know how.'

'Okay, what scared you in the water at the end?'

'Don't want to talk about it,' Trish said curtly.

'We may have a tail,' Sveta's voice echoed in their heads.

The car had split up with Prof Tripathi and Mugdha, along with Gurung right from the start, but the rest of them were together. Sveta was riding with Vishwas at the end of the group, while Brij was with Lyosha. There was momentary silence before her voice rang across again.

'Adipati says we split up at the next major crossroads. That's the roundabout at Bahadur Shah Jafar Park. I'll keep going straight, all others go left. Then Lyosha takes the first right, and the others take the second. No one is to head back to the house till they're sure of not being followed, then—' She stopped halfway through the instructions. 'Oh damn!'

Five sporty motorcycles pulled up about a hundred metres ahead of them, blocking the road. Men who wore black tactical clothing got off and trained semi automatic weapons on them, with half of them on one knee and the other half standing behind them. Adipati slowed down to a halt, and the others followed suit.

'They're coming in from behind as well!' Vishwas shouted.

Five more motorcycles pulled up a hundred metres behind them, and the men repeated the exercise with clinical precision.

As everyone got off their scooters, Adipati addressed them. 'They're not moving in, which means they're holding us till their bosses arrive.' He noticed Brij had already drawn his guns and held them in both hands. 'Vishwas...Best setting for an up-close fight.'

Vishwas closed his eyes. 'College; right side, across the road, behind the post office.'

Everyone looked at it.

'Okay, here's what will happen. On the count of three, they lose their weapons' Adipati said as he looked at Rakshit. Rakshit nodded.

Adipati looked at Brij. 'As soon as they lose them, you shoot as many of them as you can, or till your ammo runs out in the chambers.' Brij nodded too.

'Rakshit stays with him to make sure they don't pick their weapons up again. While he's shooting the fuckers, we all make a dash for the college, and they follow us inside as soon as his last bullet is fired.'

Everyone nodded this time.

'This is where we draw them in for close combat. The moment we are in, we take up suitable positions and draw our weapons. Brij, you reload and take high ground wherever you find it and shoot as many of the motherfuckers as you can when they come in. The rest of us get them on the ground. Ready?'

Hearts beat hard as everyone nodded and stood up straight.

'Three...Two...One...GO!'

The semi automatics fell through the trained grips of the men in black. As they were trying to comprehend what was going on, Brij started shooting with both arms stretched out, looking one way and then the other. He didn't make a kill but managed to injure a few. They ducked, then tried to pick up their weapons in vain, and took cover behind their bikes.

Adipati and the others made a run for it. As the men behind the bikes braved the firing toward them, their weapons that lay on ground sunk an inch or two into the road, one after the other. The others were already across the road when Brij's guns went *click* after spending every round in the magazines.

'Run,' Rakshit said. They started for the college too.

The men outside were bewildered as they saw their guns embedded in the road. Some of them drew out handguns from their holsters while others drew out blades of different sizes and rushed after Adipati's little band.

Brij came in with Rakshit to see everyone with their weapons out. Sveta held metal batons in her hands, Vishwas was screwing together a double ended spear in its middle. Trish had drawn out his swords, and Adipati drew what looked like a steel rod with intricate designs that was about three feet long. He then twisted it at the centre, and it extended two feet each on both ends. While he held it in his hands, one end started freezing while the other became red hot.

Such sights had ceased to impress Brij any longer. Lyosha already had his belts of *khukuris* in full view. Maurico pulled open a long, thin, highly flexible, steel wire rope that was coiled around his waist a few times. It looked like it had a small, conical metal tip on one end, and an etched handle on the other to grip it by.

Rakshit pulled out two beautiful, identical black hammers about two feet each in length from under his shirt behind him.

Trish's jaw slightly dropped. *Magnificent!*

Leather bound grips led to slender but strong handles that culminated into a closed fist, which appeared to be holding the hammer's head. On one side of the fist, appeared the face of the hammer which was not flat, but had slightly pointed corners. On the other side appeared the shape of a bird's beak. The top and bottom edges of the beak looked sharp as knives.

Trish was about to compliment Rakshit on the fantastic weapon he had, but saw him fall on his knees, looking weak.

'That out there must've taken a lot,' Adipati said. 'You go upstairs with Brij and rest while he shoots. You can help him if someone reaches you and it comes to close combat.'

Rakshit nodded and headed up with Brij, who had reloaded his guns and was already heading for the first floor.

The first wave of the men came in, holding up handguns. Maurice's wire rope went up over his head in a flex, and just as the tip clicked the highpoint, it invited tiny bolts of thunder on to itself out of thin air. Even as the men's hands moved in his general direction, his *whip* came cracking down on the weapons and discharged such a jolt that the poor men flew back a few metres.

Other men started flowing in, and Brij appeared to be doing a rather decent job from upstairs. The entrance was a bit choked, but he had the advantage of being where he was. After a couple of guys later, the enemy realised his position and started shooting back at him.

Brij danced in and out of the line of sight by using a pillar for his protection. Rakshit sat on the floor opposite him. On the ground, Lyosha's *khukuris* started coming out of their scabbards as he folded his hands and stood still, looking at the entrance. They lay suspended in the air for an instant before they started orbiting around him with complementing circles at angles to each other, enveloping him in a sphere of protection.

Not more than a couple of minutes after the first wave of men had come in, the rest were at the entrance, barging in together. Rakshit heard them and told Brij to concentrate on the ones he thought were carrying guns.

Back downstairs, everyone was going for the guys with whatever they had. Lyosha's *khukuris* would break orbit one at a time and fly out to puncture or hack before returning to their orbit again, while he just stood there staring angrily at the men they fought with. Whoever came at Sveta, would hear a woman shout or make a war cry behind them as if attacking them, but would turn to find no one. That was all the time she needed to break a bone or two in their bodies.

Maurice's whip cracked thunderbolts at whatever it touched. Sometimes it never touched a thing, yet as the pulse generated by his movements rode out to the pointy tip in a crescendo, it shot a bolt away in that direction. It was as if he was plucking energy from the air and discharging it through his whip at will.

Vishwas always knew where every man was and used his double ended spear to good effect. Whatever Adipati touched with the hot end of his staff caught fire and what he touched with the cold end froze and broke while he made the other end hotter. Brij noticed, as did Trish.

Trish was the only one not hacking with his blades, or even swinging or slicing them. He held the left one upside down along his forearm, blade pointing outward, with the right one close to his body. The only movement he made was getting out of his attackers' line of attack and deflecting them with his blades. His left blade moved between being parallel to his forearm and perpendicular to it. The right moved more along his body and covered more ground for him. His attackers could never touch him and only slid off his blade, getting minor cuts. In turn, he barely moved at all, unlike his friends who were all over the ground.

'Why the fuck isn't he fighting them?' Sveta boomed in Adipati's head.

'Oh, but he is, the clever, crafty little genius,' he said with a smile.

Within minutes his attackers fell one after the other. They had so many little cuts all over their body, they never realised how much they bled. Trish winked as Sveta looked at him, part perplexed and part annoyed. Then he was on to the others.

Just when they thought they had them all eating dust, reinforcements came in. Most of the new men had automatic weapons. Brij did what he could, but there were many. The others were still able to manage with what they were doing, but they were beginning to worry.

Adipati spoke in his mind to Sveta. *'We don't know how many of them might follow. It appears they're getting reinforcements rapidly. That being the case, if we stay here, we might get trapped in and lose. Maybe it's time to break out of this place. If we go outside the professor and I could try something bigger and get us time to scoot off.'*

She nodded.

Everyone heard her voice in their heads. *'Start pushing out guys, we've got to get out of here. Adi and the professor will try something bigger outside, and we'll make a run for it and disperse.'*

'I've had enough rest,' Rakshit said as he sprang to his feet and jumped off the first floor wielding his hammers. He touched the ground, breaking a man's shoulder and piercing another one's thigh.

Trish admired how well he handled his hammers. Only, he'd wear down soon the way he was going. His burst was short term, but very effective indeed.

Brij came running down and picked up some weapons. He slung two sub machine guns around him, shoved a pistol in his belt, then picked up Uzis in both hands. 'They're coming for my boy, I'm going to give them hell!' he blurted out, high on an adrenaline rush.

They mustered near the entrance. 'Eight of them right outside and making inward,' Vishwas said. 'There's more on the other side of the road holding their position, but I can't feel that far, so I can't say how many.'

'They're sending in batches while others monitor the exit, so if we manage to beat them and try to escape, they can shoot at us from the road,' Adipati said.

Maurice suggested they find an escape from the back end. 'Maybe a couple of us could hold up here just enough to let us find our way out back?'

'I'm sure they've got that covered too. No, we'll blast through these eight men, and open fire on the ones on the opposite side of the road. We'll need you again, young man' he said to Rakshit, who nodded. 'Sveta will try to disorient them by shouting as loud as possible in their heads, and if we get close enough, Lyosha can make them kill each other. In the meantime, the professor and I will try to make a rather big bang...'

They were interrupted by a gunshot followed with clicks of a gun without rounds. One of the men lying on the floor behind them had aimed at them. They saw Trishul holding his left arm, and when he took his palm off it, there was blood.

'Just grazed him,' Vishwas said as he stole a peek at it. But he realised what had happened as he saw everyone take a step back and then backed up himself.

Trish closed his eyes, and breathed deep. Adipati looked at his face with hope. When Trish opened his eyes, everyone stepped further back. He turned to the man on the floor and walked toward him, hissing in anger, glaring.

'No! No, dear God! You're the devil!' he cried. 'Your eyes! Your eyes!'

Trish knelt and gave his head a smack off the pommel of his sword. He then turned and walked toward the entrance. 'Let's get out,' he hissed as he walked in a sway.

Adipati smiled. *It had worked - the boy almost turned, but didn't lose himself. He was hissing with rage, but didn't go for the kill. The visit to the well had paid off!*

In the next thirty seconds, Trish had sliced out his way through the eight men who were making their way in, putting them to the ground. But the moment he stepped out of the exit, bullets rained around him, and he had to duck back to shelter.

'It would help if everyone had guns from the inside,' he growled back. The others lost no time and brought back as many as they could collect. 'Let's give them a round and see if we can knock a few down.'

They all stepped out for just an instant and fired away as many rounds as they could. Some bullets hit targets, others compelled the adversaries to take shelter behind their vehicles. A big bullet proof van was in their midst. As soon as they were done firing they took shelter behind the trees on the roadside to reload.

'That can work,' Adipati said. 'The first person that can take Trish out of here does exactly that. The rest of us will deal with them and make a run for it.'

'I can get out on my own,' Trish snapped, though a lot calmer now. He wasn't hissing anymore and was breathing normally.

A flurry of bullets rained in on and around the trees. 'RD is in that van there for sure. I know that's his van,' Adipati shouted over the noise of the bullet storm. 'The moment we get a break we act as we discussed.'

But there was no break. Bullets kept raining in, fewer at times while some others reloaded but never stopped.

'Damn! If they don't stop, they're going to flank us soon. We *need* a break!'

The break came with counter fire in a way they never expected. A motorcyclist came shooting off an FN P90 sub machine gun with his left hand across to the other side and snuck in between the trees to where they were, ducking before he stopped. The man looked at Trish from behind his reflective visor and jerked his head, signalling him to hop on behind him. He was wearing a Shoei helmet with red and black race leathers and riding a red Panigale R.

'Go with him!' shouted Brij. 'GO!'

Trish looked at Adipati, then nodded. He mounted behind the rider while he gave him the gun.

'Do not stop shooting,' an electronically modulated voice from inside the helmet said.

'Keep him safe!' shouted Brij, 'I'll contact you.' The bike took off with Trish shooting at the other side and disappeared before they knew it.

'Let's burn the bastards!' Adipati roared as he addressed his fellow companions.

12

«« « TWELVE »» »

'What the fuck just happened!' RD exclaimed, looking at the red bike that whizzed past their van. Two of their own chased after the red bike. 'Who the fuck was that? Are you on them, Bijoy?'

'With these bullets flying everywhere?' he quipped, wide eyed in surprise. 'There's too much noise.'

'Maybe one of them returned just to get the boy out?' Odogwu suggested.

RD was clearly displeased. 'Pull out of here. It's the boy we need. Leave your men back and ask them to continue. Try and flank them and if possible, kill every one of them. We must follow the boy. Bijoy, you try and pick them up if you can as we move out of this.'

Odogwu knocked on the roof and made a small circle with his finger in the air as the driver looked back. Within a minute they were speeding on the road with two more of their bikes as escorts.

+++

'We mustn't talk,' Trish said, bringing his head closer to his rescuer's helmet. 'And we've got to kill that engine soon, or they'll follow us.'

'Stay back and hold tight!' the electronically modulated voice from the helmet said while he manoeuvred on the road looking for an exit.

Trish gripped tight on to the bike as it sped up on its rear wheel.

+++

The van was pulling out. It took two bikes with it, but there were still some twenty odd men with automatic weapons firing at them. Adipati noticed five or six more on each side beginning to break off.

'They're coming in to flank us soon. Let's give it to them before they break up,' Adipati said, shooting at the men on his end. 'Go for the guns in the centre, Raka. It'll cause a moment of confusion. That's when everyone steps out and starts shooting at the flanks that are breaking off. The professor and I will make a run for the middle and give them something to remember. No need to bury the guns, I think we'll take them. Ready? Now!'

Rakshit poked his head out, and the guns of the men in the centre fell to the ground. As sure as Adipati had predicted, there was a break while the flanks looked at the middle in disbelief. Sveta and Vishwas took the left flank as Brij and Lyosha took the right. Rakshit and Mugdha shot at anyone from the centre who tried to pick their guns up.

Before the men knew it, Maurice and Adipati were in the centre, not ten metres from the attackers in the middle. A couple of them fled as Adipati started spinning his staff over his head, brewing up a small twister of sorts. Everyone heard a crack of thunder as Maurice stepped closer to his adversaries, flinging the tip of his whip into the twister. When he flung it back at the men, he burned them all alive with a touch of lightning extending from his whip. At the sight, whatever men had remained standing, fled like they'd seen hell from the inside.

'Pick up the bikes and let's get the fuck out of here,' Adipati said, and they all scrammed.

+++

Trish exchanged fire with the bikes in pursuit, but they were soon left far behind. The skills of this rider were unparalleled, and he had known this since the night of the race. He had so many questions. If only he didn't need to keep silent!

They manoeuvred through a few small lanes and came on to a narrow road only to be blocked by a slow moving truck. Trish was beginning to get irritated by it when its rear doors flew open. Two men slid out a thick, wide wooden plank whose end they hooked on to the rear of the truck, while the rest of it fell behind the truck making for a ramp. The bike went up the ramp and into the truck. The guys pulled the ramp back in, got off the truck, and locked the doors from outside.

Once in the truck the rider shut off the bike's engine and turned to Trish with his fingers over his helmet where his lips would have been. Trish had made the exact gesture.

Two hours of silence followed that felt like days, with the both of them dismounted and facing each other inside the truck. The rider never took off his helmet. Then the truck slowed down to a halt. Rear doors opened, and the rider pushed the plank toward two other men on the outside, who set up the ramp again. Without starting the engine, the rider drifted the bike down the ramp, gesturing Trish to follow him. Once on the ground, he pushed the bike off the road on a fifty odd metre dirt track to a small brick house, and knocked on the wooden door.

A man with a long beard answered the door and when he saw them, he returned inside leaving the door open. They pushed the bike into an enclosed courtyard as the man stepped out of a room with a long handled broom and thick bristles. Trish saw him walk back to the truck, ridding the bike's track marks till he reached the road. He then stepped into the back with the other two guys who had taken the plank up, and the truck went off on the road again.

'Come in and close the door,' the rider's modulated voice said from behind Trish.

'Are you with Adipati?' Trish asked him.

'The tall old leader of your pack?' he asked. 'Hardly. I was hired by your father.'

'To do what exactly?'

'To do exactly what I did.'

'And what was it you were doing at the race then?'

'I was casing you at the time,' he replied. 'I still hadn't taken the contract. I saw you at the race there and thought you were probably under threat from some goons or a racing cartel at best. But the money your father was paying meant you had to be in bigger trouble than that.'

'He wasn't sure what kind of trouble it would be, but he knew it would be big. He was hiring *me*, and the price offered meant even I knew it would be trouble. But what happened today...they're trained teams of killers that are after you. I have seen coups with that kind of fire power! What the fuck do you want you for?'

'I don't know,' Trish said. 'Adipati knows I think, but he insists it isn't time for me yet to fully comprehend what's going on. I know there are things I can do that they may be interested in. Maybe they want to use me to do something I would't want to do. Maybe they'd want to kill me after they've run out their use for me.'

'Well, it's bloody time you start comprehending I'd say!' he said as he brought out a first aid kit from his bike and handed it to Trish. 'Or did you not notice the gazillion bullets that rained on you today? Prepare first aid for your wound. I'll come out and dress it. The bloody leathers are killing me.'

Trish pulled open the pouch and took out a pair of scissors, bandage, some cotton, and ointment. *His father hired him.* His father was powerful, sure...he knew people and he had his way with a lot of lobbyists. Still, Trish had always figured him as someone who could get you front row tickets to the Independence Day Parade, not someone who would employ a gun for hire.

'Now, stretch out your arm and look the other way,' the guy said as he stepped out of the single room in the house. He had changed into anti fit cargo pants and a loose hoodie. The hood pulled over his head and his face was covered with a clean paintball mask. His voice was still modulated.

'You have to be kidding me,' Trish exclaimed. 'Are you Darth Vader?'

'I have to keep my identity to myself if I am to be any good in my line of work. Surely you understand?'

'Yeah, of course. But don't you ever take it out?'

'I wear a mask so that I can walk the roads a free person when I'm not wearing it,' he said. 'Now, stretch out that arm and turn your face.'

+++

'What the fuck was that you pulled out there?' Adipati demanded.

There'd been an uneasy quiet among the lot while coming back that desperately needed to be broken. Everyone came in through different routes and sat in the hall silently till Adipati finally spoke again.

'Who was that guy?'

'I hired him to keep Trish safe,' Brij replied tersely. 'I didn't know you then...not like this. We only met for the first time after I'd seen you for a brief moment years ago. And what did you have to say to me? That my son's life was in danger! I did what any father would have done.'

'He's been around that long?' Maurice couldn't believe it. 'So if he knew where we were today, he would have been following us from the very beginning, wouldn't he? Well, that sure makes us look like bloody idiots!'

'That was reckless, Brij,' Adipati cut in. 'Imagine having a tail we didn't know about. What we don't know about, we cannot hide. What we cannot hide can be monitored without us having the first clue. We can't afford variables like these...'

Brij raised his hand indicating he was in no mood to listen. If anything, he was pleased with how today went. 'Well it worked out just right, didn't it? I needed to get Trish out of there safely, and we did. That's all that matters right now.'

'What matters right now is where he's taken him,' Maurice added. 'And how we can get him back. Where's your safe house?'

'I don't know,' Brij replied. Silence hung in the air. Everyone looked at him with wide eyes, in utter disbelief.

'You don't know?' Maurice was livid, pacing up and down in front of Brij. 'You had your son, whose life by the way, is in danger, taken by someone you hired, and you don't know where he took him? Some illustration of the perfect father you are!'

'I will not be judged by you!' Brij roared as he stood up, bringing his face to Maurice's. Then he turned to Adipati. 'He does not communicate much. You give him a job, he gets it done if he takes it. I thought it would be best for us to know as little as possible too. Like I said, I knew none of you then like I do now. Put in that situation again, I'd make the same decision if I had to.'

Adipati breathed deep and frowned. 'What's done is done. How do we get him back? We can't stay here long now, you know that. We must get him and leave as soon as we can. I understand you hired him and why, but so much as our interests in saving Trish are pure, as your own wife knew, the assassin's are driven by money. And what can be bought to do one thing can be bought to do another.'

Brij paced up and down the hall. 'I need a secure Internet connection to get in touch with him,' he said. 'We will give him a place and time, and he'll get Trishul to us. That's what his instructions were in case we were in a situation like this.'

'We have Internet on the PC in the other room,' Adipati said. 'Gurung will make sure it is as secure as it can possibly be. Now, who is this guy you've hired?'

+++

'It's hardly more than a bruise,' the guy in the hoodie said. 'It'll heal in no time.'

'I'll be all right, don't worry about me,' Trish said.

'I'm not worried about you,' he replied. 'I'm worried about what shape I deliver my package in. I'm careful about my assignments.'

'Are you always as cordial with your assignments?' Trish asked him sarcastically.

'You're the first assignment of your kind,' he said. 'My assignments don't last very long after meeting me. I kill people. You're the first contract I've got to save someone. I didn't even know what to do with this request due to its unique nature. But frankly I had nothing else on my plate right now, I was getting bored.'

Trish tried to find words to say something, almost opened his mouth to speak, then kept quiet.

'So, how do you do it?' the guy asked him. 'Ride in the dark like that, I mean.'

Trish smiled nervously. 'You've got your secrets, I've got mine.'

He laughed from behind his mask. It may have been modulated, but it was clear. 'Well, you can't blame me for asking.'

'I wouldn't mind some chewing gum,' Trish said.

'What?' There was a little surprise in his voice despite the modulation.

'I know you're chewing gum,' Trish said. 'I know you were chewing gum the night of the race. I know you were chewing gum earlier when you picked me up. I know you chew gum all the time. Don't need to see your face for that.'

'See, this is why I don't take such shit jobs,' he said as he handed him a pack from his pocket. 'Now I have to decide whether what you know about me is important enough for me to protect myself to kill you right here.'

'Let's not get dramatic now,' Trish said. 'You chew gum. That's no different than knowing you are five feet seven - five feet eight perhaps...and that you are lithe and probably weigh around sixty-five kilos or so...'

'You really know how to tip the scales on a decision, don't you?' the guy said, pointing a pistol at him.

'Now, now...I'm trying to make a point about not knowing nearly enough about you to narrow you down to a million people,' Trish said, raising his arms.

He holstered his gun back. 'I'm going to sit over there. Far away from you. I don't want to lose money on destroying the package.'

'Why did you hand me the race?'

'I'm sorry, what?'

'Why did you hand me the race?' Trish asked again. 'You'd clearly won before you pulled down at the finish line.'

'Like you said, I'd already won. I was only casing you, boy. Actually crossing the line before you would bring undue attention. In case you haven't noticed yet, I'm not a big fan of attention.'

'Yeah, tell that to the guys you shot at today.'

'That was necessary for the assignment. It is otherwise imperative that I keep myself unseen. Believe me, you don't want to hire the assassin that lives downtown with a board outside his house reading *Assassin*. Anonymity is key.'

'How come you're telling me all this? Are you going to kill me now?' Trish jested with a teasing smile.

'Advertising, boy,' he said. 'Your father hired me. Considering the shitstorm that hit you today, you might be inclined to hire me yourself someday.'

'For argument's sake, let's say I did want to hire you in the future. How would I get to you? What do they call you? You must go by something if you're in a business...?'

+++

'Lorem Ipsum!' Maurice exclaimed at Brij. He turned to Adipati in stupor. 'Do you believe this gentleman here? He went ahead and hired that egotistical maniac of an assassin to keep his son safe!' He turned to Brij again. 'What is to say he won't hold him for ransom now? What is to say he won't hand him over to the highest bidder, and we lose the battle sitting right here?'

'I didn't know anyone else like that,' Brij retorted. 'He comes recommended by someone I'd trust my entire fortune to, and he's known to be a man of his word.'

'An assassin,'   Maurice said. 'That's what he is...an assassin.'

'He only kills people you can prove to be punishable by death, but beyond reproach of law as we know it,' Brij muttered.

'Unbelievable!' Maurice clapped. 'Are you advertising for him now? Who decides someone must die? A fucking assassin, that's who!'

'Stop it!' Adipati yelled. 'Enough. We don't have time on our side. Gurung, set it up. Make the connection secure as it is possible. Brij, let's try and get the boy home. Professor, you take Surbhi Ji and stand by to get the ride. Leave now. And what the fuck are you smirking about, Rakshit?'

Rakshit got up and started to leave with Gurung to help him. 'That's a really lame name for an assassin, that's all I'm saying,' he said over his shoulder.

+++

'What kind of a name is that?' Trish asked him. 'Shouldn't an assassin's *nom de guerre* instil fear in people or something? Or at least be mysterious or enigmatic? Like...The Raven, or Lucius, or The Contractor, or well... Obsidian, or—'

'I'll refer new assassins to you for names if I find some,' he said, cutting Trish short. 'Meanwhile, I am who I am. I didn't even pick it, to be honest. Someone gave me that name based on my *modus operandi*, and it kind of stuck. And you boy, stop talking to me. I'm talking too much, and I don't want to end up killing you for it.'

'You don't have many people to talk to, do you?'

'Shut the fuck up, or I'll blow your head off.'

'All right, so what's next? You can tell me that at least...'

'Now we wait for my computer to make a sound,' he replied. 'I set it up while changing inside. They will hopefully tell me where and when to deliver you. We will get out of here and ditch this bike for now. Depending on where they want you, we will either take a cheap street bike, or my other racer, and drop you off. After which we all live happily ever after. Of course, that is if my money reaches me within thirty days given your situation. Otherwise, I'll find you again, and kill you myself.'

+++

Brij opened the browser and went to an email portal. He created a new email. 'He doesn't accept communication unless it is a fresh email ID every time,' he said.

The others looked on. He then went on to a blogging website and set up a free new blog using this address.

'The name doesn't matter' he explained. There he selected default text and style, then clicked edit. While the page refreshed itself, he opened another tab on the browser. In the search bar, he typed "Latin to English", and a translator appeared.

'What message should we send out?' Brij asked Adipati.

'Tell him to bring Trish to the air strip close by at two-twenty tonight,' Adipati replied.

'What air strip?' Brij asked.

'There's one behind those trees in the university,' Adipati said as he pointed out the window.

Brij typed into the translator on his browser and wrote down its Latin translation on a piece of paper.

bring - educ
boy - puer
air - aer
road - via
near - prope
house - villa

two - duo
twenty - viginti

He went back to the original tab on the browser, with the blog ready to edit the default text, which had loaded up.

'Aaahhh!' Rakshit sounded as he looked at the screen that read in bold: *Lorem Ipsum.*

Brij scrolled to the second paragraph of the default text, then selected the line second to last. He changed it to read: *educ puer aer via, prope villa, duo viginti.*
'Apparently, nobody gives a second look to default text on a new blog,' he said as he published the blog and copied its address.

He opened up a porn site and went to its forum. There he started a new thread that read "website help". In the thread he posted 'Looking to start a new website, any ideas?' and pasted the link to the blog under it.

'What now?' Lyosha asked.

Brij turned around. 'Now we check the blog frequently. If it's taken down, he's understood and will do as asked. If there's a problem, he'll post a new blog and leave a link under my thread.'

+++

'That was your father,' he said to Trish as he walked out of the room. 'You go back tonight. Now, the house that you guys were in...was it near the university?'

13

«««« THIRTEEN »»»»

'Listen carefully,' RD said. 'They said they wanted to handle everything themselves soon. It is almost time. They'd hoped they wouldn't have to make themselves present for this and that the boy could be delivered to them by us, instead that looks highly unlikely. The first of them - the ones that are already here - should be able to present themselves directly in a day or two, and that will be the end of that. But even if that weren't to work out, they will all appear in a matter of days.'

Bijoy was unsure of what his next question should be. 'Are you saying we are not to pursue this anymore?'

RD came closer to him. 'The latest orders are that if we lose them and they escape Benares, or if we are unable to find them by noon tomorrow, our little party here is to be done away with. They will then take matters into their own hands and will have no need for our services. That would not bode well for us, Bijoy!'

'I don't understand,' Bijoy said. 'Is Odogwu supposed to pack up and leave if the boy isn't captured?'

'We will pack up, sure,' RD said. 'But nobody will leave.'

Bijoy stared back, clueless.

RD shook his head and continued. 'Must I spell everything out for you always? If Odogwu doesn't deliver, the only hope of us living longer than a week from now is if he doesn't. We would have to give them something to show for what we did about our failure. Get me Rooftop.'

+++

There was a knock on the door. Trish stood up and drew his blades. The hooded guy took out his handgun and approached the door, signalling Trish to stand beside it. When he opened it, a skinny woman in a *sari* came into the courtyard with two large plates, one on top of the other in one hand, and two big glasses of *lassi* in the other. She walked in like she owned the place, put the stuff down on a *charpoy* in the courtyard, and walked out like they weren't even there.

'Have some food,' the guy said as he picked up a plate and glass, and walked into the room.

'Alone?' Trish asked. 'Where are your manners?'

'Listen, boy...the only way you live to see another day, is not to be around when the mask comes off, you understand?'

'Well, you can't blame me for asking.'

Trish devoured the delicious food and gulped down the *lassi* in no time. He washed his hands at the hand pump in the corner and wished life was as simple as this. He sat there realising life wasn't even life as he knew it a few days ago.

Matter wasn't matter as it used to be, nor was energy, or for that matter, evolution. Hell, even gods were not gods now. And what he experienced at the well...*What was that?* After the attack on them earlier, he was certain of his companions' interest in keeping him safe. That he was in danger was pretty evident, but he still didn't know why. What was he fighting for? He felt like he neither mattered nor existed.

A drop in an ocean is nothing by itself, yet the ocean cannot exist without drops, he thought to himself. *What the fuck am I thinking?* His mind wandered back to the well. *Who am I?*

'You eat well?' the guy asked, coming out with his plate and glass to wash up.

'As well as I could,' Trish replied. He realised he was clinging tight to his blades.

The guy washed his hands and dried them with the towel they were left to share. 'Are you any good with those?' he asked Trish.

'I manage.'

'Why do people still learn that shit, I wonder,' he said. 'I mean, I could shoot you from right here before you could say shazam. What good are those then?'

'Well, you could certainly try, couldn't you?' Trish smiled.

+++

'Anything?' Adipati asked, checking with Gurung.

'The blog's down, so I guess that's good news,' he replied. 'Also, there were two videos shot on smartphones this morning making their way on the Internet. Had to fry them. I didn't have much of a choice really.'

Adipati nodded. 'Good work. These phones really make life miserable, don't they?'

'You sound like my grandpa,' Rakshit joked.

'So, what's the plan?' Brij asked Adipati.

'The plan is to not have third party variables, Brij. You must understand that.'

Brij nodded hesitantly.

'Once we have Trishul we must make haste and leave here. Very soon it will be difficult to step out much, once the real threat starts to present itself.'

'The real threat?' Brij wondered aloud. 'The fuck was it this morning?'

'These were puppets with very little skill or power, Brij' he said. 'Any time now the ones they call the twins will show up, and then the puppeteers will start coming around; the real threat. Someone has invited us over for a visit, and it is therefore imperative we visit them before all this starts.'

'Who?'

'Someone who wasn't on the agenda, but let's just say, for now, someone you do not refuse an invitation from.'

+++

'Are you ready?' the man asked Trish. He had decided it was better not to wear racing leathers, but the helmet was back on.

'Yes,' he said, rubbing his eyes. 'Didn't you say it would take us an hour and a half though? Why are we leaving with close to three hours to spare?'

'You want to sleep some more?'

'No, I've slept enough.'

'Then let's go,' he said, handing Trish a helmet. 'We have to change bikes, go through places that may be full of people looking for us, and I've got to have an exit plan at all times. Things can go wrong at every step, we've got to account for that. If we're early, we can sneak in till it's time and all is clear. But we don't know what their plan is, so if we're late, we might end up screwing all or any plans your little party may have of getting you out. Now come on and get comfy.'

'I've a better idea,' Trish said. 'One that doesn't involve using lights.'

+++

RD and Bijoy both hovered over a map of Benares spread out on a table. RD was particularly nervous. Bijoy hadn't seen him like this ever before. He had one of his best bottles of scotch out for tonight. He only did that when he was anxious. Also, he had been looking and cursing at that little notebook all evening. Bijoy had only ever seen him do one of these two things at a time. Doing them both could only mean the worst.

Odogwu walked in with a radio in one hand and his phone in the other. 'Still no movement. My men are looking at all entries and exits, and are also scattered all over the city. Grid-wise deployment ensures at least twenty men can reach any point within a couple of minutes, and more with every passing minute after that. We have a hundred and fifty strong search party in total. You need not worry, if they are still in the city, we will get them.'

'And what if they're not in the city?' RD stared at him.

'You said we have until noon tomorrow,' he replied. 'If nothing happens till then, we'll start afresh. We got them from nothing when we started trailing them...'

'From their house, you imbecile...where will you start afresh now?' RD snapped.

Bijoy stood when he saw Odogwu tense up, though he didn't know what he meant to do by standing up like that.

'Let us remain civil while we can,' Odogwu said. 'We'll think about tomorrow when it is tomorrow.'

'There will be no tomorrow,' RD muttered. 'If we don't have at least a trail by noon, we'll pack this up, you hear me? It will have proved our incompetence enough for my bosses to take over personally.'

+++

'Maurice is ready with transport,' Sveta announced as she walked down the stairs to the hall. 'He said he'll be at the rendezvous point at zero-two-twenty sharp.'

'Finally some good news! Let's just hope your assassin delivers on time too,' Adipati said to Brij. 'Maurice could wait once he's here, but he can only make an appearance for a moment or two. Time is something we don't have much of. If we do not get out of this city in time where they know we are, They will have us pinned. Tell the house help to go home. Tell them we'll leave tonight and lock up behind us.'

'So what's the plan exactly?' Brij was a little relaxed for a change. Maybe it was because of the day's success in getting Trish out in time. Maybe it was because it was he who did something that resulted in the success; something all these powerful people couldn't have done better. 'We waltz into that runway behind the trees, meet up with Trish and just leave? It was a nice decision to stay next to the LZ, but isn't there a problem here? Their guys must be all over the place, anything flying in at that hour will catch attention immediately.'

'Then we'll have to try and keep it quiet, won't we?' Adipati said sarcastically. 'Our transport had hit a technical snag, Brij. But trust us in that it was because of rigorous testing so it wouldn't fail us.'

Brij knew he didn't want to talk more on the topic. Somehow he was okay with it. He'd grown to trust him more of late. *Trish didn't go crazy when he got wounded in the morning. He must be doing something right.*

+++

Trish was going through the signals in his head as they rode without lights, with the assassin behind him. *One tap on the thigh to turn, two taps for a U-turn...left thigh for left, right thigh for right. Fist to the back to stop. Rapid taps on shoulder to speed up. A couple of taps to the helmet to slow down.* It was important they didn't talk.

Once they were parallel to the highway headed west, there was ample light on the road itself. Trish knew it was the AH1. They kept going straight for some time till they passed an auto rickshaw stand to their left. Trish felt two taps to his helmet and started slowing down. A hundred metres later he felt two taps on his right thigh and looked ahead. He saw the lane for a U-turn under the highway. As he was making the turn, right under the highway, he felt a fist to his back. They stopped.

Like parts of a clock in perfect synchronisation, ten motorcycles of a common make and model appeared. All of them wore black clothing to match theirs, and had two riders on each one. The pillion rider was wearing a bag just like them.

One of the bikes stopped right in front of them. The riders dismounted. Trish followed the lead of the guy behind him, and they dismounted as well. The two bikes were exchanged, and Trish now sat behind his companion as he took to the front seat. Within a minute of them stopping, all bikes started off together.

+++

'The red bike just showed up heading west on the other side of the Ganga,' Bijoy announced as he walked into the room with Odogwu.

'And?' RD asked excitedly, jumping to his feet.

'It stopped under the flyover for just under a minute here,' he said, pointing at the map. 'Then it made a U-turn and headed back.'

'What do you make of that?' RD was still very excited.

Odogwu intervened. 'When that bike came out from under there, ten other bikes emerged. All similar looking with two riders each that looked similar as well. Then they scattered, heading in different directions. It's the oldest trick in the book.'

'Yeah?' RD walked up to his face. 'Well, if it's so old I'm sure you know everything we are to do now, right?'

Odogwu narrowed his brows. 'It is that old and still remains in the book. What does that tell you about its success rate?'

Bijoy felt the tension and blurted, 'Can we just focus on this right now gentlemen, please?

They hovered over the map again and Odogwu began explaining. 'The red bike made a U-turn and headed back east. With it went two other bikes, one of which turned north on highway seven and the other south. Eight bikes crossed over to this side of Ganga, out of which four got off the slip road, turned around, then two went north on Garhwa Ghat road; while another two went south opposite them. Two bikes broke off at another slip road later, one heading north on Bhagwanpur road and the other heading south, opposite them. The last two are still heading west on the highway, and our guys are on them.'

'What do you mean "our guys are on them"?' asked RD, looking shocked. 'Who's on the guys that broke off and went north-south on us?'

'These are the two guys who have been on the highway until the last two bikers remained,' Odogwu explained. 'They've been informing the rest of the troops about the roads where the others headed, and the troops in turn, are trying to follow them up from there.'

'Trying?' RD walked to the map in a fit. 'How many are we still tracking?'

'The last two that are still headed west and three more. We'll get the others too as we fan out from those roads.'

'Get your men from over the river back in the city,' RD growled. 'If east is where he'd want to be, why would he come up to there and tease us so? It's just a ploy to divert our resources.'

'That sounds right,' Odogwu said.

'And get out of this room please.'

Odogwu slammed the door shut behind him.

'What am I not seeing here?' he asked rhetorically. Then he studied the map like his life depended on it. Scratching his chin, then his hair, he took a sip of his scotch. He moved his fingers over roads all over the city. It was exhausting for Bijoy to watch until his eyes lit up. 'There may be something here yet, my boy! Were they not headed through here this morning?'

Bijoy nodded. 'Indeed they were sir.'

'I remember I told you once to call me *dada*? Don't call me sir. It makes me uncomfortable, Bijoy.'

'Yes *dada*.'

'Would you say they were heading for wherever they were holed up or had their escape lined up after they ran like rats from the well?'

'Yes, that's only logical.'

'And are the bikes headed on this highway going west?'

'All but the ones that went east and you rightly suggested were decoys, yes.'

'So if the westbound bikes are heading to the safe house, and they were heading to the same safe house this morning moving south from the well, would you say the safe house is not very far from where these roads meet?'

'With due respect *dada*...' Bijoy replied. 'I wouldn't say that *is* the case, but the probability is high, no doubt.'

'Talk to that idiot Odogwu out there,' RD said in a low growl. 'Tell him to try and find that guy that took Bhagwanpur road heading north on priority basis. Let's not stop the chase after the others, but let's try and concentrate on Bhagwanpur road and the areas around it. Also, send in teams to go through every room in the university building.'

'Yes *dada*.'

'And Bijoy...call up Rooftop and tell him to try and be on the lookout in the area south of the university up to the highway.'

+++

Trish stood in wariness as the guy dumped the bike into the pond. He took off his helmet facing away from Trish while pulling up his hood as he wore the mask. Then he turned and walked back toward him.

Why? Trish gestured to him.

The guy pulled out a little notebook from his pocket and wrote on it. *250m from runway. Better off on foot. They might look for the bike.*

He signalled Trish over to a bunch of trees on a vacant plot near the pond. They went over and climbed on to the branches high enough to be covered completely by leaves, then tied their helmets on the higher branches. He showed Trish his watch. An hour and ten minutes to go. Trish asked for the notebook and wrote on it, catching some moonlight through the leaves.

House near trees lining the university. Maybe go there now?

The guy read, shook his head and wrote back: *Might be compromised. We don't know. They asked for runway.*

Trish nodded.

They sat for another half hour or so, not communicating. Trish noticed him checking his watch every few minutes. If only that could make time go faster.

He started writing again. *Which way was the house?*

Trish read and wrote back: *That way. Last house before trees. University behind trees.* Then he pointed in the direction of the house as the other guy completed reading.

Seeing Trish's hand pointing to the house, he got up and climbed higher, trying to peek through the top branches. He was scanning the houses in that direction when he doubled back down. He pulled out his notebook and started writing frantically. Trish was curious and tried to read as he wrote.

Sniper on top of overhead water tank near your house. Has clear view of the runway.

+++

He shifted his weight to one side as he inserted a ten round magazine into his AS50 rifle, cursing RD. *What a nutjob. How was he supposed to cover this entire area by himself? He doesn't even know where to start looking.*

The place had no good vantage point. The water tank was the best he could manage. At least he had only to manage a hundred and eighty sectors that way. The other side was an open field. RD had said he had men in the university building beyond that expanse. He had to manage south; the sector 090 to 270, right up to the highway.

He narrowed his eyes and could see the traffic on the highway clearly. He scanned his sector. *The fucking area is full of blind spots. This is not going to be easy. Concentrate! Not the slightest movement can be missed.*

+++

Trish's heart jumped into his mouth as he saw him through the leaves. He climbed back down to find the guy writing in the notebook. *Can't see him, but I caught a glint and movement. We have to assume it's a sniper.*

Trish took the notebook and wrote back: *I can see him. Sniper for sure. Set up facing south.*

He read, thought for a moment, then wrote back to Trish: *Must approach runway from east end. Let's go.*

Trish held him by the shoulder as he was beginning to climb down and signalled for him to wait. His father and the lot were right under the sniper's nose, less than a hundred metres from him. If they could cross over the trees without catching his eye, and they could stay hidden from him under them on the other side, ready to dash for the runway.

Once under the trees, they could crawl close enough to him for Rakshit to do something about the rifle, as they made a run for the aircraft. But whenever the aircraft came in, it would definitely get his attention and even if he couldn't shoot, he'd raise an alarm for the others with enough time for them to ambush their escape.

He needed to consult with Adipati on this. How? The other guy pointed to his watch asking Trish to leave immediately.

There was a way if it would only work. He pleaded for him to hang on for another two minutes. Then he thought hard of Sveta, picturing her in his head.

'Sveta! Please for the love of life answer back if you can hear me.'

No response.

'*I need you to hear me…Sveta?*'

'*Trish? Where are you?*'

'*Close. There's a sniper on the water tank near you.*'

'*What? Are you sure?*'

'*Yes. You think they've made the house?*'

'*Not likely. They would have attacked.*'

'*He's set up looking south, away from the university. I was thinking if you could dash across without drawing his attention somehow, you could wait on the other side of the trees inside the campus grounds.*'

'*Brilliant, Trish. We'll manage, don't worry one bit about it. How will you reach? Do you need help?*'

'*I'll be all right, no worries. I'll come from the east end and tread under the trees to you. What about the aircraft? Tho sniper is bound to alert everyone he might have nearby?*'

'*You just make it to us by two-twenty. That's all you need to worry about. You can't be late. The rest is covered.*'

'*Is Dad okay?*'

'*Never better. See you in a bit.*'

Trish climbed down with his companion and smiled as he nodded in affirmation to them leaving.

+++

'He's all right then?' Brij asked her.

'Your guy has delivered so far,' Sveta replied with a smile. 'What about the sniper situation, Adipati?'

Adipati thought for a moment. 'Can you sense him?' he asked Mugdha and Vishwas.

'Not really,' Vishwas replied.

Mugdha went over to the window to the west of them. 'Yes,' she said. 'Big rifle, set up south, another rifle lying next to him. One pistol on his hip. He's lying on the south end facing south himself.'

'Great,' Adipati replied. 'Here's what's going to happen. Rakshit will lock up the front door and help us all step out through the east wall. Once outside, Vishwas and Mugdha should both be able to sense the sniper as well. Mugdha darts across with Rakshit when he's facing south-southwest.'

'Every moment he faces in that direction after that, two of us dash across, and Rakshit helps us cross into the campus. Vishwas is the last one to join us. On the other side, we stay together and under the trees while we wait for Trish, then Maurice. Everyone on board with this?'

They all answered in affirmation. 'We can thank Trish for his help later,' Lyosha said.

Fifteen minutes later they huddled together on the other side.

+++

Trish and his companion had made it close to the east end of the line of trees. They were in a by-lane fifty metres inside the main road, or Bhagwanpur road.

The guy was really good, Trish thought.

He'd brought them there through the maze of houses, sticking to shadows, and out of the line of sight from the tank. They even encountered four bikes with armed men on them on their way, but he kept them out of sight like a pro. On reaching the tree line, he signalled Trish to watch the sniper and cross over when clear.

What about you? Trish signalled back.

He pulled out his notebook and wrote. *Contract over. Package delivered. Make for your aircraft easy...I'll set up a bang-boom south of water tank for 02:19:55.*

Trish hugged him, though he didn't know why. He looked for the sniper, saw an opportunity, signalled goodbye and jumped over. On the other side, he made a bee line heading west along the trees till he saw them all. Brij leapt up to hug him. Everyono hugged him after that.

'There are three minutes to go,' Adipati whispered.

'Is it safe to talk?' Trish whispered back.

'Yes. No one's listening,' Sveta whispered.

Trish exhaled in relief. 'I've been dying to speak something. Haven't said a word in hours!'

'Wise thing to do,' she whispered back.

At nineteen minutes past two, they felt a gentle breeze, and a plume of dust made its way from the runway on to them.

'Maurice is here,' Adipati whispered. 'We can make a run at any time.'

'What do you mean here?' Brij asked back.

'You'll see. As we run for it, Raka I want you to bury his guns into the top of that tank,' Brij said.

'I'll do you one better for calling me, Raka,' he replied. 'I'll drop his guns through the top into the water in the tank.' He winked.

'He'll appear at two-twenty. We must wait till a couple of seconds before and run toward the centre of that runway, okay?' Adipati said. 'On my cue.'

Trish tapped on his shoulder and whispered, 'We may have a better cue...wait for the fireworks.' Then *he* winked.

+++

At exactly 02:19:55 three distinct explosions occurred along the highway on vacant pieces of land, just as the red Panigale raced across the highway heading west. Rooftop took a shot at the bike, and it went skidding down the road. Whatever little traffic was on the highway stopped, and a couple of bystanders looked on in horror. One of them flung a paintball mask aside and walked off.

Rooftop was about to take another shot when his rifle fell through the concrete below him. He turned to pick up the other gun only to find it gone too. From the corner of his eye, he caught on the runway behind him something he couldn't believe.

+++

As they heard the explosions, they started to run for the centre of the runway. Their escape craft magically appeared out of thin air, sitting on the ground. A ramp lowered itself.

'What the fuck is that?' Brij exclaimed, running.

'Our escape plan,' Adipati replied. 'Better late than glitchy!'

Maurice welcomed them with a grin at the top of the ramp as they boarded. Within the minute, they were up and away.

+++

'Base – Rooftop,' he spoke into his radio.

'Rooftop – Base' RD's voice said, excited.

'Yeah! You owe me two new guns,' he said, holding a pistol. 'And we need to renegotiate terms.'

'What do you mean?'

'Right! I don't know how else to say this, but the package kinda just left in a fucking UFO!'

14

«‹«« FOURTEEN »»›»

'Do you have the coordinates?' Maurice asked Adipati while everyone else settled in. Brij and Trish were trying to come to terms with what they were in.

'16645 73323. You should find enough space to land right next to it,' Adipati replied. He then turned to Trish and Brij. 'I know you have questions.'

'Yeah, for starters let's just say I don't like surprises. I especially don't like surprises like these,' Brij said, rubbing his palms together.

'My apologies,' Adipati replied. 'Just that I didn't know what to say to you, or how to explain this without you physically seeing it first. Plus we had issues with it and didn't know for certain if it would be ready in time to help us.'

'So what? You found an alien craft and have some alien bodies holed up somewhere?' Trish exclaimed. 'And you want it kept a secret, so you wouldn't tell us unless you absolutely had to? And where are you taking us now? To the same site or something?'

'Why would you think this is alien technology?' asked a woman who wore shorts and a t-shirt, as she walked up to them. She was carrying a touchscreen tablet in one hand.

Adipati introduced her. 'Meet Karuna Brandt, Chief Scientist at Xyschema, and the real brain behind this project. Xyschema is a science research enterprise and one of the companies run by The Circuit. She has put almost her entire career into this vessel.'

'We call her Nichola,' she said with great pride in her voice. 'After Nikola Tesla. And Adipati is too modest. This wouldn't have been possible without his immense input and Maurice's understanding of energy. He's the pilot; I'm only the engineer.'

'But this is a flying bloody saucer!' Trish exclaimed.

He walked around the circular walkway that he thought would have made for the disc-like structure he saw from outside. It went around in a full circle and was about ten feet wide he reckoned, sparsely lined on both sides with gadgetry he was unfamiliar with. The centre of the craft was completely enclosed and appeared to be spherical right up to the ceiling, matching what he'd seen from outside. It was like the disc space they were in was welded on to a big steel ball at its centre.

'Yes it is.' She said, and chuckled.

'Why does it have a spherical centre and a tapering disc around it? And why the hell isn't it making any noise at all?' Trish continued. 'Then you ask me why I would think it's alien?'

'Well, at least now you're asking the right questions,' she replied. 'This is still a work in progress, and I wasn't convinced of trying it out like this yet, but Maurice told me about your predicament, and we didn't see any other alternative, really.'

'Nichola isn't ready yet, you see. We're still trying to make her work right. Why she doesn't make any significant noise is because she's running on silent, clean energy.'

'The problem we're still facing is that it has to be given a charge to keep going every now and then with batteries. You can hear her hum at that time, and you will, in a minute. We can run her without those batteries as long as Maurice is around, but our ultimate goal is to run her without any physical boost of charge at all.'

'This thing runs on a charge from batteries?' Brij asked her, his brows raised in surprise.

'Very much so We've been working on the tech for so long now and we're still not there. You see the space we are standing in goes around the central sphere. You can see the curved walls of the centre of the core there, going through the ceiling,' she explained, pointing at it. 'That houses what are our tweaks of the Rodin Coils. There's three of them in there. They're shaped sort of like doughnuts if you will.'

'We've been experimenting with the shape a bit, but this is as close as we've got. The three in there are positioned with their axes at a hundred and twenty degree angles to each other. We're trying superconductivity as best we can around them; that's what the batteries give their charge to. This is the most efficient we have come to be yet, but we're still leaking energy. That's not good news for Mr Moneybags here.' She pointed to Adipati.

Lyosha sniggered, and Sveta slapped his back.

'I know of a Rodin coil,' Trish said. 'I would love to learn from you, Ms Brandt.'

'Anyone Adipati trusts enough to share knowledge of this project is welcome to see it anytime,' she said. 'I've heard a lot about you lately too, Trishul. I'd definitely look forward to when we can show you around. Now, however, I'm told there isn't much time for all of this. You'll be getting off as soon as we arrive in Ambolgad. I'll have to take off with her. We cannot afford her being seen.'

'Sure,' Trish replied. 'Just what did you mean you want to run it without any charge at all, though?'

'The ultimate goal is to use the earth's toroidal energy to power hers,' she said. 'We are able to tap into it through Maurice, but we haven't quite done it through Nichola herself yet.'

'Toroidal energy,' repeated Trish. 'Are you talking about what is called free energy? Are you telling me it is real?'

'Call it what you want, Trishul,' she replied. 'But yes, there is energy around us that can be tapped into. Maurice does it more successfully than anyone or anything I've ever come across.'

'It's the same energy that these guys here, the yogis, channel through their own bodies when they meditate. Energy rises in from the bottom *chakr*, goes through the body and comes out through the top. This is self-sustaining and hence toroidal in nature too.'

'What is called the aura of a person is their own field of toroidal energy. Nichola works on the same principle, but only tapping in directly to it is still a work in progress. Everyone knows the earth is a giant magnet spinning at the speeds it spins at. I wonder why people have difficulty in seeing that there is energy around It.'

'It's just a lot to wrap my head around,' Trish said. 'How did you manage to keep it invisible?'

'Oh that's something a lot of people are already working on,' she said. 'It's micro cameras and plasma fabric. I believe we've done a much better job than most others, but there are better ones already in production. Ours is only good for low light conditions, so you should see it in daylight. You may be able to see through it, but you can see it right there too. Anyway, that is not my project to judge.'

Sveta and Vishwas brought coffee. 'Maurice says another half hour,' Vishwas announced.

Trish was excited about the craft. He picked up a cup and went for another question. 'Last question, Ms Brandt. Why is this vessel circular? I mean, that's not the conventional aerodynamic shape...'

'That is a very good question, Trish,' she said, sipping her coffee. 'What would you say the conventional aerodynamic shape would be?'

'Triangular, I think...maybe oblong, fanning out?'

'Okay. That would probably be it for a flying craft that had thrust at one end, and direction of travel at the other, making it aerodynamic to move toward its pointy or nose-like end. In that the direction of travel would be fixed, right?'

'I guess...'

'Now consider a bullet train that runs on one rail and travels in both directions. Where would you have the nosed end now?'

'On both ends.'

'So since the pointy ended triangle travels only in one direction, it needs a turning circle to turn to another direction, and even to turn around and come back. But the rail has a linear track which it cannot leave, thus it has no room for a turning circle.'

'Therefore, it must have two nose ends to move in two directions and thrusts in both directions as well. Now consider a small craft that can seat a few people which travels through a tunnel not much larger than itself. There is no room for turning, and this tunnel is part of a tunnel system that has branches in many directions, which the craft must take without turning. Where would its nose end be, to be aerodynamic?'

'Everywhere.' Trish smiled.

'That's what this vessel is.' She smiled back. 'And I know your next question too.'

'What tunnel system?' he asked anyway.

She beamed back at him. 'The earth is enveloped in its own energy. I hope you can understand that now, but imagine this: What if I told you if you created a disturbance in this energy emanating from the core of the earth itself, at say two different points, you'd end up in a flow of energy between the two points?'

'Like in a plasma ball?' Brij interjected.

'Well, visually it could be compared to something like that, but that's not what's happening,' she said. 'First, you can't see it and second, I'm talking about an energy flow directly between the two points where the disturbance is created.'

'Some mountains do that. They bring out an enhanced energy disturbance in the fabric by concentrating the energy going through them at mountain tops. But there has to be an energy hotspot where the mountain is for that to happen. This is most often not the case. Therefore, if I were to have a hotspot at one place on earth and I wanted to create a disturbance in the energy fabric using it, so that I could set up a flow from there to another disturbance, I would have to create something there that would concentrate this energy.'

Trish's eyes lit up as what she was saying began to dawn on him. 'Are you saying that was the purpose of all these structures all over the world that we've been trying to figure out the reason of for over centuries now?'

'I don't know if that's why they were started off, but they were definitely used for that purpose.'

'But what purpose does setting up this flow of energy serve?' Brij asked, still not quite convinced.

'Well Mr Negi, you'll be thrilled to know Nichola is riding one of these flows right now.'

+++

'They own us now, Bijoy,' RD said. "They fucking own us! I was in their debt and had I delivered the boy, I'd have been free. They asked me to deliver him to rid me of my debt. But we failed...There's only one way left to survive for now. Have you called Odogwu?'

There was a knock on the door before Bijoy could answer. Odogwu walked in. 'What do we have?' he asked.

RD beamed at him. 'We haven't lost the boy after all. They couldn't complete their ritual at the well, so they're going to the Ganga for it. They'll be on the riverbank north of *Sant Kabir Ghat* just around the meditation centre here.' He pointed to the place on the map and continued, 'I want you to be there for fifteen past three.'

'Are you not coming?' he asked.

'They're splitting up. All the others are going with the boy. The father is going to meet up with the guy on the red bike. We can take care of him. He's not special like the others. You must secure the boy. It's our last chance.'

'Why is it that the father is going alone? Are you sure they're not sending a couple of them with him? Sounds odd,' Odogwu said, his brow furrowed. The sudden cordial approach by RD wasn't helping either.

RD suddenly wasn't beaming any more. 'For once Odogwu, listen to me. I just hung up my phone. The boy is too important for them, you know that. Tonight is the last time they have got to complete their ritual. Just get the boy, please.'

More like him.

'A few of the guys were looking at the explosions and how they could have got away. I'll pull them in straight away seeing as we don't need to dwell on that now. We'll be there for quarter past three.'

They nodded at each other and Odogwu left. Outside the room, he called up one of his generals and asked him to come to the said location at the set time.

'What's the matter? You sound weird,' the man on the phone said.

'Something is not right...'

+++

Adipati came back after his little chat with Maurice to see Karuna still explaining stuff to Trish and Brij. Trish's eyes were lit like a Christmas star.

He was a delight to watch, no matter what he was doing, Adipati thought.

'Yes, that's exactly what I'm saying,' she told them. 'They used it in the same fashion. Not the men of the time, but whoever the gods were supposed to be, had perfect knowledge of this. There is an entire web of these energy flows across the planet through these sites.'

'Modern human construction has added a few too. Though almost all of them are rather weak, they're still navigable. It's like having country roads coming out of state roads coming out of highways and so on, if you will. Though the biggest highways remain through ancient sites, most modern disturbances are just noise.'

'The craft does look like a UFO,' Trish said again. 'You have to admit it. You took the structure off a science fiction film.'

'Quite on the contrary,' she said. 'We were trying everything and got stuck over and over again. Then one day I met with someone in one of The Circuit's other companies when Adipati and I were to discuss something over lunch.'

'This guy was on some project about art through the ages. When we shared with him what we were trying to do and where we were stuck, he took us to his workstation. He said we could be right about flight paths existing in ancient times and showed us several photos of art starting from cave paintings to the Renaissance, with what looked like science fiction UFOs in them. That's when I decided I wanted to try out this shape. And this has worked just fine for us.'

'Coming up in five!' Maurice shouted from the other end.

'We won't have much time,' Adipati said, addressing them all. 'The moment the ramp is down, we'll have to get off, and they'll have to leave if we are not to have a UFO sighting in tomorrow's news. Maurice will help get the craft home and join us tomorrow evening. There is still a lot to be done on this thing.'

'If at all it is possible, I'd like to come down to your workplace and understand about this gem of a craft one day,' Trish said to Karuna, offering his hand for a shake.

'Nichola,' she said. 'Her name is Nichola.' She smiled at him, shaking his hand.

'When will the world know about this?' asked Brij.

'When we want to be bought over or shut down, or both.'

'Okay, out!' Maurice shouted as the ramp lowered.

+++

'I can't see!' The man cried, trying to figure out where he was. He felt a bed under him. The side of the beds had steel rails. A PV catheter was going into the back of his hand.

'How did I get here?' he thought.

'I can't see!' he shouted again.

'Calm down, Major. It's okay.' He heard a woman say to him. 'You'll be fine. You'll see, but you had injuries. It's okay...it's okay...it's...'

As the alarm on his wristwatch vibrated, he woke up with a start and realised he had the same nightmare again. He looked at his watch. Ten past three.

Another overhead water tank. This night just didn't want to end. He'd barely slept at all and had decided to take a nap for what was to be his final orders for the day. If the money were any less, he'd have been home by now.

He put a mag into his rifle and set it up. *Any moment now...*

+++

As Nichola left, Adipati and the others stood facing the sea on a rocky cliff top. The area was largely flat and jutting out into the sea. There was no light for at least half a kilometre into the land, and the wind was moderate, gusting at times. The welcome sound of waves crashing on to rock was soothing.

'Now?' Brij asked Adipati.

'Now we wait till we are invited in,' he said.

'Invited in where?' Brij said as he looked around. 'There's nothing here.'

'I don't know,' he replied. 'We won't know where, till we are invited.'

'How will they know we're here?'

'They will know. They always know.'

Brij was perplexed. 'Where is this place?'

'It's a cliff off Ambolgad, Maharashtra, on the west coast,' he said.

'So what's here? Do we have to go to Ambolgad? I mean what's the point of standing here with not an insect to see us? Should we head for a settlement? That light looks like it's a settlement there. Maybe that's where they are.'

'Brij,' Adipati said patiently. 'This is where they wanted us. They will know we are here. And only when they want us in will we know where they are as they show themselves.

'And let me give you a word of advice. Accept whatever they offer. Ask no question till you are specifically asked to. Answer what is asked of you truthfully and to the best of your ability. Do not fuck around with them...any one of you.'

'Who are these people?' Trish asked.

'I told you they summoned us and nobody refuses their summons. The timing indicates they have something to do with Trish, and these are not people you want leaning over to the other side. They're the House of Yaksh.'

15

««« FIFTEEN »»»

Odogwu met his people near the meditation centre's building. He had six men with him, and twelve had just walked in from the north, led by his most trustworthy general. They were all heavily armed.

'Hello, Anane,' Odogwu said as he greeted him with a hug. 'We must make haste. Where are the others?'

'They are on their way,' Anane replied. 'Should be here any minute. It was a rather short notice, see?' He took out a pack of cigarettes from his pocket. 'Time to finally do this, get paid and fuck off eh? I've had enough of this country for now. I'm starting to miss the women back home a bit.'

They all laughed.

'It's not about the money for me, Anane,' Odogwu said. 'I would have done this job for free. I'm here to settle an old score, although getting money to do it anyway does no harm, does it?' He eyed the area and couldn't see his prey anywhere.

Why quarter past three? Maybe he wanted them there earlier to greet the fellows...Something wasn't right about RD's intel this time.

'What beef could you have with the boy?' asked Anane.

'Not the boy, old friend. The boy is the assignment I took on, but I had my reasons to take this assignment - to get to the man who I've been searching for all my life.' He saw some vacant wooden boats tied up to the ghats. 'Let's sit in those boats and wait for them. We can remain unnoticed till they are close enough. The others can wait till we open fire. Tell them to set up a perimeter around the area. They'll have the river on one side with nowhere to run. The boy must be breathing when we have him.'

They boarded the boats and sat down in them till Anane asked around for a lighter.

'Here, I have one,' Odogwu said, and flung one into the air.

Anane leapt up and stretched his arm to grab it, rocking the boat a bit., and Odogwu lost balance while laughing at him. They barely heard the bang, but Anane's hand split above the elbow and Odogwu's left earlobe was gone.

As Odogwu was coming to terms with what had just happened, one of his men dove at him and pinned him to the floorboard. Another low bang was heard.

Odogwu's mind was in hyper drive, processing the last several seconds. He went through the entire shot in his mind and decided that the bullet hit Anane's hand first, then him.

It came from across the fucking river! Who can shoot with such accuracy from that far away at this hour of the night? The mothorfuckor!

He remembered his two men telling him how Rooftop could see clear and far at night, from their experience with him when they staked the boy's house the night he left.

The hairless fuck!

Odogwu was torn between hatred for the guy that called himself Rooftop, and his admiration for his skill.

+++

Two shots and no kill! This day just fucking keeps giving.

He allowed himself a breath, then held it as he scanned over the boat where the guy had ducked with Odogwu.

Stand up you fucking prick. Eight more shots in the mag, he thought. *Can't take eyes off for a reload. Must fire carefully.*

He kept scanning over the boat. Another breath. Some men became mobilised, and a few shots were fired.

Fire away assholes. Even if you knew where I was, you couldn't hit me with anything.

Another breath.

What the fuck just moved? The fucker!

He noticed a hand starting the outboard motor. Even though the motor had started, he took out the hand with another shot.

Seven left.

Another breath.

The fucking boat's moving. Fuck! It's already near the end of range and going further south. They can't escape.

He fired five rounds along the side of the boat at a height above the keel where a lying body would be. Another breath.

Two left. Fuck!

A head appeared at the rear end of the boat, shouting and waving angrily.

Had he got the fucker?

He fired another shot. The shouting, waving man fell. Another breath.

Last shot.

The boat veered sharply right and ran aground at a distance on the far side.

Out of range now. Should have fired another fucking shot in the side.

There was blood in the river in the boat's wake. He'd got someone for sure.

Two heads appeared to be peeking out of the boat. Then they jumped out, carrying a body, and ran away from the river. The one behind was limping heavily as he ran. One of his legs was broken below the knee with a bullet wound.

He pulled out his big scope to verify. The man in front couldn't be identified. The one whose leg he got was not Odogwu. He waited patiently till he could see the body they carried. Odogwu!

Gotcha!

He had two wounds, one in the stomach.

He's not surviving that! Too much noise. Time to disappear.

+++

'Keep running. Don't look back for me,' the man at the back said. He held Odogwu's legs. 'If I fall, drag him over. There's a van coming. Get him out.'

Odogwu transcended back to his village. He was happily playing with other children in the bush. Nobody could run faster than him, and they all wanted him to play on their team. One of the other fast runners was at his tail, and he was running with all he had. He knew the boy would catch up to him eventually. Odogwu may have been the fastest in the village, but he had the most stamina and endurance.

'We're going too far from the village, Odogwu,' he shouted from behind. 'Your mother will smack us both if the others tell her. And you know they will.'

Odogwu looked over his shoulder, running harder. 'If you say you lost, I will stop. Otherwise, just keep following me.'.

'Okay, I lose. You are king.'

Odogwu started to slow down, as did the other boy. When they had both stopped and were breathing heavily, with hands on their knees, he jumped on him and said, 'I am king. Me Odogwu, not you.' They laughed as they rolled on to the ground.

'Father brought a big gun. He says this one can shoot from very far,' boasted Odogwu.

'He came in yesterday, yes?'

Odogwu nodded.

'So what is a separatist?'

'I don't know. He says he will help change the world. Everyone will have food. Mother doesn't care. She asks him to keep away from the city and the movement. "There is plenty you can do here", she says to him. But father wants food for everyone. Not for me and her alone. I think that is the meaning of a separatist.'

'Your father is a hero then?'

'He's my hero. I will also become a separatist when I grow up. There will be food for everyone.'

They started walking back, punching each other in the arm. They were halfway back when they heard an explosion. The village went up in flames.

'Father!' Odogwu exclaimed, making a run for it. The other boy held his arm. 'Let me go! My father just came back. My mother is in the house too...Let me go!'

The other boy held tightly, his face pale in horror. Odogwu punched him in the face and ran. No matter how hard he ran, he felt he wasn't fast enough. For the first time ever, he was slow...too slow.

It took him fifteen minutes to make it back to the village, and he ran straight for his home, but there was no home. It was difficult to say which burnt down hut belonged to who. There were bodies everywhere.

He saw a couple of trucks and a few smaller vehicles on the road, leaving the village on the other side. He ran after them, but they were gone. There were still a couple of vehicles on the outskirts of the village. He ran back in to find anyone he could recognise, calling out for his parents. A few men with guns were still in the village, but no one bothered him.

Near what should have been his house, he finally saw his father's body on the ground. He fell beside it on his knees.

'Father,' he called out, shaking his body and crying. 'Father get up.'

He wasn't burnt but was beaten, that much he could make out. *This hadn't happened by accident.*

'Get up father...who did this to you...where is mother?' he asked in between bursts of tears.

His father opened his eyes. He could see tears escape them. He couldn't talk, just looked at Odogwu and wept in silence. 'What happened father?' he cried again.

His father moved his hand ever so slightly and pointed to the boy's right. That was the last thing he did as he breathed his final breath. Odogwu wept hard. Then he looked at where his father pointed and saw a man from behind. He had a long coat on and held a baseball bat in his right hand.

He ran toward that man crying hard and jumped on him from behind. Both of them fell. The man turned. Odogwu started hitting him. The man had no expression on his face as if he was in a trance. A few other men picked Odogwu up and flung him aside. He ran for the man again but was stopped and thrown back. The man got up and walked toward the vehicles.

'Kill me! Kill me now, or I will come for you!' Odogwu yelled at them as they all left for their vehicles. He kept chasing after them, and they kept throwing him away. 'You hear me? I will never forget your face! I will come for you, you hear me?'

He chased after the vehicles till he fell and passed out.

For thirty-seven years he had looked for the man. He had no presence on the Internet and had no pictures of him anywhere he had looked. Odogwu hunted for him between every job he had, until one day RD approached him. He brought with him pictures of a boy, his father, and some people. The job was to get the boy from them alive. Odogwu recognised him the moment he saw his picture. Thirty-seven years and he looked exactly the same.

+++

The person with the broken leg carrying Odogwu's body from behind fell, but the one in front kept going. He only had to drag his body a few metres when a van pulled up and flung its door open.

'Is he dead?' someone shouted from inside as two men pulled him in.

'I don't know,' he replied, getting in with the body.

'Can't die,' Odogwu mumbled. 'Not yet...I'll be back for you...I'll be back for you Aaadddiii......'

+++

Adipati looked at his watch again. They did always have a thing for making people wait. The others were getting restless too. Save himself, none of the lot had ever visited.

'You've met them before; where did they take you the last time?' Brij asked him.

'The last time I visited was in Assam. I can bet you they're not taking us there from where we are.'

'Great! It's going to be morning soon, and nobody has the slightest clue who we are to meet, and where we're to go.' Brij kicked a small chip of rock over the cliff. 'And there is not a fucking dog here we can talk to, and there is nowhere we are supposed to move from here.'

'Who the fuck did that?' came a voice from over the cliff. Everyone walked up to the edge and looked over. An adolescent boy stood on a ledge in the dark with a jar full of fireflies. 'I'm here for Trishul Negi and his friends. If it's you fuckers, you better stop throwing shit at me.'

'That's a rather foul mouth for a young boy like you,' Lyosha commented.

'You want to tell me if it's you guys, or are you just going to fuck around wasting my time?'

Trish walked forward. 'I am Trishul Negi. This is my father, and these are my friends.'

The boy looked at him suspiciously. 'Look down there...do you see anyone?' he said, pointing downward.

Adipati stretched his neck to take a peek. It was totally dark except the splashes of water on the rock. That much he could see.

'The question was for Trishul Negi. He says he's Trishul Negi. The fuck are you looking at old man?' asked the boy.

Trish stepped to the very edge and gazed down. 'Two men with rather broad looking swords of some kind,' he said. 'Both have moustaches, one is wearing—'

'Okay, okay,' the boy said. 'You look like a fucking dork, but you must be him. Everybody follow my lead. One person at a time, these ledges can't take two. There's neither space on them nor strength.'

He jumped to a lower ledge, and held up his jar to show where he last was. Adipati ushered Brij on next. They followed in line till they were at the last ledge, which was long and held well. Everyone including the two men Trish saw, was stood in front of a big rock.

'Follow the men in please,' the boy said. 'I have things to take care of outside.'

A "please" was a refreshing change from the foul mouthed young man. They walked behind the two men around the rock into a narrow, winding cavern. About fifty metres in, they could see lights from inside. Around the next bend, their jaws dropped. They entered a huge hall with flat walls, well lit and adorned with ornate furniture.

'Please take a seat,' one of the men said. 'Lady Laranya will be with you shortly.' Both of them left.

'What the hell is this place?' Rakshit exclaimed. Everyone took seats but him. He kept trying to soak in the reality of the place, roaming all around in the magnificent hall.

'To think we stood for close to two hours on the very top of this place,' Brij said. 'They could have come a bit earlier one would think.'

'Please do not offend them, I beg of you,' Adipati said. 'That's the last thing we want to do right now.'

Just as he said this, a dusky, beautiful woman draped in white and adorned with lots of gold jewellery walked in. She was definitely *one* of the most, if not *the most* beautiful woman any of them had seen.

'How could you possibly offend that?' Brij mumbled. Trish smiled.

'You must be Adipati,' she said to him. 'I'm sorry I couldn't see you the last time you were invited. I have heard only good things about you.'

He placed his hand over his heart and bowed his head and she welcomed each of them next.

'Brijbhooshan,' she said to him as she approached. 'Pleasure to finally meet you.'

He bowed his head too. Everyone thought they heard him say "Milady". She then turned to Trish and smiled.

'Trishul,' she said, extending her arms. He looked at Adipati, who nodded; and walked closer to her. She embraced him. 'Niramayi would have been proud.'

He wanted to ask if Niramayi was who he thought she was, but remembered Adipati's advice.

'Ladies and gentlemen...' she said, addressing them all. 'It is the pleasure of the House of Yaksh to host you for the next few days. It could be one day, two, three, or as many as the Yakshini decides she needs with Trishul, and then we shall let you be on your way.'

'She says it is imperative she spends time with him and will see him at noon. You all need rest and will be shown to your chambers very soon. Please honour us by sharing breakfast with us. My children and I would love to have your company.'

She gestured to a doorway. Everyone followed her into the next hall. It was as big as the main hall and had a long dining table that Rakshit counted could seat twenty-six.

'Please, take seats,' she said. 'My children will join us shortly while breakfast is served.'

They all took their seats when Trish felt someone whisper in his ear, '*Act like you don't know me. Please don't let them know,*' as two people passed behind him.

He looked for the girl and saw the backs of a young man and woman walking away from him toward the head of the table to Laranya. As they turned, she introduced them. 'Meet my son Vidyut and my daughter Tejaswi.'

They greeted everyone with a *namaste.*

Trish couldn't believe his eyes. He tried to look elsewhere but inevitably ended up looking at her. They all sat, and breakfast was served.

'I apologise to those who prefer meat, but we can only serve vegetarian food,' Laranya said as everyone politely rejected her concern and acknowledged in unison how good the food was.

There wasn't much talk after that till they'd had breakfast and started getting up. Trish's mind kept racing, but he somehow managed to stay calm.

When Laranya offered to show the guests their chambers, her children pitched in, and they went three separate ways. Tejaswi stayed with Brij, Mugdha, and Trish. Mugdha took the first chamber, followed by Brij. He hugged his son goodnight and wished Tejaswi well before closing the door. Now it was just him with her.

'Tejaswi?'

'Trish, I can explain...I just wanted to...'

He hugged her tight. 'No need. You can tell me later,' he said. 'For now, it's just great to see you. Since the moment I stepped out of your house that morning, this is the first thing that's happened to me that I like, Natasha.'

16

«««« SIXTEEN »»»»

Trish woke up from a soft knock on his door. 'Come in please, it's open,' he said. Tejaswi walked in with tea, smiling mischievously. He grinned back from the bed. 'Have you been taking tea to everyone yourself?'

She placed the pot on a table and brought over a cup to him. 'We have help around the house, you know? I offered to help take tea for those I showed to their chambers this morning. I've seen to it already that Mugdha and your father have been served some. You better get ready Trish, the Yakshini will see you in an hour.'

'Wait,' Trish said. 'What is this place? I mean when I first heard the mention of the House of Yaksh, I thought it was your surname. Then standing in wait for you atop the cliff, I imagined it wasn't exactly that, but rather something else. Now I hear that a Yakshini is to see me. What's the deal here?'

Tejaswi sat next to him. 'The house of Yaksh has been around for millennia, Trish. You don't really know the culture of your land, do you?' Trish frowned as she continued. 'We're the guardians of knowledge and have been forever. We are all Yaksh, but there can only be one who is referred to as Yaksh or Yakshini at a time in a house. I have said enough; we usually ask, not answer questions. I like you, and you know that already, but that's the only reason I've said this much. Get ready now.'

Trish was about to say something, but she put her finger over her lips before she got up and left the room. He sat there, remaining quiet.

Within half an hour he was up, fresh and bathed. He walked out of his room toward the hall where almost everyone else was already present and talking. Laranya greeted Trish as Vidyut, and the rest of them nodded at him.

'I hope you had a pleasant sleep,' Laranya said.

Trish nodded. Sleep wasn't something that was an undeniable part of their nights now. They slept whenever they could. *When will this end?*

As the last of them walked in, Laranya ushered them into the dining hall again. Lunch was being served as they took their seats. Trish was really hungry. When he took his seat from last night, he found only a banana and an apple on his plate. He stood up for some of the delicious looking food on the table, but one of the people serving food stopped him.

'Only the fruit for you sir, on the Yakshini's request,' he said.

Trish looked at his hosts. Their faces told him it wasn't really a request after all. 'Might I have more fruit at least?'

'She would rather you did not, sir,' came the reply.

What the fuck?

Trish finished his fruit within two minutes, then sat watching the others devour their delicacies served to them.

What good would him not eating get the Yakshini?

He was amazed at how nobody cared if he was hungry as they delved into their plates. Tejaswi looked at him every now and then, but looked away instantly. He wanted to ask about what they did – Vidyut and her – but Adipati's advice loomed over his thoughts. His father was absolutely mesmerised by Laranya, and it was becoming so obvious that Trish was feeling slightly embarrassed.

All the others were still eating when a man walked into the hall and announced, 'The Yakshini will see Master Trish now.'

Trish got up; so did Laranya and her children. 'She'll come for you here, Trish,' Laranya said. Adipati got up next, hearing that the Yakshini was coming. All others followed suit. Less than a minute later, the Yakshini walked in.

She was a petite old woman who walked with the slightest hint of a stoop. Her demeanour was such that it reflected how she owned the place, if not the world. She exuded confidence, but at the same time she had a very warm smile on her face that invited conversation.

Trish thought he hadn't seen anyone like her before. She was beautiful and despite a smaller than average frame, she radiated the idea of not to be messed with. She walked straight up to the head of the table to Laranya's seat. Laranya greeted her with '*Pranaam*' and bowed with folded hands in a *namaste.*

'*Pranaam*,' said the others in the exact same fashion. She bowed ever so slightly and smiled at them.

She addressed Adipati first. 'Adi, dear child, how have you been?'

'Good, thanks to your blessings,' he replied.

'Isn't Maurice around? I thought I would see him this time.'

'He will join us tonight, should you be willing.'

'Of course, I'd be willing. Why do you think we sent for all of you?'

'Of course, my bad.'

She turned toward Brij. 'Mr Negi. It is an immense pleasure to meet you. I hope you've had good rest. This is a massive journey for you, and Adipati has a habit of withholding till he absolutely needs to spit something out.'

'Yes, I did rest well, thank you,' Brij said, wincing slightly, not sure what to make of her remark.

'Hello Trish,' she addressed him after she gave Brij a nod. 'I hope you ate nothing cooked.'

'A banana and an apple,' he replied with a sheepish grin.

'Are you hungry?' she asked.

'A little.'

'No need to be polite, son. When I ask you a question, give me the truth unadulterated.'

There it was. Politely commanding.

'I was hoping...I mean I could surely eat,' Trish replied, unsure.

Tejaswi giggled.

'Just right, then,' the Yakshini said. 'I have a question for you, son. When you were in the well, did you travel?'

Trish's eyes widened. He was the only one in the room who apparently knew what she said. He gulped and said, 'Yes.'

'Good. Then we must have a chat. Would you be so kind and follow me, son?'

He followed her, and they left as she excused them out of there. 'Please finish your meal,' Laranya said. 'Sorry for the interruption, but you needn't worry about them. He's in good hands.'

'The best hands anyone can be in,' Vidyut said proudly. His mother gave him a curt look, and he went back to eating.

I hope he doesn't speak out of turn in there, Tejaswi thought.

+++

She took him to a small room that had no windows and locked the door behind them. They took seats on a cotton mat on the floor, which was the only thing in the otherwise completely empty room, save a few objects that lay on the mat itself. There was an earthen jar, two small earthen bowls, and a wooden box to the side of the mat that she sat on.

'Do you know where it was you travelled to?' she asked.

'I don't, honestly,' he replied.

'Did you travel far?'

'Very far, for sure,' he said. 'I could see galaxies.'

Her eyes widened. 'Galaxies, you say. Interesting. I haven't met anyone in a long time who has managed that far.'

Trish wanted to ask her what all of it meant. *Damn Adipati. Why did he have to tell me not to ask?*

She placed the items between them. 'Did you listen to anything while you were in that place?'

'I was in different places, Ma'am. The mountains, the depths of the deep sea, somewhere in space, then on a never ending beach. It had water on the one side and sand on the other, and it continued forever.'

'Did you listen to anything, son?' she repeated.

'I heard someone say they could see me.'

'You heard. But did you *listen*?'

He looked confused, his brow furrowed and he shook his head slightly. 'I'm not sure ma'am. They said they could see me. They never asked me to do anything. I would've listened...'

'That Adipati will turn you into a fool like himself,' she said, shaking her head. 'All you will have remaining with yourself will be your demons chasing after you. Just as his do. There is a difference between hearing and listening. You *do* know that, don't you?'

'I guess...'

'You kids these days. Why do you guess so much? Do you know how embarrassing it is when you are the face of knowledge in the world, and no knowledge is ever to escape you...while your own grand daughter thinks she can keep things out of your knowledge?'

Trish looked up in surprise.

'Yes, I know about the two of you,' she continued. 'She was specially told not to interact with you, and I knew in that instant she would.'

Trish stared down at the mat in embarrassment.

'Listening. That is the key, son. The one true sound, the one vibration that goes through us all. Living or otherwise.'

'The one truth...the energy,' he interrupted.

'Ah! I see you've met Maurice then,' she quipped. 'Yes. The one truth. The energy. But how would you know it? It doesn't have form or factor. Sound is the manifestation closest to its own being. We all vibrate on our own; the living, the inanimate, the physical, the non-physical. All of us. And as vibrating individuals, we vibrate in the universe as one, thus making sound the one true manifestation of energy itself. The one truth that manifests into endless possibilities.'

'We all vibrate,' Trish mumbled, trying to grasp yet another face to his newfound understanding of the world.

'Isn't that what your so called modern science is now saying?' she asked, stopping his train of thought.

'Modern science...what do you mean?'

'What does the string theory propose about vibrating strings that make up everything?' she asked, looking away as she cleaned the small bowls with a piece of cloth.

Trish was surprised at her even knowing about string theory.

Keepers of knowledge alright!

'I think I know what you're saying...' he said.

'Do you now? And what brought our world as we know it then?'

'Sound?' Trish asking, taking a bite.

'In the beginning was the word, and the word was with God, and the word was God' she quoted from the bible. 'John 1:1.'

Trish looked bemused.

'Do you think it is a coincidence that our beliefs tell us that, son? How many civilisations around the world believe that the universe came into being as a result of *the three songs,* or *the seven songs,* or some such? And what is the sound of *Aum?* The one cosmic sound that is supposed to reverberate across the universe?'

'So the recital of *Aum* brought about the universe? That's the sound the universe is making?' Trish asked, his tone laced with a hint of a challenge. He immediately bit his lip.

She seemed to ignore his brazenness. 'I wish it were that simple, child. But let's just say it's the closest sound to the universe's that we can make by using our body.'

'But how does sound bring about anything? This vast universe, all the planets, their orientation, the patterns, their topography, life itself. How does sound make all this?' Trish asked her, gesturing with his hands animatedly.

'Well, we don't know everything, do we? The ancients did, but we wouldn't listen to them, and look where we are now. Trying to rediscover what was already common knowledge. Do you know of Cymatics?'

This old lady was full of surprises. Trish didn't expect her at all to know about or talk about the string theory or Cymatics, but here she was talking about stuff he himself didn't fully know of in the fields of modern scientific application.

'I know of it,' he said.

'Well, you could read about it and join them at the beginning of the cycle, or you can realise the universe for yourself. Whatever the reason, a lot has been bestowed on you, son. But if you have to realise for yourself, the key is to listen.'

'Hearing is allocating a part of your faculties, while the others work on what it is you hear. Then you process what you hear as you hear it. Processing is limited by knowledge, and that is why different people process what they hear differently, based on what they know.'

'Listening, on the other hand, means total surrender. You do not allocate a part of your faculties, but you give yourself up to undivided attention. When you attend fully with no baggage of knowledge with you, you do not process, interpret, or try to reason. You are not bound then, by any limitation at all. You don't need to use your ability to hear me to listen to me, son. Neither do you need to listen to the universe.'

Trish nodded, listening intently to her every word. *Or was it listening...hearing maybe? Damn! What the fuck was she saying?*

'Do you smoke?' she asked him.

Trish looked at her in surprise yet again. 'I have smoked. Once in a while. Not a smoker though.' He noticed she had opened the box.

'Good,' she said as she brought out a *chillum* and started fixing a joint of some kind. 'I want you to try this.' She took a puff while she lit it up.

Trish wanted to rub his eyes. The most elegant looking woman he had seen, old yet grand, extremely classy and dignified, just fixed and took a drag off of pot. He took the *chillum* reluctantly, then took a puff himself as she encouraged him to do so. The stuff was something else completely. He knew instantly that too much of this would knock him out in a matter of seconds. She poured into the small bowls from the jar and offered him a cup. Trish looked at it suspiciously and wanted to ask, but Adipati's voice echoed in his head.

She sensed it though. 'Plant extract. I won't give a guest in my house something that could harm him in any way. It is a drink of the ancients, have some faith in them.'

Trish drank from his bowl and almost spat it back out. It tasted horrible, but she encouraged him to drink, so he did. When he put his bowl down, he could feel a rather pleasant after taste in his mouth. They both had a puff each of the *chillum*, then another sip of the bowl. Trish's head started to spin a little, and he began sweating.

What the fuck is in this thing?

+++

'What did she mean by this is a massive journey for me?' Brij asked Adipati when they sat in the main hall on a large sofa. 'I certainly know about your skills at withholding, the gods know that has tested me.'

Others were seated at a fair distance too, chatting away. Laranya had excused herself and Vidyut for some urgent matter that needed immediate attention. Tejaswi stayed with them to see to their comfort, but Adipati had warned everyone to be very cautious of how they behaved and what they talked about around any member of the esteemed house.

'I don't know,' Adipati replied. 'I mean, you are Trish's father, and all this is about him at the end of the day. Maybe not about him as such, but then he is the most important ingredient in this entire soup we're in right now.'

'So I'd say it was a big journey for you, yes! Imagine everything you've been through in the last several days. And you can't begin to imagine what you've to still go through.'

'There we go again! But I guess you're right,' he said. 'It's just the way she said it. She looked into my eyes, and I could feel her peeking in my head somehow.'

'They're the Yaksh, Brij. There is no other like them. No one knows much about them, yet they know everything about everything. It's scary, and if you ask me, you should always be scared of them.'

'So what do you think she wants to know from Trish then?' Brij asked him. 'I mean, she clearly wants something. Why else would she invite us here and take him away for whatever discussion they're having in there?'

Adipati wondered for a moment. 'She may want to know something he's experienced recently, or maybe something he himself doesn't realise he knows. These Yaksh are very enigmatic, so I couldn't say with certainty. However, there's also the possibility she wants to offer him something, perhaps knowledge or something material. They've been known to do that when they so please. You can never say with these people, Brij...'

'Never say what?' Laranya's voice asked from behind them.

'I was just telling Brij how you can never say what provided Trish with the good fortune of being able to share space with the Yakshini herself,' he replied instantly, clearing his throat.

She smiled back at him mischievously, as if calling his bluff.

Did she know? They knew everything anyway. Damn!

'She made it known to me that she would love for you to visit our guest library, should you so choose,' she said.

'Of course,' Brij said. 'We would love that.'

They got up and followed her while the others remained in the hall.

'She's a vision,' Brij whispered to Adipati. He shook his head.

+++

Trish looked down at his body and that of the Yakshini, while they sat facing each other. His head was slumped, and it looked like he was not conscious. The Yakshini looked at his body and smiled. She then drank some more and took another puff. Trish looked around from up there. It was a small room with no opening other than the door. He brought his hands up, but he couldn't see them.

Oh, for fuck's sake not again!

He felt the updraught of wind and rocketed through space again. It was a sight to behold. He went through the rock that was the abode of the Yaksh and soared   infinitely upward, the world soon a tiny spec in the vastness around him.

How many worlds must there be in there? he thought. He closed his eyes and breathed deeply. He was overwhelmed again, but unlike last time he didn't lose himself to it.

When he opened his eyes, he was at the beach. Land ran behind him on both sides for as far as he could see, as did the water in front of him. He started to walk along the water on the beach, and felt the waves lapping up over his legs that he couldn't see.

This was the most tranquil place he'd ever been to in his life. He felt like he knew the place so well, but how? In the sky, even though there was daylight, he could see the stars, the galaxies, and the universe as he pictured it. On his feet, he could feel the wet sand and felt his feet sinking into it. But he couldn't see his feet. He didn't want to leave. He just kept on walking along the water.

'So this is your sanctum sanctorum,' he heard someone say. Trish turned around, startled.

'How did you get here?' he exclaimed.

'You brought me here, Trish,' the Yakshini said. 'I couldn't have come here if you didn't want it.'

'Why can't I see myself?'

'Only you can know, but I believe you must think or know that you don't need a physical form to realise you're here,' she said.

'Then why can I see you?'

'Like I said, only you can answer that. This place is yours, Trish. You make the rules, you decide what happens and how it happens. Maybe it's not yet enough for you to know that I'm here, and you need to see me. Maybe when you're ready to accept my presence, you won't need me to have a body.'

'I have so many questions,' he said. 'Where is this?'

'I don't know. You conjured this place up. This is your sojourn. I only wanted to help you get here again since you clearly didn't know how. But this is one place you need to be able to come to as and when you want. It is very important. As long as you have a refuge in the universe, you are safe. Not many people have ever been capable of this in the history of our existence.'

'What do you think I'm here for?' he asked her. 'I know I'm supposed to answer this myself, but what do *you* think?'

'I haven't the first clue. I'm the epitome of knowledge of the world, but this isn't the world I know of. This is your world. So ask it yourself...Listen.'

Trish turned to the sea and closed his eyes. He tried to listen though he didn't know how.

'Give in Trish,' she said, urging him. 'This is the safest place you can ever be in. Don't hold yourself back. Let go.'

He heard and heard but he couldn't listen. He tried over and over until he almost gave up. Just then there was this overwhelming sound. It was tearing him apart. He felt like his head would explode. He clutched on to his head with both hands as if to keep it together and let out a huge cry. He cried out at the top of his voice, but he just couldn't overpower the sound.

Listen. He heard the Yakshini's voice in his head somewhere. *Surrender.*

He fell on his knees. The sound began to filter itself out into a million voices. Distinct voices, every single one of them. He felt like everything was talking to him. People of the world. People of worlds he didn't know. Plants too...and animals. Every being, it appeared, was talking to him. And they were all saying the same thing.

I see you...

17

«««‹ SEVENTEEN »»»»

Brij was worried, and Adipati could not help but worry himself. Trish had come out shivering from the room a few hours back and had since been asleep. *'What must she have done?'* He looked at Brij and forced a smile, trying to make sure he was at ease.

The others had been asking about further plans as well, to which he had no answer. Nobody just walked out on the Yaksh. More importantly, they were a neutral party. He couldn't have them leaning the other way. It was anybody's guess what the Yakshini wanted from the boy or how long she intended to keep them. Then there was also the matter of their plans for the immediate future.

He was now beginning to wonder whether his original plan of keeping Trish at the fort in hope to wait out the rest of the days was such a good idea. After their encounter with RD's men in Benares, his faith in this plan was shaken. Sheshna was only one gateway. The fort was so close to the lake, and the thought of them being detected there was giving him insomnia. It was however, the only place he thought they had a chance of defending well. The day was getting closer too. The energies would shift and they themselves would be coming out soon.

Damn!

'We will wake him up for tea,' Laranya announced. 'Do not worry Mr Negi, what they ate together reacted with his system. Apparently, a light stomach wasn't the best idea after all.'

'Please call me Brij,' he said. 'He isn't getting up though, is he? How will we get him out for tea?'

'The Yakshini has prescribed some herbs,' she said. 'He'll be up, there is no need for concern.'

Adipati smiled to disguise his emotions. There was no way a light stomach was the reason this happened. Not with her specific instructions for him not to eat. He was growing more and more suspicious of them.

At five in the evening, tea was served. Laranya herself had gone to wake Trish up and bring him out. When he entered the hall, he looked like he'd had a good rest, and not a thing was wrong with him. He, was in fact, beaming. Brij was relieved to see his son well. Adipati, however, grew even more sceptical.

They had tea and a light snack. It was apparent that Sveta loved *pakauras* the way she always devoured them. Lyosha cracked a joke or two, Rakshit was his usual restless self, but Adipati was just waiting to get a hold of Trish alone.

Finally, he got him alone near the fireplace. 'What really happened in there?' he whispered. 'What did she do to you?'

Trish smiled playfully. 'You know the place I went to when I was in the well? She helped me get back there.' He came closer to Adipati's ear and whispered slowly. 'And now I think I know how to get there too.' He pulled back his face, expecting to see Adipati excited.

Adipati gawked at him. 'She didn't come with you, did she?'

'She did,' Trish replied, looking concerned. 'I took her apparently. Otherwise she couldn't have come.'

'No, she couldn't have.' Adipati was flustered. 'Damn!' He looked away for a second before turning back, looking really agitated. 'Did she leave something there?'

Trish became confused. 'I don't think so.'

'Think hard Trish. Did she have something on her when she arrived? Something that was missing when you returned? Anything?'

Trish thought hard and tried to revisit those moments in his head. *What was she wearing? No. That was still there. Her footwear? No. Jewellery? No. Something in her hair? She wasn't carrying anything...Damn it! Her hands!*

'She was definitely clutching on to something. There was something in her hand. I don't know what it was, but I'm most certain her hands were empty while returning, now that you mention it.' Trish had a disquieted look about his face. 'What does it mean?'

'I don't know,' he replied, nervous. 'All I know is that she doesn't do anything without reason. If she's helping you, she wants something in return. The Yaksh have always been that way. Speak of the devil...'

Laranya approached them. 'The Yakshini will see Trish if he so pleases,' she said.

'I'd like Adipati to accompany me, please,' Trish said, putting his hand on Adipati's shoulder. 'If she so pleases.'

Everyone in the room looked at him in surprise. The Yaksh were shocked. They were not used to counter requests or amendments to their own. Yogis, who knew all about the Yaksh, had not seen or heard of this ever happening before.

Laranya tried to disguise her astonishment and cleared her throat. 'I'll see what she has to say to that,' she said, then took her leave.

Trish looked over at Tejaswi. Her expression clearly said, *'What The fuck!'*

+++

'You let me in. You allowed me to see. It may have been for your own reasons...maybe you needed someone to understand, or maybe you just needed someone period. But you let me in nonetheless, and that is the only reason I've decided to overlook your audacity just this once.' The Yakshini addressed Trish as Adipati stood near the table awaiting his turn.

'I understand,' Trish said. 'Might I please be granted one more favour? I would understand completely if I'm out of line and must be denied.'

Adipati straightened himself. *Maybe it was time to pack and leave.*

Surprisingly, the Yakshini smiled. 'You never know when to quit, do you? One last time. Tell me what you want.'

'You left something behind where we were,' he said to her face that was changing to a grim expression, to say the least. 'I apologise if I'm wrong, but do you think I have the right to know? You said yourself I let you in and what happened there was all up to me.'

She looked sternly toward Adipati. He was staring at the roof, wishing for it to fall on him. Then she turned to Trish again. 'I would have told you eventually. It is not my place to interfere with your being, and indeed that is not what I intended to do at any point in time. I assure you, in fact, that I cannot interfere. You do realise I'm only interested in knowledge, I hope.'

'I do. I wouldn't have brought it up if I knew there was something to hide in it for you. I trust you completely. If it were not for you, I would have never known where I was and how to get there. But at the same time, it did make me wonder…'

'You see, I'm only beginning to understand myself and the world around me. Knowledge is your strength; you are someone who can understand better what it does to my dynamically changing world, to know something has happened, and yet not know why?'

Trish was almost apologetic. He didn't want to offend her anymore, but he needed to know all the same.

'You are tactful as you are brave, young one,' she said with a smile. 'What I left behind is an anchor of sorts. My connection to your being. It will not affect anything at all, just help me with a better understanding of the world and how it works. I haven't come across anyone in my lifetime who can do anything like this, or reach where you did.'

'I do have knowledge of this practice, but it is all handed down from previous generations. This is my way of collecting information for my own understanding, I assure you. You are most definitely a unique being, after all.'

'A cookie for my browser,' Trish mumbled.

The Yakshini laughed. *She had a very endearing laugh*, Trish thought.

'Very well put,' she said. 'I couldn't have said it any better.' She walked over to a table on the far side and brought something out from a box. 'I want you to have this, Trish. It symbolises that you have the blessings of the House of Yaksh.'

Adipati looked at them wide eyed as Trish accepted a metal bracelet, around two inches and a half wide, which had a curved plate three inches long in the middle while chain links formed the rest.

Now at least we're sure they are on our side, he thought.

The plate had the shape of a nautilus shell cut into it. It was beautiful. Trish put it on his left wrist, and it fit perfectly.

'Anyone who knows of the House of Yaksh will know that you have our blessing on seeing this on your wrist,' she said. 'Even if few people you come across know of us, they will know that you are always welcome here, going forward.'

'It was a nautilus shell, wasn't it?' Trish asked her, remembering the shell jutting out of her clenched fist. 'The one you left behind. I thought I never had a look, but I remember now.'

'It was. Now, this is what I wanted to see you about. Do you have any more questions before I retire to my chambers?'

'I do,' Trish said. 'Just one. Was it really me that looked back at me from the water in the well? What am I?'

'That is for your mentor here to help you with. If only he spent more time telling you what you really need to know than filling your mind with ideas. It's past high time he told you anyway. You have turned a couple of times already in his presence.' She turned to Adipati. 'Wouldn't you say just helping him stay in control won't do any more Adi? He has to know. He has to embrace it to be able to turn as and when he wants. He can't do it if he doesn't know what it is he is supposed to be.'

Adipati lowered his head while she spoke, then looked up. 'I agree with you. This can't be kept from him any longer. We thank you immensely for bestowing your blessings on him with this token of your welcome. I take it as a blessing bestowed on us all.'

She walked out the door and said, 'The both of you need to chat, you may use the library; good night.'

+++

'Where do I even begin?' Adipati said.

'Try at the beginning?' Trish quipped. 'That usually helps.'

Adipati breathed through his teeth. 'If only you could understand my position Trish, you wouldn't be joking about it.'

'Try me.'

'You remember how we talked about our supposed gods helping evolution along?'

'Yes. And I identify with your theory.'

'My theory, yes. It isn't so much a theory, though. The theory is that apes were transformed into men with help. The theory is we didn't just evolve from them. The theory isn't complete. Apes were not identified as the predominant species on our planet at first. There were others.'

'Our texts are full of mentions of these peoples. They even co-existed with humans and have been recorded as such, until a time our world was no longer enough for two supreme races any more, let alone all of them.'

Trish was listening intently. His ability to digest such information had grown immensely. Had someone been talking to him about what Adipati just said some days back, he would have outright ridiculed him and laughed it off. But things he never thought possible, he had now seen. Not only had he seen them, but he had also experienced them first-hand.

What he thought was an anomaly with him throughout his life when he could see clearly in the dark, somehow had to have some meaning now. The things he had felt recently were things he had never known existed. His own abilities, the abilities of those around him had left him open to just about anything.

'And what was the the first choice of species, then?' he asked. 'I know our scriptures mention so many of such races.'

Adipati looked at him, trying to frame his next words. 'The first were the reptiles. Then the feathered ones. Apes were last.'

Trish tried hard not to remember the creature that looked back at him from the well. *It cannot be.* 'Why reptiles?'

'The first amphibians were reptiles. A truly remarkable trait for a dominant species to have if you ask me. They made great progress with them, and despite someone switching to beings of flight, reptiles kept showing a lot more promise than them. Races from both these species are in recorded scripture of our past even as we came along. It was also a tussle between gods of different origins. Those that came of a certain species themselves favoured the development of their own.'

'So you are telling me some survived from the other species?' Trish became curious.

'No,' Adipati said, and got up. Trish could see his discomfort on his face as he framed the next sentence. 'An entire species survived, lived on, and is thriving.'

Trish couldn't believe what he heard. His mind kept going back to the well.

Adipati continued. 'They were obviously not going to cohabit the planet with us. That much was evident. Despite millennia of living together, having offspring with one another and sharing the same world, there was never complete harmony between us.'

'When you say between us, who do you mean? You said *an* entire species survived. Which species?'

'Reptilians,' he replied. 'The strongest of the species that were cooked up by gods. The species into which far better research was infused. The species that could exploit much more of their potential than man ever could. As they grew stronger, we grew weaker and weaker still, forgetting slowly what we were and what we were supposed to evolve into.'

'Are you saying we haven't evolved as planned?'

'Yes. That is precisely what I'm saying. Do you play video games Trishul?'

'I do...'

'Do you know how all the stages that you are supposed to progress through in a game are all written in the code?'

'Yes.'

'Yet, has it ever been that you completed a few stages of progression and realised that you missed to pick up something in a previous stage that you now needed, or else you would be stuck? Or perhaps see someone else play the same game as you and at the same level, but being far better equipped since they picked up everything there was to pick along the way, while you were busy making it to the next level as fast as you could?'

'Always,' said Trish.

'The code is written Trish, in us. There's no such thing as junk DNA, no matter what they teach you. We just never picked up all the stuff we were supposed to. The things that we thought we didn't need to advance in our evolution. The stuff that if we had picked, would have unlocked so many features we never knew existed in the game.'

'Like a fluid, we chose the path of least resistance and termed it as progression and evolution. What we left behind was everything that mattered, but we never knew existed. We shouldn't have to talk like we do.

Trish stared back at him blankly and Adipati could tell he hadn't made complete sense to him.

'I will give you an example. We call our spoken language a blessing. One that sets us apart and makes us supreme. Language as we know it is not our success. It is our failure and our way of dealing with the failure. Why shouldn't we all communicate like Sveta does? We're all capable of it...'

'We are?' Trish asked, butting in.

'Oh, come on Trish. Has it never happened to you that you were humming a song and it just got stuck in your head; and when you stepped out and met people, a random stranger started humming the very same song?'

Trish looked lost in thought. *Of course it had happened to him.*

'Don't tell me it hasn't, it happens to every one of us. How does this stranger pick that song up? We were supposed to evolve Trish, it was coded in us. But instead, we adapted, and we kept on adapting till evolution was replaced by adaptation. We got lost in ourselves.'

'Damn,' Trish said. 'I never gave it any thought.'

'That's the problem - We never do. Anyway, we are capable of realising that we missed something in our evolution. That's what the rest of us do. But we have only ever found one hidden code in us. There have been others who have found more, but those people are disappearing now. Another Shiv is highly unlikely; in the current state of affairs at least. Adaptation has killed us. Reptilians never adapted. They evolved. They tapped into whatever their code had for them.'

'So what happened then? Why could we not share our world?' Trish got up too, feeling too uncomfortable to be seated.

'There was always conflict, my dear, never accord. It was inevitable. There were wars between us, time and again, even though at other times we lived together. But the gods could see it would end bitterly, so they devised several plans to keep us apart. However, it wasn't until they discovered *Patal* that a workable solution began to emerge.'

'The reptilians were given *Patal Lok* to inhabit primarily, whereas we got *Bhu Lok*. Obviously though, after aeons of living together, however incongruously it may have been at times, we were not just going to separate overnight. We went over to their *Lok*, and they came over to ours; all the time. Some even chose to live in the *Lok* assigned to the other species.'

'Until...?'

'There's no exact specifics on the '*until*' as such. I mean it isn't recorded anywhere when exactly both sides shut gates. But it all stems from the two descending lines of Arjun.'

'Arjun, the Arjun from the *Paandavs*...from the Mahabharat...that Arjun?'

'The very person.' Adipati got to the far end of the room and poured himself water into an intricately cut crystal glass. 'Everyone remembers Arjun's son Abhimanyu; you must too. I'm sure you've heard the story of Abhimanyu and how he got entrapped and was killed inside the *Chakravyooh*.'

Trish nodded.

'The lineage didn't end there, though. Abhimanyu had a son named Parikshit who was bitten by Takshak; a *Naag*. Takshak's kingdom was vanquished and displaced by the Paandavs, led by Arjun. Not only that, Takshak's son was killed in the said battle by Abhimanyu, and his wife was murdered by none other than Arjun himself. Are you following so far?'

Trish nodded again. He went on to pour a glass of water for himself as well, wishing it was something stiffer.

'Along with the Naags lived other minority species and they were all displaced. Naags of the time could turn completely, and Takshak was a friend of the supervisor of our so called gods; the one known as Indr. He had to have revenge, and Parikohit was cursed to be bitten by a snake. Takshak fully turned; he caused the bite, and there was instant death.'

'In those times, cross-breeding was commonplace. There were lots of Naag offspring with humans and vice versa. So you can imagine the chaos all this bloodshed led to. I'll go on if you understand the chain of events so far.'

Trish nodded again and said, 'Please do. I'll stop you when I lose the plot.'

'Parikshit also had a son named Janmejay. Not surprisingly, now he wanted revenge. He unleashed hell on the Naags and had a massive plan to annihilate them. Humans, led by demigods, were also very powerful at the time. Demigods were the offspring of gods and humans, while also the same being true for Naags. They had demigods of their own. The gods had offspring with both species to produce leaders, whether they came from wombs or labs.'

'Janmejay was greatly successful in his implementation of eradication of the Naag species and even managed to drag Takshak from under the protection of Indr himself. But the gods couldn't lose that species. They were as much their creation as us, and they wanted both, whether out of love or to study the difference in evolution; only they knew.'

'The killing was finally ended by a person called Astik. He was the son of a yogi and Mansa, a Naag. That war ended there, but left open a rift that was to be exploited later.'

'But you talked about the two descending lines of Arjun. This was about the Naags and Arjun's as one lineage alone,' Trish asked.

'Yes,' Adipati said. 'And that is where the plot thickens. The rift that was to be exploited at a later stage; the one that led to the ultimate boycott between the two sides, was exploited by none other than brothers of the first line.'

'Arjun, while in exile for violating his terms with Draupadi, fell for a Naag princess named Ulupi. She took him to *Patal Lok*, also at times known as, and confused with, *Naag Lok*. There, they had a son named Iravan. Iravan was left behind by Arjun and was despised by his kin. Despite that, he helped the Pandavs in Mahabharat, only to be slain in battle. Iravan was married to Mohini as a boon, who is mentioned as the female form of a god. What that means exactly, is open to interpretation to date.'

'Thus prospered the other line of descent from Arjun, in the Naags. Where the fallout happened down the line is lost in time, but you know how fast things spiral out of control when two lines of descent from one source end up against each other.'

'So the doors between *Patal* and *Bhu Lok* were eventually shut forever?'

'Well, yes and no. Yes they were shut, and animosity prevailed, but the doors were not physical. It was just a decision that was made. Eventually, we adapted instead of evolving, forgot our true self and our connection to the universe, and could never cross over. But the *Naags* evolved. They embraced the cosmos and the power it wants to give us, and they still know how.'

'They still cross over?' Trish was both excited and nervous. He kind of knew where this was heading. 'You mean they live here amongst us too? Do they still have offspring with humans?'

'Well,' Adipati said. 'Your mother crossed, and she had you.'

18

««« EIGHTEEN »»»

It had been a terrible night. Trish barely slept at all. Adipati had brought to light facts that were so difficult to come to terms with, that Trish was having trouble breathing. He was sure his father hadn't slept either. Adipati had talked to him as well in Trish's presence after their chat, and it left him devastated from what Trish could tell. Adipati promised more answers after the night's rest, but there was probably no rest for his eyes either. Despite him knowing all this, while having an understanding of it all, Trish could see Adipati was rather disturbed too. He could actually understand what he had meant in saying that he was in a difficult position. Even though Trish was distraught, a part of him felt for the man as well.

How do you tell someone all this?

It was indeed a very awkward position to be in. It was almost morning. Trish couldn't take it any more. He got up and went to the shower. He was so lost in his thoughts that he didn't even notice Tejaswi come in behind him as he stood in the water. She hugged him. Neither of them spoke.

When they were dressing themselves after the shower, he asked her in a low voice, 'You knew?'

'That is my burden Trish, knowing,' she replied. 'Did I believe it though? Probably not. That is why I couldn't resist seeing you. I've been taught, told, and informed about the other people and hybrids both on this side and that. But I had never seen one yet, so I decided I would find out for myself.'

'When I met you though, Trish, I just got attracted to the boy I saw. I didn't care if you were one of them, or us, or another kind. I wanted to spend time with you as you were.'

'How much more do you know?' he asked, holding her hand.

'Not enough to help you at all, I'm afraid. I'm still learning Trish, but at this point, Adipati knows more that will be helpful to you than what I would know. My family doesn't even completely trust me yet.'

'Well, I don't blame them for that,' Trish remarked with a grin that disappeared fast. 'I don't know if I'm ready to understand just yet.'

'You have to be, Trish. You don't have much time. They are coming for you - the ones from the other side.'

'But if I'm part of them, why are *they* a threat to me?'

'It is best you learn from Adipati and the Yakshini. I don't want to feed you half baked information and complicate it even more for you. Now, get ready and come on out. I'll be there waiting.'

+++

Breakfast was quiet. Everyone was present except the Yakshini, who preferred to abstain and eat her meals by herself as always. They all ate, but none was sure of what to say or how to start a conversation. All eyes were on Trish and his father. They could feel them upon themselves. The tension was becoming really awkward.

Laranya decided to break the silence. 'Niramayi was a very noble woman. That is what her name was, your mother's. She and I were friends, I should like to think. She fell for you Mr Negi...Brij, and then there was no looking back. All she wanted was to be with you. She loved you so much.'

'I didn't even know her name,' Brij said. 'I don't know if I knew anything at all. I hope she loved me as she said—'

'Do not do that,' Laranya said, cutting him short. 'I will not allow you to dishonour her by even thinking that she could have lied to you. She offered to tell you everything, it was you who told her you were not interested, and that it didn't matter as long as she was with you. She gave up her life for you, Brij. She died just to be with you...'

'She died in childbirth...'

'As she knew she would,' Laranya said, raising her voice a little as she let go of her spoon. 'She always knew that bearing a child would kill her. It always kills them on our side, but she didn't want to leave you. She wanted a child with you so much...'

Trish saw a tear roll down his father's cheek. He had never seen this before, and his own eyes moistened. His mother knew she would die if she had him, yet she had him anyway.

What did that even mean?

'What do you mean it kills them on our side?' he asked.

'It is hard to explain in one simple conversation, Trish. Just know this – they come from a species of viviparous amniotes. They give birth differently, though not exactly how reptiles once did. Evolution has brought their processes and ours a lot closer, but they are yet so different.'

'The ones they approve of to bear a child on this side go through a procedure first, without which there is every chance they die in childbirth. She wasn't ever approved; in fact, she escaped so she could be with Brij and have a child with him. They wanted her to have a purebred.'

'She did know she would die,' Brij muttered. He remembered how she kept saying she wouldn't make it and that he should have to love Trish for the both of them. *"Prepare him"* her words echoed in his mind. 'She knew it as she was dying and was at peace with it. They couldn't figure out what killed her,' he said with a solemn face, but not holding back his tears anymore.

'But the Yakshini said that I turn,' Trish said. 'They have all seen that I turn. What does that mean? Why could nobody see her for who she was? I mean, if I turn into one of them, she must have looked different. Or are you telling me they can shape-shift?'

'Do you learn nothing from what you see, Trish?' Laranya asked, looking disappointed. 'What have Rakshit's abilities taught you? What has Adipati been trying to tell you all along? The food you are eating, the table you are sitting at, your body itself; these are all illusions. You don't need to be a shapeshifter when there is no shape to shift to.'

'If you know how, you can appear to be the way you want. And looking like us was part of their development programme all along anyway. Do not forget how they keep telling you that God created man in his own image. Every species was brought up to this logic. Others, in their primal form, were still not ever completely where we now are, but they can manage the imitation. We would still have managed to stay looking like our primal form, but we shunned it and are stuck with this form forever. They did not.'

'However, they still appear to be in that form when they are free and uninhibited. Being in our form limits them as there is a constant control and suppression of instinct involved.'

'You must know how...' Trish said. 'You know everything, right?'

'Knowing and being in the know are different things, Trish. Our business is to be in the know, and while we try to know all we can, we do not necessarily know all. To clarify further on your query, there are of course traits in their human appearance that can give them up, but they are hardly noticeable. Lower body temperatures, more accentuated backbone, aversion to direct light in the dark, and so on.'

'These can be disguised. But put them under threat, challenge, or discomfort, and their primal instincts take over the control or suppression they need to exercise. That is when you see them turn to their own self. It is what has been happening to you too, only your reptilian brain – for the lack of better words – doesn't know harmony, balance, or control.'

'It is so overpowering that you used to lose control of yourself entirely and let it take over. That is what Adipati sought to change by taking you to the well. He has, to a certain degree, achieved that. You now have control despite turning, but still can't turn at will.'

'Mr Mburu has arrived,' a man announced. He looked nervous having to walk in to the dining hall and interrupt them.

'I have spoken enough,' Laranya said. 'It is not my place to share information unless advised by the Yakshini on the matter. Please finish breakfast and let us all meet Maurice in the hall.'

+++

Trish walked straight up to Maurice and hugged him. 'Good to have you back professor.'

'Hey! It's nice to be back, Trish,' he replied. 'You better keep your distance from me, lad. Your energy will drive me insane.'

'Are you implying you are otherwise not?' quipped Laranya.

'My lady of the house,' he said, bowing with a *namaste*. 'It's a pleasure to see you in person.'

'Likewise, Maurice. Please make yourself comfortable. Rest as, and when you would like, you shall be shown to your chambers. I must excuse myself though, matters of the house need attending to.'

They all bowed slightly as she left. Vidyut and Tejaswi went in another direction while everyone started greeting Maurice.

Trish took a seat next to his father and put his hand on his knee. 'I won't even dare say I understand how you feel. I am not even sure how I feel, to be honest. How can I imagine your pain? The woman you loved wasn't who you thought, and now your son is something you couldn't have ever imagined.'

'She was exactly who I thought she was,' he replied, holding Trish's hand. 'What she was, doesn't matter. It was who she was that I loved. And my son is just that – my son. No more and no less.'

'You have part of her in you, son. It makes you even more special. And on the other hand, it doesn't matter if you have certain capabilities or develop skills to take on an army by yourself, I will always give you a piece of my mind when I think you deserve it.' They both chuckled, then hugged.

'I'm glad you are taking this well, gentlemen,' Adipati said as he approached them. 'We need you to be comfortable with the truth however difficult it may be. At this stage Trish, I am willing to answer any and all questions you may have that I can possibly answer. There may be some things I do not myself completely understand, but I promise to be honest and hold nothing back.'

'I apologise for trying to moderate what you have been exposed to, but think of it this way; if we hadn't exercised restraint and told you all this the very first day, would you have accepted our help? Would you have taken any of this seriously at all?'

'Do not apologise Adipati,' Brij replied. 'I owe you my trust and so does my son. You have done well, and we are forever in your debt for helping us out. We know for sure that danger lurks after that episode in Benares. Also judging by the weaponry at play that day, I know you had good intentions, and we would not have made it this far without you.'

'Your trust is all I seek,' he replied. 'There are a few treacherous days ahead, and we shall all need each other. I know you have questions, and I will try my best to answer as much as I can.'

'Let's start with where *Patal* is, shall we?' Trish said. 'I remember our conversation where you said the only reason it was said to be below us, is because of a comparison to the gods being above us. So if they're neither above nor below, where are they?'

'Right here,' Adipati replied, spreading his arms in both directions. Both Trish and Brij looked baffled. 'Let me explain. The constitution of the so called lower realms leading to *Patal* as recorded in scriptures, especially the *Bhagvat Puran*, is seven realms. These are named the *Atal, Vital, Sutal, Talatal, Mahatal, Rasatal*, and finally *Patal*. Our ancients understood the concept of time as a linear dimension, being bi-directional—'

'Bi-directional?' Trish interrupted. 'You mean going forwards and back?'

'Of course.'

'How does time go back?'

'Not only does it go back, but it also goes sideways and upwards. Time has its own dimensions, but the ancients had a full understanding of just one, assuming it to be linear.' Adipati paused to see if they were following. Apparently not, going by the blank expressions on their faces.

'They knew time went both ways?' Trish asked. 'And we don't?

'Of course, we do,' Adipati replied. 'Science is exploring all the other dimensions of time as well. It may not be taught in school, but people have spent their entire lives studying this.'

'I don't understand.'

'That is because you are limited in your understanding based on what you think you know. The fact, however, remains that you know nothing. We as a species know nothing. I can't go through a three-year course with you, gentlemen.'

'Do understand that they only knew time could go forwards and backwards, or at least that much they thought they understood. This formed the basis of the four dimensions we lived in and could conceptualise and realise in front of us. The three dimensions of our understanding of space and then time itself.'

'Why are we talking about space, time, and dimensions though? I just want to know where *Patal* is.'

'Because my dear child, the other dimensions they did not understand as being dimensions, were perceived to be these seven lower realms. Science today is exploring these very realms as higher dimensions. They called them lower realms in comparison to gods being above or higher. But both talk of the same thing. The eleven dimensions that the M theory tries to explore is nothing else but the four our ancients understood and the seven they did not.'

'You are telling me *Patal* is the eleventh dimension?'

Trish had heard and understood a lot in the past several days, but this was the most difficult bit of information to assimilate. *If all this was actually a dream, it was high time the alarm went off*, he thought.

'Don't believe the ancients, believe science if you will. The numbers match up exactly. We, in The Circuit, and Sukrit before that, have always known Patal to be in another dimension. We have known there is more than one dimension between Patal and us. We also know that some of these dimensions are highly unstable and others minuscule. What we were not sure of was how many there were and what they were till modern science started adding numbers up that matched exactly with what the ancients have recorded.'

Trish drew a deep breath. His father looked like he had given up his understanding of anything at all and fell back on the sofa in a slump.

'So when you say they cross over, you mean they cross over dimensions and appear in ours?'

'Yes. In fact, they are right here and walking amongst us in the same space in another dimension.'

'Why don't they just cross over here and grab us then? We are right here, they are right here. What's stopping them?'

'You can't just cross over dimensions as and when you like. Not unless you are the Shiv. They can't do it. There are certain energy gateways, and it is there and there alone that you can cross over. At these places too, the portal, for the lack of a better word, only opens at certain times and remains open for a few days at a time.'

'These places open up a direct crossover to the exact same place in the other dimension. The well of Sheshna is one such place and was to be in a position to be opened when we were there. That is why it was imperative they didn't find you in that place at that time. They would have taken you straight through to the other side, then transported you easily. It was also the only chance we had for you to be able to gain access to that energy so you could realise and control yourself when you turned.'

'Are there other such places?' Trish asked.

'There are plenty all over the world. There was another one open at the time at Patal Pani near Mhow. I guess that was where they initially thought they would take you if they got you. But like I said, you can only access them for a short duration when the dimensions open up at the respective locations; this is when they open up by themselves.'

'These locations change as the fabric of space-time skews, but in relation to our understanding of time, that happens once every few centuries to millennia. But they may be made to open up as well, though that is lost science, at least on our side.'

'So how do you cross over? Do you just present yourself and walk through?'

'I wish it were that simple. Unfortunately, we have lost the knowledge of it completely. No human has crossed to the other side in millennia, except when guided and taken over by one of them. They, however, have complete knowledge of it and cross over all the time.'

'Alliances on our side have been made for centuries with people of power. Their own offspring on this side have established power as some of our own, right amongst us. What we know and understand is regulated, any study into the unknown is curbed, and anything leading to them is outright blocked. Part of us losing our way to evolution has been fuelled by their agenda.'

'So no human has ever realised a dimension higher than ours?' Trish asked.

'The dimensions closest to us have been achieved. Sometimes they vibrate so close to us that we can peek into them. The next higher up would be time moving sideways. That is the dimension referred to as having parallel universes. With every decision you make when building up a new reality or new universe, people get a peek into it.'

'We have a team working on deja vu that believes it is linked to peeks into this dimension. Enter the dimension however, and you will be faced with so many realities that you will, in all probability, forget which one was yours. People have never come out of there without help. It is almost certain you would get lost.'

'Our scriptures describe this as the realm *Atal*, ruled by the son of Maya who possesses mystical powers and sorcery. They were, in their own way, also talking about facing many realities in this realm; only associating it with Maya or sorcery.'

'But there really can't be multiple realities though, right? Isn't that science fiction? If we made a decision, doesn't that automatically mean that no other decision was made, making ours the only reality?'

'Modern science has already established that these realities must exist. Not the so-called crazies any more, but the established scientists who are working on this theory. Have you heard of interactive movies, Trish? One where at every juncture in the story, the viewers are asked to make a decision for the characters, and the story progresses one way or the other depending on what the viewers choose?'

'Yes, I've heard of them.'

'Every outcome is shot and recorded. The makers obviously don't know which decision viewers will take. The first set of decisions leads to multiple story lines, which lead to multiple possible decisions that could be made. All these lead to several such multiplications, and all of these lines of story have to be shot and recorded. Now, just because you made a certain set of decisions when you watched the movie, and as an outcome watched only one reel, this doesn't mean that all the other reels do not exist.'

'That is not a fair comparison,' Trish argued.

'No it isn't. I'm just trying to explain to you, as best I can in a simple manner. The best scientists in the world are struggling with these concepts, Trish. You do understand I can't possibly explain their work of a lifetime to you in a few hours?'

Trish hummed thoughtfully. 'I'm getting the gist of it. However, there is only one question I cannot get out of my head. What wrong have I done? If anything, I'm part of them too. Why are they after me?'

'They are trying to bring back their last true god is all I know,' he said. 'This guy - this god of theirs - it is known he has immense distaste for humans. The details are sketchy, but he was lost to them in an effort from our end to incapacitate him. I don't yet know how or why, but we suspect they need you for that to be possible. Where we stand as humans, we cannot allow for this to happen.'

19

«»«« NINETEEN »»»»

Lunch was better than breakfast. Everyone seemed to have come to accept their new reality a little better. Brij wasn't as sad, and Trish was a lot calmer. The Yakshini had decided to meet everyone after lunch.

When they finished, the family decided to stay with them for the Yakshini's address. Trish looked at Vidyut, who wore a shirt with a rather wide v-neck that exposed most of his shoulders. He was a well built young man who looked fit and agile. From under his shirt Trish noticed half of his tattoo, which he thought was done rather well.

'What's the obsession with the nautilus shell?' he asked Tejaswi.

'It is one of the few species that has been around forever and remained true to its original form, unaltered,' she said.

The Yakshini walked in. 'Maurice, my dear boy,' she said. 'Finally, we meet.'

'And what a pleasure it is for me, madam,' he replied, bowing slightly.

'Oh no, the pleasure is all mine,' she said, putting her hand on his elbow. She stole a look at Adipati before continuing. 'I've always wanted to meet the man who helped ease up Adi's demons so he could concentrate on his true potential.'

Trish noticed Adipati shifting in discomfort at those words. Everyone else was suddenly uncomfortable too, including Maurice, who pursed his lips and looked down. Her comment was met with complete silence in the hall.

'The staff is a work of sheer brilliance,' she continued. Absolute silence.

She smiled. 'See, this is the kind of respect he commands. This is what I always wanted for you, Adi.'

He bowed ever so slightly, putting on an uncomfortable smile.

She turned to Tejaswi. 'Tej. Our young man here has had a lot served to him in a rather shocking manner and with no time to understand much. Trish needs to get his mind off things and breathe for a change, don't you think?'

Tejaswi looked at her in surprise, red faced and not knowing how to respond.

Why did she ask her that?

Trish tried to hide his embarrassment. She had already told him she knew about them.

'I would think so,' Tejaswi replied.

'Of course, you would,' added the Yakshini. 'Would you be a kind host for me and perhaps take him to the beach for a breath of fresh air this evening? That should allow him a few moments to relax. I am sure he could do with that.'

'Yes Yakshini, I would be honoured,' she replied.

Laranya looked at the Yakshini suspiciously. 'Maybe Vidyut could go along as well. The more the merrier. The kids can talk about whatever it is they talk about. That should help.'

'I have an important task for Vidyut. I need him to help me out with something. You know I struggle with things when it comes to technology. I need to tap into something and could use his expertise with networks.' She held his hand as she looked at Laranya. Vidyut was pleased.

Laranya was not. She knew there was nothing she struggled with. She perhaps knew technology better than her son as with everything else. She clearly wanted Trish to go out with Tejaswi alone. *Why?* It was not her place to ask.

'Do you surf?' Tejaswi asked Trish.

'I can manage a bit. I'm no good at it though.'

'Would you like to?'

'Sure.'

'That is settled then,' the Yakshini announced. 'What I wanted to tell you was that I would like it for you all to stay at least a day or two more. I haven't quite finished with this young man yet. There is still something we need to get to soon. If there is anything we can do to make your stay more comfortable, please do let us know.' She nodded and left as everyone else settled down.

Laranya started to leave them too. Tejaswi walked up to Trish. 'See you at five?' she asked.

'Absolutely,' Trish said with a broad smile that he just couldn't disguise.

Soon after they had left, Adipati excused himself to retire to his chambers for meditation.

'So, what was all that about?' Trish asked Rakshit.

'What?'

'The Yakshini said something about Adipati's demons and the professor helping him out...' Trish asked him while some of the others left for meditation as well.

'Oh, I don't know much about it,' Rakshit said. 'Just the stories one hears, that's all.'

'What stories?' Trish asked, encouraging him.

'Okay, you didn't hear any of this from me, if someone finds out you know,' he said, leaning toward Trish. 'They say the one purest manifestation of energy is sound. It is sound that transcends barriers of these dimensions that he's been telling you about. What I mean to say is, even though none of us has ever crossed over to the other side, we know that all our skills and abilities that you have seen this far are no good in the other dimension.'

'Which one?'

'Any one. Our abilities remain as long as we are bound by our four dimensions. They don't work outside. I mean, well, they work, but you won't be able to see them manifest as you do here. The only reason they seem extraordinary is that we are bound within our limited understanding. It is not the same there. We would be doing the same thing, but nothing would really happen. The only yogic power that works in every dimension is the control over sound.'

'Okay. How does Adipati fit into this again?'

'Perfectly. The last person to understand sound and control it has gone. Nobody knows where, how, or why. He just disappeared. His true name is not known to our generation, but he was known as *Achhaad* or *The Cloak.* He was known for his ability to disappear, and his last disappearing act just never ended. He went missing around a century ago or so.'

'I still don't see Adipati in your story here, Raka,' Trish said.

'Be patient, O special one,' he replied. 'Adipati was a young boy when he was spotted by the yogis, just as most of us were. He wanted to learn from Achhaad himself. Achhaad took him as his apprentice, then began teaching him about sound and how to try to master it...'

'But you said no one knew sound after Achhaad? Besides, Adipati does that temperature thing, right? Makes stuff cold or hot...I saw him do it at the fight in Benares.'

'Will you let me finish boy?' Rakshit spoke through his teeth. 'Adipati learnt and worked hard under him but could never master sound. He was touted to be the real deal and perhaps that had got to his head or something, and he couldn't take his own failure.'

'He worked day and night trying to tap into sound. But you can't select a force and work toward it, that's not how it works. You meditate and you try to be at one with the universe and in the process, you might stumble upon one of its secrets. No one can say which you might find.'

'They used to tell us when we were training that the force chooses you. In a sense that is right, I guess. I didn't choose what I can do, I discovered it just like every one else. But not Adipati. He wanted to master sound, to be the true yogi. Or at least as true a yogi as anyone living. Nobody even tries to be the Shiv anymore. That is just a dream.'

'Tell me about Adipati,' Trish said.

'Do you want me to finish, or would you rather ask him instead?' Rakshit asked him, irritated.

'Sorry, go on...'

'He found one day that he was able to transfer heat. I will not go into details, but in his quest for the knowledge of sound, he accidentally melted what he was touching with one hand while what he touched with the other froze. He had transferred the heat from one, freezing it to the other, making it burn.'

'They say *Achhaad* was impressed but he, himself wasn't. He was adamant on mastering sound. See, sound could also do what he did, yet only sound could do what I do, what Sveta does and what quite a few of us can as well. But Achhaad couldn't just hand his ability over to him.'

'They tell us an ability could possibly be transferred through genes, but not taught. Even if it were transferred through genes, it would still take the child a lot to go through with the help of yog to tap into it. Adipati, even though like a son, was not his son. He wanted so badly to become just like Achhaad, that he neglected what he could do completely and instead focused on sound alone. But that, like I said, is not how things work.'

'On the other hand, he needed to touch two things at the same time in order to transfer heat. This, he thought, was no feat at all but rather a handicap. Most others could do so much without ever touching anything. He hated the fact that if he tried to take away heat from, or apply heat to just one object, he failed. The only way was to be in contact with two things at the same time and transfer heat from one to the other. This, he considered his failure and started staying perpetually irritated and angry.'

'Did no one counsel him?'

'He wouldn't listen. Not being able to do what he wanted to do was driving him into a crazy young man. Until one day it did. *Achhaad* disappeared. Adipati blamed himself for it. They say he thought his failure was responsible for *Achhaad* being disappointed in him and leaving forever.'

'It is also said, and please do not quote me on this, that Adipati went dark for several years. He cut himself from the yogis and went around the world finding a release for his frustration. I don't know how true that is, but I know for sure it was the professor who brought him back.'

'He had worked on his own scourge for himself by then. He used it to harness energy from the atmosphere and applied his knowledge to making Adipati's staff. Adipati no longer needed to be in contact with two things at a time. Using his staff, he could take heat from or supply it to one object at a time. The opposite end of his staff stored the surplus or deficient heat. Years of their friendship brought the man in Adipati back. He owes a lot to the professor; he says that himself.'

'Who would have guessed,' Trish mumbled.

'I know...'

'Talking about guessing,' Trish said with renewed enthusiasm, 'you said that *Achhaad* disappeared over a century ago. How old is Adipati?'

'It is anybody's guess,' he replied. 'How old do you think *I* am?'

+++

Tejaswi turned up wearing a wetsuit at five minutes to five. 'I don't know if we have a wetsuit that will fit you,' she said. 'You could try Vidyut's but that is up to you.'

'If I could borrow a pair of his board shorts, I think that would do,' he replied.

They stepped outside ten minutes later when Adipati called from behind. He held Trish's swords in his hand. 'For safety' he said. 'I insist.'

'Oh, come on!' Trish exclaimed. 'Where am I going to carry these? Do you see the size of this surfboard?' He pointed to two surfboards lying on the ground further up.

'The scabbards have cross straps, you can wear them on your back,' Adipati said, not giving in.

Trish grabbed them and they walked out. It was a long walk out along the rocky trail to the beach. On their way, Tejaswi told him it was safer to go the south end of Godavne beach right over the cliff, as it was a more secluded area. There was another beach to the south of the cliff, but that one was bigger. This was a small strip of sand which was an offshoot of the larger beach further up. Pristine sand was laid across the land when they finally reached. It didn't have a single footprint on it. Tejaswi commented on how they could sometimes have huge waves, which made the place ideal for surfing. She was not very pleased with the waves they had today though.

'Better for me,' Trish said. 'I'm not a skilled surfer, I can just manage not to fall off.'

'That's fine,' she said. 'Not falling off is half the battle won.'

Trish took off his shirt and wrapped it over his swords, leaving them on the sand.

'I'm not going in with those on my back,' he said, running toward the water with his board.

Tejaswi followed behind him. Trish noticed how skilled she was. Watching her surf was breathtaking and he just stood on his board as long as he could, just watching her in awe. Time and again he fell off, got on it, then tried to stay on again. It was obvious he was no surfer. About an hour later they came back to the beach.

'That was too short,' she complained. 'We should come again tomorrow morning.'

'Maybe we should,' he said as they sat down, looking at the sea. From the corner of his eye, Trish saw movement from the area behind a line of trees.

Half a kilometre? he thought to himself. *More movement. Why am I bothered?*

'What are you looking at?' Tejaswi asked.

'I don't know.'

Something inside him was telling him not to take his eyes off it. *Why?* Something was approaching. He saw it moments later. Two dirt bikes, leaving a trail of sand in the air behind him. He got up, threw his shirt aside, and started putting his swords on him. They were approaching quickly. His mind tried to tell him something. *But what?*

He urged Tejaswi up and kept looking at the approaching bikes. Then a look of concern furrowed his brow. 'Run. Run back and tell them we're under attack.'

'I'm not leaving you,' she replied.

'They will catch up if we both try to get away. One of us has to confront them. I am better suited for that job. If I thought you were a better fighter, I swear I would have made the run. Please go...Now!'

She saw reason in what he said, so she kissed him and ran as hard as she could. He didn't draw his swords. Instead, he grabbed on to his surfboard and kept his eyes on the bikes while one of them headed straight for him. The other was beginning to open up a little, moving around to one side. Trish thought he had never felt this kind of adrenaline flowing through his veins before.

He held on to his board and started running for the bike coming at him. The other bike sped as it opened up even more. Trish knew he was going to circle in behind him. He ran faster toward the first bike, making the biker wonder what it was he was planning to do. Watching Trish run at him like that, he brought out an axe that was strapped to his leg with one hand. Just as Trish was about to meet with the bike, he dug one end of his surfboard into the sand and turned under it, holding it over his back.

The bike leapt into the air over the board and landed almost on top of the other bike that had circled behind Trish, making both riders jump off before impact. As they got up holding axes, Trish came out from under the surfboard and drew his swords. Both riders took off their helmets, stopping Trish in his tracks. They had what looked like scales on their skin and their eyes were almost entirely green, with just a slit of black in them. Trish was reminded of his reflection in the well.

They spread out until he was in between them, and both kept observing him for a while. Trish was not one for attacking first, so he moved enough to keep his eyes on both of them as they circled around him. They made subtle movements time and again to see what he would do, but he didn't flinch. Both of them smiled, looked at each other, nodded, then nodded to Trish, who nodded back not fully knowing what was going on.

With one swift motion, one of them swept the axe to Trish's chest while the other to his feet. Trish flipped and they both missed. After the attack, they kept circling and nodding at each other for some reason. Trish began to wonder if they would keep trying one move at a time, or fight with him. He flipped his swords. That got their attention. He flipped them again. It was working.

The two attacked him at the same time and in perfect sync. Even though Trish wasn't having to move much yet, he was unable to do any harm to them and knew this wasn't all they had. The fighting intensified at a slow but steady pace.

'Now the fun begins,' he thought.

+++

'What do you mean we must hold back?' Tejaswi yelled, back at the hall. 'He needs help!'

'He will help himself just fine,' the Yakshini said, raising her voice to remind her who she was talking to.

'He is still not ready to face them, madam,' Adipati chipped in. 'From what Tejaswi has described, it is the twins. They are very highly skilled to be handled by him alone.'

'He has to be ready, there is no more time. Let us go, just in case...but I don't want anyone stepping in till I say so myself. Are we clear on that?'

'She sent him out on purpose,' Adipati whispered to Maurice as they negotiated the rocky trail. 'There's no way she didn't know they would show up. I can bet you she planned this.'

'What would be the purpose of that?' he whispered back. They were moving as quickly as they could to the beach. The Yakshini was surprisingly agile and fast.

'I don't know. Logic says I should trust her judgement. But he isn't ready professor. He needs us.'

They finally came around the rocks and could see Trish fight at around two hundred and fifty metres from them. He looked like he was doing well so far.

'Here we stop,' the Yakshini said. 'Do not make a sound now, till I say so.'

+++

The two made Trish fight hard. They were also mimicking him to perfection every now and then. It was as if they forgot they were fighting and started playing with him, mirroring his every move. It was unnerving but Trish was impressing them. It was evident they had not expected he had it in him to last even as long as he did. But Trish soon realised they were beginning to understand him as they fought. Every time he went for a premeditated move, they knew it and forced him to think his every move beforehand.

Trish hadn't faced any opponent as skilled as these two before. For every successful contact he made, they made one with him. That wasn't adding up to his advantage since that meant he was only hurting them half as much. They danced with him as he wanted, but they were making him dance to their steps equally and effectively.

From a distance, they were a treat to watch. The fight was mesmerising to the audience around the corner, however, some of them became impatient. Tejaswi for one, was looking at the Yakshini and the fight alternatively, expecting her to let them go at any minute. Yet the Yakshini watched intently. Even though she was holding herself rather well, it was evident she was nervous and kept muttering something under her breath.

Adipati was getting restless himself. The twins were legendary fighters and everyone had heard of their prowess.

They were rumoured to have taken small armies by themselves and come out triumphant.

Trish wasn't ready, he thought. Not for this yet. The Yakshini had been rash in letting him take this on.

Trish managed a couple of nicks more to their bodies, but he knew this couldn't go on forever. He had begun to sense that he was proving to be the lesser warrior with the two combined. He hadn't started wearing out yet, but if this went on too long, tiredness would eventually set in. The twins were only half as worked as he was.

As if reading his mind, the twins intensified their attacks. The degree of coordination in their movement was incomprehensible. They were like one person split in two. Trish parried with clinical precision and fought back with discipline. The duo changed tactics and attacked from one side, dancing in and out in front of Trish. Four hands and four legs were fighting with him as one. He started gaining on them though, and nicked their limbs a few times until he didn't see the foot that came from behind the one in front, which landed on his chest.

The bastards had lined up.

Trish went flying a few feet and skidded backward as he touched ground. The impact was so hard, he had to dig his swords in the sand to come to a stop. He put his knee to the ground and thought to himself, *I cannot do this alone.*

Brij had drawn out his handgun and pointed it at the twins.

The Yakshini put her hand on the gun. 'Hold on for just another moment please.' Then she muttered under her breath, '*Come on Trish, if not now, then what was the point?*'

+++

Gobind had never seen this happen before. She got up in the middle of her meal. He wondered what had happened. One moment she was eating her dinner just like everyday. Then all of a sudden she stopped, looked up, and closed her eyes. He could see her brows narrow in concentration.

She opened her eyes with a start, got up, leaving her dinner half way, washed her hands and yelled, 'Get me a mat!'

He ran back with the mat. She took it and sat immediately, folding her hands. 'I need absolute silence,' she said. Everyone left but Gobind. He had never seen Amratji like this ever before.

She closed her eyes, smiled, then whispered, *'I see you...'*

20

«««« TWENTY »»»»

The Yakshini nodded and crossed her arms on her bust as Trish got back up. 'I don't think he will need help now,' she said. 'He can help himself.'

Trish got up smiling; the twins looked at each other in wonder. He looked calm again, and not worked up like how he was a couple of minutes ago. They attacked him but realised all too soon that his dance had changed. His discipline was taken over by mystique, flair, and unpredictability. The moment they tried to mimic his movements again, he moved differently, at times mirroring them instead.

The art form they had come to admire fighting the young boy had just surpassed their wildest dreams. It was now as if they were fighting two people instead of one, both much more accomplished fighters than he had thus far shown to be. He was still moving a lot less, but his movements were, even more fluid than before, which they would have thought to be impossible, were they not actually witnessing it firsthand.

The fight continued for a while, but clearly the boy was weighing heavier on them. Trish was outmanoeuvring them and never letting them settle. One axe came down on him from over his head to the left, while his left hand was still down from the previous manoeuvre. Expecting him to back up and knowing fully well he moved as little as possible, the other twin began a swing of his axe to where his leg would now have been.

But Trish moved forward slightly instead, and let the first axe pass behind him as he dug his left shoulder into the first twin's chest. The second axe fell on the first, and as the first twin fell back, his axe slipped out of his hand, due to the one that landed on it. The moment he hit his chest, Trish brought down his right sword on the second twin's forearm. He had to let go of his axe too, to save his hand.

Trish slashed upward with his left sword to his right at the second twin as he stepped further back to avoid being cut by it, and as he did, he pivoted on his left foot, swinging his right sword in a huge arc from behind till the blade landed on the first twin's shin. It cut through the flesh and broke his bone. He could have gone for the kill and finished him off, but Trish went after the other twin and holstered his blades. He was still finding his balance as Trish leapt in the air and came down on him with his knee.

His attacker barely managed to stumble out of his line of attack as he dug his knee in the sand. But as he was reaching for his axe, Trish rolled back toward him and sprang at him, punching his ribs, making him wince in pain. He then hammered his knee into his thigh and then at the same spot, hit him hard with his elbows from the top.

Both his attackers were now restricted in their movement. Trish could hammer them a little more, make them immobile, and tie them up with pieces of cloth. The fight was certainly over, yet Trish was having some sort of conflict within himself. He stretched his neck and clenched his teeth struggling with something.

+++

Amratji came out of her trance with a look of concern. 'Water, please,' she said as she relaxed her posture. Gobind rushed to fetch her a glass. She shook her head as she drank. 'Lord be with him; what was that place?'

+++

They were clearly unsettled watching him turn. It was difficult to know what was going on in their heads, but they had definitely not expected what they saw. Trish's skin started hardening a little. His eyes went black, with just a brilliant green slit in them. He practically hissed with his mouth wide open. His skin did not change in colour, but a pattern of tiny scales began to appear all over him. While all this certainly seemed to unsettle them, it wasn't until they noticed the top of his forehead that got them terrified.

Trish paced in front of them, from one side to the other. He picked up the axes and threw them at the twins, then drew his swords. 'UP! On your fucking feet!'

Not knowing what to do, but realising they were now doomed, they held their axes in their hands and limped at him.

With such speed that made his swords whistle, Trish took their heads off in a few moves. Their bodies fell to the ground as Trish opened up his arms and let out a huge roar, looking up at the sky.

+++

'He is embracing who he is,' the Yakshini said after everyone got back to the hall. 'That is a good sign for us.'

She sat on the sofa by herself, with Adipati and Brij sitting in another. Laranya took the third sofa while everyone else stood there watching Trish, Vidyut, and Tejaswi in the far corner. They thought it was best to leave the kids to talk for a bit.

'He turned at will this time,' Adipati added. 'And he turned quite a bit. We haven't seen much going on with him till now except for his eyes. But that is not what surprised me. I felt that energy shift again today like a node was around. Clearly it has to do with the boy somehow; it can no longer be coincidence, especially since it happened again as he turned. Though for the life of me I can not figure out how that is possible given everything we know about him and his history so far.'

'Maybe you don't know enough then,' the Yakshini said.

'I beg your pardon?' he said.

'This topic of discussion is for another time,' she said, dismissing his comment.

'What is a node, if I may ask?' Brij bit his lip immediately after he asked the question. They were not supposed to question out of turn like this, and never unless specifically invited to. He got a piqued look from the Yakshini, but she let it go.

'I am sure Adipati will indulge you on that. I have to go into the matter that I really invited you here for. I didn't know if I could take the leap of faith before, but I am now sure the boy is ready. It has been a burden on me for a long time now. Maybe it is finally time to hand it to someone else, someone worthy I have been waiting for.'

'Please excuse me, I will see you all after breakfast tomorrow. We shall see if Trish could be the one I have been biding my time about for.' She got up, nodded to everyone and left as she waved to the kids.

'What was that all about?' Brij asked Adipati.

'She's the Yakshini,' he said. 'How am I supposed to know?'

Laranya chuckled.

'And what was it you were saying about nodes?' asked Brij. 'You've been on about it forever. At least that, you know of, I'm sure.'

Laranya called out to the kids, then turned to Brij. 'Vidyut has a particular interest in this matter. Let us give him a chance to talk about it shall we? I never get to find out what the kids are learning.'

As the kids approached she offered them the sofa the Yakshini had left and said to Vidyut, 'Would you be kind enough to tell us what you understand of nodes?' Vidyut nodded, but looked confused. 'We have reason to believe Trish might have something to affect energy shifts like nodes.'

'But that is impossible...Unless, pardon me, you are a Naag as well,' he said, addressing Brij.

'What? I am no Naag. I'm a regular normal human being just like everyone else here.' He looked around. 'Okay, not like anyone here. But that's the point. The best I've ever done since we left home is shoot a gun, and I didn't even hit the mark every time!'

'Exactly why it shouldn't happen,' he said. 'And you are not remotely Naag. They wouldn't just approach you without having checked you out first.' He gestured toward Adipati. 'They have had your medical records since your infancy with them ever since you got married.'

Brij looked at Adipati accusingly. 'You did not...'

'I was only looking out for Niramayi and Trish,' he said defensively. 'And since you were not a threat, for you as well, in time.'

'What is a node though?' Trish asked, stepping into the conversation. 'That is what we are discussing, right?'

'Yes,' Vidyut said. 'First, let me know why you think we as humans are different from other species that we know exist on earth.'

'We are intelligent?' Trish said.

'And plants and animals are not?' Vidyut looked at him with widened eyes, clearly surprised. 'A plant beginning to lean toward a source of light in a dark chamber is intelligent. Stilt Palms actually walk toward light over several months by growing roots on the sunnier side, while the roots on the shadow side die off. A single cell slime mould stretches itself across a maze, solving the shortest route from the entry to the exit for food placed at both ends is intelligence. Life by design is intelligent. We fool ourselves with inaccurate notions of it. Intelligence is not what we alone have. It is not what makes us different.'

'What, then?'

'There are several functions that combine to make us different. Physically, obviously, our so-called evolution has resulted in our bodies to suit our interests best. But it is also how our brain processes information that makes us different. There are several parts of our brain, and most function in a similar fashion to other species.'

'Emotion is something we associate with higher order species, and it definitely puts us right up on the list. Differentiating evil from good, right from wrong, and judging are some of these functions. These are handled by what we call the limbic system of our brains. But these functions are not much different from those of other higher order species. In fact, this is considered the primitive part of our brain that had been around in our species forever.'

'What came late in evolution and was really the game changer for us, was the prefrontal cortex. This is established fact in modern science. The part of our brains that controls functions of cognition like symbolism, concept, planning, regulation, abstraction, control, and imposition of meaning, and so on. This was the step in the so-called evolution that made us human, essentially, bringing us to higher order functions I mentioned. This caused us to be the supreme race as intended by supposed gods.'

'Okay,' Trish said. 'But where are we heading with this?'

'You have, I am sure, been told a few times that evolution couldn't have happened the way we are made to understand. Whoever helped us along, finally achieved the ultimate goal by working on the prefrontal cortex to give us the supremacy over other species that we have since abused. But as it turns out, this wasn't the end of their work. It seems the prefrontal cortex could be made to work as a governor over various parts of the brain. If that could be achieved, the already supreme races – ours and that of the naags – could optimise processing by selecting a certain part of the brain to use, and shutting the rest off. You may better understand this as efficiency.'

'That sounds too far fetched,' Trish remarked.

'Have you heard of the Savant syndrome?' Vidyut asked. 'I know it isn't the best example, but it makes it easy to understand what I'm saying. People who have met with accidents have been reported to discover an ability they never had before, at the cost of losing some other basic ability or abilities. This led to the research that has since established, that this is possible by losing access to a part of the brain, making the processing power wholly available for another.'

'Imagine doing this at will. Imagine being able to stop cross talk between one part of the brain to others when you only need it and not the rest. Reduce ambient noise in the brain and select where you want your processing power to concentrate. Or, on the other hand, include another part of your brain to help out one part, so it performs better, like in the case of synaesthetes. Synaesthesia associates two senses, like coloured numbers and letters, or tastes to sounds, helping in memory. Efficiency, like I said.'

'So did they manage to achieve that?' Brij asked. 'How?'

'They kept working on the prefrontal cortex for the supreme races, out of which most perished in time anyway. The two of us that remained were intensively worked upon. Trials upon trials of batches for both species were carried out, yet human trials never succeeded. A lot of lives were lost for this, but our primitive brain – our limbic system – always won over the prefrontal cortex in a tussle between the two. It still does today.'

'What about the naags?' Trish asked. 'Were they able to achieve their goal with them? Can naags control every part of their brain?'

'Naags showed promise. Thus while humans were given up on, they pressed on with their agenda with the naags. Many more naag lives were lost in the process. Eventually, and in due time, they succeeded with a batch. Now, what happened after that has remained a mystery, but the mutation was not applied further. Just the one batch had it and passed it along to their offspring. It is said that the trials were disrupted by the very naags that they succeeded with: the one batch of nodes.'

'These beings were faster, stronger, much more agile and powerful than we can ever imagine. You talk about intelligence; there is nothing that shares space with us, that is more intelligent than them. Imagine being able to shut off all faculties of your brain, save one or two. As a rather crude example, say you were a sniper and were sheltered and well protected. Now imagine if you could put your motor skills, hearing, touch, taste, and other faculties on stand by, and concentrate on your vision. What a vision you would have!'

'And the moment, say, your mark is seen through the scope, you start up motor skills and shoot, then return to normalcy and escape. I hope you are getting the point. When you need to run you just run, when you need to listen you just listen, and so on. You would be super human. That is what they were after.'

'So they are the ones called nodes!' Brij exclaimed.

'They have been called many things,' Vidyut said. 'Yogis have been calling them nodes only since Mr Maurice coined that term. He called the shift in energy *nodal,* and thus they all started calling them nodes. Your wife was a node, Mr Negi; a direct descendant from the first and only batch.'

'But you said that this could be passed on to offspring,' Brij said. 'Maybe then, she passed it on to him?'

'That is the thing,' he said, bringing his hands together in a clap. 'There have been several instances in history where nodes have had offspring with humans. In every single case, the offspring lost that capability. Normal human DNA simply isn't compatible and rejects it outright. That is why I said unless you were a naag, he couldn't have it.'

'And yet, every time he turns, there is ambient nodal shift in energy,' Adipati said. 'I feel it all too well.'

'Oh,' Vidyut said. 'There is one more thing, and I think you will find it very interesting. In order for the prefrontal cortex to dominate the rest of the brain, they enabled it to make other brain cells react a certain way whenever the cells from the prefrontal cortex so commanded. This had to be achieved by enabling the modified PFC to use what we now call *Optogenetics*. Wherein the rest of the brain cells had neurons that were programmed to respond to certain light in a very specific manner, PFC had neurons capable of generating light. It is being *discovered* again today, and scientists are trying to use it to cure disabilities by using DNA from species that generate light and others that react to light.'

'They used biophotons?' Trish interrupted.

'Bioluminescense,' he said. 'Emission of light by living organisms as a result of a chemical reaction. That is the interesting part. We are talking about a lot of light here. Depending on the intensity of use of this new governor in the brain, they can produce quite a surprising amount of light from it. Now try to think carefully; what do the Uktena, Ganj, Riujin, Vouivre, Vasuki, and numerous similar creatures from around the world and different cultures have in common?'

'I have only ever heard of Vasuki, the serpent king. Don't know about the others.' Brij shrugged.

'They come from native American, Persian, Japanese, and European cultures respectively,' Vidyut said. 'There are numerous others from various cultures from around the world. They were all reptilian creatures with a snake-dragon descent. Also, almost all of them dwelled in water bodies. But most importantly, they were all said to have a jewel or gem embedded in their foreheads.'

'Fucking hell,' Trish said. 'The glow from their prefrontal cortex?'

'Every node has it: the glow. Though it isn't something highly visible. In fact, most often it isn't visible at all. It is only noticeable at times of heightened activity related to the optimisation of brain resources. It also causes a shift in energies that is noticeable by gifted people such as Mr Maurice and Adipati.'

'We wouldn't know, but these people feel the slightest change in energy around us. In most cases, only a slight hint of a glow is noticed around where the hairline would be, but some claim they have seen so much light it could be disturbing in complete darkness. You have no idea how many ridiculous theories were born out of this throughout the ages.'

'Wow!' Trish exclaimed, looking at his father excitedly. Brij looked like his heart had sunk. 'You okay, Dad?' he asked while he kept his hand on his knee.

Brij got up. He looked at Adipati and said, 'I will leave the reason for you to figure out, but I must tell you this.' He put his hand on Trish's head. 'I never saw it again, but I saw a glow on his head the day he was born. His mother indeed passed it on to him.'

21

«««« TWENTY ONE»»»»

'I was thinking last night,' Adipati said. 'I am sorry, I know this is inappropriate, but I must say it nonetheless. I wanted to let you know in case it ever pops up in your head, that Trish is, in fact, your son. We know for a fact, and we have all medical records to prove it. He has your DNA.'

Adipati continued to whisper over Brij's shoulder as they walked from the dining hall to the main hall. Discussions had ended abruptly the previous night, and he couldn't help but think that this could have caused unease in Brij's mind. The last thing he wanted was for him to be distraught for no good reason.

'I don't doubt that for one second,' Brij replied, a little surprised. 'She did love me. There were no secrets there. What is surprising is that you had to have it checked.'

'No, it isn't like that,' he said. 'We have always kept all medical records of you and Trish updated. This is just information that came out as a result of independent analyses of both individuals. We didn't actually go and get a paternity test done on you, but the separate reports confirm beyond a doubt that he has both your DNA and that of Niramayi.'

'It is not even worth discussing,' Brij said, dismissing the comment.

'So they say the Yakshini will see you at eleven,' Rakshit said to Trish as they took seats on a sofa. Trish nodded. 'They're saying she intends to give you something?' Trish nodded again. 'What is the matter, Trish? You're not chatty at all today. You look worried. There is no need to be, it is not a big deal. You may have got that from your mother, but if anything at all it makes you stronger.'

'I'm not worried about that,' Trish replied. 'I'm worried about what I'm turning into.'

'You are half reptilian since your mother was a naag. It doesn't have to change anything for you at all.'

'No,' he said. 'Not that. I killed two people yesterday. Okay. Not people maybe, naags. Are naags people? I don't know, but I killed someone or something, yet I don't feel a thing. Turning into this is what I'm worried about.'

'But they would have killed you if you hadn't killed them first.'

'Would they? Isn't that what Adipati has been saying all along? That they want me alive - that they wouldn't kill me?'

'He said they wouldn't kill you *yet*. The way those two were going at you, did it appear to you like they were there to capture you? They might have needed you alive, but who is to say they wouldn't have damaged you? You had to kill them.'

Trish sighed. 'That's what I've been telling myself,' he said. 'But even if I had to, shouldn't I feel remorseful? I should at least feel bad about taking lives. And this is the first time I have ever killed someone. Shouldn't that mean something?'

'It does mean something,' Rakshit said, putting his arm around Trish's shoulder and giving it a tug. 'It means you will live a little longer. You will have to kill again, Trish, just to survive. This was just the beginning, the worst is yet to come. The twins have shown up, which means the others are coming. Taking the life of some of them to stay alive should be the least of your concerns right now.'

'He is right, Trish,' Adipati said. 'Sorry for barging into your conversation, but they will not hesitate once to kill us all in order to get you. In fact, that is precisely what they are going to do. So when you fight next, do not think about this. Where it is necessary, you will have to kill.'

'Apparently, I won't have to think about it,' Trish said. 'Whatever is happening to me, I feel nothing for the twins or having taken their lives.' He got up and walked across to the library.

Brij walked over to Adipati. 'Do you have kids?' he asked, offering him a glass of water. 'I'm sorry, it never came up before, but I was wondering. You have been a beacon for him through this. I wouldn't know how to handle all this, because I have no idea about any of it.'

'I don't,' Adipati replied. 'I never had the chance to start a family. The professor is the only one of us who has a child; a daughter. She is fourteen.'

'Is she a yogi as well?'

'She is a yogi, but she hasn't found her gift yet, if that is what you mean. Being a yogi doesn't mean you are going to be like us. You could be a yogi all your life and not tap into any of the universe's energy manifestations. She meditates and practices yog, is healthy, and is sharper than anyone her age. She is very agile and fast, but that's about it.'

'Can Maurice not teach or guide her?'

'Of course, he does,' Adipati said raising his brows slightly. 'But it is not as simple as you think. He can guide her to meditate, but he cannot guide her to find the path to the universe. Since he was a yogi and had already discovered his ability before she was born, it is imprinted in her DNA. That said, she might never find it or in fact, find something else completely on her own.'

He became lost in thought for a moment but collected himself and continued.

'There have been instances in the past where the child of a yogi found the exact same ability as the parent, sometimes triggered by heightened emotion from a life changing event. But there is no conclusive theory of how that happens, and there is no pattern or consistency in it.'

Trish approached them. 'Tell me about the naags.'

'What do you want to know?' Adipati asked him, gesturing him to take a seat.

'How are they different from us?' he asked. Then he took a deep breath, staring at the floor and said, 'I don't even know if I'm one of them, or us, or what.'

'You are the best of both,' Adipati said. 'And since you were born and raised as us, you are more us than them. But to answer your question, remember I told you they evolved while we adapted?'

Trish nodded.

'Well, that is where the differences stem from. They kept on retaining whatever they deemed was an advantage from their reptilian heritage while they forsook their weaknesses. As a result of this, they can see clearly at night and over long distances without having to compromise on normal vision in daylight.'

'They have found an optimum level of development for both rods and cones in the eye. They have taken from their heritage the ability to move the eye lens forward and back by contracting/relaxing muscles to zoom in and out, though not every one of them has that yet. Their eyes have UV protection, and you already know about the stenopaic or slit-like pupil which can return to normalcy.'

'Many of their current races have infra red or heat sensing vision since they kept their *pit organs* which directly co-relate with their vision. They have kept scales as protection, though these have evolved quite a bit. Their bites are mostly poisonous save for a few of their races. Their hearing and smell are incredible.'

'While we have invented buttons to operate other buttons in the name of progress, they rely less on machines and more on their bodies. This has made them far more superior in terms of abilities of the body and mind, making them much faster and stronger. And this is just the normal naags and some of their advantageous traits. Then there are the nodes, however few, that have total control of every faculty of their brain and body.'

'Sounds like a whole lot of fun.' Trish sneered.

'I know it is not easy,' he said, then sipped from the glass of water Brij had offered earlier.

'Consider what you faced last night was only a fraction of what is to come. I don't expect you to be looking forward to it. However, you will not be alone. We will lay our lives down to protect you.'

'I have also seen the Yakshini take a lot of interest in you, and all of this on the whole. I believe she trusts in our faith that this is necessary for the survival and freedom of our kind.'

'I wonder what she wants to give you today? These people are known to bestow gifts and blessings on those they are pleased with, though there is usually some kind of test involved. I wonder if last night was the test you passed?'

+++

Everyone gathered in the hall eagerly waiting for the Yakshini. It was two minutes past eleven, and the excitement was palpable. She did, after all, mention that this was the true purpose she had asked them over for. Trish knew that if this was bigger than whatever had happened in the House of Yaksh till now, it had to be massive. Adipati said they were known to give boons to people they liked. He was sure the Yakshini liked him.

She stepped in at four minutes past eleven and greeted everyone. Behind her walked a huge man who held a stone relic. It looked like a stone carving depicting a pole arm, except it was a staff about an inch and a half thick, and three feet long with stone blades on both ends. The blades themselves were each roughly two feet long, making the total length of the object around seven feet from one end to the other. From the way the man carried it, it looked rather heavy.

'I wish to present to you this weapon,' the Yakshini said. 'If it is what I have been told it is, this may prove to be the deadliest weapon in the hands of a rightful wielder.'

Trish looked at her with surprise. It appeared the man carrying it could barely manage to lug it along himself. *How was anyone supposed to wield it? And what good would wielding do? It was stone!*

The Yakshini noticed his surprise, as did she noticed the surprise of everyone else in the room. Some even looked amused. 'Place it on that table,' she said, directing the man.

He lifted it higher with much effort and slid it on to the table, one end at a time. He looked relieved to put it down.

'Let me tell you what I have been told,' she said to Trish. 'If it is all true, what you see before you is not stone but metal. A very lightweight metal that will cut through almost anything. What looks like stone in texture is a kind of *patina*, for the lack of a better word. It has formed on the surface over millennia of the metal being dormant.'

She saw the look on Trish's face. His mouth opened momentarily to speak and he brought out his hand, but immediately shut it and pulled his hand up to his chin.

'Yes, what is it?' she asked.

'When you say dormant, does it mean it was in some way active?' Trish's eyes glinted with excitement. 'An active metal of some kind?'

'Not active,' she said, smiling deviously. 'Alive!'

Trish took a moment to comprehend and assimilate what he had just heard. There was no way the Yakshini was bullshitting him, yet there was no way it made sense at all either. But then nothing had made sense of late. His own being was something he would not have believed in some days back. But still, *living metal?*

'You find it shocking that a metal could have life, and it is obvious why,' she said, running her finger over the object. 'We all find it surprising. I haven't seen living metal myself. However, as part of my being in the know, I have been handed over knowledge of what used to be referred to as *Jaivdhaatu.*'

'I have heard of it and possessed this weapon forever, but have neither seen a metal with life nor this one come to life with my own eyes. I was told someone rightful would come to me one day and I would know that I had to hand it over to him or her.'

'We do not expect life to exist in any form other than the forms we know of. That is what our problem is; looking for water and oxygen on other planets to establish whether they have life. We continue to be shackled by our knowledge. Why should another life form need exactly what we need to live? We are so ignorant in the matter that we even ignore how there are several life forms on earth itself which need no oxygen, or are anaerobic.'

'Yes, but metal is inanimate,' Trish said.

'Is it? Why must it be inanimate? Because we know it to be so?

'Metals from other worlds have had life, and our supposed gods have handled them in their times. There are recorded instances in so many words which will tell you exactly that. The first and most powerful such instance was in the creation of *Asi* when the supreme gods conjured a being so powerful and deadly it shook the earth, and trees fell as a result of its energy. This being was cast by them into a fine edged sword. It was named Asi and was known to be born, and even has a parent constellation and a *gotr.'*

'Tell me what turns into a sword or a weapon? Flesh and blood, or metal? There are similar instances of beings turned into weapons of solid metal in various cultures. Ours had many more too. The Asi was so powerful, it could not be wielded by any of the so-called gods. Eventually, it had to be given to someone greater than the gods themselves to tame it.'

'The Shiv!' Trish exclaimed.

'The Shiv indeed. What you see here also came to the earth, shaking it and felling trees. In fact, it came in so hard, that the god it was bonded to had to disengage himself from it before it made impact.'

'You see Trish, this metal here isn't as powerful as that of Asi. It lives, but cannot live by itself and needs a kind of a symbiotic relationship. That is why it has been dormant for all this time. When it was about to impact the earth, whoever it was bonded to disengaged themselves, resulting in a portion of its mass breaking off.'

'Where it impacted on earth, therefore, you find two craters. One large crater made by impact from the large chunk, and another smaller one made by the tiny chunk that broke off. The bigger portion was cleared up by the gods; probably used for their weaponry. But the smaller one went unnoticed and was lifted by demigods a few millennia later and forged into weapons for themselves. The two craters can still be seen around seven hundred kilometres north-east of here in a place called Lonar.'

Trish listened intently. 'So this is one of the weapons that were forged from the smaller chunk of the metallic mass, or meteorite?'

'The only one remaining from that chunk, and one of the only few weapons made of *Jaivdhatu* that are still on earth.'

'How few?'

'You can count them on your fingers. On one hand.'

Trish was certainly excited but also perplexed. 'How am I going to use this thing?' he asked, looking at the said weapon.

On closer inspection, he could see under the patina that the shaft was not cylindrical, but was actually made up of what looked like a set of twisted vines. Some of these vines were thin, and some were thicker than others. These vines then knotted up to make for the quillon near the blade, before opening up and spreading out to hold the blade on either side, thinning down progressively and embedding themselves into the blade itself.

The blades were perfectly identical but faced the opposite direction to each other. At five inches wide at its widest part, the curved blade looked fabulous, and the entire weapon was made with magnificent finesse. He looked at the Yakshini, then asked for permission to pick it up. When she nodded, he gripped the weapon with both hands and lifted it. It was so heavy. He turned around to look at everyone, then put it back.

'This is no weapon,' he said, slightly exhausted. 'I can barely lift it. Wielding it is out of the question.'

'Now herein lies the test of whether you are to be the one to wield it,' the Yakshini said. 'The legend I've been handed down with the weapon is that it splits into two swords and morphs into one weapon as it is at present, at its host's will. You will get one chance to make it split into swords, and if you can, it will forge a bond with you forever. If you cannot, it will remain dormant till someone who finds it can.'

'I have no clue about the whats and hows of it. I haven't seen It happen ever in my lifetime and I don't know who it belonged to before. All I know is, I believe you may be the one to will it to bond with you. If not, I will pass it on to Laranya before I leave this body, with the knowledge that has been bestowed on me.'

'But how do I will it to split up?'

'I don't know. I can give you a room to yourself to figure it out. Just remember, do not try to pull the swords apart till you know you have cracked it. If you do, you may lose your one chance, and it is over before you know it. Frankly, I simply do not want that and would love to get rid of this burden on the house.'

Adipati smiled. She didn't just want to get rid of it. *It must be imperative that Trish has this weapon, and only she knows why.*

'I will give it a shot,' Trish said. 'I don't know what to do, but the worst that can happen is that nothing will happen. If I don't have the weapon, that doesn't change a thing about our situation as it stands now anyway. So yes, let's have that room.'

'Would you mind if we could see you from the other room?' the Yakshini said. 'You won't even know. There will be very tiny cameras and tinier microphones, so you won't even notice. The room is soundproof, and you will not be disturbed in any way.'

'Must you?,' Trish asked.

'I am just curious about the whole thing,' she explained. 'No one who lives has seen anything like this. We haven't had anyone wield one of these around for millennia now. If this indeed is what it is, you will be the only one handling one of these on the planet today.'

'OK.'

+++

Fifteen minutes later they were all standing in Vidyut's office in front of monitors, watching the room Trish was to enter. The Yakshini requested total silence, and the sound on the speakers in the room was turned up. They saw the door open, and a man gestured Trish inside.

Trish walked in, remembering the Yakshini's advice. *'Listen. Listening is the key: complete surrender.'*

He walked to the centre of the small room with the weapon in his hand and looked around. She was right, he couldn't spot a single camera or microphone. He breathed in deep and started turning around slowly, trying to decide which way to face. Finally, with his back to the door, he sat down on the floor folding his legs and lay the weapon across his thighs.

He kept looking at it for a while, then straightened his back up, and drew in a deep breath while closing his eyes. When he opened them a few minutes later, he was sitting on sand at the endless beach. The sound of the waves calmed him somewhat. He looked at the weapon again and said, 'All right, what are we to do with you now?'

As the others watched him on the monitors, the Yakshini knew he was gone. His body was still; like he was made of stone. They looked at him sit like that for over half an hour.

Then Vidyut broke the silence. 'Turn up the sound. Is he actually humming?'

22

Trish had been humming for over four hours. He wasn't humming a song or a tune. He was humming flat on a single note for several minutes, then was on another random note. At times he went silent but even when he wasn't, his hum was hardly audible at all despite the speakers being brought up to full volume.

Everyone wondered what was going on. Some were getting bored to death. Rakshit signalled to Lyosha that he was hungry, only to get a disapproving look from him. Every now and then a couple of them went to the back of the room and whispered to each other. The wait seemed endless. Only the Yakshini had hardly blinked all this time and kept looking intently from one monitor to the other.

'Nobody has a clue what's going on,' Sveta whispered at the back of the room. She had not once communicated in her usual way since they had stepped into the House of Yaksh. On Adipati's instructions, she had stuck to talking by way of speaking.

'I don't think even the Yakshini has a clue this time around,' Vishwas whispered back. 'I had from the beginning believed that Trish was going to have a difficult time trying to assimilate the world around him. Turns out, I'm having a difficult time myself.'

They all heard a commotion near the monitors.

'Another hum?' the Yakshini asked. 'Are you certain?'

'Absolutely positive,' Vidyut said, staring at one of the monitors. 'Between C and C#...he had been holding that for the last thirty-three minutes and eighteen seconds, or interestingly thirty-three decimal three minutes after which I can say with absolute certainty I have two sources of the same vibration in the room at 136.1 Hz.' He moved to a monitor on the far side.

'Look here,' he said, pointing to a series of graphs. 'This is the hum he has been holding, and this is the one that has appeared now. They're definitely two sources interfering with one another, however, they're of the same frequency.' He paused for a bit, then his eyes widened. He pointed to the second wave form. 'Unbelievable. The new source starts, interferes, then stops only to start again.'

'What does it mean?' Adipati asked.

'It's trying to synchronise itself to be in phase with Trish's hum,' Vidyut said as his jaw slightly dropped. 'Trying to achieve a state of what we call constructive interference.'

'Are you saying it is trying to sync with Trish and amplify his hum?'

'Very much so,' Vidyut replied. Everyone crowded over the monitor, trying to get a glimpse. A little while later he declared, 'They're in sync.'

Everyone exchanged looks with one another, while also looking at screens in between, wondering what to expect next.

There were sets of monitors at three different workstations. One set was being supervised by Vidyut, which he would show the others from time to time. The two other sets of monitors were where other members of staff were seated, facing each other, about five feet from Vidyut's station.

A man stationed at one of the monitors facing backward called out to Vidyut, 'You need to see this.'

They went over to his screen where he had zoomed in on Trish's lap. His hands clenched the object's shaft just like before, but they noticed something new. The object was vibrating; and not just that, the patina on its surface started coming off gradually and dropped to the ground as dust.

The Yakshini smiled as the real beauty of the object began to show itself. *So it was all true.*

Minutes later the vines that made the staff of the weapon, parted at the centre and receded toward the blades. In doing so, the broken ends scraped Trish's palms as they passed through them and drew blood. At about six inches from the quillon, they knotted up in a ball, making for the pommels of two individual swords.

Trish came to with a start, realising his palms were bruised. He then saw the two swords on either side of him and picked them up. The one to his left had red vines, the colour of his blood, and a black blade. The one to his right had black vines and a red blade. He picked them up and was surprised at how light they were, almost as if they were made of cardboard.

As he held them in his hands, a pattern began to emerge in the blades. Where the vines tapered into them, they continued throughout the blades in a beautiful motif completely flush with the blade's surface. Along the top of the ridge of the blades appeared writing in the Indian script of *Devnagari*. Part of it was inscribed on the red blade in black and the other on the black blade in red. Trish swung the swords in a *downward flower* a few times, cutting figure eights in the air around him. He beamed with delight.

A couple of minutes later, Adipati knocked on the door and opened it. The Yakshini walked in to find Trish grinning.

'It worked,' he said, gawking at the blades. 'Look at this thing!' he exclaimed with joyful admiration for the weapon.

'It is not a thing,' she remarked, beaming back at him. 'For one, the weapon has a life or consciousness of its own. There is *praan* in it. And secondly, they used to have names back when this one was forged, and a personality, even if they had no *praan* in them.'

'What is this one called? Do you know?' he asked excitedly.

'They tell me this one was named by a demigod and the forger together,' she said. 'You are holding in your hand The Ulka.'

'Meteorite! Isn't that what it means?'

'Yes dear child, it does.'

Adipati took a closer look at the blade. 'Let me read what is inscribed on it.'

'On her, you mean,' Trish said with a wink.

Adipati smiled. 'Yes, let me look at it please.'

On the two blades, he found written in halves what he read out as one.

निंसदेह, इदं ध्रुवं सत्यं यत् वयं परस्परं रक्तेन बद्धाः परं किमिंद आवश्यकं यत् अहं भवताम् नेतृत्वेण अनुसरणबद्धोsस्मि

'What does it mean?' Trish asked him.

Adipati pondered a moment and then announced, reading off the blade: 'As we are bound by blood indeed...So shall I follow however you lead.'

The Yakshini nodded in affirmation as Trish's smile grew immensely.

'These are the scabbards,' the Yakshini said, pointing to a man who carried them. 'You have not had anything to eat since breakfast. Let us all have a snack and some tea. You can spend some time practising with Ulka later.'

She had barely finished speaking when Rakshit grabbed the scabbards and started putting them over the blades. 'Best idea I've heard all day,' he said. They all burst into laughter.

+++

In the hall, while they were finishing up with tea and refreshments, Vidyut turned to Trish. 'So what made you realise that you needed to hum?'

'I was to what now?' Trish asked, looking clueless.

'You know...the thing you did in there. When you started humming, then stuck to just one note before the weapon started vibrating, what prompted that?'

Trish looked bewildered. 'What note was I humming?'

The Yakshini stepped in and stopped the conversation in its tracks. 'You should try and see if you can will it back together.'

'Will it together?' Trish looked at her questioningly. 'How do you mean?'

'See if you can make it into one weapon as it originally was,' she said.

Trish walked up to the table where the blades lay and picked them up. He held the pommels together with the blades facing away from each other and tried to concentrate. *Nothing!* He tried again. A third time, to no avail. He turned to the Yakshini, looking clueless before trying one more time. Nothing happened.

'Any suggestions?' he asked everyone.

'We are all seeing something like this for the first time ever,' Adipati said. 'It is up to you to figure what to do just as you did to bring it back to life.'

'Her,' he said, correcting him again. 'Bring *her* back to life.'

As he said that, the knots that made for the pommels began to untie themselves. Everyone watched in amazement as both ends of the vines began to grow outward, entwining themselves with those of the other blade. Seconds later Trish was holding the seven-foot weapon again. It was as light as the blades and not heavy as before. The staff made of entwined red and black metallic vines and both blades faced opposite to each other; one red, the other black.

'See,' he said, 'she doesn't like to be referred to as an object.'

Everyone present had a look of awe on their faces. Rakshit extended his arm, seeking permission to hold the weapon from Trish. Trish nodded and held it out to him with his right hand. What he offered effortlessly with one hand, Rakshit found difficult to hold with both of his.

'This is so damn heavy,' he said, trying not to hurt his own pride.

'What?' Trish said. 'It is not! It's as light as cardboard.' He gestured for Adipati to try holding it. Adipati took it with both hands and immediately tightened his grip on it.

'I think only you are supposed to wield it,' he said through gritted teeth. 'It is indeed heavy for us.'

Trish took the weapon from him with his left hand, spun it around, then rolled the shaft between his palms, rotating the entire length of it vertically as if it had no weight at all. 'Well, so long as she is light in my hands...she did choose me after all.'

The Yakshini looked pleased. She had a calm and a light smile on her face. 'My duty and the purpose for which I sought your visit is now fulfilled,' she said. She then looked at Adipati. 'You must stay till tomorrow and are welcome to stay as long as you so wish, but I shall hold you here no more.' She bowed slightly, smiled at Trish, took in a deep breath, then left.

Adipati knew well what that meant. They were to leave the following day.

+++

'It is late in the night,' Sveta said to Trish. 'I know you are excited about your new acquisition, but you should rest now.'

Trish was in the main hall, practising with Ulka. He had sought Laranya's permission and moved the furniture back to make space for himself to dance around and try the new weapon he had. After all, it was a massive hall.

'We're getting to know each other,' Trish said. 'She is learning as well as I. It is difficult to believe, but I think she is beginning to understand my every move and anticipate it before it happens.'

'How do you mean?' asked Sveta .

'Would you be kind enough and attack me? A friendly bout, if you will. I'll be able to demonstrate better what I mean.'

'I must warn you, I could kill you in a friendly bout by accident,' she quipped.

'I'll be sure to keep an eye out and beg for mercy before you do,' he said with a wink.

She chuckled and drew out her batons. 'Well, what the hell. I need some exercise anyway.'

Trish held the weapon as one, gripping it near the centre with both hands two feet apart. She attacked him playfully at first but knew soon that he was not moving his feet and gave her a rather bored look. He urged her to up her game a bit and soon what started as jest, turned into spirited combat. She realised how good he was while he defended himself without attacking once. It started to embarrass her a little till she decided to give it all she had.

Trish was definitely impressed, but he hardly broke a sweat as he kept deflecting her blows with practised ease. It was then that Maurice walked in. He watched them for a while and sat smiling on the sofa that was pushed against the far wall.

'Find something amusing?' Sveta asked.

'No, dear,' he said. 'It is encouraging to see you help the boy practice.'

'I am not practising so much as trying to understand the weapon, while she understands me,' Trish said. 'Would you care to join, Professor? The more difficult it is for me to stand my ground, the better. Not to say I don't already have a stiff challenge, but I want to see how far I can go with Ulka here.'

'Might I join in?' he heard Rakshit say from behind him as he walked into the hall. 'It couldn't hurt to get a little exercise and if I get to help make you eat dust, I couldn't really ask for more.'

He winked as Trish nodded.

As the vines disengaged and shortened, Trish held the two swords across his front. 'I will try not to cut anything.'

Rakshit drew his hammers and presented Trish with his profile, while facing Sveta and nodding at her. She went first as Trish parried her advance with the red sword, stepping forward to engage Rakshit with the black one. Rakshit spun about himself, bringing a hammer down fast on his left shoulder. He moved ever so slightly to let it slide by him as he punched his sword's pommel into his forearm.

Sveta was already charging from behind him to land a blow on the right side of his rib cage, but her baton met with the flat of his sword as he stepped back again to hit her elbow lightly with the other sword's pommel. They knew he was pulling his punches and having fun with them.

They tried different lines of attack but the result was always the same. He stood in between them while they danced around him, trying to get through his defence. Every now and then he would land a little blow on them and make them wince for a moment. If he was any good before, he had only become better.

Sveta decided it was time to bring her abilities to better use. As Rakshit engaged him, Trish heard a loud cry from behind.

He swayed and swung his sword backward to tackle whatever was coming at him, even as Sveta charged from the other side. Though he was still looking over his shoulder, his sword swiftly flipped around and blocked Sveta's oncoming baton. There was nobody behind him.

'How did you do that?' she said. 'I made that cry from behind you. You almost fell for it. Hell, you even kept looking for something behind you, yet brought your sword in to block me just in time. No one has not fallen for that before.'

'That's the thing,' he said, nodding at the weapons in hand. 'I didn't do it. I was still looking for someone behind me and had swung the sword to tackle the attack, but she understood, so she turned back on her own! She's beginning to learn. That nudge she gave you after the block; that wasn't me either. She has been learning as I defended myself against you. This is incredible.'

'That thing acts of its own will?' Rakshit exclaimed as he stopped to catch his breath.

'She is not a thing, Raka,' Trish said. 'She just saved me a certain blow to the ribs. What the hell was that trickery anyway? I thought we were fighting fair.'

'And why is it not fair to use whatever is at your disposal?' she quipped. 'You have a sword that lives. I say if you using that is fair, so is me using what weapons I have.'

'Fair enough, I guess,' he said with a shrug. 'But did you see that? It is unbelievable! Imagine the kind of snake ass I can kick with her by my side.'

Maurice got up and walked toward them. 'Let us see her sweat as you then, shall we?' he said, pulling his whip from around his waist. 'Would you be up for all three of us against you lad? I'll be sure not to hurt you too much.'

Trish grinned. 'I thought you would never ask.'

What followed was a pleasure for all involved. All three of them knew it wasn't going to be easy, but they were having fun trying. Sveta and Rakshit took solace in the fact that even the Professor couldn't do much to bother Trish. He had found a new energy within himself. He moved a lot more and they knew full well he was still pulling his punches.

It was difficult to say what Trish was doing as a result of pure intent and what he was doing as a unit with the weapon. It wasn't until Maurice decided to bring in his additional faculties to the match that things heated up. Trish felt a jolt as he managed to let the tip of his whip pass him by. No one could say whether that took him by surprise or annoyed him for being unfair, but whatever the case, Trish was now attacking.

Trish put Rakshit and Sveta down without injuring them by means of making them lose their balance and tipping them over each other, but he went hard for the professor's whip. It was as if he wanted to cut the whip clean with his blades.

Maurice found it rather difficult to anticipate his movements and kept falling back with half a mind of yelling at Trish to stop. Then, in a moment of frustration, he managed to jolt the boy again, heavier jolt this time.

Trish became berserk. He moved so fast that they couldn't see the blades any more; it was just a dance of red and black around him. Soon enough, the whip was out of Maurice's hand, falling lifelessly to the floor. Trish's blade went straight for Maurice's neck, in a move that was sure to take his head off clean.

'NOOOOO...' Trish yelled as the blade turned right before making impact and ended up hitting him broadside under his ear. Maurice fell wincing onto the sofa next to him.

'I am terribly sorry, Professor,' Trish said excitedly. 'I did not sanction that. I guess she must have misunderstood my aggression toward the whip. Forgive me please.'

'Don't worry about it kid,' Maurice said. 'You called her off in time. That was a close but good call. I think you will do famously well together. Just give it time and practise with her as much as you can.'

'Yes. I shall. I think it best we retire now. I will see you all for breakfast.' Trish bowed apologetically to them and left with Ulka back in her scabbards.

'That is some weapon, that one,' Rakshit remarked.

'They are,' Maurice said. 'Not the blades and not Trish, but them together are too strong a force to face. Trish's skills are already known to us, but with this new addition to his abilities he grows stronger by the minute. The more they practice, the stronger they will grow.'

'Well, that can only be good news,' Sveta said throwing herself onto the sofa. She felt drained by the combat. *Man, that kid is fast.*

'He isn't fighting us at the end of the day. And we would love to see him win over whoever he fights. Perhaps we should get to bed too.' She said her goodnights while Rakshit followed suit and left. She got up to leave behind him.

Maurice sat down on a sofa. *Good news it is, so long as we can save him and he can save himself. But with this weapon by his side, if we lose him to the other side, we lose the weapon to them. And they are already bonded. This fucking thing was a boon so long as it wasn't a bane!*

23

««« TWENTY THREE »»»

After breakfast the next morning, everyone returned to the hall to find it arranged just as before. Adipati informed them that they were all to leave at noon. Laranya had offered an apology on the Yakshini's behalf, saying she wouldn't be able to see them off, which upset Trish a little. He had grown to like her somewhat. Also, he wasn't sure when, or even if at all, he would see Tejaswi again. She seemed unperturbed. Maybe it was because she was trying to put up an appearance in front of her mother, but then again, maybe she didn't care as much. He wasn't going to ask.

'Will you end up getting trouble since the twins have located this area?' Trish asked Laranya.

'We will be here no longer once you have left us,' she said. 'This place does not exist, and once we are gone it will be solid rock and no more.'

'How does one find you?' he enquired.

'One does not,' she replied. 'We find whoever needs to be found.'

He gave Tejaswi a glance, but she looked away. 'Well, thank the Yakshini for me, please. I could never repay her if I tried.'

'I will be sure to thank her, but she did not see you, or make you understand and realise yourself, for repayment. It had to be done and she knew it. Think no more of it, Trishul. The house's blessings are with you in your future endeavours.'

'Thank you,' Trish said, looking at the bracelet the Yakshini had presented to him.

Maurice was having another conversation by the mantle at a distance. 'Do you realise if we lose the boy now that he has bonded with that weapon, the weapon goes into their hands too?' He whispered to Adipati. 'We will end up giving them not just the boy, but the powers he has gathered as well. It makes me happy to see that he is being equipped to face what is coming, but if he is lost...'

'Well then, it is more important we do not lose, isn't it,' Adipati whispered back. 'In any case, if the boy is lost and what is said is to come true, it wouldn't matter what else they do, or do not get.'

'But you are still taking him to the fort, are you not?' he asked. 'The journey is treacherous and long, and there is every chance they will track us, should we encounter them on our way. Above all, there is no way we might not encounter them at all, now that they will start showing themselves. The gates are open, Adi. The proverbial bloody shit has hit the fucking fan.'

'There is no place else we can defend better professor, and you know it. The chances of them discovering it may be far greater than we had previously imagined, but we wouldn't be able to defend at all were we to be found elsewhere. I wouldn't advise leaving positions of advantage. We were exactly on top of Sheshna, but see where that got us.'

Maurice was about to say something else, but Adipati dismissed it. 'We cannot fear the worst and wish for the boy to be weak if we were to lose. We must hope he is strong and triumph in the end. No more on this please, Professor.'

+++

Once they made it to the top of the cliff, led by the foul mouthed boy who had shown them in, they saw Gurung with others standing beside three SUVs, parked close to the edge of the cliff.

'We must make haste,' Gurung said. 'The villagers know that the cars have come out this way. We can't stay here too long. If we leave immediately, they might think someone got adventurous for a bit then left. Besides, we could cross Aurangabad before midnight and stop for the night somewhere. Ms Brandt will be expecting us where you had me tell her we'd be.'

'We cannot afford to stop anywhere except for short durations to freshen up, and for refreshments,' Adipati said. 'Let us leave immediately and make a stop for an early dinner somewhere. Vishwas, Mugdha, and Trishul must catch up on sleep before midnight and drive after Aurangabad without lights till daylight. We must keep moving and get to them as soon as we can.'

Everyone nodded and started boarding the vehicles. Maurice checked all the provisions for the journey and saw them distributed equally between the three vehicles. They began moving onto the road.

Trish cast a last look at where they had stayed for the last few days. 'Where are we headed?' he asked Adipati.

'To the north west end of Satpura National Park, north of the Tawa Reservoir, and east of Tawa river. That is where they will wait for us; in a secluded spot, engulfed in the fold of a ridge.'

'Who will wait for us there?'

'Karuna Brandt, with the Nichola. They can't make the flight this far without the professor on board, but it will make a couple of pit stops in secluded areas to meet us there by tomorrow. It is the only way we can make it to our destination quietly.'

Trish was pleased to hear about Karuna and the prospect of travelling in the Nichola again. 'Where is the destination, though?' he asked. 'Don't you think the time to trickle information down to me at the rate of one conversation a day has long passed? Do you still think I will be unable to process anything you throw at me now?'

Lyosha looked back from the navigator's seat and sniggered. Adipati gave him an amused look and turned to Trish and Brij. 'We call it The Fort. Our guru resides at the premises, and a lot of training and guidance is provided there for people with potential, and those who have had their initial brush with yogic abilities.'

'It is not a school or an institution of any kind. It is like an *ashram* or hermitage, and we as The Circuit are its prime patrons. There is, of course, the vested interest of recruiting for our cause. The guru, however, has no concern for it, or The Circuit as such. He only believes in meditation to conjoin with the one truth, and remains to be the source of energy for the place for more than the last five hundred years.'

'Somehow the mention of five hundred year old men doesn't seem to bother me that much any more,' Trish said. 'And I'm not entirely sure that is a good thing.'

'To be able to take truth at its face value cannot be bad in my opinion,' Adipati replied. He looked out of the window momentarily as he began speaking. 'The human body was designed to be able to last at least twice its current expectancy, under as they say, standard test conditions.'

'But just as your car does not give you mileage similar to that advertised for it due to your driving style and non-standard conditions, the body doesn't last that long either. Over millennia our lifestyle and the things our bodies endure have changed drastically for the worse. To top that we take no care of it, and it has resulted in the health of the body to deteriorate faster than ever.'

'Sure, life expectancy has been increased of late by medical science, but the health of the body has not. Meditation slows down ageing of the body if done right. And if done to perfection, it may even give you immense control over the ageing process.'

'I remember you said you were older than a century yourself,' Trish said. Brij looked highly surprised.

'Let us not get off topic here,' Adipati said, cleverly avoiding the subject. 'What you wanted to know was where we were going. The Nichola takes us to the fort, which is in the mountains. That is also where she rests when not in use, or under further study.'

'The mountains you say,' Brij said, finally speaking. 'Where exactly?'

'Ladakh.'

+++

They had travelled for eleven hours straight, stopping only twice to change drivers and stretch their legs, while they sipped on tea at small stalls along the highway. It was time, however, to stop for dinner. They had crossed Aurangabad a little while back, and Adipati had suggested they stop near Ashrafpur. Soon they pulled in to a small roadside restaurant, where they ordered food. Adipati had instructed everyone to talk about random stuff or not talk at all. No mention of the House of Yaksh, their true names, or their present situation was to be made.

They ate their food mostly in silence. A few truckers would stop by every now and then. Some would stay for a meal, others didn't stay long at all and drove on. Some had been there before they had arrived, yet nothing seemed out of place.

Lyosha finished his food first and got up to wash his hands at the hand pump. On walking back, he bumped into a man who was leaving. The man's wallet fell on the cot next to them, which a few men were having their dinner on. Lyosha apologised and bent to pick it up. A man on the cot also turned to pick up the wallet, and Lyosha touched his hand as he grabbed the wallet first. They smiled and handed it back to the owner, with Lyosha apologising again. He then thanked the man on the cot and shook his right hand while he patted his back with his left.

As he approached his seat, he smiled at Adipati and gently whispered, '*snake*'.

Adipati and Sveta looked at each other for a moment, then everyone heard her voice in their heads. '*Make no haste, but finish your meals, and let us leave here soon.*' She got up to go and wash her hands, but they could still hear her as she walked. '*Act normal. Do not look alarmed, but be vigilant. There are naags here.*'

A few minutes later they had all finished up and thanked the staff while they boarded their vehicles one after the other. It was Trish's turn to drive, along with Mugdha and Vishwas.

Once on the road again, they switched the headlights off as Trish questioned Adipati. 'What does this mean? They were there, but they didn't attack. They saw us, and in all probability, came to know that they had been made, yet they still let us leave. Why?'

'We will be attacked,' he replied, wringing his hands together. 'We will be attacked soon, or they wouldn't have let us go. If we make a run, they will just keep following us. The only way to throw them off is to stop when confronted and fight. We must disable or even kill all of those who attack us if need be. The trail must end here. We cannot afford to be followed to the fort.'

Maurice's voice echoed through the speakers. 'There is no major detour we can use to throw them off our scent till Sillod.'

'They will not wait till Sillod,' Adipati replied. 'My guess is they will come soon after Phulambri, where there is a secluded patch along the road.'

'Should we stall at Phulambri then? Or go west for a bit?'

'That will only prolong our agony, Professor,' he said. 'It will also give them more time to execute the attack and gather more force. We must keep going and destroy whatever blocks our way.'

+++

There was a truck parked broadside to block the road. They knew of the vehicles that were following them too. One had been in pursuit since dinner, and two more had joined in at Phulambri. 'Good I ate light,' Vishwas's voice said through the speakers. 'I can feel at least thirty of them ahead of us. Add to that five each in the vehicles behind us, and we have close to fifty naags to face.'

'Hold nothing back,' Adipati replied. 'Kill when you must. Let's get this over with.' He stepped out of the vehicle before it came to a complete stop. Everyone followed and formed a periphery along the vehicles facing out.

'Just the boy,' a deep, firm voice said. 'Hand him to us, and the rest of you can go about your business. Everybody wins.' A rather tall, dark, and extremely well-built man stepped to the front. 'Or this could get very ugly, very fast.'

As he said his last words, he grimaced and turned to his other self. The scales on his skin were large and looked impenetrable. He made for a really intimidating figure. Brij clasped on to his son's hand, while his other hand was on his gun.

'Just the one thing we cannot do for you, Varadh,' Adipati said. 'We cannot let the boy go, and you cannot let us go with the boy. Let us face it, friend. There are not many choices left.'

'Adipati Ji,' he replied with a slight nod of his head. 'My god needs him, you know that. You have seen more years than I. I do not wish to end your life.'

'As I, yours. But both of us cannot leave here with what we want. I have respect for you, dear boy, but when it comes to this I must take your life.'

'It shall be a worthy death, if that is what happens. Dying in line of duty to my god at the hands of as great an adversary as you is more than what I can ask for. Should I have to end yours though, I must ask for forgiveness now. Others of my clan are not as understanding of you and I. Very few of us believe we should have coexisted on this planet any more. If it is you who takes my life, I must apprise you of the danger that awaits next. They are coming at you with all their might.'

'I would expect no less for such great a matter, son. We are but a few, however, we will do whatever is in our capacity to stop your god from claiming his prize. Now we must fight and be on our way.' Adipati made a slight nod.

Varadh smiled in acknowledgement. His scaly face and reptilian eyes looked sinister, but his smile defied his looks. 'I will give you two minutes for you to confer with your party and be ready. Then we fight.'

Everyone drew their weapons. There were a few questions bothering Trish, like who this Varadh was, and what was this exchange of respect that took place between him and Adipati.

And who the hell talks like that?

But this was no time for it. Not that Adipati had said much either. He just reminded them that they were to kill and not hold back. What else could he have said? Just to watch out for themselves and Rakshit to be alongside Brij at all times.

Two minutes later Adipati and Varadh nodded at each other, and it began.

Every person with Trish fought many of the naags off. But they were not as easy to deal with as the mercenaries they had fought off in Benares. These were strong, highly skilled beings who were not getting hurt as easily. Every blow from them was heavy and powerful.

The ones Brij shot did not fall or even stop, they just kept coming with the bullet lodged in them. It did injure them though, and together, Rakshit and he were making a good team. Adipati was astonishingly swift for his apparent age, which if what he claimed was true, was much less than how old he actually was. Trish didn't think him highly skilled with the staff as such, but he handled it well. Besides, it wasn't just any staff. The slightest touch would give the naags a burn or a frost bite instantly. Had it been humans it would have completely burnt or frozen the parts of the body it came in to contact with. These beings, on the other hand, were far more resilient and recovered quickly from its effects.

Trish himself was very highly skilled. He used the Ulka as a combined weapon, rotating it in front of him by using both his hands as he waited for his enemies to attack. Then, as they approached, he spun it in figure eights around him on both sides with one hand, to fend them off using small, gyrating movements of his upper body. The attackers were left looking for a rhythm so they could break in. The moment they found it, Trish noticed their footwork change to accommodate a strike, and he brought in the second hand and altered the rhythm then spun slightly.

While this would not get him anywhere and he would have to strike eventually, he was making them wait and playing on their minds to frustrate them. When they caught on to his new rhythm, Trish moved himself forward, inviting some of them to come around behind him. His weapon then started covering his back as well in an entirely new rhythm, while it never stopped spinning. He started moving it around him as he pleased with one hand at some times, then with both hands at others. He could now see them getting agitated and waited for one of them to make their first mistake.

Eventually, they thought they had waited long enough, and one of them lunged forward in a bid to break into Trish's ever-spinning weapon. It had built a protective cascade around him, but he had to move the one weapon to cover every direction they could come from. No matter how fast he was spinning it, any skilled warrior would want to break in when he thought he had cracked the timing.

That was the first attacker's undoing. The weapon cut through his arm at the elbow without a hint of resistance to its momentum. Even Trish was surprised. He hadn't exactly cut anything with the weapon before this. The attacker winced in pain and others stole a look at where Trish was. Others were barely causing bodily harm to the naags with their weapons, yet Trish had taken a limb off.

Other attackers around him took it upon themselves to break through his defence. This was the time to make them disengage from a formation. Trish leapt into the air. As his weapon spun around him continually, he hopped, skipped, and jumped, cutting through two more and scaring off the others. His weapon had become rotating blades of death, and the formation and coordination between his attackers fell. Even as he executed a cartwheel spinning his blades around him, he emerged from the massacre holding not one but two weapons. It was time to attack.

Cries of horror came from the ones he cut down as they saw not a boy but a naag once he had turned himself. But what really surprised every single one of them was the glow on his forehead. They gasped while being attacked.

Varadh saw it too, from a distance. Adipati could see the immense surprise on his face as well. It was apparent that the boy being a node was a surprise to everyone, even the naags themselves. Everyone took advantage of the surprised naags as much as they could and inflicted blows on them.

Trish leapt and spun in the air, bringing down his blades on those attacking him. He wasn't his regular rigid self in letting them attack him to take advantage of their commitments any more. He was fluid and brought the action to his adversaries by hitting, cutting, and killing them. No sooner had he finished with his own attackers, that he started taking on others as well. He leapt to help his father and Rakshit first.

Brij hadn't seen his son completely turned up close. The monster he saw killing the other beings was still his son though. With only two of the opposition left standing, Trish went on to help Mugdha next, then Vishwas followed by Sveta. He kept moving from one set of attackers to the next, leaving his companions to deal with just one or two before helping the next one.

While Trish helped Lyosha, he noticed one of the attackers moving toward Adipati, who was busy fending off Varadh and a couple of other naags. He had to make a move for them. To stop the oncoming naag, he would have to fling a sword onto his chest in time to reach the one whose blow was going to fall on Adipati's shoulder in a matter of seconds, which meant losing one sword momentarily.

While he thought this, the vines on his left sword unfurled at the pommel and gripped his wrist. For the first time ever he could feel his weapon communicating back to him. He didn't hear anything, but just knew what he had to do.

He flung his left sword to the attacker that was running in toward Adipati, still making way to where he was himself. The vines grew, making for a long rope attached to the sword as the blade lodged itself in the attacker's chest, even as Trish ran toward Adipati. He then yanked on the vines, raising his right blade to ward off the raised hand that was to land a blow on Adipati's shoulder.

The entire proceeding lasted a few seconds, but the attacker running in had fallen, with the left sword back in Trish's hand. The right sword had sliced clean the fist that was raised above Adipati. Trish landed with his right knee dug into the ground, while his left sword parried an attack from another.

In the meantime, Adipati had landed a huge blow of his staff to Varadh's chest, which almost froze it. As his enemies chest began to thaw, Trish flipped and chopped off his left arm, and Varadh went staggering backward from the shock. Adipati took the opportunity to hit hard with the frozen end of his staff on his chest again, and he fell on his back, gasping for air. He then flipped the staff over and thrust the burning end into his mouth, then held it there with all his strength, looking skyward while letting out a huge roar. He didn't ease up till Varadh's head exploded.

Everyone else had put their attackers down, with none left standing. Brij looked like he was possessed while he walked around shooting whoever was left alive, in the middle of their foreheads.

'What?' he roared at Lyosha who looked at him in stupor. 'They were not to be left alive, right?'

Trish, on the other hand, looked aghast at Adipati. He hadn't imagined him like this ever. When he turned around though, he noticed a tear in his eye. 'He was a good person,' he said, referring to Varadh. 'He died for what he believed in, just as we do.'

'I thought I saw one of them run off into the fields when the fighting had just begun,' Maurice said.

'We can't go after him,' Adipati replied. 'We just do not have the time. We must make haste.' He looked around. Most of them had bruises and minor wounds, but Vishwas was hurt. He was on his knees and his left arm looked flaccid. 'Get word out that they must bring Fakru along as well. We need him.'

+++

'I have placed it on the engine,' he said, panting. He had run hard and long from the place of the little battle. 'So long as the engine does not go cold, we will know where those vehicles are going.'

'Is there any chance they might find it?' asked the one in the hood.

'It is organic. Not like their tech. They won't get it in a scan. They might see it if they pop the hood open, but they will not know it from the filth.'

'Track them,' he replied.

'Don't you mean follow them?'

'No. We will catch up with them in time. Right now there is more important news to be delivered. The weapon that boy has, and more importantly that the boy is *varshaapit*, it will please the Lord.'

24

«»«« TWENTY FOUR »»»»

'By now word of you being a node must have reached their council,' Adipati said. 'They will catch up with our route soon; I know it. We must make haste in leaving as soon as we meet with Ms Karuna.' It was breaking dawn, and they had already passed Khandwa. 'We must not make a lengthy stop till our destination.'

'We will reach there before noon,' Maurice said over the speakers. 'Surely you are not planning to take off in daylight, and will wait for nightfall? If we leave past midnight, we would still be at our destination in less than three hours. I can give it everything I have.'

'But that will exhaust you,' Adipati said. 'We do not want to exhaust anyone.'

'I can rest when we reach. Don't worry, I've been through much worse. It is still much better than flying around in daylight. We will be all over the news before you know it.'

Adipati agreed. 'We must keep our heads down through the day then. Are we sure we do not have a tracer on us?'

'I have run a scan thrice. There is no sign of anything on us,' Gurung replied through the speakers.

'Still, we must let the vehicles go the moment we get off them,' Adipati said and looked outside. 'And they must not stop at all, other than to let us out. No more than half a minute.' If the others have rested enough, let them pull over for a quick tea and stretch their legs. They should take over the wheels now.'

They soon stopped at a shabby stall by the road off Bedia. The stall keeper was rather talkative and tried to make conversation with everyone, but he gave up though, seeing as nobody was interested in idle conversation.

The drivers popped up the hoods of the cars as Gurung stood by for inspection. 'Looks like something died on it and melted,' one of them said.

'Take it off,' he replied. 'Burn it.'

+++

'You are certain of it?' asked a burly man who sat in the shadows.

'Absolutely, master. I saw it with my own eyes. He is *Varshaapit*, just as we had wished for him before his mother abandoned us for the human.'

'She did abandon us alright; she had the child with a human, and yet he is blessed with the curse despite being born of human blood. The Lord must have known. So it is His will. The world works in strange ways to make the promised word come to life. This is indeed good news.'

'If I may...' the one in the hood added hesitantly. 'Will this not pose a threat for the word to come true? He is going to be a far more formidable force to reckon with now. And with that weapon of his...'

'He is to be the Lord's revival. What is his, will be the Lord's. It is only for the better, my child. No doubt it would have been advantageous if we'd had him since his birth, and he would live to end himself for the Lord. However, he is as we would have liked, and that is a sign in itself. Follow them to the end of their path. It is time we hit them with all our might for the day is drawing near.'

A reptilian ran into the room. He was young and agile. He bent his knee to take a bow in one single motion.

'Rise, my boy,' the one in the hood said. 'What is it?'

'They must have found it, the owner of my life,' he said. 'We have lost them.'

'Where?'

He took out a map from his pocket and pointed at it.

The huge one in the shadows rose from his seat, and his menacing scaly face showed itself in the thin ray of light. 'I will give you ten of our best huntsmen. Send them over and track them down. We must know of where it is they are headed. I will arrange for the *Abhishri Battalion* to be at the ready for your signal.'

'As it pleases My Lord,' the one in the hood said, then he bowed and left with his servant.

+++

Adipati had instructed them not to cut across to Itarsi but to keep going onward to Hoshangabad, then head east-south-east through Babai and Managaon. After they had disembarked, the cars were to carry on through Ranipur, heading south to Betul. That is where they were to make a stop for lunch, then drive on to Nagpur to get rid of the vehicles and disappear.

'That should throw them off a bit if they are still on to us,' Adipati said.

Half an hour after they passed Babai, the cars stopped for no longer than half a minute as Adipati had instructed, and all of them got off east of the meandering Tawa river and the railway bridge across it. From there they trekked eastward over a small ridge where Nichola sat. Invisible from a distance, yet easy to make out from the top of the ridge.

Ms Karuna had been right about it not being the best camouflage in daylight, Trish thought. But no one was going to get this close, and from a distance it was invisible.

As they approached her a door opened. Karuna walked out wearing her favourite outfit; shorts and a t-shirt. She welcomed everyone and ushered them inside. After they all crowded inside, she greeted them all with hugs. 'We cannot be seen, so it's best to stay out of sight and in here.'

When Karuna hugged Trish she smiled. 'How wonderful to see you again, Trish.'

'You are looking rather conspicuous,' Maurice remarked.

'Passing cloud,' she replied, letting go of Trish 'We had to save energy as we didn't know for certain when you would arrive, so I put the cameras offline. We blend in perfectly with the captured images projected so long as there are no changes in ambient light. That cloud has darkened the area a bit, and we are still projecting the images from before it showed up.'

'Let me worry about energy now.' Maurice took off his jacket and disappeared behind a door. There was a light hum for a second or two, then it faded away.

'Adi, my dear friend,' they heard him say, as Fakru walked toward them from around the bend of the vessel's core. Adipati hugged him and patted his back. 'Heard you had an encounter with the others on your way here. Let me look at him.'

Lyosha and Sveta helped Vishwas onto a table where they lay him down. 'If you could all go over to the other side, I need to spend a little time with him,' he said. Everyone shifted to around the curve where they wouldn't disturb them any further.

'I hope you made it here comfortably,' Adipati said to Karuna.

'Yes,' she replied. 'The last minute change, and getting him in the middle of the night was a bit of a challenge, but we found a place to land quietly. It just put us back quite a bit energy wise. I was worried a little that we wouldn't make it here and would have to relocate the rendezvous. But it all worked out in the end.' She looked at Trish. 'What is that you are carrying?'

'Weapon,' he replied. 'The Ulka. She and I are getting to know each other. She is really something.' He smiled.

'I should like to know more about her, then. And see you working in tandem. She is alive, right?'

'How did you know?' Trish asked, surprised. A living metal wasn't something he would think a scientist could accept so easily.

'I was at the fort to pick Nichola up. They know of it there. That is all everyone could talk about. Now, I am no yogi, but I've been around these people long enough for the horizons of my mind to broaden a lot.' She winked at Adipati. He smiled back.

'Well then, maybe when I come to see you about Nichola, we could talk about Ulka as well,' Trish said, patting his weapon.

Karuna broke into a laugh. 'Absolutely.'

Coffee was served with some refreshment. Rakshit was the first to attack the food, to the amusement of his peers. They were all relaxed a bit. Lyosha took off his shoes half way and spread his legs a bit as he slouched into his seat.

Maurice had stepped out briefly to inspect the outside. 'The cameras are all online, and we are blending in much better than before,' he said as he came in. 'We should sustain till nightfall. I must rest now since I need to give everything I have to make good time for tonight. Excuse me.' He nodded to everyone, then went further up the curve to pull out a sleeping pod. He crept in and locked himself in it.

Fakru walked up to them with Vishwas in tow a minute later. There was not a scratch on him and all his wounds were fully healed. Fakru looked around curiously. 'What is the diameter of this thing?'

'Nichola is twenty-five metres in diameter and ten metres high at the very centre, while she's a metre and a half thick at the circumference,' Karuna said, pointing to the respective sections as she explained it to him. 'Of course, sitting down on her legs extends one metre below her belly, making her crest eleven metres above ground.'

'I apologise for calling her a thing.' Fakru sat down, smiling apologetically. 'Yes, she does appear quite large compared to her previous prototype. That was eighteen across, wasn't it?'

'Indeed it was.' Adipati smiled at him. 'You say you are not with us, but you are as interested as any of us in matters of our cause.'

'Nonsense. I never said I'm not with you, just that I'm in service of people more than anything else. I'm at your disposal as and when you need me. You know that. I don't understand why you must agitate me so.'

Adipati chuckled. 'You make for such a sight when agitated.' He rose up and excused himself. 'We must all rest a little. It was a long and tiring journey. We must leave past midnight tonight. Let's chat over dinner, which we have to eat out of packets as well. Two of us can keep watch over the monitors while others sleep. I'll take over when someone wants the next shift in three hours.'

+++

'They did not talk much sir, I don't really know much at all.'

The stall keeper did not get many visitors that matched the description these men had given him. It was clear to him immediately that it was in his best interest to tell them everything he knew or could remember. There were four cars in their convoy, all with dark glasses for windows. Not one soul other than the two men standing in front of him had stepped out, but he was sure the cars were full. They were polite, yet he knew they were trouble somehow. The man in the hood was so heavily built, he had never seen another such man; not even in movies.

'I think I heard one of their drivers say "*jungle*",' he blurted.

'Jungle, you say,' the hooded man said. 'Now that is something I can use.'

He looked at the lanky lad next to him and nodded. Then he patted him on his shoulder and turned to his car. The other lad handed him a bundle of currency notes.

'No one will bother you any more,' he said. 'You have done well.'

He turned as well, then they all left in their cars. Twice in a day he had seen such big fancy cars. *What were the odds of that?* He told himself it was probably government looking for fugitives, though he feared the contrary. He looked at the notes in his hand.

That's enough to rid me of all my miseries forever, he thought. *Praise the Lords in the sky.*

+++

While the sun went down, dinner was served in packets from a hot box just as Adipati had said. There were some pleasantries exchanged and stories shared with Karuna and Fakru. There were also a few hushed exchanges between the seniors in the group and some looks exchanged by others. Everyone was aware of the impending danger, but it was clear no one knew what it was and how it would befall them except for Adipati. Trish had a notion he knew a little more still.

After dinner, Trish found Adipati away from the others just for a moment. It was a moment he wouldn't lose. He walked up to him to talk before he returned to where everyone was seated.

'You know more,' Trish said. 'I know you know more, and it is no longer time when you should hold anything back from anyone.'

'I do not know much, son. Whatever little I know I am not going to keep from you. I was myself looking for an opportune moment to talk to you, for whatever I know will only cause unrest as it is nowhere near enough.'

'He said his Lord needed my life. He said you knew,' Trish said while he held Adipati's elbow. 'What does that mean?

You said you would do everything to keep his Lord's prize from him. That would be me, right? The prize?'

Adipati sighed. 'Do you remember how I said it is believed that the first of the nodes were responsible for the destruction and the end of that programme? Well, the one who led the rebellion won the favour of the gods who had not approved of that programme.'

'He needed to side with higher powers of the time to keep standing after what he had done. They, on the other hand, needed someone from outside themselves to stand up to the other faction in their interests. He was made the Lord of the Naags for the time and was given what no other in their species had got before.'

'What?' Trish asked.

'Unending life. He was bestowed with *blessings* such that his body would stop ageing forever and heal itself for perpetuity. So he went on to be known as *Duhsheertatanu,* the one whose body cannot be destroyed.'

'He is the one sending these creatures after me?' Trish asked, looking disturbed with a frown on his face. 'Is he coming for me? What have I done to upset or anger him? Was it something my mother did?'

'He is not in a position to come for you, son.'

'What?'

'Duhsheertatanu went on to marry two women. One was naag and the other human. He had sons from both wives. I do not know much about how and what happened next, but it would seem he was tricked by his human wife into giving away his *praan*. Even as he did, he vowed to return one day to unleash his wrath on humankind for its betrayal, and tasked a council to ensure his return.'

'But he couldn't be killed, you said. What does it mean when you say he gave away his praan? Did he die? If so, how is he to return? Is he coming back from the dead?'

Trish was more nervous than afraid. He felt he'd been developing a taste for this adventure lately, yet it never ceased to surprise him, or even shock him time and again.

'His body could never be destroyed,' Adipati said. 'But the body as a vessel needs *praan* to run it. Just as it is *praan* in the metal that makes your weapon live. Since he could not be killed, he was made to give away the *praan* in him. His body still lies, aged, and not a single day more than it was when he lay it down in their highest temple, awaiting his promised revival.'

'That is all I know. He must need a way to get *praan* in his body again, but why it has to be you, I have no idea. If they wanted *praan* in him and had a way of returning it to the body, why did they wait for so many millennia? It is a question that has plagued us all. Not only could they have used anyone they wanted, if it was his bloodline they were after, they could have had so many before you.'

'What I know is that you are the key, and that his revival means the end of everything we know. If he does get his way, there will be no more living as we have been. He has vendetta and whatever peace we have had for so long will be gone. There will be war, and it would augur much worse for us than for them.'

'None of this makes any sense at all,' Trish said shaking his head. 'Even if it was me they wanted, why did they wait till now? They could have taken me as a baby or a kid. Wouldn't that have been a lot easier?'

'For that, I may have an answer. Though I am not sure if it is exactly how I think it is, it would make sense if you thought about it.'

'Pray tell me,' Trish pleaded.

'When he got blessed with the boon of never ageing, he was twenty-one years old. He lived long after that boon, but even after he gave his *praan* away, the body that lies with them is still that of a twenty-one year old.'

25

«‹«‹ TWENTY FIVE ›»›»

He saw them from the top of the ridge. It wasn't really high but it was high enough. He knew for sure they would still have been on the hunt, had it not been for the stall keeper. Adipati had left a false trail as was expected and though they would have got here eventually, it would certainly not have been this soon. One of the huntsmen started coming back toward him.

Finally.

'Certainly here,' he said as he approached. 'They didn't leave too long back. Must have waited for nightfall, we think. They were definitely here for a while, my Lord Nishoodak.'

'Can you trace them? Or better still, follow them perhaps?' The one in the hood was clearly in a rush.

'It is different from their normal technology, more ancient than modern in their terms we think. There has been a disturbance in energy around this place. We can track that, but it will not be nearly as fast as they left. My Lord, what it means is, the ripples may die down in the time we take to follow them. We may lose the trail near the end.' He bowed, then looked up.

'Hmmm...Well then, we must not be wasting time discussing this. Get to it immediately and tell us where to go.'

+++

It was dark inside, save for the glow of a few dim lights from the electronic controls at the station manned by Karuna.

'No lights on the outside,' Maurice said. 'We can get by undetected so long as we are not in close proximity to towns where some night crawler with a smart phone is shooting stars.'

'It gets dismissed as soon as it is produced anyway, even if there is a video of it,' Karuna added. 'No one can handle this kind of truth. That is good for us, or we would see the end of this before we knew it.'

'Why do you think that happens?' Trish asked.

Adipati was cleaning his weapon. 'It is all about control. The powers that rule the world need to manage what information is available to you and I. They can't have saucers flying through channels of free energy around the earth. Neither ours nor any from outside the planet.'

'So you are saying there are some from outside then, aren't you?'

'Well, they've been around. They always have been. How much they meddle in our affairs, I do not know, but they definitely visit us. Would you not be curious about how something you created was faring on its own if you were them?'

'Aliens?' Trish looked at him in exasperation. 'Seriously? You are going back to aliens again?'

'Aliens, gods, what does it matter? Someone created us. They have to be intrigued, don't you think? If you were to worship the gods as they have been documented, where do you imagine they are? They were right amongst us here on this planet, and then what? Did they cease to exist?'

'Hardly any explanation exists at all. If they were all around, why don't they show themselves any more? Or, maybe they are here now; maybe they look at us from where they are and curse themselves for ever creating us. Maybe they are waiting and hoping they won't have to destroy us and start over. Isn't that what our scriptures tell us?'

Karuna came over leaving her engineer behind with Maurice at the conning station. 'We have slipped into a weaker stream. There are a couple of weak streams to navigate with a lot of noise around them. The professor is best suited for navigation at the moment. I will take over the final leg before we land.'

Adipati nodded. 'Let us concentrate on what we know, rather than what we don't for the moment. Trish, I think it might be a good idea if you could try and meditate with your weapon when we reach the fort. If ever there was a place where the uninitiated could meditate successfully, it is there. You, on the other hand, have had an experience most others never have. I think you could bond with the weapon far better if you meditated.'

Trish grinned. 'I was thinking that myself. I should practice with her in the place the Yakshini visited me. Haven't had a chance to do that yet. I just hope we can find time for it How long do you think it will be before they discover us?'

Adipati's expression changed. There was a look of concern on his face. 'It would be too optimistic to think we might stay hidden long enough for your capture to become irrelevant, but I'm hoping for the best. I believe they have one shot at doing whatever it is they intend to do, and it has to be done at a specific time.'

They all felt turbulence but Maurice looked back at them reassuringly. He then spoke to the engineer and came over. 'All yours Ms Brandt. Final leg. Please cross check the coordinates 3516 7788 for landing.'

'Thank you professor,' she said. 'I know the coordinates well. We will land in the middle of the triangle and hop over a hundred metres to hide her in the gorge north of the LZ. This isn't my first tango.'

'I apologise, my dear. It was not my intention to doubt your abilities. I merely—'

'Oh please, Professor,' she said, giggling, 'relax, I was only pulling your leg.'

+++

'Where to now?' Brij asked. They stood in a triangular plane; that of a rock face nestled amidst snow peaked mountains. Nichola was over the rocks north of them, being buried in snow by Lyosha under the watchful eye of Maurice, with Karuna by his side. Heaps of snow rose from around the place and dumped themselves on to the vessel. It was invisible before long.

'Follow me please,' Adipati said as he led the way.

The triangular plane they stood on was oriented with its apex pointing west. The ridge to the base of the triangle formed a straight line running almost north to south. Near the middle of the base of this ridge were two big rocks facing each other at a metre apart. Adipati walked into the gap between them and disappeared. When Trish peeked in, he could see the passage between the rocks but not Adipati.

'Come on then,' Adipati's voice said from within. Trish slowly started creeping up the passage. After a couple of metres in, he saw a fissure about a metre and a half high, and half a metre wide in the rock to his left. Adipati was inside it.

As Trish slithered in, Adipati started walking down what was a narrow stairway carved into solid rock. He followed him downstairs while the others came in behind him one at a time.

At the bottom of the narrow, winding stairway, there was space enough for one person to stand. There was no flat surface that could have slid to one side as Trish had half expected, but the stairway abruptly ended. There was jagged rock around the tiny space where Adipati stood, and Trish could see no possibility for a doorway anywhere.

Adipati looked at Trish. 'Open up please,' he said, still looking at him.

The block of rock directly behind Adipati moved out and made space enough for one man to enter behind it. 'Welcome to The Fort.'

The newly made space led to a walkway that hung over a huge hall, which was half the size of a football pitch. They walked on the walkway as it ran along one side of the hall and transformed into a ramp at the far end, which was all carved out of the rock that housed the hall. The ramp wont down to the floor of the hall on the end diagonally opposite to the entrance.

In the hall, people had started gathering to take a look at their visitors and welcome them. The murmur of their hushed conversations echoed in the hall. There were men, women and children from what appeared to be of all races in the world. What surprised Trish though, was that while they were cold in their jackets themselves, some of the people in the hall were wearing minimum clothing. A few men were bare chested wearing shorts, some women had shorts and T-shirts on, as did a few children.

'Are they not cold?' he asked Adipati. 'How are they surviving in this chill?'

'The same way yogis always have,' he replied. 'It is yog. They have control over their bodies. Those who don't are wearing jackets; see? Perhaps your brain is too conditioned to see a yogi in a saffron shroud near snow and not wonder, while not being receptive of yogis in shorts?'

'I guess that is it. I even keep forgetting you bunch are yogis too. Practices yog, is yogi. I'll try not to forget.'

At the end of the ramp on the hall's floor stood a few people with hands folded in a *namaste*. At their very front a woman in white tunic and black slacks stood barefoot. 'Welcome Adi,' she said. 'This has to be Trishul.'

Adipati chuckled. 'He doesn't like it when people say that.'

'No, it's fine,' Trish interrupted, flush with embarrassment. 'I am Trishul, miss. You are right.'

'What a pleasure to meet you in person,' she said. 'My name is Dafna. I am the present keeper of The Fort.'

Trish looked up at the wall behind her. The enclosure was three stories high and there were several small balconies on the face of the wall overlooking the hall. People stood in them too, looking down at the newcomers.

'You shouldn't call this a fort. This is at least a township, if not a city. How many people live here?' Trish asked.

'We can accommodate just under a thousand people at any given time, including permanent residents such as myself,' Dafna replied.

'That is a lot,' he said. 'Are they all here to find what they can do?'

'We help them meditate. Some find that they can harness their meditation to connect with the universe, some do not. No one can help another with that. This place has immense energy, and it helps in channelling the mind.' She took his hands in hers. 'You are a funnel in yourself.'

Trish blushed. 'I don't know about that,' he said sheepishly. 'How did you ever manage to create all this?'

'The ancients did. They have done much better with much less, and at times much earlier than this place's creation. The good yogi, our guru, happened to chance upon it and has been here since.'

The rest of their party were all in the hall now, meeting and catching up with friends and acquaintances. Only Trish, Adipati and Brij stood talking to Dafna.

'Come, let's get you settled in first. There are many who wish to talk to you.'

+++

Trish had bathed, changed and eaten. He was, along with the others, to meet with people who wanted to talk to them. Everyone appeared to be calm here and Trish wondered if it was the effect of meditation. He was actually quite keen on having a chat with some people.

It would mostly be Adipati talking, he thought.

When he reached the hall, he half-expected there to be an address of some kind delivered by Adipati for them. But it looked more like an informal chat, with clusters of people crowded around one or the other of his *team*. He saw his father with one such group talking animatedly, so he decided to approach him.

'Don't you ever take them off?' a young man asked, stepping out in front of Trish and pointing at Ulka. The man happened to be not much older than Trish himself.

'She has been alone long enough,' he replied with a smile. 'Besides, she is too powerful to be left without supervision.'

'There are two swords you are wearing. Which one do you mean when you say *she?*' the man asked, looking a little unsure. Nervous even.

'Oh come on boy,' an elderly woman said, who stepped closer behind him. 'Don't tell me you haven't yet heard of the weapon that lives. Those two swords are the one weapon everyone has been talking about.' She bowed to Trish in a *namaste*. 'Pardon my son, dear. He has been meaning to talk to you but is afraid.'

Trish returned the *namaste* with a smile and bowed slightly. 'Afraid of what?' he asked politely, trying to hide his surprise. He stole a look at Adipati. 'Has anyone told you not to speak to me, friend?'

'Afraid of you, of course,' the woman replied. Trish couldn't hold his surprise back any more. She noticed. 'Well, there are all sorts of stories doing the rounds here, my dear. My son is new here; it's only been a week since he arrived. This place does surprise you, you know?'

'You don't say,' Trish said, with the hint of a smile. He looked around the hall once more, then turned back to them. 'I'm afraid not much surprises me any more, after the recent past.'

'So you...' muttered the man, hesitantly. 'You have seen them then? The others. The ones that come from the other place. It is not just a story, is it?'

'Of course, he has,' the woman said as she left them to chat. 'They are, after all, coming for him.'

Trish had a smile on his face, but the man in front of him could sense he was saddened by his mother's remark.

'My name is Jacob,' he said, presenting his hand for a shake. Trish obliged. 'I own a meditation and yog centre in Kerala. Mother has always practised yog, and that is what led me to meditation. I decided there was a market in our town and set up my own centre for it.'

'My sister and I ran the place, while mother decided to retire here. She never said where she was, but visited us often. Then a few months back while meditating, my clothes caught fire. I didn't understand at first and kept mother out of it. But when it happened a couple of times after that, I finally mentioned it to her. I thought she could probably explain what was going on, having been a practitioner her whole life.'

'That was when she told me about this place. I didn't agree with her initially, but have since given up trying to understand it myself now, and came here a week back. My sister Lisa is running our place by herself. To be completely honest, I'm still not fully convinced about being here. They say they will help me. I think I will give them a month.'

'I'm sure you are in the right hands,' Trish said.

'Is it true? Is he really one of them?' Trish heard murmurs behind him. *So that is what they were scared of.*

'I was leading a perfectly normal life too, a few days back,' he said to the young man. 'Everything changed so suddenly for me, yet I had good counsel in Mr Adipati and his friends. This despite being on the run. You are in their sanctuary, friend. I have complete faith you will be alright.'

The man nodded and thanked Trish. They shook hands and he started towards his father again.

Most people walked away as he looked at them, while some smiled and moved on. He felt a tug on his pants and looked down behind him. An adorable little girl stood looking up at him. She looked no more than four or five years old.

'Hello little one,' he said to her as he crouched to meet her at eye level. 'What is your name?'

'Syra,' she replied, beaming. 'What is yours?'

'Trishul. But friends call me Trish.'

'Are you my friend?' she asked.

'If you want me to be. Do you want to be my friend?'

She nodded, then pointed at his swords 'Can I see that?'

'Well, since you are my friend, I must show you if you ask,' he said as her smile widened. 'But you must promise not to take her out of her cover, okay? She's sleeping now.'

'Okay.'

Trish removed the scabbards from over his shoulder and placed them on his knee. 'You can touch her if you like, but she must rest in her cover. She is also my friend.'

She touched the scabbard and moved her hand over to the sword's grip. Then she looked up at him, beaming with joy. He smiled back but felt like something was amiss. He looked at her feet and noticed they were a few inches off the ground. He looked back at her in surprise.

'Sometimes when I'm happy, I fly,' she said, radiating happiness.

A woman came for her shouting her name and held her. 'Forgive her please,' the woman said to Trish. 'I hope she hasn't bothered you much. She doesn't have much company her age here, I'm afraid.'

'Not at all,' he replied. 'Not only is she adorable, she is indeed incredible too.' She stopped floating and stood on the ground.

'Ah yes. That is why I brought her here. Her grandmother, I am told, could levitate as well. She was no more alive when I got married to her father. He knew of this place. He couldn't leave work for a long time, so I got her here. He visits often. He works for Mr Adipati's company now, and not only does he have his support but also his discretion on this matter.'

'Yes, indeed,' Trish said. 'Discreet. That is one thing the old man is.'

'We must move along now,' she said. 'Say bye to Mr Trishul, Syra.'

'He's my friend,' she replied. Then she waved at him. 'Byo Trish.'

'Bye Syra.' He replied, feeling like he breathed fresh air for the first time in quite a while.

+++

'You are sure?' asked the one in the hood.

'Absolutely,' he replied.

'That is good news. You shall let Lord Parimanyu know at the earliest. He will be delighted with the news.' He turned hastily, but then stopped. 'Leave it to me. I will convey the news to him myself. There is also some explaining to do regarding our shortcomings in the chase. It will take some tact to deliver the good news.'

'If I may be pardoned, owner of my life...' He waited for him to acknowledge.

'Go on.'

'Why are they headed in the same general direction as us? I would have thought they should take a path leading as far away as possible.' He bowed, submitting to the will of his master.

Lord Nishoodak took his hood off. 'They exploit the same sources of energy the planet provides as us,' he said, his red eyes gleaming in the light from the torch he held. 'I can bet you, their stronghold will not be too far from the lake of the serpent itself. All we need to do now is to nab the boy and take him over. Our best soldiers are at the ready. Go find me their hiding place, and it shall all be over soon.'

««« TWENTY SIX »»»

Trish spent most of the next day meditating with Ulka, where they both stayed on the beach in his place of refuge. When he reached there, he saw the nautilus shell that the Yakshini had left behind. He never touched it but practised nearby. It was a mercy he never got tired in this place. Maybe it was because his body was actually not here but was meditating back at the fort.

Where was this place? Could it be that this was the other dimension? He was part naag after all. He looked around nervously. Nothing. *It couldn't be another dimension. He never left his own, only rocketed out somewhere within the known dimension itself. Or did he?*

He told himself it was best to keep practising and not waste available time procrastinating. Both Trish and the weapon were communicating almost seamlessly now. She understood his mind and read his apprehensions and plans, while he had come to know of her abilities a lot better. The vines that made the hilt grew or shrank as he needed, could be stiffer than a steel shaft or flaccid as a fibre rope. She perceived threats too, apart from him and if she did, he knew immediately. They were beginning to think as one every time he wielded her.

The next time he sat down for a break, he closed his eyes and thought of the one person who would appreciate his skills with Ulka as much as himself. He longed to see her too, even though he had thought he'd never miss her ever.

Amratji came to his rescue when he was fighting the twins. *Maybe he could call on her again?*

'What is this place?' she asked him. He found her sitting next to him when he opened his eyes. 'You asked me here before, and I knew you were in trouble. This time it doesn't feel so.'

He touched her feet in respect. 'I don't know what this place is. But it is the only place I can be where I find peace. So much so, I can hear anyone, and anyone can hear me apparently.'

'Why did you summon me, Trish?'

'Summon you? Trish looked apologetic. 'It was never my intention to summon you at all. I just wished to see you.'

'You are troubled, son,' she said. 'What is the matter?'

'Why did you send me away? You know I would never hurt you on purpose.'

She took a deep breath. 'When my husband died, there were stories that I heard. Stories that made no sense to me or to anyone else. We knew that he was an able fighter even at the age of seventeen. He would never hesitate to stand up for righteousness, as he did that fateful day.'

'There was no way two unarmed men could kill him, not while he still had his sword with him. But they did, and the stories people told about them were figments of fantasy to me. Told, I thought at the time, to glorify my husband and honour his defeat. I had put that all behind me Trish, buried under immense hatred somewhere within myself.'

'Then during our duel, I saw your eyes turn as they had said theirs had done before they killed him. It was all true. You were one of them, or at least had some connection to them. I did not send you away because I feared you could kill me. I sent you away because I knew I would kill you.'

A tear rolled down her cheek.

'I am sorry,' Trish said, looking away, while trying to hold his own tears back. 'I had no idea. I am one of them, it would seem. But they are the ones I'm fighting to survive.'

'I know that now, from your last ordeal where you sought help with the two you were up against.'

'I have a partner now though,' he said, patting Ulka. 'Her name is Ulka. I will explain what I can about myself to you in a bit. First, let me show you what we can do together.'

+++

Adipati had been summoned by the guru, and was to meet him alone. While he was in a meeting with him, the others waited anxiously. It wasn't customary for the guru to summon anyone. He usually kept to his meditation and met people if they sought guidance.

Dafna paced up and down in front of the group, which was most unusual for her. The others talked amongst themselves since they did not know what to think of it. Trish had been in meditation for over six hours already, but no one was to disturb him. Adipati had made himself clear about that.

When he finally emerged, Dafna almost ran to Adipati. 'What did he have to say?'

'Trish is drawing too much energy. He said anyone could make the deficit easily and be upon us in no time. Whenever he ends his meditation, we must ask Trish to discontinue immediately.'

Dafna looked concerned. 'Why don't we ask him to stop immediately? Why wait for him at all if it is such a big risk?'

'I don't yet understand his meditation and transcendence completely. I can't be sure if it will be okay to disturb him once his meditating has begun. Let him finish this session. I will talk to him immediately after that myself.'

'Talk to who? What's going on?' Adipati turned to find Trish walking toward them. He looked radiant, peaceful, and had a calm about himself.

'Oh good, you are out, Trish,' Adipati said. 'The guru advised me against you meditating with the Ulka. You were drawing too much energy, and he said that could practically be a beacon for trouble.'

'Yes, I realised that myself,' he replied.

Brij stepped forward and gripped his shoulder. 'Maybe you could practice here instead of focusing on your meditation session?'

'I don't think there is any more need for it,' he said. 'I think we understand each other well enough now.'

'I would suggest from first-hand experience that you think that over again,' Maurice said.

Trish laughed. 'I'm sorry Professor. What happened the other night will not happen again. She does not act on impulse any more, and we communicate really well. I did just spend close to thirteen hours with her. I know.'

'Just over six hours, you mean,' Brij said.

'What?'

'Six hours and twenty-three minutes,' Dafna said. 'That is how much time you spent in meditation, son.'

'I had a watch with me,' he said, pointing to his wrist. 'See...Damn! I swear it's gone back in time. I spent just under thirteen hours there. And it felt every bit that long too. Though I felt neither tired nor hungry, or even thirsty.'

'We know nothing of your transcendence, Trish. Time can be relative when it comes to that. Now is not the time to figure it out, however. Right now, we must conserve our energy.'

'Okay,' he said. 'So what's the plan?'

'The plan is to remain undetected here.'

'That is not a plan. That is wishful thinking. What is the plan?'

'That is the only one we have,' Adipati replied.

Trish looked shocked. 'You can't be serious. They are going to find us.'

'Let us hope they don't.'

'Hope? What if they do?' Trish said, his voice shrill with displeasure.

'Then we fight if we must. Every last one of us in here will lay our lives down to see that they don't get you.'

Trish looked at him in horror, completely baffled.

+++

'So how much time do you think, then?' his voice asked, booming out of the weird looking radio.

'We should be upon them in two days,' the one in the hood replied into it.

'You had better,' his voice replied back. 'We are running out of time. If he is not here on the fourth day, we will lose the opportunity.'

'He will be there in three, my Lord.' The effect of the one on the other side of the radio was such that he bowed even as he spoke into it. Then he switched it off and turned to his disciple. 'Tell me we have them.'

'The trackers picked up disturbance, owner of my life,' he replied. 'We have it down to the area. If the disturbance continues, we might even be upon them tonight itself. If not, we will still have them by the morning after tomorrow.'

'Send word to the Abhishri commander. Keep him updated at all times. He must head for the area in question and be ready to strike at the moment when we have a precise location.'

'He has been informed, my Lord. He knows our every progress. He is closing in as we speak and sends his regards to you. He has assured us he is ready to strike at the first command from your Lordship.' He bowed, took the radio off him, then left.

This could well be the break he had been looking for. Reason enough to seek and destroy this hideout the yogis had right under his nose. It was time to give Adipati a demonstration of the powers he had been meddling with. He wished they wouldn't give the boy up till the very end. If they did, he would have to abandon his onslaught on the yogis to deliver the boy as soon as possible. If they stayed hidden in the pit, however, he could destroy it before taking the boy.

Adipati would count on a sacrifice to save the boy. He was counting on Adipati to do just that.

+++

'No,' Trish said. 'We are not bringing the battle here. There will be no discussion on this.'

'But our best chance is to stay hidden,' Adipati argued. 'This is the only place we can count on at the moment.'

'These people have no idea what is lurking out there,' he said, pointing toward the residences, his eyes bloodshot. 'We cannot bring war upon innocents. They have nothing to do with any of this. They can't even handle themselves. Most of them don't know how to.'

'We have no other option, Trish.'

'But there are children here.' Trish looked over his shoulder at Syra. She held her mother's hands with a smile on her face, standing six inches off the floor. 'If you will not come with me, I will step out by myself. Sveta says they will be in the vicinity tomorrow night. I will draw them away from this place and fight to my death.'

'If they get you, all these people are doomed anyway. All of mankind might be drawn into war. If Duhsheertatanu rises, it will be the fall of peace and equilibrium. You will allow that, but not this?'

'I intend not to fall into their hands. If they get me, however, and kill me or incapacitate me in whatever way, I shall have no control over what befalls these innocent people. I can die with that, but I cannot live with having so much innocent blood on my hands. If I'm dead and cannot prevent their wrath, then that's that. I'm dead. But so long as I breathe, I cannot wilfully put innocent lives in harm's way just to survive. I have been brought up better than that.'

'We could fight them,' Rakshit chipped in.

'Do not encourage him, boy,' Adipati snapped, clearly angry.

'I am not so comfortable with bringing them here either, to be honest,' Lyosha said.

Adipati was enraged. Blood made it's way to his face and the veins on his forehead began to show. He tried hard not to shout. 'You think I want this? We are out of options. This is statistically the safest bet we can make.'

Everyone in the hall turned to look at them.

'Yeah, I don't much care for statistics lately,' Trish quipped. He stepped in front of Adipati and held his shoulders. 'We all know you have the best interests at heart for everyone. But please understand, I can simply not have this on my conscience. Yes, I still have one in case you wonder. I'm not completely from the other side.'

Adipati held the back of a chair for support. 'We won't stand a chance. Not with what I expect is coming for us.'

'Then we die fighting like men,' Brij said. 'All of us. My son and I, if it comes to that. We will all die fighting to preserve what it is you are trying to preserve. Not like cowards using innocent lives as a buffer to prolong our own.'

 Trish hugged his father when he saw a tear escape his eyes. 'Your mother would have expected no less either,' he whispered to Trish. 'I am proud of you son.'

'And I of you, Dad,' he whispered back.

+++

'In this gorge here,' Maurice said, pointing on a map. 'Two kilometres to the west.'

Everyone looked at each other and nodded.

'If we lose, all this would have been for nothing,' Adipati said, his head hung low.

'Cheer up old man,' Lyosha said as he thumped his back. 'Let us show them what hell might look like.'

Adipati forced a smile. 'Let us indeed.'

Sveta stood up. 'They will be very close by tomorrow night. If we don't have them drawn away by then, it will be too late to keep them from finding the fort. We must be ready to lead them to the gorge before that.'

'Let us draw them tomorrow while there is still light,' Maurice added. 'They will be far more formidable in the dark.'

'No matter when you draw them, they will not strike before nightfall,' Adipati said, pacing next to the table they had placed the map on. 'If I know anything about them, they have their best battalion out for us, and the operation will be overseen by a Lord of repute. My money is on the Abhishri Battalion and Lord Nishoodak. He will wait for nightfall to strike.'

'Whatever the outcome, let us draw them away as soon as we can tomorrow,' Trish said, leaning over the map. He saw Adipati pacing uneasily and stood up straight.
'I suggest we set out in the morning and draw them out once we are there in the afternoon. Then, if they attack, we fight. If they don't, we wait. At least this place will be left safe.'

Adipati realised the boy was having to step up and that he himself was not helping at all. He stopped and sighed, then he looked at each one of them in turn and said 'We must take a good, long rest tonight. We are putting everything on our abilities tomorrow. They are pressed for time, and if we can defeat them somehow, we might just get done with this cursed quest for good.'

««« TWENTY SEVEN »»»

In the morning, they said their goodbyes. Everyone in the fort said they would meditate in favour of Trishul. Trish thanked them for the positivity they promised. He met Dafna with the others but wanted to meet Jacob and Syra in person, all on his own. He asked Jacob to keep faith in the establishment and meditate and practice as directed. They were his best chance at conquering his difficulty.

Trish told Syra he would be back soon. She levitated above the ground with a big smile on her face. 'Finish your work fast,' she said. He kissed her forehead.

'What do we need food for?' Brij asked Adipati as they slung the day packs over their shoulders.

'If they make us wait till sundown as I believe they will, I would like to have something for lunch,' he replied with a nervous smile.

They waved to everyone in the hall as they exited through the stairway one after the other. Soon they were out walking toward the gorge.

'What will they do with me?' Trish asked Adipati. 'If they get me, I mean. What then?'

'There are places in both their dimension and this one that are exactly the same. Of course, there are gateways and portals like the Well of Sheshna and Patalpani and the others, but the other ends to them are not identical to ours. I mean, if you were to be taken through the well, you might come out of water on the other end, but it wouldn't be a well like on this side.'

'There is a lake not very far from here that is exactly the same as it is on the other side. This I only know of as I have been told, I have never been to the other side myself. The body of Duhsheertatanu lies not too far from the lake. That is where they would take you if they had you here.'

'Where is it? The lake?'

'It is a small lake around eighty kilometres East-North-East of the fort. It has been known as the lake of the serpent for millennia.'

'Eighty kilometres East-North-East? Wouldn't that be deep in the...'

'Disputed territory? Yes, it is. Don't tell me after everything you have seen and been through recently, that you are worried the Chinese will find you being taken by Naags within disputed territory.'

Adipati still looked uncomfortable with what they were going to do. Trish realised he would rather have them stay in the fort. But deep inside he knew they had taken the righteous decision, if not the right one.

They kept on walking and made small talk, trying to keep their spirits high. Everyone knew what was to come next was the final frontier. It would be much more than a few from the other side trying to capture a boy. If what they had seen of them on the highway was anything to go by, the onslaught of their best in huge numbers wasn't something to look forward to.

'How many are we expecting?' Lyosha asked.

'Their battalions are usually four to five hundred strong, but if I'm right and they have the Abhishri on this, expect two fifty of their best. They try to keep a smaller, tighter unit for better precision. Also expect nodes, trained for years together just to fine tune their nodal skills.'

'Doesn't sound very encouraging,' Mugdha muttered.

'That is because it isn't!' Adipati snapped back.

'We are here,' Sveta declared from up front. They stepped into the gorge and walked to the centre of the expanse before them.

Adipati looked up to the ridge on the north, then to the south. 'I guess this spot is as good as any. Time to draw them out.'

+++

'We have them, my Lord,' the young one declared as he rushed in the tent.

'Good,' he replied, taking his hood off. His scaly face had a triumphant smile on it. 'The Lord Medhavin has been informed then?'

'Yes, owner of my life. We shall reach alongside them in a couple of hours.'

'You have done well. This will not go unnoticed, I promise you.'

'I do my Lord's bidding. Shall we commence?'

+++

Trish opened his eyes and looked up at the top of the northern ridge. They had arrived. He could see at least a hundred of them. There was no mistaking the fact that they were generally larger and better built that humans, but then these were a battalion of fierce fighters. Trish could see that far easily and could make out the scales on their bodies. *Did they turn or were these ones always in this state?*

He saw Adipati was looking at them as well while the others were still meditating.

He got up and looked to the southern ridge. There was at least a hundred more of the reptilian foes. Adipati was right about the numbers, which implied he might be right about the battalion's skills as well.

Sveta opened her eyes and nudged Lyosha and Vishwas. They, in turn, nudged the others. They knew this was coming, but to see it now in front of their eyes as battle loomed over them was something else. There was a lot of nervous energy and for the first time Trish felt it too. Not like he would have done by looking at their body language previously, but he actually *felt* the energy like he imagined Maurice would.

'Should we draw weapons?' Trish asked.

'They will not attack without a declaration,' Adipati replied. 'Honour and the rest of it. Just like Varadh did, remember? They will have someone deliver a message of their imminent attack first.'

'Didn't seem like that in Benares,' Brij quipped.

'That wasn't them,' Adipati said. 'It was RD. Human. They will not do it. What the twins did was man to man combat, so that was different. But a battle is never going to happen without a forewarning first.'

They could feel their gazes upon them, as every adversary looked down from either side while the few stood defiantly in the middle of the gorge. Adipati looked around as if looking for someone in particular, perusing through them till he stopped and squinted. He bowed slightly and nodded in acknowledgement at someone. Two reptilians repeated the gesture. Trish could see one of the two give instructions to someone from the party behind them. A couple of minutes later, three soldiers darted downhill toward them.

Adipati cautioned the others not to engage as the approaching party was expected only to deliver a message. 'Do not let them in my head when they communicate,' he instructed Sveta.

When the three messengers reached them, they bowed to Adipati, then one of them offered his hands to him. Adipati took his hands in his own and closed his eyes. They held hands for an uncomfortably long minute. Sveta broke sweat, trying to concentrate hard. They eventually let go and nodded to each other as the messengers turned and darted back upwards, never slowing down.

Adipati turned round to face everyone. 'They give us until sundown to hand Trish over, after which they will attack. They will mark the declaration of an attack by firing a single blazing arrow toward us. Once the arrow hits the ground, we will be at a point of no return. They shall come charging at us from both sides.'

'I wonder if it is best I walk over to them and see where that goes?' Trish muttered.

'I have heard enough from you,' Adipati snapped. 'Let us eat and rest for a few hours. One person keeps watch as we take turns. At sundown, let us give them all we have got. Nobody gets Trish till they have got us all.'

+++

'Will they give him up?' asked Lord Medhavin, commander of the Abhishri.

Lord Nishoodak looked at him as he slipped the hood off his head. 'They would have given him up long ago if they had the slightest doubt in their minds about fighting us. No, they will not give him up. Look at them having lunch. They await the onslaught. One must credit them for valour if nothing else.'

'In that case, we will have the boy not now, but tonight. That is all the difference it makes.'

'But it isn't, Lord Medhavin,' he barbed at him. 'The bastards gave themselves up so as not to give up their stronghold. We will have the boy tonight, but victory would have been so much sweeter, had we got the hideout as well.'

'I could spare some of my men to hunt for it till dusk,' he replied. 'They could return in time for the charge. Even if you want for them to keep hunting and not return, I could do this with half my strength.'

'Do not underestimate them, Lord Medhavin. Anyway, the boy is what we want. The stronghold would have been a trophy, but the mission is the boy. Let us stick to the task at hand.'

+++

Everyone waited anxiously at sundown for the arrow to be shot. They had rested enough, and by this time they had all come to the same state of mind. It was inevitable, but the wait only made it more agonising.

'Bring it on already,' Rakshit muttered.

They saw a flame at the top of the ridge on the north. Silhouettes all around looked like the enemy was huddling in for a discussion. Someone lit an arrow.

Here it comes.

The arrow went flying in the air and gained altitude. All eyes followed it in the gorge as it went higher than they had imagined. At the crest of its trajectory, it was already halfway toward them. Then they saw it heading straight for where they were.

'Who the fuck can shoot this far with a fucking bow?' Brij exclaimed.

'Node,' Adipati said.

'It's going to reach us.' Lyosha looked straight at it, scratching his chin. There was admiration on his face.

'Fuck!' Brij exclaimed again.

Adipati noticed Trish smiling at the arrow and shifting slightly in his place. *What the fuck was he up to?*

The arrow came whistling down toward them. Trish leapt into the air – slightly to his right – then caught it airborne, three metres above the ground. Before anyone could utter a word, he turned around once and landed on his right knee, breaking the arrow in two on his left thigh as he did. He then stood up, waved the arrow and gestured at the ridge, beckoning their adversaries.

'The fuck was that for?' asked Lyosha.

Trish smiled. 'They said the arrow would hit the ground. I just didn't feel like it.'

'Who shoots an arrow this big?' Brij asked, having difficulty coming to terms with the feat he had witnessed.

Atop the ridge, they saw Trish waving the arrow and gesture at them. 'The boy is audacious, I can certainly see that,' Medhavin said.

Nishoodak turned to address him. 'I assure you, he is not an unworthy adversary, which only makes my faith in the council stronger, to be honest. There is no doubt in my mind that the Lord is finally within our reach.' He then turned to the archer who had shot the arrow. 'Good shot, Pateeyati. You know we are counting on you to deliver tonight. You cannot fail the Lord.'

'As I shall not,' she replied, kneeling on one knee in respect. Her eyes, however, were fixed on something. The gleaming bracelet on the boy's wrist that reflected the flames of the arrow, burning her heart and filling her with rage. She could see the nautilus shell on it.

Motherfucker!

+++

Before they knew it, the naags were upon them. There was crackling of thunder in the gorge as Maurice snapped his whip like never before. Feet sank into firm ground as Rakshit moved through some of them, cracking his hammers down on their bodies. Some froze while others burnt as Adipati led from the front with shaft in hand. Vishwas and Mugdha negotiated attacks on them with deft moves and counter attacks.

The disoriented naags tried to cope with cries from every direction as Sveta brought down her batons onto them. Not many could come very close to Lyosha thanks to his rings of flying khukuris. Whoever tried to break through them got cuts and stabs; others got fingers and limbs cut off while a head became severed. Brij played the trustworthy wingman to whoever he could help effectively, with both his guns.

But none of this was as spectacular as a whirring Trish with his weapon. Held together as one, his blades were doing the worst damage. The only split second he ever was still for was when he changed the direction of rotation of either himself or his weapon. His weapon was like the blades of a helicopter moving through the air as if being offered no resistance at all. It went through limbs and bones like a sharp knife through paper. All eyes in the small clique atop the ridge were on him.

And he had not yet turned.

'Beautiful,' Medhavin remarked, admiration clear in his gleaming eyes. 'The Lord is almost home.'

Nishoodak smiled back and looked at him with a raised brow. 'Still think you could have done this with half your strength?'

'I wouldn't yet discount us,' Medhavin replied, watching the onslaught in awe. 'But I have no hesitation in admitting they are admirable and far better than I could have imagined.' He looked back at him and saw Nishoodak addressing Pateeyati.

'Ready yourself young lady,' Nishoodak said. 'Let him wear out a little and spend that time well, study his every move. When the time is right, I shall seek your ministrations as it were. We are depending heavily on you. This is what you have trained for I am sure, for as long as you can remember.'

She nodded, bent her knee once, then went to the edge. She planted several arrow tips down into the ground, held her bow, and lay down next to them. Fixated on Trish, she took a deep breath.

That bracelet should have been on my wrist. Those conniving Yaksh. They say they are on nobody's side, but they favour you rats and have done so for as far back as time goes.

She held her breath, became motionless with her eyes fixed on him. There was a flicker on her forehead as she lay still.

+++

After an hour into battle, nearly three platoons of the Abhishri were either dead or unable to move. Devastation had rained on the attackers that had been sent, while the little band at the centre of the gorge sustained no real damage. Whatever was left of the first onslaught, Adipati and his crew were running over admirably.

'We need to send them all in,' Nishoodak said, pacing along the ridge near their command post. 'Our strength is in numbers. I cannot, for the life of me, imagine why you would hold out.'

He looked up at Medhavin who turned away, looking into the battlefield. Nishoodak walked up to him and placed his hand on his shoulder. 'Forgive me Lord Medhavin. I do not doubt your leadership or strategic prowess. I guess I have been away from battles too long and forgot my place. The corridors of the council can change you like you wouldn't imagine.'

'It is no bother. We are doing alright for now, though I must credit our enemy for being far more formidable than I had thought so far. They have gone through three dozen of my men. I am sure we will lose many more tonight, but this is a loss we are all willing to bear for success.'

'A few minutes more, if you will, my Lord. Let them finish with the remnants of the first platoons and build their hopes up. I will send in everyone soon enough.' Medhavin turned and called out to his lieutenant who was keeping a distance, should his Lords have to discuss matters above the scope of his role in the battalion.

He came rushing to his master's side and bent his knee. 'At my command,' Medhavin said, his brows narrowed and his eyes devoid of emotion, 'I want the *Atibal* to attack from both sides at once, and the *Dhanvin* to take positions at the feet of the ridges. Pateeyati and the other three will remain with us.'

The lieutenant nodded, thumped his chest as he rose, then left.

All foot soldiers to attack at once and the archers set up to cover them. Nishoodak finally saw some merit in the plans. It was now looking like the battle would be what he had wanted all along. *They would get the boy.*

Medhavin turned to where the nodes were. He wrote something in the snow in front of Pateeyati's face. *Be ready* she read without moving a muscle. He signalled two others to their positions and called out to the fourth.

'Come with me,' he said to her. 'I will need you to communicate with the troops.'

She sat on her feet by his side as he put his hand on her shoulder. She closed her eyes, and her forehead began to glow.

'Stand by my brothers,' he said in his mind. *'It is almost time to show the Lord home.'*

The lot of them thumped their chest and nodded.

+++

'Why are they holding back?' Brij questioned rhetorically as he took aim at a naag crawling toward Vishwas. He was about to shoot when Vishwas' spear swung behind him, embedding the rear head into the enemy's chest.

He turned to Brij who was finishing the last of the ones he was fighting. 'What's the play here?' he asked. 'I'm sure there's something fishy.'

Adipati approached him as the others started coming too, since a flash had emanated from atop the ridge. 'The real onslaught is coming,' he said, changing his stance, then looked at Trish. 'Here they come. I don't know if you can yet turn at will now son, but now would be the time to do it if you can. Show no mercy.'

They turned to face the enemy who was almost upon them as a barrage of arrows rained from the skies on both sides. 'To the death,' Adipati yelled as his staff started glowing amber and blue. They all yelled out their fierce defiance in the face of oncoming danger. Trish roared like they had never heard before while he transformed his physical form and split his weapon, holding one sword in each hand.

They dodged arrows and fought through scores of unrelenting, fearsome warriors who targeted each of them in different formations. Adipati knew their commander was guiding them from atop the ridge. They moved in infallible sync, which could only be achieved with the entire army conforming to one mind. Besides, he could see the loom of light where the commander was, and every time it flickered, the troops changed formation.

The Abhishri had managed to wedge distance between them and they were no longer fighting close to each other. At least that bit of their ploy was working for the naags. They didn't seem to be gaining much on the individuals yet. To the credit of the archers, the *Dhanvin* were shooting regularly without their arrows ever brushing any of their own. Arrows came straight for one of the yogis every single time. Though they were doing much less damage than they were intended for, the gradual bruises on the yogis from the brushing of the arrows began to show.

When Medhavin was satisfied with the distance between Trish and the rest of them, he walked over to Pateeyati. *Now,* he wrote in the snow in front of her eyes. The flicker on her forehead steadied to a mellow glow. She stood up, moving for the first time since she lay down.

'There is no pattern,' she said, 'but it can be done.'

'It must be.' Their leader placed a hand on her shoulder, looking intently into her eyes. 'We are banking on you to deliver, Pati,' he said in a softer tone. 'You cannot let us down. You cannot let me down.'

'Yes father,' she whispered back. She picked up an arrow, drew it on her bow, then steadied it as her forehead exhibited a soft flicker again. A couple of seconds later, she let the arrow fly.

+++

Trish enjoyed himself amidst his attackers. His effortless dancing with the swords kept baffling them. Every time they thought they were weighing in on him, it turned out he was only making them dance to his tune. Their strikes were coordinated, and he knew well that he wasn't really fighting that unit of soldiers, but was fighting only one person. Someone was choreographing their moves.

As he flipped against a rock to land behind the naag to his back, two of them flanked him from the left while the ones on the right drew him toward themselves.

Really, now?

Trish jabbed with his right hand as if playing into their ploy for a second, while his left hand readied for the assault behind him. Without pulling back on his jab, he leaned back as the sword in his left arm sliced through bone. He sprang backward as if uncoiling a wound up spring within him, then landed his right sword on the other assailant. His head rolled even as he sprung up again to slice the incoming arrow in half. He looked at the ridge top and hissed before he continued with his rampage.

+++

Pateeyati let two arrows fly this time. Medhavin was not amused with the ease with which the boy had tackled the first one. He was exactly where the arrow came down on him, which meant she didn't do anything wrong. She just had to do better. He saw them both land on him. The first was where he was and the second was where he had shifted to avoid the first. She had done brilliantly, but he stepped out of the way of one and despite ending up exactly where the second landed, he deflected it with a deft touch of his sword.

Damn! Three arrows next. *They were all spot on!* Pateeyati had been flawless with her aim, yet he didn't even look at them while deflecting all three.

'How?' he muttered rhetorically.

'It is as if he is two persons,' she replied. 'I can imagine how he will move, but he knows where the arrows are without looking at them.'

Nishoodak walked up to them. 'The weapon,' he said, gritting his teeth. 'The weapon fights in tandem with him.'

'So it is the weapon that senses the arrows?' asked Pateeyati, half exclaiming. *The fucker has everything!*

'The weapon can act in his defence, but it has to learn from him. It is the boy. If he didn't ever see them, he must be hearing them coming, at least once they're near. He is after all, one of us as well. Then there's the communication between him and the weapon; together they are proving to be quite the nightmare now, aren't they? What do you suggest we do next, Lord Medhavin?'

Medhavin stared intently at the battlefield, trying to find a breakthrough. He looked at each of his enemy, one after the other. The one with the hammers, the one with batons, Adipati with his staff, the other one, and the other, the father and so on.

The vulnerable father looked the most promising. He would be an easy target if he hadn't anyone teaming up with him. The father could be used to make the son yield, however difficult it might be. After all, what was he without the help of the others he was with? Within the three minutes he'd been observing him, the father had already been saved twice by the crack of the dark one's whip.

His brow furrowed. *That was it.* He looked back at Nishoodak with a wicked smile on his face. 'I know what we must do.'

+++

Adipati noticed how the bigger arrows were shot by the node from the ridge. He'd already started wondering how they were planning to make it work, but the arrows had stopped. They were surely having a discussion on their next move up there.

He was busy dealing with the odd arrow coming down at him while fending off the foot soldiers, but Adipati's primary focus was on the strategy in play by his adversaries. He took note of how each of his friends were placed from the corner of his eye, and tried to keep himself abreast of their movement. They all seemed to be doing rather well, but there was nothing exceptional about the onslaught they were facing. This wasn't all there was; he was sure of it.

The node's arrows were the only extraordinary feat so far, and it hadn't worked. He knew something bad was coming for them. *But what?*

He moved closer to Trish while going through the unit that was upon him. Freezing, burning, then freezing again, Adipati realised two other nodes had started firing the long arrows from the other ridge. They seemed to randomly land in the middle of nowhere.

Something was up.

Adipati tried to edge toward Trish a little faster, but resistance from that end started getting stronger, leaving the side opposite open. He took a step back and noticed this was happening to the rest of them as well. The long arrows started making their way to where Brij and Maurice were, till they scared Brij enough to have to fall away from Maurice.

'Brij! They are going for the father to get to the boy,' Adipati thought.

For everyone else, the archers on the ground let loose a volley of arrows that made the sky rain intermittently. Fighting the troops while avoiding the arrows consumed them enough not to be able to make ground toward Trish or Brij. Maurice was between the two, with Trish less than a hundred metres east of him, and Brij closer to the west.

In a bid to separate Brij from him, they appeared to be pushing Maurice closer to Trish. The foot soldiers of the Abhishri were being choreographed into enveloping Brij, Maurice and Trish in one big ellipse, while the others were kept out of their reach within their own smaller rings. From above they appeared to have taken a shape similar to a knuckle duster. But the soldiers that formed the ellipse had already started driving a wedge between Maurice and Brij, and it was apparent to Adipati that Brij would soon be in a rather tight spot all by himself. His bullets alone were not doing much harm to the attackers anyway.

He looked at Sveta and communicated with her.

'Rush to help Brij,' her voice echoed in all their minds. 'Trish still has Maurice. As soon as Brij is safe, we will all regroup with them and fight together as a unit.'

Each one of them started pushing harder to get through to Brij. They concentrated their efforts in one direction which also meant the resistance from that end began to weaken ever so slightly. Lyosha was closest to Brij and was the first to break through.

With Lyosha by his side, Brij started making some progress with his guns. He would injure, while Lyosha would let a blade fly onto the wounded. The others were making their way as well, and appeared to be sure of breaking through soon enough. Then, clearly on a cue, the Abhishri let them all in at once to where Lyosha and Brij were.

'What the fuck just happened?' Adipati exclaimed. The others were equally clueless.

In the meantime, the archers on ground started advancing toward them, shooting arrows to cover for the large number of retreating foot soldiers around them. They were all heading for Trish and Maurice.

What had they missed?

The two nodes started shooting the longer arrows at the larger group now. They missed most of them, but the arrows were raining in hard. They were not going for accuracy, Adipati decided. They were going for scores of arrows instead. To keep them heavily engaged, obviously; but to what end?

He stole a glance over at Trish and Maurice amidst the barrage of arrows. They faced a change of strategy as well. Some archers kept cover while others darted in and out of their encirclement, almost taunting Maurice.

Why were they concentrating on Maurice?

Soon enough, Maurice did get irritated as was evident by the way he went berserk with his whip. Unleashing fury at every single one of them trying to dart toward him, his whip made unprecedented thunderous sounds as it charged, then discharged immense amounts of energy from the atmosphere.

Adipati realised it was too late when he saw the loom of soft light atop the ridge. He shouted at the top of his voice, but it was lost from the deafening thunder Maurice unleashed. Even Sveta couldn't get through the charged space between them. Maurice was unstoppable.

Pateeyati rained down every arrow she could one after the other at such speed, that her arms did not appear to be moving, from a distance.

Trish noticed the others trying to say something and rushed in to Maurice's aid, only to calm him down. He sliced his way through half a dozen soldiers he was fighting, missed three arrows that came for him, deflected another two, then leapt toward Maurice.

The sixth arrow went through his right thigh and pinned him to the ground while the seventh went through his right shoulder and came out of his gut.

28

«««« TWENTY EIGHT »»»»

As Trish fell, everyone else fell apart. Maurice hesitated for a bit when he realised what had happened. In that moment he heard Sveta in his mind and froze for an instant, as the result of his deafening assault dawned on him. A few of the Abhishri took advantage and managed to knock him down. They were almost upon him when Rakshit broke through and came to his rescue, filled with rage over the sight of Trish on the ground.

A few of the assailants started pulling Trish away while others stood together as a wall to defend them. Adipati's motley band of yogis started breaking apart instead of fighting as a unit. Brij made a dash for his son, only to be dealt a blow with a heavy club on his chest. He fell to the ground on his back as Lyosha rushed in to his aid. If the blow weren't as mistimed as it was, it would have killed him, instead it made him black out, and Vishwas tried to drag him to safety.

'Thoy mustn't yet away with him,' Adipati yelled, but they were.

The yogis' own disjointed efforts to defend their fallen comrades kept them busy. They had all seen the unbelievable speed of the Abhishri soldiers when they had dashed down with their commander's message. There was no way they could keep up with them, now that they had Trish.

Adipati cursed himself for not seeing through the enemy's plan, and rushed everyone to Brij. In the moment of self-loathing, he took an arrow to his right arm. Sveta took another to her shoulder, while trying to push him out of its trajectory.

Trish was halfway up the ridge by the time this had happened. Two soldiers followed behind him and his captors, lugging his swords with all their might. Adipati nodded at Sveta and turned around so she could pull the arrow out of his arm from behind him. Vishwas and Mugdha covered them, while heavily bruising themselves.

Sveta then pulled the arrow out from her own shoulder and winced. Adipati leapt toward the nearest soldier and rammed an end of his staff into his chest, freezing it. Vishwas buried his spearhead into the frozen chest. Adipati touched his own wound gently with the other end of his staff, cauterising it and repeated the action for Sveta.

They were going to lose Trish. That was certain now.

He looked around and realised that a sizeable portion of the remaining Abhishri had left. They were weak but could manage to fight off the remaining troops. If only they could do it fast enough to give chase to the captors, they still might have a chance of saving him.

+++

'Let us head back immediately,' Nishoodak said.

Medhavin looked disgruntled. 'We have the boy. We can launch a full-scale assault on them with all the men we have. The Dhanvin can also join the Atibal in close combat. They have become frail. We can finish them off and have nothing to look back over our shoulders for.'

'Oh, and we still have time. I do not want to leave those soldiers there by themselves. They are the best we have.'

'Of that, I have no doubt,' Nishoodak replied after patiently letting him finish what he had to say. 'Therefore, they are capable of winning on their own, but we must make haste.'

'They might still not last against such formidable adversaries by themselves. My men are injured too.'

'How to fight your battle is your decision to make, Lord Medhavin. Whether to fight or not is mine. We leave now.' Nishoodak turned to Pateeyati. 'Ask me for anything, and you shall have it, child. Anything.'

'I want that bracelet,' she replied, pointing at the nautilus bracelet from the House of Yaksh.

Nishoodak laughed. 'Kids,' he said, looking at Medhavin. 'She could have asked me for anything in our worlds here, and she wants the bracelet. Go ahead child, you can wear it.'

'I have no desire to wear it,' she said. 'I deserve it, but with dignity, not by stealing another's. It's just that I can't stand him wearing it.'

'We are ready,' Medhavin said, his tone brazenly demonstrating displeasure.

+++

Adipati and the rest made a final assault with all they had left on the remaining assailants. The Abhishri were admirable fighters. They were skilled and utterly resilient; not to mention much stronger and gifted with heightened senses owing to their origins. But the coterie of yogis they were up against, were no mere humans and they were losing to them.

Not fast enough for Adipati though. He knew they were losing time and would have to chase the naags soon if they were to have another shot at saving Trish. He looked at Sveta and heard her in his mind. 'Too risky. They will have no weapons and will land in the middle of this. We have to finish the last of these soldiers before we can summon them.'

Maurice's voice echoed in. 'We can hold these fuckers. The rest of us can stay for this, while you could start falling back with Lyosha and Sveta. Call them over and leave.'

'I'm in for this plan,' came Mugdha's affirmation.

'Me too,' Rakshit re-affirmed. 'I can kick their butts by myself if you like. Go get the kid.'

'I'm staying,' Vishwas said, joining in.

"Then it is done. Take Brij with you. He can recover in their care when you drop them off,' Maurice said with finality in his tone. He unfurled his whip toward the sky as a bolt of lightning met its tip. As he cracked the whip, unleashing shock at the soldiers before him, everyone heard him shout, 'Down with you fuckers.'

Adipati nodded at Sveta. She closed her eyes as Lyosha and Adipati fell back with her. They managed to put a decent distance between themselves and the others within five minutes. The odd arrow that made it to them met with Lyosha's orbiting *khukuris.*

They all heard the thrum and felt the turbulence as they looked up behind them in surprise. A not-so-disguised amateur looking version of Nichola flew in and landed heftily west of them, then a door fell open.

'Sorry,' Karuna yelled, 'I had to get him too...there was no time to get Nichola along.'

Fakru gestured at them to run along, from behind her.

'You are a godsend,' Lyosha said as they ran into the craft and shut the door behind them.

Brij had to be helped along and could barely speak. All he could manage was, 'Trish.'

'So where is Trish?' asked Fakru.

'They got him,' Adipati replied with a sense of urgency, helping Karuna take off again. '35397822,' he said to Karuna, who nodded as the craft took off.

She had real concern on her face - her eyes welled up a little and her lips trembled. But she turned around with a sense of urgency and headed straight to the navigation console.

'We are a small unit on a craft, and they are too many,'Adipati explained. 'With some luck, we should be able to intercept them before they make it to the lake. We have no hope otherwise.'

He looked grim, and his wound made him uncomfortable. Fakru came over, but Adipati stopped him, gesturing toward Brij. 'Him first. He is in bad shape.' He then turned to Karuna again. 'Drop us at the lake even if they're there and return to the fort. Be at the ready for our help, should we make it back.'

'You will,' she said, assuring herself more than the others.

Brij had come back to his senses. 'I'm going in,' he said. 'I don't care if I die there. I'm not staying over as long as my son is in danger.'

Adipati deliberated on this for a bit, then hesitantly nodded. 'Alright,' he said.

Lyosha and Sveta looked at him in surprise. Lyosha almost said something but held back. *Now was not the time.*

'Fifteen minutes,' Karuna declared. 'But we will slow down considerably, so I'd say twenty. She isn't Nichola.'

Brij sat on a stool as if nothing had happened to him, loading up his guns and checking for extra magazines. Fakru moved to help Sveta and was almost done.

'I'll try to get a fix on them,' she said once Fakru had finished. As he turned his attention to Adipati, she sat on the deck and closed her eyes.

'Time to heal that wound,' Fakru said.

'Nothing can heal my wounds, friend. But you could take care of this hole the arrow left in my body.'

+++

'Must we carry his weapon with us?' Medhavin asked Nishoodak as they prepared to enter the waters.

'If we have it when the Lord returns, it will be *his* weapon. Must I tell you what that means?'

'The lake on this side shrinks,' Pateeyati mumbled.

'They are eating away their home, the foolishly arrogant bastards. They will have no lake here in some time.' Nishoodak said with disdain in his voice for humans. 'The pilferage of their world affects ours too. That is why the Lord must return. Their ways must end with them.'

'We have everything all assembled, Lord,' Medhavin said. 'We have a periphery set up and are good to go.'

Nishoodak nodded. 'We are a large unit. The egress will be massive and could remain open for a couple of days...'

'I am leaving the nodes here,' Medhavin interrupted. 'They will lay hidden and keep a watch on the lake, and take care of any humans attempting to enter. I will also have nodes at the ready on our end to come over and take care of it should they be alerted from here.'

'Let us proceed then,' Nishoodak said as he stepped into the water. 'The boy comes with us; and Pateeyati. She is a hero, and our people need to know that. We will send a couple of nodes over in her stead the minute we are on our soil. And I know we all want to return at once, but let's try and keep the egress as small as we can.'

Medhavin rolled his eyes and shook his head. His daughter pursed her lips to keep from giggling.

+++

'They are crossing over,' Sveta exclaimed. 'From what I can tell, Trish already has!'

Adipati frowned. 'We must go in right after them, if not with.'

'But do we know how?' Karuna questioned. 'I mean, the lake is sitting right there, but how does one cross it?'

'They were entering the lake,' Sveta said.

'Then we must enter too.' Adipati slammed his fist onto his palm.

'They have a portion of the army in a periphery. They are going in slowly, making sure there is an adequate number to tackle any of us. Maybe enough to delay us till their portal closes or something?'

Karuna listened intently, thinking with her fingers on her chin. 'How big do you imagine the portal is?'

'There is no way to say,' Adipati replied. 'We don't know anything about this crossing over to the other side business. Why?'

'I was thinking if we dived in, right behind them with the craft...I mean, there are scores of them going in right? It can't be an aperture. It has to be big.'

'How big though? We know nothing for sure. What if we don't make it across?' asked Lyosha, making a valid point.

'I am open to a better solution.' Karuna shrugged.

'I am willing to take the chance,' Adipati said. 'Karuna, you and Fakru take the crash pod off this thing now. I do not ask any of you to try this either. Please leave if you'd like. There isn't much time.'

'Oh, just because I asked doesn't mean I'm not doing this,' Lyosha said, crossing his hands over his chest.

'I'm coming,' Sveta said.

Karuna smiled. 'She cannot be steered outside the energy grid. We will have to go close enough at a precise velocity and switch her off to make a drop into the lake. You can't do that by yourself, Mr Srivastav, however, I can.'

'But it will be a treacherous expedition with little to no chance of survival. You don't even...'

'I don't even have the skills that you do? On the other side, your staff is just staff...her batons are just batons...his knives are just knives...and...' She looked at Brij.

'Don't look at me, I'm as good as ever; this side or that,' he said, cocking his guns. 'Bullet's a bullet. No inner piss hanky panky there.'

She couldn't help but laugh despite the rising tension in the air. 'I'm coming,' she reiterated.

Adipati turned to Fakru. 'There's nothing you can say that will make me reconsider you taking the pod out of here, old friend.'

'How about I don't know how to get out of the damn thing?'

+++

The three nodes had positioned themselves on the ridges southeast, southwest and northwest of the lake. The last couple of units that stood guard around the lake were now going in. Their foreheads flickered before settling in on a soft glow as they lay next to their long arrows planted on the ground, touching the fingers of their drawing arms. In the other hand, each one held their bows. A gentle breeze brought a chill with it. They were ready for any attempts at the egress, and their counterparts on the other side stood by for any indication of danger.

In the distance, they heard lightning. Two seconds; no more. No sooner had the lightning stopped they heard a whir. Unbeknownst to the soldiers by the lake, all three nodes were on their backs with arrows drawn and ready to shoot at whatever was coming from above by the time tho whirring stopped. The disguise on the poor old craft was not match for Nichola's advanced capabilities. And even Nichola wasn't equipped enough to remain hidden from a node.

As the craft dropped in from over the southwest ridge, the node at the summit fired a flurry of arrows at it. Between the second and third arrows hitting the craft, it lost all stealth capability. Now it became one large target for the arrows coming from the other two ridges that all hit their mark. By the time the Dhanvin started shooting at it, the large, free-falling chunk of metal had hit the surface of the lake and made a colossal splash. They heard engines as it pushed further inward, coming apart at the seams all over its body.

The nodes twisted the bands on their wrists, rotating their outer bezels and ran toward the lake. It was time for the other side to join in.

+++

Adipati drew an extensive breath, then coughed and spat as he came out of the water. He crawled to the edge of the lake and collapsed, panting hard. He could see bodies lying in the short distance; a couple of them still at the edge of the water and others just outside. With his cheek to the ground, he could see beautiful snow laden birch and aspen trees as snowflakes fell in the distance.

He couldn't get himself to move. There were no trees before, so far as he could remember. Had they made it? Was this the other side or was his mind playing games with him as he lay dying?

After what seemed like hours, yet he knew only a few minutes went by, he decided he could not just keep lying there any more. He started pulling his body with his hands, dragging himself toward the other bodies a couple of feet at a time. He kept looking up, adjusting his course to reach the first one, while breathing heavily and coughing. It looked like it was Lyosha.

His hand caught something. He lifted his head up a little to look at it. A shoe. A rather weird looking shoe. He tried to lift his head up a little more but could not. With a lot of effort, he managed to turn himself over on to his back and looked straight up. A scaly face stared down at him.

'First trip to the other side?' Medhavin jested.

Adipati turned his face to the side and vomited.

'Happens to the best of us on our first travels,' Medhavin added. 'No need to be embarrassed.'

29

«««« TWENTY NINE »»»»

Adipati woke up to a splitting headache. He blinked as he came to, and tried to make sense of where he was. What he saw above him was a crudely carved out roof in solid rock. He started to get up and saw Lyosha and Brij looking at him. They wore warm clothes. He realised he was cold.

'Not so yogic on this side,' Lyosha said, then threw him a coat made of leather and fur.

'At least we made it,' he replied, looking around. Karuna and Fakru were huddled up together in the corner, and Sveta sat beside the bars of their cell, looking out at the wall facing them.

'Yes, we made it here, but to what end?' Lyosha said, not sounding so pleased at all. 'They have my blades, her batons, his guns, and your staff. Not to say they were going to be the same on this side anyway. But I mean, what do you think we will do? Don't get me wrong, I can still take them on in a fist fight, but I don't believe for a second that they are going to fight us with their fists.'

'We are here,' Adipati said. 'Trish is here. That is more than what we could have asked for a few hours ago when they got off with him.'

That shut Lyosha up for the time being. He could be quite agitating if he got to it. Adipati looked around again. No more than a niche cut out in a rock. Outside the bars was what looked like a tunnel, and it was dark. The only little light they had was from a source far away that wasn't visible.

'What are you looking at?' he asked Sveta.

'Someone is watching us,' she replied. 'I do not have my yogic abilities, but I haven't lost my senses. There's someone in the shadows out there stealing a peek at us every now and then.'

'Curious? Or watchful?' Adipati asked her.

'Can't say.'

Adipati moved over to her side. 'This fucking headache is killing me.'

'Wish I could help you,' Fakru said from the back. 'Seems I can't make mine go away either, though.'

'Don't worry about it old friend. Let's just keep our wits about ourselves for now.' He looked out at the corridor. There was no sign of a soul.

'He's there,' Sveta said. 'Or she...someone's out there.'

Adipati turned around and put his back up against the bars. *What kind of bars were these anyway? 'Where the hell are we? And why doesn't anyone show up? What the hell is going on and what are they doing with Trish?'* he thought to himself. *I better not think out loud.*

Just as he was about to say something to Karuna, he heard someone speak. He didn't know what they said, but someone spoke in a hushed voice. He signalled the others over.

'Someone is saying something,' he whispered to them. They heard it again, clearer this time, but no one could make sense of what was being said. It was a male voice; that of a young man. He spoke again.

This time though, Fakru replied in a language none of them understood. A young fellow stepped out from the shadows. He had a green scaly body.

Did Fakru know their language too?

Adipati had heard them speak before, yet this didn't sound like their language. He spoke again, addressing them all. Fakru replied. Adipati wanted to ask what was being said, but he trusted Fakru completely. To interrupt didn't seem right.

They heard footsteps in the distance, and the naag disappeared into the shadows again. When no one appeared for the next few minutes, Adipati asked Fakru what had happened.

'The boy was speaking *Koshur*' he said, clearly delighted. 'What a beautiful language. I would pay just to talk to him.'

'Kashmiri?' Adipati said, scratching his chin. 'Maybe that is all the exposure he's had with humans.'

'He was very fluent,' Fakru said. 'As if he speaks it every day.'

'What did he want?'

'He asked if we were human, to which I obviously said yes. Then he asked me whether we had plans to rescue the human boy, or just wanted to get out of here and back to our side. I said the boy was taken from us and we followed him here. Then we heard the footsteps, and he was gone.'

Adipati was curious. 'I really do not understand this line of questioning. If he does not want to be seen talking to us, he clearly isn't questioning us on their behalf...'

'Maybe he's just curious,' Brij interjected. 'Maybe it doesn't mean anything.'

They heard footsteps again. This time they were coming toward them. Everyone could hear at least two of them talking. What they said they had no idea, but everyone heard them approaching until someone wearing a large coat with a hood pulled over his head stood in front of them. There was another large figure right behind him, the one Adipati recognised when he passed out at the lake on this side. Medhavin. Behind them, stood three more guards.

As he pulled his hood back, revealing his scaly but handsome face, the one in the front spoke. 'My name is Nishoodak. You have already met Lord Medhavin, commander of the Abhishri.' He gestured toward his companion.

'Where is Trishul?' Brij growled.

'The boy is alive and being taken care of.'

'If you so much as harm a hair on him...'

'You will do what, exactly?'

Brij reached out with one hand through the bars to grab his collar. He couldn't reach that far.

'That is what I meant,' he said. 'You can do nothing. You serve no purpose for us and should have been dead by now, but since you *are* here on this auspicious day with us, the council has decided to let you marvel at our Lord's genius. You can bear witness to the most significant event this world has ever seen on either side since the gods last dwelled with us. Of course, you can then die.'

Lyosha jumped at the cell bars. "We will not let you kill the kid no matter what.'

'Kill the boy? We don't want to kill the boy!'

'What then?' Adipati hissed. 'What has all this been about?'

Nishoodak genuinely smiled. Not to incite anything in them, but truly revelling in his belief in whatever he was planning to do. 'We only want to take his life, so he may then live forever.'

+++

It had been over half an hour since Nishoodak and Medhavin had left, which meant they were close to another five hours before they would be taken to witness whatever hocus-pocus was planned for the day. There was nothing they could do from within their cell, and making a run for it whilst in transit to the event would yield little result since they would have to make it to Trish anyway. It would have to be at the event when Trish was in sight. They would have to think of something impromptu.

'What are we going to do?' Sveta asked, almost as if she could still read his mind.

'We don't yet know, do we?' Adipati said. 'What is important right now is that we are here and as long as we are, we have a chance.'

The young naag who visited earlier called out again in a hushed voice. Fakru responded and they moved toward him.

'Why do the others not understand when I speak your language?' he asked Fakru.

'They do not speak this language,' he said.

'What do they speak?'

'Other languages.'

'Are they not human?'

'They are. They speak other human languages.'

'Do you have many?' he asked him, looking very curious.

'Yes,' Fakru replied. 'Where did you learn Koshur?'

'We used to live on your side when I was little. I was, in fact, born there. Before we were brought back, we had been living there for four generations. I would have been the fifth. My father worked for the council on that side, living amongst humans as so many of us do.'

'This is the language we used to speak where we lived. My mother still speaks to me in this language. I don't remember everything from my time there, but I didn't realise you had other languages too.'

'What does he want?' Adipati asked Fakru, growing ever so curious.

'He has lived on our side,' Fakru whispered back. 'His mother still talks to him in Koshur. There may be some empathy here. Let me try to see if this can lead somewhere.'

'What is your friend asking?' the naag boy asked, becoming slightly anxious.

'Nothing,' Fakru replied with a calming smile. 'He is just worried about your intentions.'

'What did you say to him?'

'I told him you fondly speak of your time in our world. That you cannot mean to unnecessarily hurt us.'

'That is right,' he said. 'Not unnecessarily. In fact...'

'What, dear friend?' Fakru urged him on. 'In fact what?'

'In fact, I can help you get away if you promise not to go after your boy.'

Adipati knew something was up. 'What does he want?'

'You are making him anxious, Adi,' Fakru said calmly. 'Do not get excited anyone, please. He is offering to help escape if we do not go for Trishul.'

Everyone nearly jumped but tried to keep their cool. 'Why would he help us?' Brij asked.

Fakru turned to the young man. 'You have to forgive us but there is apprehension, as you can understand. We want to be sure this isn't going to land us in even more trouble than we already are.'

'What could I do that would make more trouble?' he asked. 'You are already imprisoned. They are definitely going to kill you; it is a miracle they haven't already Why would I offer to free you so you could be captured again? I genuinely want to help you. The only condition is that you forget about the boy, and get back to where you came from. Doom is upon your kind. Nobody can change that. But if I could help you live just long enough to get back to your people...'

'Why, though?' Fakru politely asked, but he had to be sure.

'I do not have all the time in the world, but I will tell you this. There was a battle of some kind when we were still on your side, just before we had to be brought back. I don't remember everything; I was too young.'

'We were discovered by a soldier from one of the fighting armies there. He came to realise we were not human but still saved us. He brought us to safety, but my father and he had taken a lot of injuries. My father was certain he wouldn't make it and wanted to save the soldier instead since he had saved us all.'

'It wasn't something your kind could do, you see? He wanted to save him by donating his organs, but your organs can't just be replaced with ours, or something to that effect. I do not know exactly.'

'There was a procedure to be done, and my father knew one of ours who could do it. He saved that soldier's life. But the surgeon was ordered dead by the council when they learned of this, and my mother and I were brought here and banished from ever crossing over.'

'My mother tells me most of this. She didn't want to come here. She wanted to live on the other side where she was born and had lived her entire life. She is the one who sent me here to help you.'

Everyone listened intently, trying to make sense of what was being said. They hadn't a clue though. Fakru gestured to the boy and turned to the others, explaining to them what he had said.

'Well, we are going for Trish, that is for sure,' Brij said. 'At least I am.'

'And you think we came all this way through all of that, and will now just walk away to leave you fighting, because he is your son and we couldn't care less?' Lyosha interjected in frustration. Sveta held his hand to calm him down.

'Can we please try and not scare away the boy who wants to help?' Fakru said calmly as Brij raised his hands apologetically.

'Try reasoning with him,' Adipati said.

Fakru turned to the boy and held two of the bars in his hands, then brought his face between them and came closer to him. 'The boy is really important to us.'

'Then I'm afraid I cannot help you,' he replied as he backed up.

'Wait,' Adipati said, stretching his arm out.

'Why don't we tell him what he wants to hear and get the hell out of here first?' Lyosha grumbled. Adipati looked at Fakru, then tilted his head.

The boy seemed to sense what was going on. He looked perturbed, hesitated for a second, then came over to Fakru and put his hands on his. 'If you escape, they will still need to concentrate on the ceremony with the boy, and once that is complete, none of this will matter. There will not be a need to look into how you escaped. But if you disrupt the proceedings tonight, even if you do not succeed and are captured, the first thing they will do after the ceremony is find out what happened. And I promise you they will find out. My mother works in the chambers of tho council. She Is constantly under observation. She has sent me to your help in good faith. Would you let us both die in return?'

Fakru put his forehead between his hands and looked at the ground, repeating for the others what the boy had just said.

'Let him go,' Brij said. 'We will take our chances when they take us there. I will not let a son and his mother die to save my own son. We don't even know how successful we will be in our efforts.'

Lyosha came up to him and hugged him. Sveta put her hand on his shoulder, and Adipati nodded. Fakru conveyed their decision to the boy.

'You are righteous,' the boy said. 'Foolish not to run while you can, but righteous. Mother was right about you. If you ever, by any miracle, pull something off or even fail at the rescue and manage to flee, get to the three rocks by the lake and I shall leave you instructions wedged in them on how to cross over.'

'The egress might still be open if you reach there soon enough. They are big rocks, one lying atop the other two, and hard to miss. I will go now and find out the situation of the egress. Check in the rocks.' He backed into the shadows and said, 'I wish you safety,' then left.

+++

They didn't know what to expect when they were being taken away. When the guards came, they blindfolded them and led them on by their shoulders. But once outside wherever the reptilians had been holding them, they took off their blindfolds. They turned onto a street which was met with a wide road fifty metres long. Once on the road, there was a small crowd awaiting their parade. They shouted and gesticulated wildly at them while they were made to walk as prisoners.

Among the crowd, they spotted the boy who had visited them in their cell earlier. He yelled at them too, probably hurling abuses to blend in. But while gesticulating, he kept repeating four particular gestures. Pointing downward he swung his arm along the road where they were walking. *This road*. He then pointed to the direction opposite to where they were being taken. *That way*. Holding his up palm facing sideways to his nose, he brought it straight down in an arc, pivoting at his elbow. *Straight*. Then he held his fists in balls at his chest, then rotated them cyclically and out of phase. *Run*.

Run straight in that direction on this road.

Now, if only they could run. Adipati started taking a note of landmarks as they turned. A tree...a big tree: right; the building with what looked like a minaret: left. All their buildings were stone and wood. They hadn't yet seen any signs of concrete, steel, or any other modern construction materials or methods. But the buildings were sturdy and grand, made out of solid precision-cut rock and exquisite wood. He had noticed, however, that the guards carried technologically advanced looking weapons, not the spears, arrows, and swords that the Abhishri had.

'Yes,' a guard said to Adipati, noticing him looking at his weapon. 'You better not think of trying anything funny. We have the real weapons here.' His language was not perfect, but he spoke decently well. 'It is our honour to uphold our Lord's wishes to this day, and not use any technology for weaponry on your side. Honour. Not something you know much about, do you?'

Adipati didn't say anything. *'Was that a well? It looked like a well. Left from the well.'*

It did not look like a city. The buildings were spaced out, and there were a lot of deciduous trees around. Not much construction, so it was probably a village. The small crowd that had greeted them with abuses at the road was accompanying them on their march. The boy, however, was not in it any more. They followed them on either side of the road, their shouting and screaming dying down to almost a murmur at times, then picking up again.

At the end of the road in a cul-de-sac, massive gates ahead protected a building that looked like a small castle. It had fortified walls with turrets at the corners and was made entirely of stone. The towering keep peeked over the gatehouse and men were stationed on the ramparts.

The gates opened as they approached. The crowd stopped at a distance, but a male from amongst them continued to follow them. The guards at the gates shouted at him, and he hesitated for a bit, but marched onward again. The guards taking them inside turned round, and the one that was previously talking to Adipati pulled out his weapon. It was holstered in a tubular sheath and looked like a tube itself.

The guard inserted his fist into the top end of it, then held it by what seemed to be a grip inside, and pointed it at the offender in a flash. The male hesitated again for a second, but started coming closer, shouting louder than before. The guard lifted his hand and fired in the air. They could all feel the pulse go out, but there was hardly any noise. They could also see the path that the pulse took through the air. It stopped the miscreant in his tracks. They didn't start moving again till he had backed up.

'The Professor would love this thing,' Adipati thought. *'If we could get our hands on one of those tube-guns...'* He noticed he wasn't the only one in their party who thought on those lines. The others looked impressed as well, their brows raised and eyes wide.

The gates opened into a small driveway splitting around a fountain, then leading to the building. The men on the ramparts were sparse, more for observation than defence, it seemed. There were some men in the ward, but they were neither wearing any uniform nor did they look like soldiers. They paid little attention to the humans being escorted in. The main building itself had the most intricately carved doors any of them had ever seen. They were made of solid wood and were thick and heavy, they could tell.

Once the doors opened, they were in a huge hall. In the centre, they saw a bunch of people looking over a bed of stone where Trish lay. Everyone twitched and tugged at their binds to no avail. Brij shouted his name but realised as they moved closer that he wasn't awake. His head was propped up over an incline in the bed. There were probes in his body, and a series of narrow tubes came out of a flat contraption that pinned round him, hugging the nape of his neck all the way to his forehead. There was other machinery next to the bed, and a few more of the others were working on something on another bed nearby.

'What are you doing to him?' Brij growled. 'Let him go! He's only a boy.'

'But he is to stay with us forever now,' Nishoodak announced, walking forward. 'Our Lord has waited for millennia for this day, to be reunited with himself. To walk and breathe amongst us, so He can rule us and guide us again. And to exact His vengeance upon your scheming, unscrupulous race; the reason behind Him giving His life up in honour of His word.'

'We haven't a fucking clue what you are on about,' Adipati said. 'Whatever delusions you have about this Lord of yours, I'm sure they have nothing to do with Trishul.'

'Not with his body, no. You may take it once we are done here; it is his *praan* that we want. It is the one thing that is our Lord's revival.' He gestured to the other bed as the others moved aside, to reveal the body of another young man who was handsome, strong, and around the same age as Trish. 'Our Lord, the one known as Duhsheertatanu.'

«‹«‹« THIRTY »›»›»

'As the council presides over tonight's proceedings,' Nishoodak said, 'I will give you the opportunity to appreciate our Lord's erudition.' He addressed the captives from a distance. They were bound to the wall and could see past him to where the bodies lay. There was no obstruction save him.

Adipati counted six reptilians as they came in and took seats in a gallery directly opposite them, overlooking the beds where the two bodies lay. They sat close to the balustrade, stretching their necks to get an unobstructed view of the evening's proceedings.

'Allow me,' a deep voice echoed. They turned to see a huge figure enter the hall, followed closely by a few others who went straight for the equipment next to the bodies. 'My name is Parimanyu. I am chief of the council for our Lord. While the procedure takes effect, I will answer any questions you have but will answer only one of you. Who wishes to speak for your lot?'

'What are you doing to my son?' Brij shouted before Adipati could frame his first question.

'There is no reason we cannot be civil, Mr Brijbhooshan,' he replied. 'You address the council. And I suggest you check that tone of yours.'

'What are you doing to him?' Brij growled.

'As you may have realised, we have kept him alive, but you must forgive us for having to heavily sedate him. We could not afford delays. Do you see that cylinder between the two bodies?'

They saw the glass cylinder that had two tubes connected to it, leading into the tubing on the heads of each of the bodies. It had a small, red sphere suspended inside it halfway to the top.

Parimanyu continued. 'The red plasma-like substance inside is the sap from the Tree of Life. Of course, as all other bullshit that is handed down to us through generations, there is no tree, and there is certainly no sap. It is matter that meets certain parameters, enabling it to be able to be affected by the *praan*. Our Lord kept some for himself while the gods had his services. We want the boy's *praan*, and we want to introduce it back to our Lord, who is its rightful owner.'

'My boy's life is his, and his alone,' Brij spat.

'But it isn't,' he replied. 'Our Lord was tricked by the vicious human queen into giving his *praan* up, as it was known his body could never be destroyed. It is time he got it back.'

'But why Trishul? You could have got it from anyone,' Brij retorted.

''No, we couldn't have,' he replied calmly.

'We are ready,' someone from behind him reported.

'Begin,' he commanded. Then he turned back to Brij. 'We will help Trishul's *praan* escape his body and enter the cylindrical encasement you saw earlier. The sap of the bullshit then begins to rise. However, we are unable to contain *praan* independent of a physical form. It must remain tethered to the boy while we link it to our Lord's body.'

'The valve on the side of the boy will now open. When the sap reaches the top of the cylinder, the valve on our Lord's side will open. On establishing a link to his body, the *praan* will detach from the boy, closing the valve on his side. This is brilliant engineering; very precise and beyond our understanding even today. The prototype was engineered by our Lord himself.'

'Stop it right now!' Brij shouted as he saw the valve opening.

'That is not a question,' Parimanyu said. 'I said I will answer questions.'

'So why do you want Trishul's *praan*? Why not someone else's?' Adipati asked, calmly.

With his mind racing, Adipati tried to go through all his options. Their weapons were laid out for display on a round table close to where the beds were. Ulka lay next to Trish on his right. The equipment on his left was close to his head. Then there was Duhsheertatanu on his bed, and to his left lay a beautiful looking sword, unsheathed.

His weapon, probably.

There was no way they could come off their shackles and reach the middle. Their feet were clasped and chained close to the wall, as was their waist, and their hands were chained to the clasp on their waist. The maximum they could do was to move their hands and stretch them out straight. That was the end of their hands' reach. Maybe if...

'Only one of you,' Parimanyu said. 'Must I repeat everything?'

'Tell us what we want to know,' Brij said. 'You know all our questions.' His eyes were fixed on the little red sphere which seemed to have risen just a tiny bit.

'Very well,' Parimanyu said. 'You are aware, I believe, that the soul escapes the body at death until it is assigned a new body. Bodies disintegrate, the soul starts over with a fresh one. This random reassignment of the soul, or chi, or *praan*, or whatever the hell you want to call it, is not that random after all, it would seem. Finding this was our Lord's end with the gods. He reported this...how do you say it? Bug?'

'He reported this bug in their algorithm and several other shortcomings which made their system vulnerable. There was already debate over his involvement with them, and this drove them to believe he was learning too much. Anyway, to cut it short so you know everything before he rises tonight, he found that *praan* could be tracked. With the procedure he had discovered, and the arrangement you see here today, he also learned that *praan* could be transferred manually by overriding the system if certain parameters were met.'

'So, you see, we have been tracking his *praan*, waiting patiently through millennia so he could have it back. Before he gave it up, he had set up this council and tasked it with this sole purpose. He taught us everything he could in the few days he was given before he had to give up life. He made sure we could bring him back when it was finally time. We have borne this weight through generations for this day, as we can only transfer *praan* that has resided in his body before.'

'Why didn't you take it from the first person that got it after him?' Brij demanded.

'I told you certain parameters had to be met. The most important being that this procedure cannot be done till his *praan* is not back with his genetic signature. Trishul here, is a direct descendant of his bloodline. The pure bloodline, not the one corrupted with the human queen.'

'Why do you think we wanted Niramayi never to cross over or breed with a human? We had kept the bloodline pure to the very end, till she decided to malign it with yours. Oh, battles were fought to keep her here. Adipati knows; he's been around. We wanted the child to be *Varshaapit*, and no human offspring with a *Varshaapit* naag can sustain the blessed curse. But it appears miracles still happen, especially in the name of our Lord. Your son got it anyway! The unthinkable has happened.'

The sphere was almost halfway between the middle and the top when they heard someone call out to Parimanyu from the beds. 'His sedatives are wearing down.'

'It doesn't matter now,' he replied. 'By the time he comes to, he won't have enough life left in him to be able to move.'

'Let him go!' Brij shouted. Adipati noticed he was shivering. Whether from anger or the fear of losing his son, he could not say with certainty.

+++

'Summon her,' the Yakshini commanded.

Trish was knee deep in the water; curling his toes, trying to catch sand in them. He didn't look back. 'How did you know I was here?' he asked her. Then he shook his head and said, 'The shell, of course.'

'Summon her Trish,' she repeated.

'I cannot move a finger,' he replied.

'Not there you can't, but here, Trish. Summon her here.'

'To what end?' he asked. 'As long as I can't move over there, it doesn't matter what we can do here. How is she supposed to help me if can't do a thing myself?'

'Talk to her. Maybe you can work something out together. I don't know how you will summon her or what you will do, I can only remind you that you can.'

+++

Brij had shivered and hurled abuses at the council, and whoever he could see, and finally he had fallen silent; his head hung, and his spirit low. Adipati was still trying to find a way to break free of his chains and somehow escape with Trish, even though his mind kept telling him there was no way out.

The others were also looking for some miraculous way of escape, and if there had been a way to communicate, he thought they might have come up with something. But Sveta was as helpless as any of them. They kept stealing a look at the cylinder every now and then. The sphere was now almost all the way to the top.

Words were exchanged again between the captors and the captives, and an argument ensued, until they all heard the sound. The other valve had started to open. Parimanyu clapped in delight and Nishoodak went right next to the cylinder to observe it closely. He looked up with a smile and nodded. 'And so it happens.'

'I think,' the one closest to Duhsheertatanu's body said, but then stopped, probably for fear of being out of line.

'What?' Parimanyu growled.

'I think he moved a finger,' he said, gulping.

Everyone in the gallery stood, hailed the occurrence, and started walking downstairs. The rest of them hovered over his body and waited with bated breath for him to open his eyes.

On the table next to Trish, the pommel of one of Ulka's swords unfurled. The vines grew and entwined themselves around Trish's right arm. Once tightly woven around it, the ends of the vines dug themselves into his hand. Adipati noticed. He yanked his chain to get Brij's attention and signalled him toward Trish. Brij's eyes widened, then his jaw tensed up. The others noticed too, while the naags were too busy with Duhsheertatanu.

Trish opened his eyes. Swinging only the hand Ulka was attached to, in one quick motion, he cut through the tube leading to the other side. Everyone at the other table turned immediately to try and do something, but it was too late. The second valve began closing again, and the sphere started to fall. Trish lay motionless, his hand bleeding from Ulka's intrusion.

'No...NO...Nnoooooo!' Parimanyu cried out. 'Do something! We will not have another chance!'

There was a scurry amongst the ones overseeing the operation. They pulled out another tube and began replacing the end attached to Duhsheertatanu's skull. By the time they were done, the valve was shut, and the "plasma" was falling faster than before.

Brij was excited. His eyes were full, and his body shivered again. All the others yanked at their chains, hoping against hope to get free somehow.

'Kill the boy!' Nishoodak yelled. 'Kill him. He is of no use to us any more. Our Lord may have to wait yet again, but he must not breathe another breath.'

A couple of the reptilians tried to pull apart the tube connected to Trish, but to no avail. They looked at each other in horror. The tube wouldn't come apart. They kept struggling and looked at Nishoodak apologetically.

'Cut it!' he shouted as the sphere returned to the centre.

'Nnooooooo!' Brij roared at the top of his voice as they grasped things to try and cut the tubing.

Adipati felt his eardrums move.. His eyes widened as he stared at a shivering Brij. 'No way!' he muttered and signalled for the others to copy him. He instantly lowered his head as much as he could to bring them within reach of his hands and covered his ears. The others followed.

There was a marked drop in pressure in the hall, which everyone experienced. Parimanyu and Nishoodak looked over to their captives. 'Oh, shit,' Nishoodak mumbled as they saw Brij.

Every single human felt the pulse that emanated from Brij and went through them. All hands went to their ears immediately. Things shattered, shards and splinters flew everywhere, and people fell. Adipati's chains fractured, as did the others'. They helped each other free while guards rushed toward them.

Brij lurched over to his son, who was now awake. He wasn't shivering any more; he was calm. He saw them try to approach Trish again and narrowed his eyes then took a deep breath.

Another drop in pressure was felt across the room. Everyone braced themselves. After the pulse, the yogis rushed to their weapons. They couldn't use them as they would have liked on this side, but they were weapons nonetheless.

The councilmen left the chambers in a hurry. Parimanyu was the last to leave, shouting orders at Nishoodak. 'None of them must survive. You hear me? None!'

Nishoodak rushed to activate an alarm while others by his side fled. The yogis positioned themselves on both sides of the doors leading to the hall with raised weapons, ready to attack whoever came through. Trish struggled to his feet and hugged his approaching father.

Brij broke into tears. 'My son. I love you.'

Trish kept regaining his strength by the second. He lifted his other sword with his left hand the moment he saw a guard head toward them. In one swift motion, he cut through the incoming threat while still in his father's embrace.

The doors flung open and guards from outside stormed in. They were immediately met with an ambush by the yogis, who couldn't do much damage to them but made sure they were relieved of their weapons. Trish broke his father's embrace and joined Ulka into one while heading for the main door. Brij picked his guns up.

'Use your ability!' Adipati yelled to Brij. 'It is the only thing that's working here. We really need it.'

Trish had already started cutting through a lot of them with vengeance in his every move.

Brij concentrated, focused his energy, and let go. Nothing. He missed a swinging sword by a whisker. 'I have no clue how,' he yelled back and opened fire on the naags.

'Fuck!' Adipati exclaimed, knocking down a weapon from a guard's hand.

Thankfully not all of them had these tube-guns that they saw on their guard outside before coming in. Lyosha picked the weapon up, inserted his hand in it, then clasped onto two bars inside, one with his fingers and the other with his thumb. He pointed the weapon at one of the naags and squeezed. Nothing happened.

'You have to be a naag to be able to use these,' one of them said as he struck Lyosha on his shoulder with a mace.

'Still too bad for you though.' Trish picked one up himself and shot the naag, blowing him to bits. 'I like these' he said, amused.

'That was just so awesome' Karuna said. She was the only one not skilled enough to fight well, and they were mostly protecting her behind them. 'Wonder if those would work on our side.'

'Pick some up even if you can't use them,' he said to the rest of the group, blowing one naag after another while he held Ulka in the other hand.

'Watch out!' Sveta yelled.

Nishoodak moved toward Trish and swung his sword at him. Trish turned a little too late, and the sword cut him, making a huge gash across his chest and stomach, which cut his insides as well. Trish fell to his knees, and his head dropped. Brij shot furiously at Nishoodak, but did little damage to his armour. Nishoodak had a sinister smile on his face and never stopped looking at Trish even though he was under fire. His smile melted away when Trish looked up. His wound quickly healed over as he rose to his feet.

'No!' Nishoodak exclaimed. 'You were supposed to give to the Lord, not steal from him!'

Trish quickly put their weapon to his head and squeezed. Nishoodak's head blew to bits that splattered over everything around.

'Let's get out of here,' Trish said, wiping his face.

He took a slain guard's shirt and walked toward the door, shooting his way out. The others picked up a few of the weapons and followed him. Soldiers started to come in instead of the guards, but Trish kept shooting, realising it would be difficult to keep up with the numbers that were beginning to muster. Also, the number of attackers with firearms was slowly increasing.

'We need out fast,' he said. 'Do we know where to go?'

'Yes,' Adipati replied.

'That looks like some kind of vehicle,' Karuna said, pointing to a three-metre long contraption at the side of the gates.

It was about a metre and a half wide and had vertical bars that rose from its floor which had handles to hold on to. There was one such handle seemingly for the driver and eight others to hold on to while on it. It had, however, no wheels.

They rushed toward it amidst the crossfire from a few of the naags. Trish spun Ulka with his left hand, deflecting arrows shot at them while shooting with his right hand. Brij fired to give him cover. The others dealt with the remaining one or two *naags* that made it closer to them.

When they reached the vehicle, Trish found out his weapon wasn't shooting any more. 'Knew it. It had to run out of whatever was powering it. Anyone keep any more of these?'

Lyosha handed him one, and he fired again. They had all kept a couple of the weapons. However, Karuna couldn't get the machine to start. There were no buttons or anything at all other than the handles. Trish stopped for a second and handed the weapon back to Lyosha. He gripped the driver's handles. They could hear a slight hum and felt the machine come alive, but it still didn't move.

'Fuck,' he exclaimed. A shot at the vehicle from one of the naags rendered it lifeless. Trish got back to firing and deflecting arrows. 'Do you see anything else?'

'Yes,' Fakru said, pointing to Medhavin, who was charging at them on horseback.

'We need the horse. Can you throw those with your hands as well?' Trish asked Lyosha, looking at the *khukuris* on his belt.

'Better than with my mind,' he replied.

'Let's see if you can hit a man on horseback with one.'

Trish ran diagonally across from where Medhavin was charging on. Medhavin started shooting arrows at him. Trish kept running even though a couple lodged into his shoulder and back. Just as Medhavin turned to follow him, he yelled, 'Now!'

Medhavin caught sight of the incoming *khukuri* in time to avoid it, but it was followed by another, and then another. He couldn't concentrate on Trish any more, but he let an arrow fly at Lyosha. The arrow missed, but Trish had enough time to leap at him to cleanly cut off his left leg.

Medhavin shifted in pain and fell off the horse, getting dragged by his right leg that was caught up in the stirrup. Trish got on the horse, slowed it down, then kicked Medhavin's leg off. He wanted to shoot him, but decided to ride on instead.

'Tighten the breast strap,' he said to Adipati. 'Lyosha, we need your belts. Tie the vehicle to the rigging ring at the back of the saddle. Who can ride a horse?'

'I can,' Lyosha said. 'My left shoulder is sore anyway. I'm best off riding the horse with the reins in my right hand.'

'Okay. Let's get the fuck out of here.' He pulled out the arrows from his body, and almost instantly healed. No one said a word about it.

They got to the lake within a couple of minutes. Lyosha rode in the front while they trailed in the back of the dead vehicle. Everyone held the handles tight, but stayed in a crouching position. Adipati told him when to turn and fended off anything they drifted too close to at the turns with his shaft.

Trish was the only one facing aft. Ulka was holstered on his back, and he had the reptilians' weapons in both his hands. He shot at anything that moved behind them, while Brij shot with his guns at anything moving in front.

They saw the three boulders by the lake and went straight for them. Fakru jumped out and leapt toward the rocks. He found a piece of paper there, as promised.

'Allah be praised,' he said. 'It is written in Sharada!'

'What does it say?' asked Adipati.

Fakru looked up, horrified. 'It says the portal is open, but to find it, we must follow a dying soul into the water. Not dead, dying.'

'What the fuck is that supposed to mean?' Adipati asked rhetorically. 'Where do we find a dying soul?'

'The horse,' Lyosha interjected. 'Kill the horse.'

'What?' Fakru asked, looking at him with widened eyes and an open mouth, terrorised.

'Do you want to get over to our side or not?'

'Let us think about this, shall we?' Adipati said.

'They'll be upon us any minute now,' Lyosha said. 'Kill the fucking horse, and drag him into the lake.'

'We are not killing the horse,' Trish said. 'What has it ever done to us?'

'We need to get out of here. Now.'

'Let me get someone,' he replied and mounted the horse. There are a few of them behind those trees.'

'It is risky,' Brij said.

'I will be back in a couple of minutes. Be ready.' He rode off.

+++

'That monster must not escape!' Pateeyati yelled. Her father lay on the ground, getting treated. 'I am going to kill him myself.'

As she got up to leave, Medhavin held her hand. 'He will not die.'

'I will chop his head off before I smash it and see how that goes,' she said, mounting a vehicle similar to the one the yogis had taken. This one was smaller, with space enough for two. She took another look at her father and sped away to the lake on the hovering automobile.

+++

'Are we just going to slit his throat to find our way back?' Fakru asked in disgust.

'Better him than the horse,' Trish replied, holding the arms of his captive behind him. 'Besides, I just killed three others to get this one here. How is this different?'

'He is not attacking you.'

'Okay, let us let him loose, and then when he attacks me, I'll slit his throat. If that suits you better.' Trish signalled Sveta over to the horse. 'Would you cut the reins from the bridle and tie his hands and feet please?'

She nodded and proceeded to do so.

'They're coming,' Adipati said.

'Then it is time to go.'

As soon as his limbs were tied, Trish slit the captive's throat and hurled him into the water. Fakru asked for forgiveness. Lyosha reminded him to hold on tight to the loose end of one of his belts since Fakru couldn't swim. Adipati dived in first behind the dying naag, and the others followed. Trish stood guard with the reptilian weapons in both hands. He could see a lot of them approaching, but before he dived in last, he shot several times at the oncoming enemy. When he exhausted both weapons, he cast them aside, then took the dive.

Pateeyati fell off her mount, but regained her balance and ran hard for the lake, along with several others. She saw him dive in and signalled everyone to run faster. They all heard the massive electronic sounding hum. She never stopped running, even when she looked up and saw the orbs gliding in over them in the sky above, glowing orange in colour.

'For fuck's sake,' she said, 'be on our side this time.'

+++

Seconds after the body came afloat on the surface of the water, Adipati surfaced as well, gasping for air. The others followed one after another. They swam arduously for the shore and crawled onto it. Lyosha pulled Fakru up with all his might. Brij spat water and Trish was the last to come out.

'I think we are on our side, but they were right on our heels' he said. 'Expect them to show up anytime now.'

Trish wasn't panting; he just sat straight, with his two swords in his hands at the ready. He sat like that for a few seconds when he heard an incoming whir, which turned into a flash. Big black arrows flurried toward them from three directions, hovered over them, broke in the middle, then fell to the ground.

'It is so good to be back,' Lyosha said.

'Where are they coming from?' Brij demanded.

'Remember the slew of arrows they shot at us while we were making our drop into the lake?' Adipati said. 'It appears their nodes are still manning their posts at the ridges since the portal is open.'

'Why aren't they coming?' Trish remarked, looking at the lake.

Another barrage of the black arrows met a similar fate. Then they heard thunder. Lightning befell the ridge to the west. Trish kept alert by the lake. The next time the arrows came in, there were none from the western ridge.

'You don't think...' Sveta said.

'I am positive,' Adipati replied with a smile. 'That was the professor.'

Soon the arrows from the southern ridge dried up as well, then the last of the arrows from the south.

They lay for twenty minutes in anticipation of movement from the lake before Maurice showed up. 'Let us get you home,' he said, beaming. He dragged them into a hug. 'There is plenty to learn from you lot.'

'It is so good to see you again, old friend,' Adipati said. 'We are still wary of our pursuers though. They were right behind us on the other side.'

'We will have someone watch over the lake,' he replied. 'We must get you home to the fort now. I brought Nichola to pick you up. She's resting shy of the southern ridge. The others will be there soon too.'

'What others?'

'Rakshit took care of the east ridge, and Mugdha took care of the south. We decided to meet back at the craft.'

'I can't wait to be back with Nichola,' Karuna said as they started walking south. Trish kept looking over his shoulder toward the lake.

As soon as they were near the craft, Rakshit ran over and hugged them. Mugdha joined him in a huddle with Trish. Then they hugged the others.

'What happened back there?' Rakshit asked. Then just as Trish was about to say something, he spoke again. 'That was rhetorical you dumbfuck, tell me later.' They all laughed after what seemed like ages.

They boarded Nichola and Karuna took her off. Maurice walked over to Adipati. 'Brij is sweating in this cold, is he all right?'

'Oh, he's more than all right. He's primarily the reason we are back here. Trish is not a node by coincidence. Brij isn't just any other human. He's a yogi, and he has sound,' he said, not being as warm in his narration as he ought to be. He sounded rather sceptical instead of thankful. 'We must look at the whereabouts of the Achhaad in the years around his birth.'

Maurice immediately looked concerned.

An escape from an ordeal such as theirs and this is the first thing that comes to his mind!

He was afraid for his friend and feared a relapse of his obsession. 'We will see about that soon enough. Let us get him help first and see if he can't understand his capabilities.'

+++

There was a grand welcome for them at the fort. Everyone cheered at their return and greeted them with warmth and a feast. Vishwas was injured but was under the care of Liu, who was learning to heal just like Fakru did. Syra came over to Trish, and he kneeled to hug her.

'You came back,' she said.

'Just as I said I would,' he replied.

She levitated and beamed with joy.

Adipati didn't talk much. He sat sipping on wine and stole a look at Brij every now and then. Maurice noticed, so he walked over to Trish. 'We will need to talk about Adipati. I fear the worst for him. Whatever happened there has taken a toll on him and—'

'And you are afraid he will start obsessing over his failure to control sound again,' Trish said, cutting him short.

Maurice was surprised. 'How much do you know?'

'Not enough,' Trish replied. 'I do know about the Achhaad, and that Adipati went through a tough time.'

'Then you do know of the possibility that your father...'

Trish nodded. 'What exactly happened with Adipati though?'

'That is a tale for another time, my bonny lad,' Maurice replied. 'For tonight we toast.' He raised his glass to Trish's, and they both drank to a battle won.

31

«««« EPILOGUE »»»»

Pateeyati looked up at the sky, furious. 'You cannot keep fucking with our worlds forever, you know?' she yelled. The orbs had disappeared once the egress was shut. They had tried to re-open it to cross over but couldn't. Hundreds of soldiers stood at a distance, unsure of what to expect next. Pateeyati was furious, and their leader was injured.

Medhavin lay beside her on a stretcher, supporting his weight on his elbows. 'We can't just cross over with an army and attack their entire world,' he said. 'That kind of a thing has repercussions. Our world cannot exist alone. We can't rid ourselves of the duality. You know all this.'

'I don't need an army for him,' Pateeyati muttered through gritted teeth. 'We had them - we had them right here and I would have finished them all. But these fuckers had to show up and close the egress behind them. How long will they keep screwing around with us? If it was so important for them to run the show on this planet, why did they ever leave?'

Medhavin was in pain. His severed leg pained him less than losing his station though. 'There are suitors for my position, daughter. But I know one day you will take this mantle. You have to lead the Abhishri in time, and rise to much greater power soon after.' He looked up at the sky. 'They did what they did. The serpent lake is shut now, anyway, my child. Forget about it.'

'This isn't the only egress,' she replied. 'This isn't the end of it.' Pateeyati pulled out the metal bracelet from her pocket and clenched it in her fist. 'I shall return this to your corpse, Trishul Negi. I promise you that.'

+++

'Did you find anything out on the Achhaad?' Adipati asked Maurice as he continued to pace up and down the office, like he had all day.

'We are still looking. The man has been gone for a century now, Adi. You know he disappeared.'

Maurice could see his friend hadn't lost it, but he was definitely irked. Thankfully the years since they had first met Niramayi, she had healed him enough not to cause a relapse. But he was certainly not himself. What he had always wanted, Brij got without even knowing it. That couldn't be easy on him.

'Don't worry about me, old friend,' he said, sensing Maurice's fears. 'I am not going to turn away again. I just want answers.'

Karuna walked in. 'We will be running the next set of tests on Nichola starting next week. With your permission, I would like to invite Trish to the facility. He starts his internship on Monday anyway.'

'Of course,' Adipati replied. Invite Brij too.' He saw Maurice staring at him from the corner of his eye.

+++

'Do we have surveillance round the clock?' Odogwu enquired.

'Yes, of course. He came to the office today - had a meeting with the electric whip guy. We are watching him.'

'Good. I do not want to make a move till I know everything about him. Then, I will find him and strangle him with my own hands.'

Odogwu was back in his village. *It had changed so much*, he thought. The only thing that hadn't changed was that his parents were taken from him. Now he finally had the man responsible in his crosshairs. If he didn't kill him, everything he had done in his life would be for nothing.

'Are you well, Odogwu? You seem to wince when you stand up.'

'This pain is nothing, my friend,' he replied. 'It will go in a week, according to the doctor. The pain I have lived with forever, however, it is still with me. Very soon, though...very soon I shall be relieved of it as well. Once healed, I will head back to kill that bastard. You must never lose sight of him at all, you hear me?'

Half a kilometre away, a man wearing a hat clicked off his radio while looking through a scope. 'Then I shall await your return and have you at home on my turf,' He said. Then he took off the hat and patted his bald head. 'Can't have a man alive to tell he was shot by me. I have a reputation to keep.'

+++

'I wish you could stay,' Amratji said. 'It is the weekend, surely you could spare some time?'

Trish was happy to be at the school again, but he wanted to get going soon. 'I would love to, but I have to prepare.' He looked at his watch. 'I must leave in an hour. I start with my internship on Monday, and I'm really looking forward to it. They are doing some fantastic work in the field of science, and I have so much to learn.'

'Your sword is definitely the best weapon I have ever laid eyes on,' Amratji said. 'I could still beat you, though. Even with that.'

'You wouldn't stand a chance,' Trish said, then laughed.

'You would have to stay and fight to back that claim.'

Trish smiled. 'I promise you I would if I could. Maybe another time? I'll stay, and we can practice together, so you can give me pointers. Maybe I could give you some too.' He winked.

'Oh!' Amratji exclaimed. 'Someone thinks they can outshine their guru. We will see about that, whenever you're ready to kiss the floor.'

Trish's phone beeped. It was an email from a blogging site. 'Thank you for signing up with us. For tips on blogging click here. To visit your blog click here.'

His eyes lit up, and he clicked to visit the blog. *Lorem Ipsum.* Trish opened another tab on the browser to translate. He looked at Amratji a moment later, hardly able to contain his pleasure.

'I swear I will make up for this next time, but I must leave. I have somewhere to be and an old bet to settle.'

ABOUT THE AUTHOR

The author, Shobhit Dabral is a Master Mariner, Captain of merchant ships, keen science enthusiast and a fan of mythology from around the world.
Educated in schools in Dehradun and Delhi, he studied Nautical Science in South Shields, England.

His travels in his profession have helped him to understand different cultures and their understanding of mythology from their respective regions.

Always one for telling stories to family and friends even as a kid, he thought of the idea for his first novel quite a few years back. Hoping not to get information in the story wrong, he began researching on various aspects of science and mythology till he was convinced he could put his ideas to a story correctly.

To engage with people with regards to his writing, he has been writing some short stories to be read for free and posting them online at shobhitdabral.com/blog.

It is his belief that science and mythology are two faces of the same coin. He has explored various scientific concepts and tried to look at mythology through them in a story that is set in our time, but has origins in the history of humankind.

DID YOU ENJOY THIS BOOK?

If you did, would you spare a few minutes of your time in helping spread the word?

A little gesture on your part could go a long way in helping the author reach more keen readers such as yourself.

You could…

1. Take a selfie with the book

And/ OR

2. Tag the author on social media with your post about the book and what you liked.
(Use the hashtag "#forbiddenlore")

The author's social media handles are:

Instagram	-	@shobhitdabral
Facebook	-	@dabralshobhit
Twitter	-	@dabralshobhit

3. Leave a review on

- Amazon
- Goodreads
- Your favourite site/ blog

- THANK YOU -

Made in the USA
Las Vegas, NV
12 March 2021